I0824669

·TROLLHEIM·

a world of hope & magic
planted by
Björne
grown by artists

BASED ON FEELINGS
EVOKED BY
ANCIENT NATURE

· TROLLHEIM ·

TALE OF SÝSTIR

GEORGIA SUMMERS

TITAN BOOKS

)

Trollheim: Tale of Sýstir
Print edition ISBN: 9781835416648
E-book edition ISBN: 9781835416655

Published by Titan Books
A division of Titan Publishing Group Ltd
144 Southwark Street, London SE1 0UP
www.titanbooks.com

First edition: March 2026
10 9 8 7 6 5 4 3 2 1

A CIP catalogue record for this title is available from the British Library.

EU RP (for authorities only)
eucomply OÜ, Pärnu mnt. 139b-14, 11317 Tallinn, Estonia
hello@eucompliancepartner.com, +3375690241

Designed and typeset by Richard Mason.

Printed and bound by CPI Group (UK) Ltd, Croydon CR0 4YY.

·TROLLHEIM·

A WORLD OF HOPE & MAGIC
GROWN FROM THE MYSTERY OF THE DARK FOREST
ROOTED IN THE WONDER AND THRILL OF THE UNKOWN

www.trollheim.com

To Tiveden

"I've always thought as forests as relatively static shapes in our landscape – unless humanity intervenes – but now I know that this couldn't be further from the truth. Instead, it is breathtakingly alive and changeable, with its history written in the shape of its trees and under its earth. There is a story here to tell, for those with the care and experience to read it."

GEORGIA SUMMERS
Tiveden ancient forest, Sweden

12 June, 2024

· PROLOGUE ·

Against the black of night, Sýstir is running.

Her hand is fisted in her older sister's, their breath twinned in a synchronised rhythm of terror. Behind them, smoke coils thick and fat, visible in the moonlight. Ash glows like fireflies, drifting lazily upwards from the centre of the village.

For thirteen years, the village has been Sýstir's world. But no longer.

Later, she will remember this very differently. She will dream of the neighbours who had overnight become strangers, of the crackle of burning wood and the unspeakable cries that followed. But in this moment, the night is beautiful in its vastness, and it seems so cruel that she must notice its beauty, even in her terror.

The shouts grow fainter.

Still, they run.

I

· LITTLE BIRD ·

· ONE ·

Sýstir's breath comes in short puffs, her lungs pistoning as her sister urges her onwards. Under the night sky, the darkness is a weapon wielded against them. Every shadow hides a man, a monster. Even the moonlight above shines like the edge of a knife.

"Come on," Ada says, squeezing her hand tighter.

They run for what feels like forever, the ravenous shouts of men chasing at their heels. They move off the road, clambering over fences bordering fields to reach the wilderness proper. But Sýstir's legs are no match for her older sister's, and her feet start to flag. She stumbles over a rock, then another. Her older sister's grip is iron, keeping her up, dragging her forward.

Half drugged with terror, Sýstir barely notices when they slow from their breathless run to a walk. She only realises they've stopped when her sister's hand slips from hers. Then they collapse, a tangle of heaving limbs sprawled against the grass.

Almost immediately, Sýstir sits back up, to better drag air into her starved lungs.

"It wasn't Mother," she gasps. "They *lied* – if we explain – we have to go back—"

Ada takes her by the shoulders firmly. "There's no going back," she says, and Sýstir is startled by her sister's expression. "Listen to me. She's gone."

Sýstir flinches. "Don't say that."

"She's *gone*," Ada says again, and this time there's no questioning the hitch in her voice.

It has to be a lie. A mistake. But the men pursuing them from the village are no fantasy, and neither is the smoke from the pyre, still clinging to their clothes. Stray embers have speckled burns across their cloaks.

They shouldn't linger. But neither of them can face the thought of climbing to their feet. Once they're on the move again, decisions must be made.

"Where will we go?" Sýstir asks.

Ada bites her lip. "I don't know."

They have cousins in the next village over, and more family beyond that who could take them in. Then Sýstir catches her sister's gaze straying to her hidden tufted tail, the slight billow at the back of her dress, where the curve of her body falls inward.

Ada could go. But Sýstir, with her long cow's tail and the hollow in her back, cannot. Because huldras are unwanted. Dangerous.

Sýstir isn't dangerous. She brings home birds with broken wings and nurses them back to health. She releases spiders outdoors when Ada can no longer tolerate the webs inside their cottage. She nursed their goat by hand when its mother rejected it. But it won't matter that she's wept over the spoils of a hunt, or that she's as much kin to her cousins as Ada. They only care about the other half – the Väsen half that whispers of the enigmatic *other.*

If she were braver, she thinks, she would have the courage to say *go without me.* She waits for the words to arrive on her lips, to wrestle with selfishness and fear.

Instead, Ada finds Sýstir's hand and helps her to her feet. Already the sound of the village men is drawing near again.

"We have to keep going," Ada says, and so Sýstir follows.

If there is a singular mercy, it's this: one foot in front of the other, until Sýstir is so tired she can't think beyond the simple act of moving forward. Her head swims, her limbs ache, and just when she thinks she can go no further, her sister takes another step. So she continues to follow, drawing deep into reserves of strength she had no idea she possessed.

At last, Ada deems them safe enough for the night. She spreads out her cloak on the grass and there's just enough space for both of them to lie on it.

They have no pack of food, no pillow to rest upon, and it's too dangerous to attempt an open fire. Sýstir rummages in her pockets just in case she left something useful there, and comes up with three stones, each with a hole bored into its centre, that she'd meant to show her mother and forgot. A loose thread of spun wool, a knotty splinter of wood she'd intended to carve into beads, a dried wildflower that has largely disintegrated.

The flower she loosens to the wind, but Sýstir holds on to the other objects. She takes off her cloak and nestles close to her sister, so that it covers them like a blanket. Her stomach rumbles, but even if there were anything to eat, she's not sure she could face it.

She turns to look at her sister. Though it's easy when they're side by side to note their differing fathers in their features, there are more similarities than not: the same long, tapered fingers; the same dimpled smile; the same laugh.

Ada's eyes flicker open: warm hazel, the same colour as their mother's.

"Try to sleep," she says.

It's a gentle night for early winter, and so the wind is barely a ripple across the long grass. The sky is clear, and a hundred thousand stars stretch out before them. Their mother called them freckles across the night's face, and behind every constellation, a story perfect for telling by the hearth.

Sýstir mumbles their names to herself until her eyes slip shut.

. . .

Sýstir's mother is standing in the doorway, her back to Sýstir. It's early evening, but light bleeds red through the open doorway, speared between her mother's feet. The sound outside is a roar: wind, people, flames. Their devouring hands wrench her mother from the safety of the cottage, and her eyes are alight with fear.

Vala. Witch.

Sýstir tries to get up, to pull her mother back. But her legs refuse to work, in that syrupy way of dreams; every step is a mountainous effort, and all the while, her mother is slipping further away.

The flames crowd the doorway, but this time, it's for *her*—

She bolts upright from the grasping sting of the nightmare, her heart racing, reeling with fear. She reaches out for her mother, but her hands only find grass and damp earth. Every texture is wrong, the charcoal scent still clinging to her. The wind rattles through her bones.

She bites down on the first sob, but she can't hold back the second one, or the tears that follow. Ada must already be awake because she finds Sýstir quickly, reaching across the little ground that separates them. In the cradle of her sister's arms, Sýstir cries.

"I want to go home," she sobs.

She wants the quiet warmth of their cottage. She wants the hazy glow of the fire, the crackle of fresh bread between her fingers, the soft rug beneath her feet. She wants their mother to chide her for clumsy stitching, to poke her teasingly with the broom, to sing, to laugh, to stand with her hand on her hips, head tilted to the side and say, *My daughter, you are the world's most beautiful puzzle.*

This time, Ada doesn't scold her. Instead, she pulls her more tightly against her chest, Sýstir's head tucked under her chin, as they did when they were young. Ada's shoulders heave, and now Sýstir can't tell whose tears are on her face, or who's crying harder.

"We have no one," Sýstir says.

"You still have me," Ada whispers fiercely. "And I still have you."

Always, always, always, Sýstir thinks. Reciting it like a promise.

. . .

The morning is still infant-new when Sýstir is shaken awake. She rolls over on to the grass and groans. Her eyes are puffy from tears and exhaustion. Ada hisses as she shifts, gingerly examining her arm. When she rolls up her sleeve, the skin underneath is an angry snarl of burns.

"You're hurt," Sýstir says.

Ada swallows. "It's nothing."

"You should bandage it," she begins. "Or—"

"Later. We can't stay here," Ada says. "Come on."

Sýstir knows what she means. From this hill, they can still see the village, the houses a brown-grey cluster in a quilt of fields. The men will have sated themselves on their mother's death overnight, but the morning will bring a renewed appetite to hunt down the daughters of the vala.

It used to be that to have a vala in the village was a blessing. A vala's healing touch could ease ill health and save a difficult birth. They could read small futures in palms and slightly greater ones in the stars, so a long winter might be accounted for with extra stores of grain. Or a man might go on a journey knowing that his family would come to no harm in his absence.

But Sýstir had seen the suspicion in the villagers' eyes, the resentment as they handed over coin. They were jealous, Ada had said, that their mother could barter her healing for what their garden didn't supply; that more than one man had tried to court her, even though she rebuffed them all; that their house was always rich with laughter and joy. And, more than anything, that their mother could not share the nature of her blessing, or take an apprentice – because some things simply can't be taught.

Then, two weeks ago, a child went missing, and the rumours turned to accusations. The accusations turned into a search, then a hunt. But they had not hunted the merchants who had passed by, with their heavy coats of foreign furs, seeking a youngling to take with them, to no avail, or the visiting men of Oden, who had frightened half of the village with their demands for cheap provisions. No, the village had returned to their cottage again and again, until it became very clear that what they were looking for was not the child but evidence of guilt.

Two weeks. That's how long it took for the villagers to stoke their hatred, to build a pyre, to drag their mother from their cottage.

Just two weeks, for their lives to turn to ash.

Ada is already re-braiding her dark hair, pulling errant wisps back into order, albeit slower with her burnt arm. The sight of her sister doing something so ordinary gives Sýstir an unexpected twinge of hope. If there can be normality here, against every single odd leveraged against them, then perhaps there is still a future for them beyond this hill.

"Ready?" Ada asks.

Sýstir pulls her own cloak over her shoulders and nods tightly. She's not ready, but for her sister, she will be. Reluctantly, she tugs on her slippers and brushes down her dress. Her feet are still sore from last night's terrified run, but today, they will walk yet further. She turns once more to glimpse her home, before Ada urges her onwards.

Slowly, the village tumbles over the horizon and is lost to view.

The sisters move at an easier pace, the sun wicking dew from their cloaks. Sýstir quickly shakes off her body's stiffness from the night sleeping outdoors. Her arms swing at her sides; her gaze traverses the landscape. Aside from the hill they slept on, the land is largely flat, an endless vista of green pockmarked by dark forest.

But her curiosity is soon replaced by tedium, and then discomfort, as they trudge forward. By the time they come across their first stream, the sun has already crossed its apex. Sýstir falls upon it eagerly, too thirsty to care that she's kneeling in mud, or that the water tastes brackish. When she's had enough, she splashes it against her face, droplets running under her neckline.

Next to her, Ada kneels more delicately, avoiding the muddy bank. She fishes in the pocket of her cloak and comes up with half a loaf of bread that she splits in two. Wordlessly, she passes one half over.

Sýstir tears into it with sudden, ravenous hunger, spurred by the icy water. The bread is stale and squashed after a night in Ada's pocket, but it's the first food she's seen all day. She finishes it in several quick, tough bites, though it's not enough to loosen the knot of hunger.

"That's all I had," Ada warns. And they cannot risk returning to the road in search of the next village or a town. Not while the pyre still smoulders, or when so many are on the lookout for the daughters of the Vala. If they want to eat again, they'll have to forage for themselves.

"Are we far enough?" Sýstir asks.

Ada glances behind her and Sýstir follows. Although the sun still shines down on them, storm clouds are gathering on the horizon.

"Not yet."

As dusk approaches, they stop again. But this time it's hunger, not men, nipping at their heels. Ada is far too pale, and Sýstir doesn't feel much better. Her stomach gnaws at her, and not for the first time, she wishes she'd grabbed something on the way out of their cottage, the way Ada had. She thinks of her mother's stew, growing cold and congealed above their long-dead hearth.

Grief, a second later, hits her like a punch. The feeling is obliterating, devouring—

No. She needs a distraction.

"I'm starving," she says.

Ada looks at her wearily. "Well, I already told you, there's no more food."

"Then I can find us something to eat," she suggests.

"We should stay together."

But Ada looks badly in need of a rest. There are dark circles under her eyes, and Sýstir realises she doesn't know if her sister even slept last night.

"You're famished. We need food. And I won't go far." Sýstir points to a cluster of trees in the distance. "Promise."

Sýstir can tell that Ada is relenting even before she nods. "Be careful, understand?"

Ada lies back down on the ground as Sýstir readjusts her cloak. She unloops her tail from its usual hiding place, a pouch sewn into her shift by her mother's dextrous fingers. The ache subsides in her spine.

"Don't be long," Ada warns.

Sýstir shoots her a quick smile. Then she's off, an arrow flying across the long grass. The gulf in her chest is a little less vast with every stride.

If Ada's strength is her fearlessness, then Sýstir's is her knack with nature. Foraging down to the very last day of the season, tending plants away from their deathbeds, knowing the best places to collect the sweetest nuts and the biggest clusters of mushrooms. She's tried to explain it to Ada before – that nature, like everything else, has its tells. But no matter how many times she's pointed out the signs, or shown her the best approach, her sister has never quite got the hang of it.

Sýstir reaches the trees quickly enough and lopes through the undergrowth, searching for berries. It's late in the season, and most of the bushes have been picked clean by creatures smaller than she, but Sýstir finds a few untouched, perfectly ripe. She pops one in her mouth, savouring the sweet burst. Then she thinks of her sister, and plucks as many as she can to fill her pockets.

Something knots in her stomach, worse than hunger. Ada wouldn't be hungry – or cold, or tired – if she'd chosen to keep walking to the next village. There, she would meet their cousins, and be gathered into their arms, with a roof over her head and a fire beside which to lay her damp cloak.

Sýstir has met her cousins exactly once, shortly before her aunt had pushed them all back into the confines of their house, away from Ada and Sýstir – or more specifically, Sýstir.

Ada wouldn't be hungry if she was at their cottage. She wouldn't be hungry if she went alone.

She wouldn't be hungry if you weren't her sister.

The thought catches Sýstir like a slap. Just as quickly, she shakes herself free of it. Thinking like that, their mother had told her a long time ago, never led to anything good. Besides, as long as Sýstir can prove that she can look after Ada just as well, there'll never be any need for their cousins. She can learn to be useful, she thinks, with renewed determination.

Sýstir has just started searching for mushrooms when she hears a noise. Hastily, she ducks down into the bushes, ignoring their thorny prickles. She debates running back to Ada, then shuffles closer instead to the source of the sound, careful to stay hidden. It might be travellers willing to make a trade. It might be something wilder, stranger – cousin enough to Sýstir to bargain with, perhaps.

Useful, she reminds herself.

The strangers draw closer, the sound bleeding across the silence. She glimpses a person, then another, their faces damningly familiar. Her stomach drops.

The villagers have found them.

· TWO ·

Sýstir presses herself further into the bushes, wishing herself invisible. Nothing more than an errant breeze through the trees, or sunlight glinting off a lake.

The men are almost all recognisable to her: farmers who had asked for their mother's help – but only ever in secret – when the strenuous harvest exacerbated old aches; the miller who had sold them flour that was often more sawdust than wheat; trappers who had looked at their cottage and crossed the road for fear of cursing their hunt. More than one of them are those her mother had gently rebuffed; Sýstir remembers the way they had looked afterwards, poisonous with dislike.

But how could they have pursued the sisters so quickly? Then Sýstir catches movement, and understanding follows: horses, snorting and pacing uneasily by their masters. Most are familiar shaggy carthorses, better suited to tilling the earth, or walking packs from one village to another. But she spies one or two that have the powerful, streamlined look of a more expensive breed, with glossy coats that suggest better fodder than anything a villager could pay for.

Even though the sisters have been quick and light on their feet, the men have managed to track them here. The gods must favour the sisters, though, because the men are on the wrong side of the grove, hiding them from each other's view. Sýstir breathes a small sigh of relief; perhaps they'll never meet, and she and Ada will slip out of their clutches, and then memory, altogether.

But her gaze drags to a man's bare arm, and she presses her hand against her mouth to stifle shock. Halfway down his forearm is the circular brand of Oden. This explains the silky warhorses, the voracity of the hunt, the clean shine of well-honed weapons, the relentless pursuit of the sisters' blood – because for the men of Oden, any human tainted by *other* is not worth suffering to live.

Sýstir knows, then, that they will not stop until they find what they've come for.

The men laugh and talk, loud in the grove. Confident in their impending victory. Sýstir begs for them to start a fire and settle down for the night, to sit and drink themselves stupid as the villagers might have done without Oden's influence, but the branded men merely adjust themselves on their horses and light torches against the encroaching dark. Something bays, and Sýstir catches sight of a hunting hound, chuffing the air.

As soon as the men move on, Sýstir wriggles out of her hiding place. Hastily tucking her tail away, she runs back to Ada, berries spilling from her pockets. She flies across the land, wishing her feet were lighter still. Thank all the gods, Ada is still sitting out of sight.

"Men," she gasps. "Horses – and hounds."

Ada shoots upright, reaching for her cloak. "Already? Are you sure?"

Sýstir nods. "One of them bears the mark of the One-Eyed God."

For a second, Ada's expression changes to rare uncertainty, and Sýstir is reminded with a jolt that her older sister is barely out of girlhood herself. But the moment passes quickly, replaced by a look of thoughtful determination. *Ada will know what to do*, Sýstir thinks fervently.

"We will lose them in the dark," Ada says eventually. "We'll just... keep walking."

"All night?" Sýstir says, half question and half protest.

But Ada is already striding ahead, and Sýstir has to hurry after her.

The sun tints everything a bloody red as it creeps slowly below the horizon. Too slowly. Their shadows lengthen, prominent against the scrubby ground. *Ada will save us*, Sýstir thinks, though it feels less like a certainty and more like a fragile hope.

Against the horses alone, perhaps they might still escape. But

Sýstir's seen first-hand the single-minded nature of a hunting dog. She recalls stumbling across the end of a hunt once, the men triumphant with their spoils. The hares that had dangled from their belts, bloodied and limp. The relentless energy of the hounds, undiminished by the long hours already spent tracking prey.

Somewhere behind them, a man shouts triumphantly; they've found the sisters' trail. Sýstir's heart stutters with alarm.

Ada grabs her hand, wrenching her forward. "Come on!"

They break into a sprint. But the land before them is flat and unforgiving, too sparse to hide in, with no hill to duck behind or valley in which to lose them. Even spattered in mud, grass slicking their slippers, they're easily visible. Her sister glances back, and Sýstir catches the naked fear on her face.

The horses are moving steadily now, growing closer with every second.

They have run so far, endured so much, only to go no further than this. It's not fair, Sýstir thinks bitterly, anger briefly eclipsing her fear. Whatever happens to them – and she's trying desperately not to think of that – the men will go back home tonight. To their cottages, their wives, their children. They'll eat the meals cooked for them by another's loving hand. They'll fall asleep in the comfort of their beds. And they won't even care that they've snatched that all away from someone else.

Sýstir clenches her fists, the hollow in her back aching. Fairness is a child's argument, but it's the truth: *it's not fair.*

She tries to look back at the horses one more time – and fumbles her footing. She crashes to the ground, the momentum pulling Ada with her. They land hard; Sýstir's knees sting wetly. Behind them, the sound of hooves striking ground is thunderous.

Sýstir gets to her feet first, ignoring her bloodied knees. If the men want to take them, she'll put up the biggest fight they've ever seen. Never mind Oden and his armies; it's of Sýstir they'll tell the most frightening tales.

Then her eye snags on a dark mass, crouched on the horizon ahead of them, and forgets all about her fearsome vow. It's a forest. And where there's forest, there's a chance to escape. She and Ada glance at each other. *Can you keep going?* hangs unspoken between them.

Not without you, thinks Sýstir desperately.

This time, Sýstir reaches for Ada's hand to pull her upright.

The men might not have spotted them yet, even if the hounds have their scent. And there are ways to slow them down.

As they run, Ada tears at the hem of her cloak, holding a fistful of tattered cloth. She leaves one strip embedded in the gorse, as they zigzag the other way; another she loosens entirely to the wind. It might buy them a scant few minutes, but every second between here and the forest is crucial.

Sýstir's lungs are burning, spent, by the time they're close enough to see the individual trees prickling at the sky with tall, spindly branches. Behind them, someone blows a low call on their horn, and excited shouts erupt. The horses break into a gallop, the thud of their hooves echoing over the landscape.

"Vala's get!" someone roars.

Sýstir lets out a terrified sob, and Ada tightens her grip, as if to say *I know.*

The long, dark stretch of trees rises to meet them, a thin mist snaking low across the ground. Despite the calamity behind them, Sýstir's heart twinges with foreboding. But Ada is already leading the way, pulling her through the thicket of gorse into the undergrowth.

The horses whinny and stamp their feet; the hounds howl, clear and loud at their quarry. Someone shouts a curse.

Sýstir turns one last time to look at the men arriving at the edge of the treeline. Men she'd once called neighbour, if not friend. Only strangers look back at her.

Then Ada tugs Sýstir forward, and she twists away. She braces for a hand closing over her shoulder, or the punch of an arrow or teeth through tender flesh. But neither come. The forest is difficult terrain, a struggle for horses. And although the hounds will stop at nothing for blood, the men might be more cautious.

Night closes over them as they pick their way through the woods, too afraid to do more than squeeze each other's hands. Every rustle, every crackle of branch sends fissures of terror through Sýstir.

Not everything that walks in the forests surrounding the village is person… or creature.

Ada stumbles, landing hard, and it takes her a moment before she climbs to her feet again. Even in the little moonlight filtering through the dense canopy, Sýstir can see the pallid colour of Ada's face. The sound of hoofbeats have vanished; either the men are on foot now, or they've decided to make camp for the evening. Or, Sýstir hopes fervently, they've turned back, their quarry slipping like minnows through their fingers and just as insignificant.

We are minnows, she thinks fiercely. *Moths, field mice.*

"We should stop," Ada says. "I just need a moment."

Without waiting for Sýstir's answer, Ada slumps on to a nearby fallen log. Cautiously, Sýstir joins her; the log bows underneath her slightly and then settles.

Sýstir shivers and cups her hands to her mouth to warm them. The cold is digging its heels in, a little early this year. Mist clings to everything. She waits patiently for Ada to gather herself and get up, but she just sits there. Her hand, Sýstir notes, keeps moving over, but not quite touching, her burnt arm.

"Where are we going?" When Ada doesn't reply, Sýstir nudges her. "Should we make a fire? What are we going to do about food? Ada—"

"I don't know!" Ada snaps. "Just – stop talking! I don't know, understand?"

Sýstir flinches.

Ada's shoulders tremble, and there are the soft hitching sounds of someone trying not to cry. When she lifts her face, tears glimmer at the corners of her eyes.

Ada presses her fingers to her temples. "I'm sorry. I'm just..."

Sýstir leans her head against Ada's shoulder. "I know."

She doesn't, though – not really. But Ada's breathing evens out, and Sýstir consoles herself that anyone might snap after the last couple of days they've shared. A familiar guilt stabs at her again, harder this time. She's asking Ada for too much without giving anything in return. She rummages in her pockets for the berries she'd collected, but most of them have congealed to a sticky mass.

She glances at their surroundings, trying to see it with a forager's eyes. Her head pounds with exhaustion. Then she spies the tops of a mushroom cluster, peeking out from ferned undergrowth. She doesn't recognise it – and she's not yet so desperate that she would risk poisoning herself, or worse – but where there are one kind, there may be more.

Sýstir.

Sýstir startles, instinctively turning to her sister. But Ada's eyes are closed, her mouth pinched against the cold.

"Did you say something?" Sýstir asks.

Ada shakes her head. Then her eyes flicker open, alarmed. "Is it the men?"

"No, I just… I thought… Never mind," she says, clearing it from her thoughts.

Ada leans back and rubs her eyes wearily. "They won't come after us now. Tomorrow, maybe... But we'll be gone by then."

Sýstir's shoulders slump. More walking. She waits for Ada to say that all will be well, or that the men will give up, or that the sisters will find another home because there is simply no other alternative. But Ada just looks into the distance with an awful, unfamiliar expression on her face.

"It's going to be alright, though, isn't it?" Sýstir prompts.

Finally, Ada turns to her. "Those mushrooms look good," she says. "Why don't you see if you can find some food for us? I'll make a fire."

Sýstir brightens, though that odd, uneasy expression hasn't left her sister's face. She climbs to her feet and stretches out her tired limbs. Once they've eaten, and had a few hours' rest by a warm fire, the way forward will be clearer; she's certain of it.

She leaves Ada on the log and starts towards the mushrooms. The night has a hazy quality to it, everything shrouded in shadow. She searches for a more familiar variety, but the mushrooms only yield more of the same, with no way to tell what effects they might bestow besides a full stomach.

Their mother would have known if they were edible.

When Sýstir glances back to Ada, she's kneeling in the dirt, pulling twigs towards her for kindling. If Ada can do something useful, then so can she.

The mushrooms trail ghostly white into the forest, but Sýstir spies a flash of dull orange hidden in the undergrowth. If she's correct, *that's* a mushroom they can eat. Her stomach rumbles encouragingly. She steps behind the tree, briefly eclipsing Ada from view.

"Don't go far," Ada calls out.

"I won't," Sýstir replies.

She takes a few steps forward at a time, careful to keep one eye on the path behind her. The forest looms, dark and unknown, the trees above stretched tall so that most of the moonlight is captured in their branches. What's left is barely enough to see by, even with Sýstir's keen eyesight.

"Ada?" she calls uncertainly.

After a beat, Ada's voice comes muffled through the trees. "I'm still here."

Another few steps in, a bird calls in the night. Sýstir puts her hands on her hips and surveys the ground. The splash of orange is nowhere to be seen; just endless waxy green, punctured by the glossy white mushrooms. She squints into the gloom, tuning out her hunger, her exhaustion, the weight of the future, shattered and uncertain, bearing down on her...

Sýstir.

She freezes. Her name again.

Without thinking, she surges towards the sound in a frenzied few seconds, pushing past ferns and thorny bushes. She tumbles out of them, wide-eyed and heart thumping. The forest closes in on her, silent and foreboding.

"Mother?" she says.

No one answers.

Of course no one answers; what did she think she heard? Sýstir's name is already more than half susurration; it'll have been a nocturnal bird taking flight, or some creature bolting underneath the leaf litter. Annoyed, she kicks at a stone and it skitters into the distance.

It's only because she wants to hear someone else say her name, she thinks. What she would give now for her mother to call for her in her soft, lilting voice, even if it would be to hurry her inside for chores, or in frustration, or for some punishment assiduously evaded.

Tears brim and she wipes them away angrily. She's supposed to be helping Ada. Not thinking about their mother.

She abandons her search for the edible mushrooms. It's too dark now, even for her eyes, and anyway, her hands are sore from the cold. Ada will have a fire going, surely, and even if she's going to bed hungry, at least she'll be warm.

She turns around – and stops.

The path back to Ada is gone.

· THREE ·

Sýstir curses herself as she retraces her steps through the forest, a hard thing to do in unknown territory, and even harder in the dark. The ground is at once knotted with tree roots and slick with moss, and all the more treacherous for both. She calls Ada's name twice, then cuts herself off; even if the men are camped outside the forest, she has no wish to give them an extra lead. But her voice must vanish with the wind because Ada doesn't reply.

She's probably asleep, Sýstir tells herself, lulled by the warmth of the fire she'll have made by now. She should let Ada rest; it won't be difficult to find her. And perhaps it'll be better this way, sleep eclipsing hunger – and Sýstir's failure to fix that. *Be useful*, she thinks irritably.

Something crackles underfoot, unseen and unfamiliar. Sýstir pauses, pressing the arch of her foot against it through her thin shoes. She's used to navigating terrain through the feel of it underneath her feet; she's always known where the end of the lane to their cottage switches to the main road, or where the tilled fields give way to the land beyond the boundary line. More than once, her mother has suggested that she could walk the village end to end at midnight and not get lost – not knowing that she already had.

But she doesn't remember this root under her foot.

"Ada," she calls out, and this time it seems as though the forest is deliberately swallowing her voice.

Ignoring the unease in her stomach, Sýstir continues forward.

Perhaps it's just that she's tired and cold and hungry – all the things that make it harder for her to concentrate. Anyway, Ada might not have Sýstir's fleet-footed instinct, but she's always had keen ears. And she didn't go far, Sýstir thinks, nervousness now tugging at her. Just slightly out of sight.

Then she thinks about the wind calling her name, the way she'd crashed through the bushes, unheeding. Maybe she'd walked further than she'd intended. Or maybe she'd somehow got tangled up in the wrong direction.

Overhead, the moonlight hangs like the curve of a scythe, peeking through rain-laden clouds. Sýstir glances up, but the light is too slippery to hold on to, and with the sky mostly obscured, it's impossible to gauge her direction from the stars. Even if she could, where would she go? She should have paid more attention when she left Ada.

But she's never had to pay attention before. She's always just *known*.

Something wet lands on her neck and she slaps at it, before realising that it's water. Another drop falls, and soon the forest is blanketed in a thin drizzle of rain. Sýstir shivers and tugs her cloak tighter to herself.

Maybe, she reasons, it's Ada who's wandered off. Ada who decided that there would be better wood for the fire elsewhere, and it's only unlucky timing that she's just out of sight. Or Ada might have started to worry about Sýstir, and left the log to find her. But she wouldn't have gone far enough to be so thoroughly lost that a five-minute search wouldn't rectify it.

A five minutes that has ticked past more than twice over by now.

"Ada?" she calls, and then again.

No response.

Something awful and panicky claws its way through her before she can fight it down. The same sickening dread that had coursed through her seconds after she'd accidentally dropped their mother's favourite vase. The silence that had succeeded the ceramic shattering, hundreds of fragments skating across the floor of the cottage. That awful desire to do something, *anything* to turn the clock back just five seconds, so that she hadn't bumped the dresser upon which it stood, her arms full so that she couldn't steady the vase as it wobbled precariously. The fatal knowing that what she'd done couldn't be undone, and that there was only the world before, in which she'd not yet broken the vase, and the world after, the vase smashed into unsalvageable pieces.

"Ada!" Sýstir shouts, no longer worrying about men or hounds. "Where are you?"

She shouts until her voice is hoarse. She circles back twice, retracing her steps one by one. But the trail of mushrooms seems to have been swallowed up by the ferned undergrowth. Even though she's absolutely certain of her surroundings – she knows she tripped over *that* root, and caught herself on *that* tree – the forest melts and shifts in front of her.

The rain intensifies from a drizzle to a downpour, so that it becomes impossible to see more than a few steps in front of her. She'd meant to grab her winter cloak on her way out of the cottage, but there hadn't been time, and while this one is serviceable until the very last months of the year, it does little to stop the rain soaking right through. Sýstir shivers, but she can't tell if it's from the cold or panic.

Maybe she needs to stop. Maybe if she stays where she is, Ada will come to her. She sits on a mossy rock and shakes out her hands, trying to restore some warmth. Her hair sticks to the back of her neck, and for a few moments, she fumbles with re-braiding it. Ada has always been much better at this.

The shadows thicken and quiver. Sýstir's gaze snaps up; although she can't pinpoint it, *something* is watching her. She pauses, breath catching in her throat. It's probably harmless: a nocturnal creature, going about its day the way she would go about hers.

But if it isn't…

Something howls in the forest, and she jumps. It doesn't sound like the baying of the hunting dogs, or anything else Sýstir would recognise. It sounds like something older, wilder. Starved – and scouring the forest for easy prey.

Something snaps near her. A breath brushes against her neck.

Fear burns through her, hot and impossible to ignore. She stumbles backwards, then turns and runs. Brambles and thorns reach out for her, ripping tender skin and snagging on her cloak. For several, terrified moments, she pelts through the forest, not caring where her feet land, or how far they take her. Only that she has to get away.

Finally, she stops, gasping for breath. The sky has taken on a hazy grey quality, no longer midnight black. Dawn is cresting above the treetops.

Sýstir has no idea where she is.

...

As the light shifts to the bruised lilac of morning, the rain doesn't let up. Even though Sýstir's face burns numb with cold, she forces herself to keep moving through the forest. She tears the hem of her cloak into strips and ties them to branches as she passes by, just in case Ada happens past them.

The last time they'd been separated for this long was when Sýstir had tried to run away, two years before. She'd got as far as the next village in one night, which is no mean feat for anyone, never mind a girl of eleven. There had been an argument – she's already long forgotten what it was about – but she'd declared herself finished with them all: the family, the cottage, the village and its small-minded inhabitants. It had been easy to start walking, and easy to keep going. And all the while she had seethed, a small, cooling part of her had kept moving just to put off the inevitable punishment that awaited her.

Their mother, of course, had been angry twice over: first for the leaving, and second for travelling so far. *Unnaturally far*, some of the villagers had muttered. Their mother had only laughed, and if Sýstir hadn't seen her pinched with worry for the two days it took them to walk back, she would have never believed it anything but genuine. *She hitched a ride on a wagon. Can you believe it? Children.*

But it was Ada who had been furious without the tempering worry, who had shaken her and then not spoken to her for a week, except to call her clod-headed when their mother was out of earshot.

You put yourself in danger, she'd said. *And when you do that, you put us in danger, too.*

Sýstir hadn't quite grasped the scope of this danger until a few days ago, already far too late to heed it. And now here she is again, clearly unable to learn her lesson. What was the last thing Ada had said to her? *Don't go far. I'm still here.*

She calls Ada's name until her throat hurts, both with the

effort and the frosty punch of air that settles in her lungs. Now, a million potential fates race through her head, the same way their mother must have fretted over Sýstir's whereabouts. Ada might be terribly lost, unable to fend for herself. She might be too cold to move, her limbs slowly locked into place. Sýstir thinks of that terrible howl in the night and quickens her pace again.

By midday, she finds that she can barely speak at all. Each breath feels like needles in her chest. She has to stop and cough, then stop again. But when she can, she calls Ada's name. Still no answer.

When was the last time she drank, or ate? A small part of her suggests that now may be the time to pause in her search, just long enough to look after herself. That hunger and exhaustion are preludes to worse things.

But the rest of her continues doggedly onwards because an entirely different kind of worry starts to encircle her thoughts. What if Ada is worse than lost? What if the hounds had managed to slip between the trees, honed to the sisters' scent? What if the men decided to break camp and keep going in the middle of the night? *What if?*

Sýstir has always loved that the future is never entirely predictable: that each day is a gift precisely because of the unknown treasures it holds. She's never understood why Ada and their mother had craved the same thing, day after day, like mundanity was something to celebrate. Not until now.

As the sun peaks and then starts its gliding descent – so early at this time of year that it feels like the day has only just begun – Sýstir tries to situate herself in the forest. They hadn't strayed far from the edge, but she's walked for so long that she's surprised she hasn't come out on the other side already.

Ada. Sýstir's breath curls in the air, followed by a cough. Her body aches. Even though the sun has burned away the bitterest of the cold, it still nips at her hands, the tip of her nose.

A thought that has nagged at her like a bad tooth, wormy and fearful, surfaces. Perhaps Ada isn't lost. Perhaps she hasn't been found by Oden's men, or their hunting dogs, or any number of other things that may happen to lone young women in forests.

Perhaps Ada is gone... because she wanted to go.

Perhaps she grew tired of Sýstir's weight around her neck, Sýstir's complaints of the cold and the lack of food, Sýstir's need for someone other than herself. Perhaps she thought about that short, nebulous time before Sýstir's birth, when it was just Ada and their mother – her mother – in a cottage built for two, with no sense of the storm about to descend upon them. Perhaps she thought about all that lay before her with a huldra for a sister, and how, when she removed the huldra from the image, the future grew clear and bright and *real*.

There it is, Sýstir thinks. They both know what Ada could have without Sýstir in the way: a home, a warm bed, a fire, a meal. Sýstir considers her sister's expression again, and how she'd worn it like a badly sewn shirt.

Not unease, but the anticipation of… something. *Of leaving.*

And can Sýstir blame her, really? Ada's already lost most everything; why stay and lose yet more?

As night blankets the forest once again, Sýstir tries to search for a spot to rest, her exhaustion finally too overwhelming to ignore. She discovers a rocky incline, jutting outward to create a few dry spots. The rock is ice cold and hard, and the dirt beneath is so damp it's really mud, but at least it shields her from some of the harsher elements.

She crouches on the ground, briefly indecisive. If Ada was here, they would share out the cloaks as they had done the night before. But there's no way that Sýstir can sleep on the ground without getting muddy. Her shoes are already caked, her feet freezing in their stockings.

She wraps herself in her cloak as best as she can, cringing at the brackish smell of mud. Then, pulling her hood over her head to protect herself from the worst of it, she lays down, trying to find a comfortable spot. Her stomach howls with hunger, her heart sore with grief.

Weeping, Sýstir curls up. Alone.

· · ·

It's at night that all the worst stories from the villagers come to her, told with a wicked glee: *Be a good girl, or else the monstrous Väsen will get you.* The undead Draugr who rise from their graves to stalk their prey, rotting skin sloughing off skeletal frames; the trolls with their bodies built for crushing and fondness for sucking marrow from human bones; Oden's army of wicked creatures, who only wander the earth between dusk and dawn.

But this is a nightmare from which she can't seem to emerge. Time starts to slip from her fingers, as the cough that is no longer just a cough settles deep in her chest and probes curiously outwards. During the day, the trees rustle in unfriendly conspiracy, every sound stretched and warped into new, unrecognisable terrors. In the evening, strange lights taunt her, flickering like the torches wielded by the villagers, until she gets close – whereupon they vanish. She wakes with bark woven into her hair, and the ties of her shoes knotted several times over, as though something has been toying with her while she slept. She cannot bear to think about who – or what – might have stumbled across her, vulnerable and alone.

By the time she comes to a river, the water flat and black, she thinks she has been in the forest for three days, perhaps more. The bank beyond is thick with mist, but even so, Sýstir hears the faint steps of something too loud to be deer, too clipped to be wolf. Across the water, the trees rustle, as if a huge creature is passing through. Her imagination supplies what her gaze misses, and she shudders.

Her mouth prickles with thirst – a reminder that she hasn't drunk water in far too long. She cups her hands and lowers them to the water's surface. As she lifts them, someone – *something* – tugs on them.

Sýstir reels away, tumbling backwards. A pair of eyes, luminous and set too far apart to be human, look back at her. She sucks in a breath, ready to scream, but it devolves into a coughing fit. By the time her coughing subsides, the eyes are gone.

On the fourth day – she thinks it's the fourth; time skips and stutters across her thoughts – she finds that she doesn't have the strength to keep walking. Every time she tries to catch her breath, her body spasms with hacking coughs. Her head is reeling.

She stays on the shoreline for the afternoon, waiting for something of herself to return. *I'll just lie down for five minutes*, she thinks. Five minutes to gather enough strength. Five minutes just to let her mind empty. Her eyes slip shut.

When she awakens, the sun has largely disappeared behind the trees. And even though it's freezing, her skin is damp with sweat. Her thoughts are foggy and slippery, twisting out of her fingers.

The rain comes again. And this time, it doesn't let up. It patters like a hand playing on her forehead, cool and soothing.

She should get up. She has to get up. *Get up*.

She closes her eyes and lets the rain wash the world away.

• • •

In the middle of the night, she wakes, soaked to the skin. A figure wavers in the trees, a staticky silhouette with no discerning features that she nonetheless recognises. It's in their posture, the way the figure tilts their head, their arms opening wide. This cannot be real, she thinks, at the same time as the rest of her screams, *this must be real*. Because how could it not be?

She climbs to her feet, dizzy. The world feels far away, stretched to a dreamlike thinness. Though there's no sign of fire, charcoal lingers in the air. She blinks and the figure flickers.

Mother, she tries to say. But illness has closed a fist around her throat; every swallow is lightning racing into her lungs.

She staggers towards the figure, away from the river, and the trees melt in her presence, parting for her. The branches twist into an overhanging roof, vines splay into pots and pans, leaves twine inwards to form a lantern that is always lit – and this, too, she recognises. *Home*. In front of her, the hearth burns merrily if strangely, the flames a curious blue that emit no smoke. She lifts her hands close to it, and although they still feel cold, the thought that might question this is so very far away.

Her mother bends down to whisper something in her ear. The charcoal scent is there again, accompanied by a meaty smell that sends her stomach roiling with nausea and hunger all at once. She reaches for her mother, but however much she tries, she can't seem to close the gap between them.

Get up, her mother says. *You have to get—*

Sýstir blinks once, twice, rain clinging to her eyelashes. The forest shimmers through her vision, dark and wet. Ever-present. She's not sitting by a fire at all, but on the ground. There's no one else with her.

How did she come back here? She remembers the river, the eyes watching her, rain...

She starts for the direction of the river – at least, she thinks it's the river. But she only gets a few steps in before her legs give out. She lands in the mud; her chin clips a rock. The pain barely touches her. With effort, she turns her head to one side, blinking mud from her eyes.

Her gaze lands on a tree, black from what must have been a

lightning strike. Although most of the tree stands, albeit dead, the trunk has been hollowed out by time. Sýstir drags one foot after the other, and collapses halfway into it. The moss nestled within is soft beneath her body, closer to a pillow than she's had in days.

Unable to get up, she sweats, she shivers. And then she is travelling away from the forest, back to her beloved cottage. The hearth is empty, her mother absent. Instead, Ada is there, looking pensive, as though she's on the cusp of working out a problem. But when Sýstir calls her name, Ada turns and her face is that of a villager, screwed with hate.

Sýstir flinches. In the seconds between movement, she stands in the village square. The gallows are to one side, as they've been every day of her life, though they're seldom used. But then they're not gallows at all, she realises. The timber crackles, and there's a pyre in front of her. The crime must be a grave one; green rushes hem the pyre to slow the flames and prolong death.

Then she looks up, and it's her mother. Ablaze with light.

Sýstir screams. She runs towards the pyre, but in between one footstep and another, a crowd throngs her, pushing her back. Or no – towards the fire. The flames roar, grasping for her. A huldra daughter to burn with her vala mother. Sýstir bucks and cries, but the crowd shoves her forward.

You must get up, her mother says, and there is that foreboding scent of charcoal again.

Sýstir's eyes flutter open. The dark outline of the hollow stares back at her.

Dimly, something inside her registers that she shouldn't be feeling this absence of cold – not when there's frost on the ground, and her fingertips are a ghostly white-blue. Even her thirst has receded, though she hasn't drunk anything. All that's left is a consuming numbness, too vast to even entice fear.

A shadow falls over her. She blinks, glassy-eyed, but reality keeps slipping from her. It's her mother, clutching at her burning clothes. It's Ada, come to find her at last. It's the men of Oden, with eyes like flames, and crow feathers stitched into their skin. They're singing to her, a haunting sound that reverberates inside her own head. And even though the song is not one that she knows, it envelops her like fire.

Two large hands reach for her, but she's slipping, slipping.

She drifts, and falls.

· FOUR ·

Sýstir sleeps, wakes, sleeps again.

In her dreams, a figure slips through. Sometimes it looks like her mother, and she cries. Sometimes it looks monstrous, and then she screams. Her skin burns at every touch; her chest sparks with hot coals; her mind conjures flames.

She's not sure when she finally emerges from her fevered nightmares. Only that she can no longer smell the sweet charcoal of flesh, or hear her sister calling her name, and the darkness under her eyelids no longer blooms with haunting visions. She takes a shallow breath, and although her chest aches, it's a dull throb rather than stabbing needles. The bed underneath her – and it *is* a bed of sorts – is soft, piled high with furs. Warmth tickles her skin, and she can hear the pop and crackle of a fire nearby.

For a second, Sýstir can almost believe she's back in the cottage. Ada will be on the other side of the hearth, mending something or other. And her mother—

Then Sýstir opens her eyes, and disappointment lances through her joy like the worst kind of thief. There's no sweet smell of thatched roof because the ceiling above her is rock, burred with delicate carvings. A crude skylight is slotted above her head, made with the kind of thick glass panes she's seen in the village tavern. But there's little in the way of a view except grey sky.

With effort, she rolls on to her side to survey the rest of the cave. A fire spits merrily in the hearth wedged into the corner, smoke vanishing through some sort of chimney. Cured meat hangs from the ceiling alongside bone flutes and handfuls of dried wildflowers and herbs. There's very little furniture, but what is there is carefully made: a stool of knotted wood; stone mortars and pots; a collection of decorative wooden carvings stacked on a stone recess. Pelts and furs line the floor, with more heaped into a pile near the fire.

It's not her cottage. It's not anyone's *cottage*.

Maybe she really died in that hollow, after all.

"Girl." A gravelly voice, deep enough to shake mountains, startles her.

She turns to the source of the noise. A figure stands in the entrance to the cave. Black eyes sit in a weathered face that is mostly nose. Two curled ears rise up like horns from long, thick hair, gathered simply into one braid and strung through with gold beads. Several pelts have been stitched together to form a sturdy tunic, enveloping a frame that seems to unfold like an accordion as the figure looms in front of her.

A *troll*.

Sýstir tries to shout for help, but all that comes out is a breathless rasp. The figure rolls his eyes. He must sense her terror, though, because he stays where he is, on the other side of the cave. Not that Sýstir is in any fit state to fight him back; he is more than twice her size, outmatching even the burliest man in the village by several feet. He could crush her where she slept, and she would be helpless to stop him. She eyes him, her heart beating rabbit-quick.

"Fortune must favour you that it was I and not worse who found you," he says. "And more fortunate still that frostbite did not carry off the tip of your tail."

This time, Sýstir can't stifle her gasp, even though the paltry force burns her throat. He knows what she is.

Something softens in the troll's gaze. "You have no need to fear me. Do you know where you are?"

Sýstir shakes her head. Even the motion is enough to make her feel queasy. For a horrible few seconds, the cave spins.

"The Dark Forest was made for those like *us*," he says. "Väsen."

Sýstir scrabbles for anything she knows about the Väsen, besides the fact of herself. There are stories passed down between generations, half myth, half fancy, but always with that edge: that maybe, maybe they could be true. Her mother described the Väsen in equal measure of awe and fear, with the conviction of truth borne from experiences she refused to discuss – only to say that

Sýstir should always be cautious. Ada said they lived in between human spaces: spirits to keep the hearth and home tidy; fickle creatures who could bless a farmer with a bountiful harvest, or blight fields in already desperate times. Her neighbours muttered *monster*, as the men of Oden polished their blades.

Sýstir knows she is technically Väsen, in the same way that she is technically made up of bones and muscles and sinew. But it has always seemed like some subterranean other, to be weighed to a stone and sunk to the bottom of her heart. She has never seen any of herself in the stories that her mother told her, even the good ones. Because even the good Väsen are capricious and unknowable, their blessings bestowed as haphazardly as their curses. Sýstir couldn't be capricious or unknowable if she tried.

She shivers, her skin hot under the covers.

"I am Agagkantor of the Skóug Trolls," the troll says.

Silence. He looks at her expectantly.

"When someone tells you their name, it is considered good manners to reciprocate," he says.

"Sýstir," she croaks, and passes out.

...

Over the next few days, Sýstir becomes, if not used to, then less afraid of Agagkantor's hulking silhouette. There are still mornings where she flinches at the sound of his approaching footsteps, but only because it was her mother who used to wake her, and the memory cuts deep to the bone every time. Her voice is still raspy, so she mostly contents herself with watching him potter about his home, gathering questions like wildflowers in summer.

Other things she learns from observing him. He spends much of his time on a stool by the fire, mending or stitching pelts together with long needles of bone, or else carving spoons and other utensils, curls of wood gathering at his feet. Sometimes he sings, and the low rumble sets the bone chimes above humming in tune, with a lovely, clean resonance at odds with their appearance.

But there are hours when he's not in the cave, and time crawls by, second by second. Sýstir finds herself tracing the carvings on the walls with her gaze, or the bone chimes that sometimes whistle even when there's no breeze. When she's well, she thinks, she's going to have so many stories to tell Ada—

Then she stops, before her mind can torment her further. She might have all the stories in the world, but there's no point in holding on to them because she has no one to tell them to.

Sýstir is sitting in a makeshift bed, soup bowl cradled on her lap, when Agagkantor pulls up his stool next to her. Up close, the firelight paints his face in exaggerated lines, and it occurs to Sýstir that he might be terribly old – older than she thought *anyone* could be. It's been long drilled into her that to ask someone's age is impolite, but what is politeness to a troll?

"You did not arrive in the Dark Forest through chance," he says, a statement as much as a question.

Sýstir sets her spoon down, dread lancing through her alongside the memories of the last few days. One tear falls into the soup, then another. She scrubs at her face, but it's no use. She stares at her half-finished bowl. She has rolled the story around her head like a piece of gristle, but she has no idea where to begin. The story starts at the pyre; it starts at the missing child; it starts at the first stinging jealousies of their neighbours. Go far back enough, and it starts at Sýstir, the child who had always been just a little different.

"It was... our neighbour. Elise," she says. "She accused my mother of – of stealing a child. Because she was a vala. And valas are..." *Other.*

How quickly it had unravelled from there.

Slowly, she recounts the story, in halting, stumbling steps. The fever has stolen certain details, but left others painfully untouched. Agagkantor says nothing as she mentions the missing child and the subsequent search, the neighbours turning on her mother, and her mother unable to turn to anyone else to prove her innocence. Because with a vala's skillset and a peculiar daughter – though the villagers could not yet fathom the true nature of that peculiarity – their family had always been tainted by the outside.

Then, the pounding at the door.

Sýstir has to stop and collect herself, then collect herself again when she tries to describe what happened in clinical facts, rather than the muddled terror she recalls. Their neighbour, Elise, claimed to have found the child's mitten inside their gate. The villagers believed their mother had killed the child, to use his bones in the service of witchcraft. The punishment for witchcraft is death by burning.

For the most part, Agagkantor sits quietly, listening with few interruptions. His questions are gentle, but even so, by the time she's finished, her eyes are red and aching, her body desperate for sleep.

"To know humankind is to suffer," he says. "And how you have suffered, Sýstir."

Her entire body unwinds in sobs, helpless tears between her fingers. But Agagkantor doesn't tell her to shush, or that only children cry, or that she should be grateful for being saved at all, given the circumstances. Instead, he starts to sing, low and thrumming with a language she has no knowledge of. It's the same song, she realises, from the fever dream of the hollow, warmed through with something that she can't quite yet identify.

Slowly, her sobs dissolve into soft hiccups, and then stop altogether.

As she drifts off, she catches him contemplating her, his gaze reflecting gold firelight.

• • •

The next day, Sýstir is awakened by Agagkantor's low cursing. He startles when he sees her watching him, as though he'd forgotten that he'd rescued her.

"My apologies, Sýstir," he says, her name rolling with an unfamiliar burr in his mouth. "I did not mean to wake you."

Sýstir struggles to prop herself upright. Agagkantor has furnished her with what might generously be called pillows, but are really just a few sacks stuffed with scraps, hastily put together. That he'd scrambled to put together a space just for her is oddly touching.

"What were you singing?" she asks. "Last night."

"It is an old song handed down between Skóug Trolls, meant for protection. Think little of it," he says gruffly.

Before last night, Sýstir had no idea that trolls could sing so beautifully – and until this very second, she'd considered Agagkantor an outlier.

"There are more of you?" Her voice quavers.

Agagkantor huffs in what she thinks is a laugh. "Are you the only one of your kind?"

Sýstir shakes her head, though in truth, she has no idea. That other huldras might be out there has only vaguely occurred to her.

"Then I am not the only one of mine." A shadow passes across his face. "You will meet them soon, I suspect. My little secret has already escaped."

The next day, Sýstir is well enough to climb out of bed, and the day after that, Agagkantor sets an enormous wooden basin in front of the fire, brimming with water. A *bath*. Sýstir's entire body itches with the remnants of the forest.

When Agagkantor trudges back outside, Sýstir weakly strips and washes herself by the fire. It takes much longer to do it than usual, but there's immense satisfaction in watching clean skin peek through the layers of mud and grime. She unbraids her hair and dunks her whole head in. The water turns grey and opaque.

Agagkantor has left an old tunic for her, a belt that's served better days, and a shirt that looks like it would fit a grown man. When she pulls them over her head, the tunic sits well below her knees, closer to a dress, and she has to roll up the sleeves of her shirt several times before her hands peek out from the cuffs. She's too tired to pull her hair back into a braid, so she settles for twisting it into a thick knot at the nape of her neck.

Then she glances at the shoes. They're unquestionably the ones she was wearing before, though someone's taken the time to soak the mud from them and stitch patches over the threadbare parts with a beautifully delicate hand. She picks one up and holds it to the light, where the neat stitches glint at her alongside her own more clumsy efforts.

Before she can examine the shoes further, there's the slow thud of footsteps and she hurriedly puts them on. At the last second, her tail brushes the back of her legs, and panic sears her. Hastily, she pulls her tail up under her tunic and cinches it around her waist, securing it out of sight with the belt. Her bones ache at the extra stretch, but several *someones* are coming, and it's too late to do anything about it now. She'll just have to grit her teeth at the discomfort.

A second later, Agagkantor thunders through the cave. But his footsteps aren't the only ones. Sýstir's breath catches in her throat.

"Hilda," Agagkantor says curtly, and steps aside.

Three skóug trolls enter the cave, two behind the first. The first one wears a combination of fine furs and fabric, stitched together in a complex pattern of thread that seems to shift with the light – more delicate than anything Sýstir's ever seen. Thick gold bangles bracket her arms, carved runes glinting in the firelight. Her belt buckle is of polished antler. Behind her, the others straighten in clearly protective postures, though Sýstir can't imagine what kind of threat a sick girl could pose.

Although Sýstir has never seen armies or royalty, she's reminded of the time a nobleman had passed through the village. He'd been flanked by several warriors, their leather breastplates oiled but scarred from some battlefield. She glances at Agagkantor, but every line of him is drawn taut. For the first time since waking properly, a chill of fear steals down Sýstir's spine.

The first troll inclines her head to Agagkantor. "Well met."

"I would not presume that, Hilda," he replies, crossing his arms.

Sýstir glances between them, but there's too much going on in their expressions for her to follow. Hilda, though, just shakes her head and turns her attention to Sýstir.

Obediently, Sýstir takes a step closer, her legs trembling beneath her. The room spins sickeningly, and she fights to keep on her feet. Hilda looks at her for a long moment, then waves a hand. Sýstir perches herself on the edge of the bed, trying to find a spot where she won't sit on her tail.

"Tell me, child, how did you come to be under Agagkantor's shelter?"

Haltingly, Sýstir tells her the story. She'd thought it would get easier with the telling – that it would be robbed of its power – but her heart burns with grief. When she reaches the point where she lost Ada, she has to stop and swallow back tears.

Hilda doesn't console her, but she doesn't berate Sýstir either. As Sýstir continues, she sneaks a look at the troll every now and then. Though there's nothing she can pinpoint as hugely different between Hilda and the other trolls, there's something about her that makes Sýstir sit up just a little straighter. Her story told, she offers a tentative smile, and Hilda returns it, even if her gaze is distant.

"And you are staying with Agagkantor now?" Hilda asks.

"Yes," Agagkantor cuts in.

Something warm glows inside Sýstir's chest. Agagkantor has already taken her in, fed her, clothed her. If she can leave a good first impression, then maybe there's a place for her here, after all.

Hilda straightens up and turns to Agagkantor. "This is a terrible mistake."

It takes Sýstir a second to realise that Hilda is talking about her. She feels as though she's been slapped. Hot shame races up her, searing her face crimson.

Sýstir is a terrible mistake. Ada knew it first, and now the trolls are coming to the same conclusion. A *mistake*.

Agagkantor looks unimpressed. "She's just a girl-thing. Would you rather I left her out to die?"

"She is a human."

"Hilda—"

Hilda cuts him off with gentle admonishment. "Am I not your queen?"

"She is not human, *Queen* Hilda," he says, with exaggerated patience. "She is Huldra."

Sýstir shivers at the name. Even though Agagkantor is Väsen – they are all Väsen, she keeps reminding herself – she can count on her hands the number of times she's been called by what she is, rather than who. Even when her mother had gently explained for the first time what it meant to be huldra, and therefore what she could never be, it had sounded like sorrow in her mouth.

They will not want a huldra, she thinks. They will cast her out, back into the cold, with no miracle reprieve this time.

"I'm not worried about the huldra," the queen replies, frustration tinging her voice. "I'm worried about the other half. The human half." A pause. "She has spent her entire life with them. Would it not be a kindness to return her?"

"No!" Sýstir says, before she can stop herself.

Every gaze in the cave swivels to look at her. Bright spots of red bloom on her cheeks. But she holds her ground. She can't lay Ada with another burden.

"They don't want me," she says quietly, shame scorching.

Agagkantor gives Queen Hilda an indecipherable look. "You see?"

Queen Hilda looks unconvinced. "I hesitate to suggest that you, of all, are best placed to—"

"Do you have dominion over all living things now, Hilda?" he demands. "Do you think you know better than the Dark Forest?"

Behind her, the two trolls stiffen. But Agagkantor is unrepentant. He steps between Queen Hilda and the bed, so Sýstir's view is suddenly one of his gravelled back. She shrinks against the wall.

She won't leave. She can't leave – because there's nowhere else to go.

Queen Hilda raises a hand. "Peace, Agagkantor."

The trolls behind her settle, though the tension doesn't quite leave their shoulders. Agagkantor moves to one side, just enough for Sýstir to see by.

Queen Hilda sighs. "I cannot say I like this, but I suppose I don't have to. The Dark Forest has chosen her. If she wishes to choose it in return, she may."

Sýstir takes a second to parse through Queen Hilda's meaning. Hope flickers faintly in her chest.

"You mean... you're not throwing me out?" she asks.

Agagkantor kneels by the bed, so they're at eye level. The frightening gleam in his eye has vanished, replaced by the gentleness she's grown used to.

"You have a choice, little huldra," he says. "You may return to your humans, if you wish. I will lead you out of the Dark Forest myself."

Sýstir considers leaving the warmth of this room behind, the soft bed, the firelight licking over dark stone. There will be the journey through the forest, harder with every day that they sink into winter. And what happens at the end of that road? No cottage, no bed, no hearth. Only a vast landscape, her sister a speck somewhere beyond the horizon. How big is the world?

Her entire body shudders.

"Or," he adds, "you can stay here. With me."

Relief floods through her – followed by vast, bitter guilt. It is, without question, the cowardly choice. Leave, and she might find Ada. Leave, and there is that vague notion of justice, or revenge – or something that gives her mother more than a pyre to be remembered by.

But she is so tired, and so cold. The crackling in her lungs has only just stopped.

And maybe, a voice whispers, finding Ada won't be the worst part. No, the worst will be that meeting: Sýstir at her cousins' door, Ada on the other side of it, with that same pinched expression of despair.

It doesn't have to be forever.

"If... if Ada comes, can she stay, too?" she asks.

In case their cousins are as cruel as the village folk. In case her sister dreams of Sýstir's face, the same way she dreams of Ada's every night. Just... in case.

Something flashes across Agagkantor's face, and Sýstir doesn't understand why it looks like pity. But then it passes, settling into one of assurance.

"Of course," he says.

"Then I would like to stay," she says, her voice small.

Agagkantor looks at Queen Hilda and the other trolls triumphantly. "She stays."

Queen Hilda's expression is solemn. "So be it."

· FIVE ·

It takes Sýstir more than a week to recover. But even after the long nights of coughing have stopped, she can't muster the will to get out of bed for more than a few moments. The brief burst of energy after Queen Hilda's visit seems to have fizzled with the waning sunlight. She lies listless, watching snow accumulate on the skylight until the room is awash in a dim blue glow. Most of the time, she drifts in and out of sleep; in many ways, it's easier than being awake.

Because awake, she has to think about everything she has lost.

Agagkantor waits by her bedside. Sometimes she catches him singing: a low rumble of melody that reminds her of rockfall. Other times she catches him sitting on a low stool, his hands working deftly across some carving or tool.

On the tenth day, he sits on her bed with a sudden huff. "It is time to make yourself useful, girl," he says. "Can you sew? Can you weave?"

Cautiously, Sýstir nods, but inside, her stomach is churning. She's had her fill of fairytales where young maids are imprisoned by their monsters, destined to drudging servitude. But we are both monsters here, she thinks before she can stop herself.

"Can you chop wood? Can you carve?"

This time, Sýstir shakes her head. Agagkantor huffs again, but it's hard to tell whether this is a sign of displeasure. Most of the time, the expressions on his face pass before she can comprehend them.

He props her upright with his large hands, setting her on the edge of the bed as if she's nothing more than a doll. "Then there is still something to teach you, I see."

At first Sýstir works hunched in her bed, unravelling frayed rope for Agagkantor to re-braid, or sorting dried grass into various lengths. The fibres cling to her skin, prickling her long after he's whisked away the grass. She loathes the tedious, irritating process, but where she might have escaped outside to play in the fields, Agagkantor always seems to have one eye on her.

Winter, he tells her, is a time of replenishment.

"I know that," she says, unable to keep the irritation from her voice.

Wistfully, she thinks of only a few months ago, when she and Ada had taken turns to make jam in their mother's large copper pot, while their mother had strung garlic from the rafters, and packed flour away into their pantry. Wintertime in the cottage always meant the delightful smell of dried lavender and thyme and rosemary – all the scents lifted by the constant fire. Or, when it was cold no matter what they did, piling into the same bed, layered under the covers.

"Not just of the hearth and home," Agagkantor says. "What about the head? What about the heart?"

Sýstir mutters something about food being filling enough, but either he doesn't hear her, or he chooses to ignore her remark.

"It does the heart good to sing, sometimes," he says.

Sýstir shakes her head. "I don't do that."

He gives her a curious look. "No?"

No. Even though Sýstir loves singing. Even though her voice is high and clear, with the pretty resonance of a bell. Even though she long ago memorised all the folk songs their mother sang for the sheer joy of sharing them.

Singing got her into trouble, the same as her slightly wide-set eyes, or that indefinable aura of other that seemed to linger, even though the hollow of her back and her tail were kept well hidden. Singing meant that all the village children wanted to play with her, even though they had shunned her seconds before she opened her mouth. Singing meant that parents took narrowed-eyed notice of her, until her mother suggested that perhaps songs were best left to the comfort of their home.

Singing means power, in the mouth of a huldra. Because it means magic.

So no, she won't be singing again.

As her strength returns to her, she spends more time out of bed, making herself useful where she can. She discovers that the cave in which she's spent so much of her time is called the hart, with a long corridor leading outside. There are a few carvings along the seam between the hart and the corridor, detailing stories that she can't yet parse.

The first two days out of bed, she tries to perch on Agagkantor's spare stool, though it – like everything else in the hart – is built for him, more so than for a thirteen-year-old girl. On the third, she wakes up to a beautiful new stool by her bed, made exactly for her height.

"To make rope," Agagkantor says.

Despite herself, Sýstir groans. Then her hand flies to her mouth, too late to stop it. She should be grateful. She *is* grateful. Ada would give her the Look – one inherited from their mother with mimetic precision – if she saw Sýstir complaining about chores, when only a few weeks ago, she'd been lucky to eat a fistful of berries.

What she would give for Ada to look at her like that again.

Tears prick at the corner of her eyes, and she has to look at the ceiling to stop them from falling. It happens like this, often: Sýstir's hands ghosting over an action that she's done a hundred, a thousand times, only with a second pair of hands beside her; the soft scent of warmed pine wood, or the sound of fire crackling, just like home; a memory that has nothing to do with Ada or their mother whatsoever, and yet it still strikes true.

All at once she feels exhausted. Tired of being sad. Tired of crying *all the time*.

Agagkantor, as usual, misses nothing. He sets her to working on dinner instead, with the most rudimentary of instructions. But this is something Sýstir knows well, and at least if there's not satisfaction, there's not frustration, either. For two hours she chops vegetables and kneads dough, skins a snow hare and boils its bones clean for stock. She feeds the fire, stirs the pot, presses garlic and dried rosemary into the risen dough, and sets it cooking. By the end of it, her body aches with premature fatigue. But there's a stew and fresh bread waiting for her.

Agagkantor has left a bowl and spoon to the side. She pulls apart the crackling bread, dips it in the stew. When she takes the first bite, uncomplicated satisfaction washes over her.

Later, it will occur to Sýstir that not once in those two hours has she thought of Ada.

. . .

For several weeks, the snow refuses to let up. Agagkantor keeps her hands busy – not more rope, thank the gods – but with everything else. She spends a good few hours meticulously washing her dress and cloak, so that although they're no longer as pristine, they're fit to wear again. When she asks about her shoes, Agagkantor only shrugs.

"You were asleep for many days," he says. "It took me but a few of them to set right."

The distraction of chores only works once; her mind still wanders. But there's certainly less empty time to feel her family's absence so keenly.

Then, one day, Sýstir wakes to faint sunlight pouring like honey through the skylight, and an uneven, thumping beat through the ceiling. Moments later, Agagkantor tramps through the door, shaking snow off his boots. He's whistling a melancholy tune that makes the fire pop and spit.

"How do you fare?" he asks.

Sýstir wiggles her toes experimentally. "Good."

Between her chores and the hearty food, her strength has returned to her in its entirety. Even though her limbs still feel rusty with lack of use, her skin pallid from so long inside, she no longer feels dizzy every time she stands up or exhausted after a few hours of work. She feels like herself again, in as much as she could ever feel like the girl who lived in a cottage, and not a cave.

"Then get your cloak," Agagkantor says. "It is time you meet the Dark Forest."

. . .

Sýstir stumbles outside, wrapped in her scarred but clean cloak. After weeks in the warm gloom of Agagkantor's home, she's unused to even the weak light, made brighter by the drifts of snow piled up around her. As her eyes adjust, Agagkantor stomps around, tamping down the snow.

"Careful," he warns, as Sýstir steps out from the shelter of the cave.

Icicles as long as herself dangle overhead, but she slips between them easily, following Agagkantor's footsteps. While she's been recovering, the snow has fallen thick and fast in the forest, and mist blankets everything in a thin layer. Any leaves remaining are glazed with frost.

At the end of the path, Sýstir falters. Even though she's recovered, she hasn't forgotten the fevered haze of wandering across the forest, nor the various creatures that had watched her.

Agagkantor places a warm hand on her shoulder. "The Dark Forest is to be respected, not feared. But you have had much of which to be afraid." He kneels down to look her in the eye. "I will keep you safe. That, I promise."

Sýstir clings to his shadow tightly as he walks in front of her, treading through the snow. Even though the forest looks indistinguishable from every direction, Agagkantor seems to know where he's going, because he strides unwaveringly through the hip-deep snow, pausing to adjust at certain, unseen markers. She follows in his wake, like ripples after a rock thrown in water.

She has considered the forest almost entirely uniform, with only the sheer mountains in the east, but as her gaze tunes in towards the finer details, Sýstir picks up on the gentle undulation of the landscape or the black mouth of a cave, almost entirely hidden by snow. The path veers downwards into a shallow gulley, overhead rocks forming natural archways. Then she hears it: a faint buzzing sound. Noise. *Life*.

"What's that?" she asks, unable to help herself.

"Hilda's Rise." Agagkantor's eyes darken. "It is not for us."

Sýstir remembers the way the troll queen had looked at her. *A terrible mistake*. No, even if she wanted to see the Rise, she wouldn't be welcome there.

"Are you part of a Rise?" she asks timidly.

Agagkantor shrugs. "It is a Rise of one, perhaps." Then he glances at her. "Now two."

He explains a little more as he walks. Sýstir learns that every troll has a Rise because every troll is one of many. Not just the Skóug Trolls, he says, but Moss Trolls and Hasl Trolls and more besides. Trolls within the same Rise will largely live together in one cave, much as the larger families in Sýstir's village exist under the roof of one cottage. But Agagkantor has chosen to live alone, without a Rise, away from the others.

She senses there's more to the answer, but his pace is quickening, and she hurries after him. Slowly, the forest gives way to higher ground, the trees thinning. The climb up the hills leaves Sýstir breathless and warm underneath her cloak. Agagkantor's strides swallow up distance easily, but he waits patiently for her as she clambers after him. The blanket of white gives way to snow-topped boulders, most of them bigger even than Agagkantor.

As they pass one closely, he stops her. He reaches out to brush snow off it, unveiling lines criss-crossing over the stone, weather-beaten and soft with time.

"They were once trolls, and now they have fallen into the eternal sleep that takes us all," Agagkantor says. "From that which we were, we will become again."

Sýstir hesitates, then wipes some of the remaining ice off the boulder. It would be difficult to see the features of a troll sculpted in the rock; Agagkantor is right in that this being has truly returned to its original state. But she fancies she sees the curve of a round, protruding nose in the smoothness of the rock, or a sturdy foot peeking out in the ridges at the bottom.

Most of the rock is layered in grey-green moss, springy to touch. This troll must have been exceptionally old, she decides. But perhaps they had smiled a lot in their exceptional elderhood, for some of the wrinkles in the stone look like laughter lines.

Her gaze drifts past to the other hefty rocks with renewed interest. So many trolls, all gathered here.

"Was there a battle?" she asks.

Agagkantor shakes his head. "When our time comes, we are moved here and laid to rest, amongst kin."

Sýstir nods distantly. Indeed, there are worse ways to find one's eternal peace.

As they crest the hill, Agagkantor stops, giving Sýstir enough time to catch up to him. In the uphill climb, she's grown hot enough to pull at the collar of her cloak. She's distracted, so she doesn't notice when Agagkantor continues to wait. Still fiddling with her collar, she starts her descent when he stops her.

"Wait. Look."

He unfurls his hand, gesturing to the sweeping valley below, and Sýstir's eyes follow. The canopy is frosted in white, punctuated by the sweep of a waterfall from a cliff opposite, and faint sunlight glitters on a nearby river. Sýstir's gaze snags on a clearing where an ancient tree sits in the centre, large and sprawling.

"Do you see?" Agagkantor asks.

Sýstir tilts her head this way and that. "Maybe?"

He laughs, a pleasing rumble. "You will."

As they descend into the valley, the trees thicken once more, but Sýstir finds herself walking easily through them, no longer fighting deep snow or rambling undergrowth. For the first time, she's on a gently discernible path, worn smooth by feet before her.

They stop some metres above the clearing, so they have a good view. An enormous tree stands tall in the centre, its branches fanned out in every direction. Even from here, she can see that the trunk is thicker than two men stood side by side together, arms stretched from fingertip to fingertip. As she gets closer, she's certain she can feel some kind of hum from it, resonating through her ribcage, familiar and uncertain all at once.

Sýstir becomes aware that Agagkantor is watching her.

"This is Nattaskur," he says, and even he sounds awed. "The heart and soul of the Dark Forest."

He settles himself some distance away from the tree, across from the river, and she perches next to him to watch. A few skóug trolls gather in Nattaskur's shadow, music and laughter drifting from their merry party. She watches as they leave a wreath of bark and pine needles around a particular branch, reverence written across their faces.

"The branch is grafted from their family tree," Agagkantor says. "When they come of age, each Väsen of the family returns to honour their branch, and join themselves to the Dark Forest. Even if they die, and their memory lost to all who knew them, Nattaskur remembers, and through its remembrance, so too does the Dark Forest."

Sýstir glances at the great tree again, trying to imagine the branches as entire families, stretching back generations. Each one representing uncounted Väsen of the Dark Forest. Each one like *her*. Something twinges in her heart.

"It's beautiful," she whispers.

Agagkantor chuckles. "There is yet more to see. I wish to show you something."

Reluctantly, she tears herself away from the tree, and follows him past Nattaskur, along the side of the valley and the river twining through. She keeps twisting around to look at the tree, though. Behind them, a cheer goes up, and the valley echoes with delighted sounds.

"Which one is your branch?" she asks.

Agagkantor is in front of her, so she can't see his expression, but his tone turns cold. "I claim no family tree."

Sýstir can tell when she's pressing too hard, and she resolves not to ask any more questions. But it doesn't stop her thinking about Nattaskur, or what kind of branch she might pick for herself. Most of the trees she's seen in the Dark Forest so far are spruce or pine, tall and imposing. None of them look like the sparser, stouter trees in the village, for which they never had a name because they never needed one. Maybe, she considers, an apple blossom from the orchard, at the height of summer – though she would have had to beg one of the farmers for it.

She finds that she can still think in this way – in hypotheticals and what-ifs – without bringing down the obliterating pain of recent events: a world pared from this one, suspended in perpetual stasis.

She's still mulling this over when the path noticeably narrows to cliffside, so that she has to walk single file behind Agagkantor as they climb upwards. Somewhere ahead of her, the quiet is broken by a rushing susurration. A waterfall, ribboning from the cliffs behind Nattaskur.

Even though it's winter, the waterfall is a roar at the lip of the rock, spray flicking into the deep pool below. She's suddenly reminded that the long walk has worked up a fair thirst, and she wets her lips in anticipation. But Agagkantor's turns and places his hand on her shoulder, rooting her in place.

"Listen to me carefully," Agagkantor says. "You must never drink from Nivir's waters. *Never*, do you understand? If you are thirsty, choose another river. If you must bathe, bathe elsewhere."

"Why?" is out of Sýstir's mouth before she can stop it.

"Queen Hilda would have you believe that the laws of the Dark Forest are infallible. That her law is *the* law. And if you drink from Nivir, then yes, that is the truth. You will not be able to shed blood, not even if your own death bore down upon you." His gaze hardens. "We are not of her Rise, nor would we be offered her mercy. Why be shackled to that which would not protect us?"

Sýstir looks longingly at the water, but Agagkantor is right; she shouldn't be beholden to something she doesn't know, and moreover, doesn't want to know *her*. She's already seen what happens when she lives under a law not made for creatures such as herself. She shivers, nothing to do with the cold.

"I won't drink from it," she promises.

Something in Agagkantor's expression shifts. "Then you will walk free from her laws, and have nothing to fear."

The walk back is long and tiring, the sun setting behind them. As they wind through the trees, Sýstir becomes alert to every sound. The Dark Forest, home. It seems like such a preposterous idea, but over the last few weeks, she's had to get used to her fair share of preposterous ideas becoming reality.

She touches the trees lightly as she passes, with a tentative hope. Home, she thinks again, steadier.

And although the sound is nothing more than the gentle snap of branches in the breeze, Sýstir swears she can hear them whispering to her.

Welcome, Sýstir.

· SIX ·

Winter has stretched its fingers across the Dark Forest for so long that Sýstir is astonished one day when she emerges from the low-slung doorway of their home to find that the snow has started to recede. Water is a constant musical refrain as icicles drip merrily from the overhang. Her first step goes sliding out from underneath her, and there are a few panicked attempts to right herself before she wheels backwards into a slushy snowdrift.

The days are starting to slip from her hands. Agagkantor keeps her busy, so that she often tumbles into bed exhausted in the evening. She learns how to weave rope, how to build furniture and carve joints that never need a nail to hold firm, how to etch runes and play the tricky fingerings of the bone flute. And where the gap between troll and human comforts widens, Sýstir manages to bridge it. She insists on making her own mattress, even though it takes weeks of finicky work, picking apart old sacks and stuffing them with whatever material she can find.

When Agagkantor sees her efforts, he rolls his eyes and mutters something about human follies. But he doesn't stop her, and soon she has a nest that feels comfortable enough to call home. Through the skylight she catches glimpses of faeries – fleeting Väsen of more kinds than Sýstir can name, barely larger than the span of her hand – carving patterns across the frost, or leaving tiny fingerprints in condensation.

It's only at night, when Agagkantor's steady snoring fills the hart, that her thoughts drift unwillingly, like clouds scudding across the sky. She presses her hands together, fingertip to fingertip, and imagines that one hand is Ada's, in anticipation of the game they would play when neither of them could sleep. They would push back on each other as gently as possible, each trying to get the other to yield, so that eventually their fingers would look like the curved branches of the tree outside. She wonders if Ada is playing the game with their cousins, whether they all sleep in the same bed because it's winter, a tangle of mussed hair and cold feet pushed into calves to elicit shrieks.

Sometimes, the wonderings merge into dreams, and it's her mother, not Ada, who presses her fingertips to Sýstir's, murmuring too low to hear. Flames, smoke, cries lancing through the air.

It's then that she wakes up screaming, or sobbing breathlessly. But Agagkantor is there, stroking her forehead or singing with his low rumble. Most of the time, he simply sits on the end of her bed patiently, until she's ready to accept the mug of water in his hands.

"Grief is like a stone," he says, after one of her nightmares.

They're sat opposite one another: Sýstir upright on her pillow, half-drunk water in her hands; Agagkantor on his stool at the end of the bed. The fire in the hearth flickers dimly, throwing shadows against the walls.

She sniffs and wipes her eyes. "Everything is like a stone to you."

In reward, she catches the twitch of his eyebrow – a sign that he's trying not to smile.

"Imagine your grief is a stone," he says again, with exaggerated patience. "Sometimes it's a boulder, larger than a troll, or a giant, or even Jörmungandr itself. Can you expect yourself to move? Can you expect yourself to bear its weight?"

Sýstir tries to picture the World Serpent winding around her chest, crushing her. But its enormity is impossible to imagine, never mind bear. She shakes her head.

"No, it is impossible," he agrees. "But remember the burial hills by Nattaskur? Time whittles us all down eventually – even your Jörmungandr of sorrow. The wind will smooth its edges. Time will carry away its sediment. Until it's small enough to hold in your arms, or even fit into your pocket.

"But time can play tricks on us," he continues gently. "Some days it will still feel like Jörmungandr. Yet there may be many days when it feels like the lightest of tjärn faeries, unnoticeable."

Sýstir's not sure she believes that. She takes a heavy, hiccupy breath, though the immediate threat of tears has passed again.

"Will it... ever go away?" she asks.

Agagkantor looks at her for a long time. "Do you want it to?"

Sýstir thinks about the relief of shucking the weight of grief. But she cannot imagine any way to do it except to forget entirely. Forget the pyre, her mother pressing a frantic kiss to her forehead – the last one she will ever have – and the long days of hunger in the forest without Ada. But...

To forget is to also forget her mother's unrestrained cackle of laughter, which would always set off Sýstir giggling, too. Forget Ada showing her how to fish in the river, or giving her a piggyback home after she cut her foot on a sharp stone. Forget returning from an errand, battling wind and rain, and seeing the cottage lit up within, the shadows of her family flickering across the windows like birds in flight.

She'll never forget that – for as long as she lives. She *can't*.

"You will carry it with you for the rest of your life," Agagkantor says. "After all, grief reminds us that we loved, once, and were loved in return." He takes away her mug and tucks her back into bed. "Remember that."

Sýstir falls asleep just before dawn, and this time her dreams are full of pebbles, turning smooth and soft at the bottom of the river.

...

With winter's easing, Agagkantor starts to take Sýstir on more trips into the forest. Most of the time, he leads with that uncanny sense of knowing where the paths lay, despite a lack of distinguishable signs. But occasionally he tells her to go first, to show him the way to the local river, or past the Rise's cave to Nattaskur. Most of the time she is hopelessly lost within a few minutes, before Agagkantor's quiet cough lets her know that she's missed a tree with cleft branches or a pattern of lingonberry bushes that signalled the path.

Today, Agagkantor is taking her deeper into the forest through a new route. Sýstir struggles after him, picking her way over rocks and fallen trees, icy puddles and pervasive mud. Though she's never thought of herself as clumsy before, every movement compared to Agagkantor's feels ungainly, as though she's a fawn learning to walk. For such a large creature, he moves with a sure-footed deftness that she's never seen before, while she scrambles through the undergrowth alongside him.

"Giants make less noise than you," he remarks, as she trips over an errant branch yet again. "Are humans supposed to hop in this way?"

When he's not looking, she sticks her tongue out at him in response.

At the base of her spine, her tail twitches with vestigial instinct. Despite Agagkantor's eye rolls, she tucks it back into the sewn pouch every morning when she gets dressed, before pulling her dress over her chemise. Theoretically, she knows she's safe to free it. But it's theoretical in the same way that the nightmares she still wakes from gasping aren't real. Every one of her mother's warnings prick at her.

They walk for most of the morning, stopping only once for Sýstir to chew hungrily at the strip of dried meat in her pocket. More than once she's longed for the slow appetite of a troll; these days, it feels like she can never quite get enough food to satisfy her, even though Agagkantor provides plenty.

Finally, they come to a halt. A solitary menhir stands like a spire amidst a mossy clearing, ringed delicately by snowdrops still emerging from their hibernation. The trees rustle with the breeze, as if sensing their presence.

Agagkantor sinks to the ground in a crouch, perfectly balanced. Sýstir folds, somewhat less elegantly, into a cross-legged position. The ground is cold, but not unbearably so.

"Close your eyes," he says. "Listen."

Obediently, Sýstir closes her eyes, and the world narrows to the other senses. The last of the snow hits cold in the back of her lungs, then the peaty scent of the dirt underneath her. A fine drizzle starts up, rain seeping into the collar of her cloak. The silence sprawls between the gaps of sound: the pause between her inhale and exhale; the coiled moment of relief from the breeze; the rain blurring into a susurration.

The seconds tick by, long and slow. Her nose itches; her muscles cramp.

Sýstir cracks an eye open and squints sideways. Agagkantor is in the same position, his breathing almost imperceptible. From this angle, he seems more rock or tree than anything else, the craggy lines of his skin dappled with moss. As though he has always been here, grown up from the ground. A few spinn faeries gather curiously at the tips of his ears.

"You're supposed to keep them closed," he says without opening his eyes.

Reluctantly, Sýstir squeezes her eyes shut again and tries to breathe like Agagkantor. She tries to pretend that she's a sapling, rooted to the earth. Her breathing slows; her heartbeat fades to a dull thump that washes into the background.

What does she hear? The felted beat of faerie wings. The rain pattering on her shoulders. The breeze teasing at the trees, setting their branches crackling together. There's something else, underneath the hush, that makes her pause. She lets the rest of the world wash away, seeking the source.

This time, when she opens her eyes, Agagkantor is watching her closely.

"Did you hear it?" he asks, and he doesn't need to elaborate further for her to nod energetically.

She strains to catch it again, but there's nothing except the clearing around them, just as before. Yet for a second, she had felt *something*, like an unfinished song, the melody snatched away.

"What was that?" she asks, awed.

His eyes crinkle. "The trees."

"That was..."

Not the trees, she thinks. Or at least, no tree noise that she's ever heard. Yet there was something distinctly... green about the way the sound had made her feel. Like a sapling in truth and not imagination, straining upward.

On their way back, Agagkantor explains more fully. Sýstir learns that the susurration is Elfdalian, the language of the trees. Proficiency in the language takes decades; mastery takes hundreds of years – a lifetime well beyond that of a human.

"But a fraction compared to the trees' lifespans," he says. "Queen Hilda might believe herself the law of the Dark Forest, but the trees are its true memory keepers. Nothing passes through without their knowledge."

Sýstir thinks of all the trees might tell her. The stories, the magic, the wonder. A smile creeps across her face. It might take hundreds of years for someone *else* to master Elfdalian, but she's willing to try and beat those odds.

• • •

Other days, Agagkantor gives her free time to use as she pleases. At first she lingers near the cave, afraid to venture much further than its near-invisible boundary lines. But soon curiosity overtakes her fear, and she spends more and more time outside.

Her favourite place, it turns out, is the river where she'd spent several freezing, miserable days at the height of her illness. Without the fever haze, it's lost much of its terror, and what's left is a place that is at once both tranquil and energetic, calming and effervescent. At this time of year, the river is awash in snowmelt, and remnants of ice floes skate gently by like clouds upon the water. On the other shore, she catches a glimpse of another Väsen, luminous against the snow. So much she didn't know – and never even knew that she didn't know it.

She sits on a rock cushioned with moss and watches the river go past. Without meaning to, she finds herself humming: some old folk ballad, warning about a river guardian and a girl. She'd picked it up from travelling musicians the winter before, though they had moved through too quickly for her to learn its name.

The words come back to her slowly, unlocked by the melody. When the musicians had played, it was with a nyckelharpa, buckskin drums, a flute, harp – and several more instruments that Sýstir hadn't recognised. With the instruments, the song had sounded full and merry, but in Sýstir's high, sweet voice, there's something melancholic twining through the words. Mist dances on the water, inching closer – tjärn faeries, hand in hand with one another.

She sings through the folk song, then another one – and another, just because she can. It feels good to stretch out her diaphragm, to feel the rise and fall of her chest with purpose. Like tuning an instrument until everything shines clear and bright.

"You have a fine singing voice," someone says behind her.

Sýstir jumps, almost falling into the river. Agagkantor saves her at the last minute, pulling her on to the bank. The tjärn faeries scatter, dissolving back into mist.

"I didn't – do you—"

Sýstir can't quite catch her breath. But Agagkantor, as always, seems to intuit what she means.

"Yes, your music has power," he says. "So does mine. But not all power is bad; it is how you channel it."

Sýstir links her hands together tightly to stop them from shaking.

"I just… don't want anyone to get hurt," she says quietly.

Agagkantor lifts an eyebrow.

Her voice gets smaller. "It's what happened last time."

It's what had alerted the entire village to her… *otherness*. Up until a point, she had been like every other child. Her tail had not yet come into its full length, so there was no need for secretive pouches. She had been, to every passer-by, normal.

And then abruptly, she hadn't.

Agagkantor considers this plea. "Would you rather live without singing for the rest of your life? Or would you see yourself knowledgeable about your magic, so that you can sing as much as you please without hurting anyone?"

Sýstir has to concede that he has a point. And not singing is like deliberately hewing off a part of herself every day, with no respite. With another's guidance, she could sing without harming anyone – and better yet, she may even be able to help others.

She pretends to mull it over. "But who will teach me?"

He must know she's joking because he rolls his eyes. "Who else but the long-suffering?"

Sýstir springs off the rock and immediately trips. She windmills for a few seconds before she rights herself. Agagkantor looks at her flatly.

"You hop like a bird; you sing like a bird." He puts his hands on his hips and sighs. "Are you sure you weren't born with wings?"

"I could be a bird," she declares, then considers. "But only a little one."

Large birds inevitably gather interest – to be captured and presented as a gift to some jarl, or else hunted for sport. But a sparrow or a finch – no one ever pays attention to those.

"Then come, Little Bird. Let us fly home."

• • •

The biggest surprise of all doesn't come until the season is halfway spent, and the forest's ice has returned to water. For the first time, Agagkantor wakes her before dawn.

"I have a treat for you," he says.

Sýstir follows him as he winds his way up the burial hills towards Nattaskur. The ground is damp from the last night's rain, water clinging to ferns in fat droplets. With dawn just fringing the horizon, the trees' shadows stretch long, like ribbons trailed behind them. Sýstir darts between them, her own shadow soaked up by theirs, as though she has slipped into a secret within a secret.

From a distance, she can hear the steady thump of footsteps. Her heart picks up, somewhere between anticipation and nerves. She's not seen the Skóug Trolls since that day at Nattaskur, during the grafting of branches. But as she and Agagkantor descend into the valley, they find themselves amongst company, slipping through the trees alongside them. Dawn emerges in truth, revealing not just trolls, but Väsen big and small. Two sprýg gnomes pass by on a squirrel, almost soundless, while a young giant strides overhead, matching one pace to Agagkantor's five.

It's been some months since they last passed by Nattaskur, and she still hasn't lost her awe for the sheer spectacle. But all of the branches had been bare then. Now, its small shoots have unfurled into verdant leaves. The entire clearing smells like something fresh and green after the rainfall. Like hope, carried on the breeze.

"The coming of spring happens one day every year," Agagkantor says. "I would not miss this."

No one seems to be missing it. Sýstir hasn't seen so much activity since she left the village, and she cranes her neck to ensure none of it escapes her. She had no idea the Dark Forest could contain so *much*. There are Väsen with packs on their shoulders or strapped to their mounts, as though they've travelled days to see the spectacle. Closest to the trunk of Nattaskur, she spies Queen Hilda, an easy expression on her face. Sýstir shuffles a little further behind Agagkantor.

She sticks with him as he winds his way effortlessly through the crowd, unwilling to be separated. Though one or two Väsen give her a lingering look, most offer her only a passing glance before returning to their own chatter. It's a far cry from the village, where she was used to suspicious sneers and muttered disdain. Here, she is just another Väsen.

Agagkantor stops where the crowd thins a little. But the branches of Nattaskur are close by, green fingers stretching outward. She inhales deeply, shadows dappling her face, and tastes the lush, earthy scent of petrichor. Vitsippor in shades of creamy white blanket the ground, still dewy. There are no words for this feeling, she thinks.

Two woodland gnomes confer to one side, glancing at Agagkantor every now and then. Their knitted hats are pulled down over their ears for warmth, dyed in all the soft colours of the forest. Sýstir notices as Agagkantor looks back and waves one hand in greeting.

He touches her shoulder. "I will be but a moment, Little Bird."

Without Agagkantor, Sýstir feels oddly vulnerable, as though his steadying presence is all that keeps her on the ground. Here, with the vast enormity of Väsen before her, it's easy to be reminded of how little she knows. Who are long-standing allies or friends; who are bitterest enemies but for these exceptional circumstances. Who might welcome her presence... and who might resent it. By the trunk of Nattaskur, Queen Hilda raises her head to glance at Sýstir; she flushes and looks away.

But not all the skóug trolls are with Queen Hilda. The younger ones cluster together near Sýstir. She can tell they're youths from their more coltish builds, as though they've not yet quite decided to be like the rocks from which they came. All limbs and stretched proportions, their movements quicker than their elder kin.

She doesn't realise she's hovering on the edge of their conversation until she coughs and one of them catches her eye. A troll with mossy green eyes, impenetrable as the bottom of the river. She looks surprised to see Sýstir there.

"Agagkantor's ward," the troll says, and the others turn.

Sýstir feels the childish urge to retreat and hide behind Agagkantor's imposing figure. But instead she forces herself to stay where she is. Even though Queen Hilda has declared her a mistake – *a terrible mistake*, an awful voice echoes in her head – she has as much a right to be here as the other Väsen.

"You are Huldra," the troll says.

Sýstir takes a deep breath. "I am."

It still feels like a curse to say it out loud. One day, she resolves, she'll be able to say it without that accompanying wince.

The troll tilts her head curiously to the side. "Why hide your tail?"

Something hot and unpleasant sticks in Sýstir's chest. She thought she would leave this behind in the village, in the hands of the cruel boys who had mocked her. She folds her arms tightly across her chest and tilts her chin up defiantly.

"I don't see how that's any of your business," she says curtly.

"Humans are often prone to such ignorance," a second troll says, with more than a hint of a sneer. "They know nothing but shame, and anger where shame fails to curb a Väsen's nature."

The first one shoves his shoulder pointedly. "Grendel, enough. She is Väsen."

"A Väsen who consorted with humans? Who cannot stand to be herself?"

"I'm not – I—" Sýstir stammers.

But words fail her. She's spent so much of her life defining herself by all that isn't Väsen: human enough to be her mother's daughter and Ada's sister; human enough to live in the village; human enough to bleed by their laws. And what wasn't human to be weighed down inside of her. It's only in the last few weeks that she's tried to describe herself as anything else.

But she is not quite Väsen, either. Not like these trolls.

She bites down on her lip hard. A sick panicky feeling rises within her.

"Let her be, Grendel," the first troll says, steering the others away.

Sýstir waits until the trolls are out of sight before heaving a shuddering breath. She didn't cry. That's something, at least.

Moments later, Agagkantor returns, looking thoughtful. He pockets something and comes to stand next to her, his head craned upwards at the branches.

"How are you enjoying yourself?" he asks.

He looks at her so hopefully that she doesn't have her heart in it to tell him the truth. That she'd been so thoroughly dismissed by the trolls, it feels as though she has been flayed to her core and still found wanting. It doesn't matter, she thinks fiercely. As long as she has Agagkantor, she'll never need to deal with the others. She's only ever lived in a world for a few – that's all she's ever needed. If not herself and her tight-knit family, then herself and Agagkantor, and the whispering Dark Forest.

She forces a smile. "The flowers are so beautiful."

Hidden away, her tail aches in painful response.

· SEVEN ·

The Dark Forest grows hot as summer shakes off the vestiges of spring. Sýstir wakes half tangled in her bed, the humidity clinging to her skin. She takes to going barefooted, the sleeves of her dress rolled up to her elbows, her hair pulled into a knot at the back of her head. There might have been a time when someone would have accused her of impropriety, but the trolls are indifferent towards the intricacies of human clothing.

Agagkantor still gives her lessons: in the art of Elfdalian, in singing, in the markers of the forest as they shift with the seasons. But lately his attention has been diverted. He leaves the cave for days at a time, with no indication of where he's going or why. She asks the first few times, but when no answer is forthcoming, lets it rest. They're all entitled to their secrets – and the gods know that Sýstir has more than a few of her own.

But even without Agagkantor's commanding presence, she's learning. Slowly, the Dark Forest is opening up to her, with all its possibilities stretched out at her fingertips. Every corner seems to brim with some new secret, whether it's the impenetrable black mirror of a lake, or the shimmer of a spiderweb strung like a curtain across a cave's entrance. With no snow on the ground to flatten the scenery, the pathways become easier to distinguish, from clusters of mushrooms peeking through mossy groves, to shy wildflowers, to a tree with a particular knot in its trunk. And where her navigational skills sometimes fail her, the trees do not. They tolerate, too, her clumsy forays into their language, though she's less clumsy with each passing day.

Most days, she finds herself returning to the river once her chores are finished. It's the best place to practise her singing, using Agagkantor's exercises of control and intent. Sometimes she brings along a bone flute instead, though her fingers still lack the deftness and strength required to pull out some of the more intricate melodies. Not that it matters to her – not when the true joy is to be found in learning at all. How much wider the world feels after a scant six months in the Dark Forest.

Six months, a quiet voice reminds her, *without Ada*.

Even though the sunlight never quite reaches the ground in the Dark Forest, the river still glints faintly, dragonflies zipping over it. The whine of insects punctures the air. Occasionally, the silvered belly of a fish surfaces, but otherwise, there's no one around.

Sýstir sings for as long as her voice will allow her, then sprawls out on a flat rock in the shadows of the overhead trees. She closes her eyes and lets the sounds of summer wash over her: insects humming on the air, the brush of wings, the low whickering of a doe to her almost fully grown fawn. When the heat becomes just about intolerable, she opens one eye and squints at the river, temptation itself. Agagkantor had warned of drinking from Nivir, but she is perhaps far enough from the waterfall for anything ill to have long-since dissipated. It's a small enough risk that she's willing to take it.

Unable to resist, Sýstir strips down to her cotton chemise and dives in. The first sensation is the needle punch of cold, stealing the air from her lungs. The ghost of winter claws at her, terrifying. Then her head breaks the water and she sucks in breath after breath. The summer warmth fractures the chill.

She rolls on to her back and lets herself bob in the current, face turned up to the sky. Her chemise floats weightless around her. The ice sluice of the water against her body diminishes to a pleasant cold. She lifts her hand up to her face and splays her fingers, admiring their pruny whorls.

Years gone by, she would watch longingly as the other children shucked their clothes and pelted through the village towards the rocky banks of the river. Sýstir would go with them – given a choice, she would always follow – but her tail was too conspicuous, with too much risk of discovery, never mind the hollow in her back. The water, as with so many things, was not meant for her.

So the summer would tick over as it always did. Ada would stay by her side in solidarity for the first few weeks, chaining wildflowers together into necklaces and crowns, or entertaining her with all kinds of stories about the capricious Väsen who lived at the edges of the woods, or in the ditches surrounding the fields. When the heat proved too fierce, they retreated to the shady orchard that overlooked the river, where Ada would persuade an apple off the farmer, or forage for the first pick of blueberries along its edge.

Eventually, though, the lure would be too great, and Ada would snap her book shut with a pained sigh, or she'd gently pull the wildflower crown from her hair and place it next to Sýstir.

"Keep it safe for me?" she asked.

And Sýstir knew she wasn't really asking about the crown or the book. But she'd smile anyway and pat the ground next to her.

"I'll be here," Sýstir said, and she'd watch her sister run towards the river, her braid unravelling in the wind.

It always hurt, though, just a little. Like pressing down on a cut deliberately to see whether it would bleed again.

Later, at night, when the heat was wicked away by dusk and all respectable children corralled into chores, their mother would bring Sýstir and Ada back out to the river, giggling as they cut soft-footed through the long grass. Then, and only then, Sýstir would ease her toes into the water and feel sweet, blissful relief.

Until a few weeks ago, she'd never been in the river during the day. It's every bit as delicious as she'd imagined it to be.

For a while, Sýstir is content to play. She floats, slips below the cool water, floats again through the dappled shadows of overhanging branches. She fishes for leaves, twirling them wetly in her hands. She dives for as long as her lungs will let her, occasionally straining to brush the algae-slick stones on the riverbed. The river at home – *not home*, she thinks, with a pang – is shallower than this one, even at a glance. But she'd never managed to touch the bottom.

Feeling daring, she fiddles with the pouch that keeps her tail tucked away. There's no one around to see her. She unloops it and it flicks free in glorious defiance.

Her tail steers her like a rudder, keeping her from the other bank of the river. When she dives again, her body is one synchronised line, honed to the same purpose. She touches the riverbed easily, and when she surfaces, she's clutching a small pebble, smooth and gleaming. This must be what it's like, she thinks, remembering the lean arc of her sister drawing herself across the water, stroke by stroke.

She dives again – and again, just because she can.

She's just come up for air when she spies movement on the shore. She sloshes upright, her heart pistoning. For an awful second, her vision tunnels white with fear. Her tail is free; *she's not alone – she'll be caught—*

Then her mind catches up to what her eyes have been telling her all along. It's a group of skóug trolls from Queen Hilda's Rise, laden with nets woven from grass and branches whittled into thin poles. Although she's still learning how to distinguish between them – what might pass for delicate features on one, or a handsome smile scrawled on another – she's sure she recognises at least two of them from Nattaskur's blossoming. They are talking to each other in quiet, unhurried voices. Then one of them points – right at her.

Sýstir sinks further into the water, but it's too late; they've already noticed her.

A smaller troll, with the juvenile colouring of someone close to Sýstir in age, stares at her with undisguised curiosity. It was the one who had asked her about her tail, she realises, her stomach turning sour. Another one nudges the troll, and she glances away.

The largest of them looks at her, unimpressed. "You'll scare away the fish."

Then he jerks his head upstream, and the rest of the trolls follow. The younger one looks at her again. Amongst the trolls, she seems small, but she had been head and shoulders taller than Sýstir. It's a long time before their footsteps fade.

Even though they're just trolls, she feels too exposed, with nowhere to hide in the vast water of the river. As soon as they're out of sight, she clumsily wades out, grabbing her dress. She curses herself for not being more careful, even though she avoids thinking about what specifically requires her care.

Her dress clings to her over her waterlogged chemise as she makes her way back to the cave. She's so irritated with herself that she's almost relieved when a wailing peep echoes in the forest, distracting her. Then she hears a slightly longer wail from the ground and stops.

A fledgling nuthatch, cushioned in the wide hammock of a

fern's leaf. It mouths at her, tufted with the first brush of feathers. Sýstir cradles it in her hands as though she is handling glass. Carefully, she checks for signs of broken bones or bruising, but the fledgling is miraculously unharmed.

She glances from the fledgling up to the tree, tracing its arc. Halfway up the tree, her gaze snags on a nest. An anxious winged shadow scores lines across the sky. She looks at the bird again, pink and open-mouthed, searching for food.

If she leaves it here, it'll die. That's just nature.

But Sýstir thinks about the long, hard death, even in the tree's cool shade. Hungry and thirsty. Alone.

"Come on, little bird," she whispers, as much to the fledgling as herself.

She lines her pocket with soft moss and places the fledgling inside to keep it safe. She pushes up the sleeves on her dress and ties a knot in the skirt, so that the material slings low over her hips. Carefully, she flexes her toes.

Her tail would be useful for balance, a stubborn voice tells her in the back of her head. But just as quickly, she dismisses the thought. She's been able to scale trees just fine without it, and it's not that far up.

She begins to climb.

The first few branches are easy, low and more than strong enough to support her weight. Between Agagkantor's chores and her persistent exploration of the forest, her body has been honed to a sinewy strength, and it's not long before she's halfway there. She pats her pocket, and it peeps in response.

But the tree is taller than she'd expected from her vantage point on the ground. *Don't look down*, she thinks, a beat before she looks down anyway. The forest floor swims in her vision, and her heart flutters. But if she climbed down now, the fledgling would die. And although that's the way of all things, it seems like fate for her to have chosen this precise moment to walk through this part of the forest, and to have paused when she might not have. For the fledgling, she can be brave.

With one final effort, she hauls herself on to the last branch and swings her leg over the side to straddle it. The nest is within arm's reach. Inside is a treasure of feathers, leaves and broken eggshell – and two more fledglings, gloriously, beautifully ugly, like most newborn things.

Carefully, Sýstir retrieves the fledgling from her pocket and places it back with its siblings. There's a flurry of peeping from the nest. Above, a cry from the circling bird.

"Don't fall out again," she says mock sternly.

Sýstir's muscles ache with tense fatigue, but unless she wants to spend the night up a tree, she has to make her way back down. Carefully, she descends, feeling for every step. Her legs shake, muscles cramping and already exhausted from hours of swimming. *Just a little longer,* she pleads.

She's nearly down when her dress snags on peeling bark – and she loses her grip. *I'm going to fall*, Sýstir thinks, in terrifying slow motion. Her stomach swoops in surprise.

She falls.

There's a split second of too much air – of the earth rushing up to meet her, of her scrabbling to catch a branch to slow her descent – and then she hits the ground. Her teeth rattle in her jaw; her knees bloom with pain, hot and instant. She lets herself sink entirely on to the dirt, trying to wrest control over the shock.

I'm fine, she thinks. She's *fine*.

One by one, she tests all her limbs, and then stands shakily. Nothing broken – just sore. Her knees protest, and when she glances down, blood splashes bright across her skin.

Above, there's a rustle of wings, as the nuthatch circling above perches on the edge of the nest. Safe, at least. But Sýstir is covered in dirt, and there's a sizeable tear in her dress. Wearily, she makes her way back to the river.

Her knees singing with pain, she wades into the water to wash the worst of the blood away, biting back tears as she does so. Not for the first time, she longs for the warmth of her mother's hug, or Ada's pragmatic hands ready with a cooling poultice. It's no use going to Agagkantor; she knows very well what he'll think of her escapade. *How did you fall?* and then *what did I tell you?* He's already told her more than once that her tail is there for a reason. A reason that she'd ignored because she's always ignored it.

The fledgling is safe, she tells herself. That's what matters.

When she emerges from the river, dripping, she reaches for her shoes, left on a smooth, flat rock, and pauses. A large scrap of fabric is pinned underneath, an iridescent emerald entirely at odds with anything she's ever worn before. But it's just long enough to mend the tear in her dress.

Sýstir looks around, but there's no one to thank. Still, she winds a strand of her hair around her finger and pulls. The nearby woodland gnomes like the hair to stitch with: finer than horse hair and less precious than silk, but still hard to come by.

Her heart squeezes in fondness. She doesn't see the woodland gnomes often, but she's forever leaving out gifts they might consider useful. In exchange, they've often gone out of their way for her, whether it's to return a missing button or leave a splinter of antler with which to craft a needle.

Sýstir flexes her shoulders, feeling the ache of every muscle. She did good today, she thinks more brightly. She walks back to Agagkantor's cave soaking wet, letting the dappled sunshine dry her, her mind lingering on the fledgling. She has no idea if birds recognise kin, but it was worth it, just to see them huddled in their nest together. And it's true that a storm might still carry them off, or a cold night, or a predator. But at least they're facing it together.

She's still thinking about the birds when she becomes aware of a pair of eyes on her. She stops and turns. A figure, almost a mirror image, is watching her, crouched in foliage.

A huldra.

For a long moment, she and the huldra stare at one another.

There's something familiar in her pointed chin, her eyes set slightly wide and lined with thick black lashes. In that wiry composition of limbs, the soft scoop of the hollow in her back and the striking shadow that dapples the ground in front of her. She is so beautiful that Sýstir can barely breathe for daring to look. It is the kind of beauty that might make someone stop in the street to gape, or have a husband questioning his vows to his wife.

If there's any human within her, it's only in the slight crease of puzzlement as she contemplates Sýstir. Every single other element, from the way she cocks her head to the flick of her tail, and even the way she seems to linger in shadows, is Väsen. So wholly a creature of the forest in every imaginable way.

The huldra must be a little older than Sýstir, she thinks wondrously. But they are unquestionably sisters, in all the features that Ada has never shared with Sýstir. Tucked into its pouch, Sýstir's tail twitches in response.

Cautiously, Sýstir waves.

Then the huldra vanishes with a nimble leap, one long, elegant line with the grace of an arrow shot through the forest. There and gone, with only the faintest rustle to prove her presence. Agagkantor has told her before that she is unlikely to come across many of her half-sisters, solitary as they are. Even her own quiet presence is enough to spook them from this part of the Dark Forest.

For a while, Sýstir stares at the spot where the huldra had crouched, but she doesn't reappear. What little Sýstir knows of her father was squeezed out, line by line, from her mother. She knows that he was a Väsen: a river guardian or spirit of some kind. That he was beautiful, in the same way that bears could look beautiful from a distance.

All her other features she's had to piece together from what was missing from her family – and who was to say that something didn't come from a long-deceased relative, skipping past generations to her? But seeing the huldra was like seeing the second half of a map, or a dozen puzzle pieces finally assembled into the final picture. Herself, fully realised.

As Sýstir heads back, the huldra replays in her mind, the slick water ripple of her gaze, the warm freckle of her skin, her irrefutable beauty. And that leap. Truly, breathtakingly effortless. Everything Sýstir has wanted from the Dark Forest emphasised in one sinuous arc.

With careful, trembling fingers, Sýstir reaches underneath her chemise for the pouch. Her tail slips free, curling around the hem of her dress. It swishes, testing the air. Sýstir rolls up her sleeves past her elbows, letting the sun warm her skin. She flexes her toes in the dirt, feeling the ground beneath her feet.

She jumps, and it feels like flying.

· EIGHT ·

Sýstir sits cross-legged, mending her cloak. It's starting to take on the colours of the forest: mottled greens, glistening amber, the blue-black of the mirror-like lakes. Using fine gold stitching, she's also started to weave in the runes for her story: a girl, lost in a forest, and the troll who saved her. At her request, Agagkantor has added several stitches of his own along the hem, in a sturdy hand that she would recognise anywhere.

Her newfound forays with her tail have been exciting, but not entirely without mishap. More often than not, she's bounded through the forest only to be rudely sent sprawling by her cloak catching on a wayward branch. She's tried to go without, the way the other huldra had, but she likes the reassuring weight of it against her shoulders. As a result, her cloak is looking much worse for its wearing, with a large and ungainly rip down the back. The mends Sýstir has planned, though, should ensure that it looks even more beautiful than before.

If this were the village, she might be able to buy reams of wool from the farmers' wives, to spin for herself into yarn – or else wait for a passing trader for finer silk and other wares. But she's come to realise that there are no human traders who would ever find themselves in the Dark Forest, even if she's not entirely sure why. Perhaps they've heard rumours and stay away; perhaps it's simply difficult to find. In any case, the best place to ask for help is at the nearby Revel of sprýg gnomes.

Today, Sýstir is after something slightly different to her usual requests: a wooden frame in which to keep the fabric of her cloak taut while she sews. With it, she should be able to work in finer stitches, with a more even tension.

The sky is overcast, and rain mists the air as Sýstir sets off. She picks her way through the Dark Forest, careful to watch for the pathways, their markers changing with the season. In her pocket, she carries a handful of trinkets that might be worth gifting: among them, several river stones that she's polished to a high shine, bright feathers collected over a season, and rarest of all, a seashell, glossy and strange.

Sýstir knows she's close to a Revel of sprýg gnomes by the sound: a quiet burr of activity that's almost indistinguishable from music at a distance. She pads quietly over the moss, her tail lending her extra balance, careful not to disturb the ground of their dwelling. Though the Sprýg Gnomes are generally forgiving of any physical blunders, she would rather not break anything.

Two sprýg gnomes she recognises pass her on a squirrel with a cheery wave, their luvas fluttering in the breeze. Sýstir is still learning which Väsen are less inclined to talk to her – the trolls are a given – but the sprýg gnomes are always friendly. They often linger by Agagkantor's cave for her singing or for stories late at night – particularly in the summer when Sýstir climbs over the boulders to eat her meals outdoors. They've already exchanged a few gifts between themselves, and Sýstir has grown used to their presence, though it's rare she sees them out in the open.

A few months ago, she had stumbled upon a Revel and their dwelling accidentally, still unversed in the Dark Forest's signs. Now, though, it's so obvious that she wants to laugh at her past self for her own clumsiness. Their wooden homes are set comfortably like nests in the treetops, branches carefully pruned to make them easier to scale, with bridges strung between them. The forest floor is a whirl of activity; elsewhere, foliage and ferns are cleverly positioned above paths to hide sprýg gnomes from enterprising birds. But anyone else – her human self – would only see another stretch of wild, untamed forest.

Her friend Thróttr is waiting for her outside of his home, perched halfway along a low birch tree branch. His luva sticks out behind him like a twig, a hat made out of fur so fine that it could be mistaken for felt at a glance. She stands on her tiptoes to hand him one of the feathers in her pocket, alongside a few tiny wooden beads that she whittled herself.

"I've come to ask a favour," she says.

Thróttr beams and ducks back into his house. This exchange of favours still surprises her, both in the level of generosity and in the fundamental way it seems to happen – as though a life without favours gifted and bestowed is not just unthinkable, but a kind of un-life. Though Thróttr looks old enough to her, he's still considered a child to the rest of the Revel. A thousand favours bestowed to gain adulthood, he'd told her. The last time she spoke to him, he was on six hundred and something – a specific number that she forgot moments after he told her.

"How do you keep track?" she'd asked.

He'd just tapped his luva thoughtfully. Later it had occurred to her that she wasn't entirely sure if he'd meant that he simply remembered, or whether it was marked on his luva in some way. It seems like a much nicer way to note the passage of adulthood, more so than time – or at least, Sýstir can think of more than a few people in the village who might have benefitted from such a system.

Something whistles past her ear and she ducks instinctively. A zip line, strung together from spinn faerie silk. The sprýg gnome is there and gone before she can catch a closer look at how it works.

"Ah, here it is," Thróttr says, emerging from his house again.

The wooden frame is almost the same size as him, but he carries it with ease. Sýstir thanks him, stowing it in her pocket. Between the frame and her existing store of thread, there's more than enough for a good few weeks of work, and by the time she returns, she'll have more new and interesting items to share with him.

"There is a favour I wish to bestow upon you," he says.

Sýstir cocks her head to one side. "A favour? But I'm already asking for one."

"A different favour."

"And you're asking me... if I would take the favour?"

Thróttr smiles. "If it would please you."

Intrigued and yet puzzled, Sýstir nods her head. Thróttr descends from his house, landing with a soft thump amongst the ferns, and motions for her to follow. She holds her breath as she walks, stepping in between fences that would only look like stems if she didn't know better.

She's exchanged favours with Thróttr before, but something about this feels... different. He leads her towards the very edge of the dwelling, where their paths blend into the forest, so that no one might ever guess that they're here at all. She takes another step forward – and stops.

Two sprýg gnomes are trying to placate a lynx kit. Now she understands why Thróttr has brought her here; even though the kit can only be a few months old, it's already taller than them, with a careless energy that anyone would struggle to contain. The kit squirms free and bounds towards the dwelling, but before it can cause damage, Sýstir kneels down to scoop it into her lap.

"This is the favour?" she asks.

Sýstir looks at the furry, wriggling creature in her hands, then back at the sprýg gnomes. Its ears are tipped with dark points, the body robust under the kit's fuzzy coat.

"He is the runt," he says. "His mother rejected him. We cannot keep him here, so we could let the forest take back what it's owed, but..."

It's an odd kind of favour, and she's not entirely sure if she's the recipient or the giver. Sýstir hears the echo of Agagkantor's words. *She's just a girl-thing. Would you rather I left her out to die?* And all the implications in Queen Hilda's response.

She pulls the kit more firmly into her lap. She might not have looked after a lynx before, but she was there when the neighbour's cat gave birth to a litter twice over. And all creatures need the same things, she's found: warmth, food, shelter. Love.

"Will he eat meat?" she asks.

Thróttr nods. "And milk."

They ply her with as much as she can carry, with the kit coming last in a rather ungainly sack. She cradles him as best as she can. He's much too big to feel like a kitten, but too wayward to set down to walk beside her and too small to be protected from the forest's larger creatures. A singularity.

On her way back, she tries to conceive of every plausible reason to be returning with a lynx kit that might pass muster with Agagkantor. It's true that it's a grave thing to refuse a favour from the Sprýg Gnomes, even one with as much ambiguity as this. And it might be useful to have a lynx – once he's grown, he can help take down larger hunts, or track animals in places Sýstir might otherwise find impossible. Truthfully, she has little idea of how a lynx might be useful, but the Sprýg Gnomes wouldn't bestow a favour if they didn't think it was truly favourable.

When Agagkantor sees her, he only sighs, as though he'd been waiting for this to happen. He's probably right; her mother was no stranger to Sýstir coming home with all manner of birds out of the nest too early, stray kittens still mewling for milk, or once, memorably, a fox cub that had tried to bite everyone except Sýstir.

She sets the lynx kit on the floor and he tumbles out of the sack. After a cursory investigation of the cave, he returns to her arms, if only because she's tempting him with food.

"He is a wild thing, lest you forget," Agagkantor says. "And he will not be a kit forever."

Sýstir presses her forehead to his, feeling the soft tufted fur, whiskers tickling at her face. He meows at her, a screeching sound that's a far cry from the domestic cats she's used to.

"What happens if he goes wandering?" Agagkantor continues. "He will flee eventually."

"He needs a name," she says.

Agagkantor gives her a look that tells her exactly what he thinks of this endeavour. Wild things don't have names, and the kit is as wild as they come. There's every certainty that come spring, he'll simply run off from the cave, never to be seen again. But at least it'll be spring, she reasons, with every chance of survival, and not the unforgiving winter. As long as she can keep him occupied until then, she'll have fulfilled her favour.

Sýstir stays up late that night pondering the kit's future. He shifts in his sleep with a fitful, skittish energy that reminds her of her own first few weeks under Agagkantor's watchful eye. What did she want, at that time? To be smaller, less than nothing, because even nothing can be noticed. Only less than nothing survived, she'd believed at the time.

"Fenrir," she declares the next morning.

Agagkantor's ears twitch. "A wolf's name?"

They both look at the kit scarpering across the floor, chasing at the shadows thrown by the fire. In the dim light, his own shadow stretches out, twice as large as his true self.

"The biggest wolf," she agrees.

"As you please," Agagkantor says, with a sigh.

But Sýstir knows that he understands because he doesn't protest any further.

That night, the kit curls up next to her head, his nose pressed wet on her forehead. He smells like animal, like a child of the Dark Forest. She gathers him in her arms.

"Fenrir," she whispers to him, and there is a low rumble that might be mistaken for a purr.

May you be bigger than all the wolves at your door, she thinks.

...

Those first few weeks – that month, really – Fenrir feels less like a favour bestowed and more like one that Sýstir can come to collect from the Sprýg Gnomes in time. He wakes her up in the middle of the night, pouncing at her toes with painfully sharp claws. He demands food, attention, sleep, more food – and when it's not from her, it's from Agagkantor, whose patience wanes thinner than Sýstir's, and by greater degrees. Fenrir gets into *everything*.

It's one of those days where the rain is more like sleet when she wakes up in the cave to find that Fenrir isn't with her. It'll be weeks before the sleet turns to snow, before winter digs in and calls itself as such. But the weather is too harsh for a little lynx kit. If she'd left him with the Sprýg Gnomes, he would have long been swallowed by the forest, doomed to a runt's short, hard fate.

Sýstir scrambles into her shoes, flinging on her cloak. Outside, sleet pours from the sky, thunder groaning in the distance. The sun is a rain-soaked blur, with barely enough gloom to see by. The weather is changing, biting deeper.

She tries to track him, the way she's learning to do. But the sleet has churned everything into a mud wash, with so many prints it's impossible to tell who or what they might belong to. Panic crawls up her stomach. He surely can't have gone far in this weather.

She'll find him. She has to.

For the entire day, she looks for him, searching in all the places that a kit might roam. The slender gaps between boulders that she is almost too tall to squeeze into, hollowed-out and fallen trees almost invisible under moss, dense ferned undergrowth where it's almost too dark to see. She even returns to the Sprýg Gnomes' dwelling, in the hopes that Fenrir has simply decided to go back to his original home. But the dwelling is far too quiet to have encountered him, the sprýg gnomes curled up in their warm and dry houses.

She passes by the river, where the water gleams dark and impenetrable. A huge knot of terror chokes her. What if he didn't wander far at all? What if he overestimated his strength? There are so many ways for a forest to take its own.

By the time night falls, Agagkantor must notice she's missing because he comes looking for her. He finds her almost blue with cold and soaked through, teeth chattering, still calling Fenrir's name.

"Go back inside," Agagkantor says.

Sýstir looks at him, so sodden it's impossible to tell what's tears and what's rain. "But—"

"Inside."

Sýstir would protest further, but Agagkantor is already ushering her in, and she can barely stay on her feet. He sits her down by the fire, taking her cloak from her. She shivers, stifles a sob.

"A wild thing has no business being tamed," he mutters.

But he turns around and trudges back into the sleet, leaving puddles behind.

Warmth comes back to Sýstir bit by bit, though it's a long time before she stops shivering. Guilt devours her, even though she knows that not all kits survive to adulthood, that the Dark Forest may take what it's owed, that the cycle of growth and rot is inevitable. She knows just how fleeting life can be – she *knows*.

She puts her head in her hands and tries not to cry.

Two hours later, heavy footsteps sound in the corridor. Sýstir can't look up.

Agagkantor will have given up. It's too dark, the weather is too bad, and Fenrir so, so small despite his name. She was lucky to have him as long as she did. *You have failed again*, a cruel voice sings at her from the back of her mind. And it's true, isn't it? Because with Ada—

Agagkantor shoves a soaked, mewling thing into her hands, smelling strongly of wet fur.

"More fool us all, but he will live," he grumbles.

Sýstir lets out a ragged sob. Fenrir wails at her, and no sound has ever been sweeter.

"He will live, Little Bird," Agagkantor says more gently.

...

The next day, Agagkantor presses two rocks into her hand, with holes bored into the sides, and a twist of metal coiled into a spring. When Sýstir pushes them together, the sound is an instant clack.

"It is how the lilvätt tame their toads," he says. "For when you wish to call upon your... Fenrir."

Sýstir glances at the lynx kit, still fast asleep by the hearth after his wearying day outdoors. She can't imagine a time when she'll feel safe letting him out of the cave, much less out of her sight. She leans over to press her face into his fur, and he meows in complaint.

"You're smarter than toads, Fen," she whispers to him.

"He cannot stay inside forever," Agagkantor says.

"I know," she says.

It's not an instant success, but the rocks help in small ways, and then larger ones. Sýstir spends several weeks trying to get Fenrir to come when called, associating the sharp sound with food. And with the promise of a meaty treat, her efforts start to work. She still doesn't trust him roaming too far outside, and more often than not, she bundles him up with her, always keeping him close.

Even inside the cave, Sýstir is reluctant to leave Fenrir for long periods of time. But Agagkantor shoos her outside, plucking the kit from her.

"It is stuffy with your fretting," he says. "I will take your charge."

He's right – he's always right. When she leaves the cave, she takes a deep breath, one that perhaps she has been holding on to for too long. Even though the sky is overcast, the sleet has abated, and she spends a glorious day in all of her favourite spots.

She's returning and in the corridor of the cave when she hears the sound of laughter. She stops in the entryway and peers around the edge.

Agagkantor leans over his footstool, dangling a piece of string in front of him. Below, Fenrir bats at it with his over-large paws, entirely focused on the sliver of meat tied to the end. When Fenrir successfully grips it with his needle sharp teeth, Agagkantor chuckles. Sýstir presses a hand over her mouth to avoid revealing her own laughter, afraid to break the spell of the moment.

For all his gruffness, it seems Agagkantor isn't quite done with taking in strays.

· NINE ·

Winter is unfolding from her hibernation again, the light waning with it. Sýstir wakes one morning to find that the water trough outside is frozen over with a thin skin of ice. It only takes a small tap to dislodge it, but the water makes her gasp with its fierce cold. She splashes her face and neck, then strips to her waist and douses herself, shivering. It'll be a long time before she'll be tempted to bathe in the river again.

She's told herself she hasn't been paying attention to the turn of the season, golden-leaved autumn giving way to winter, but her body remembers what her mind refuses, keeping track on her behalf. Her thoughts drift reluctantly.

This time last year, a child had gone missing in the village. A little boy, from one of the larger families. The alarm wouldn't go out until the day after; that day, they were still assuming that the boy was with some neighbour or another, or out in the fields with the other children. Sýstir wouldn't even know the boy was missing until later, when search parties went out and returned with nothing but rage in their fists.

What was she doing that day? The memory is hazy, suffused in the blanket of fever that tugs across more than its fair share of time. But she was probably doing what she always did: collecting eggs from the hens; milking their one stubborn goat, or straining out its curds for cheese; weaving a new blanket or rug if the weather was too unpleasant to venture outside. Grumbling at Ada's criticism of her stitching, or bristling at her mother's complaint about the mud tracked in.

Normal things – and fragile, as it turns out.

Now, she's been in the Dark Forest for an entire year. She tries to imagine what life might be like if the boy hadn't gone missing, if she'd stayed in the village. But for the first time, that future feels cold and distant. Yes, she would still have her mother and Ada, but what else? A village who would never have seen her with anything but suspicion at best – and who might have hunted her as a monster at their worst.

Whereas the Dark Forest has welcomed her into its home, monster and all. She might not be well liked by the other skóug trolls, but she's never been able to rely on friendships before, so that's no great hardship. And she has Agagkantor. She has the trees that whisper their secrets to her, the Sprýg Gnomes with their clever crafting hands, the Faeries that linger at her music – and Fenrir, of course. Her tail swishes behind her freely.

When she returns inside, Agagkantor is busying himself at the hearth. He hasn't seemed entirely himself for the last few weeks; he is snappish and prone to headaches. Sometimes looking at him, she has the awful sensation of watching a stranger wearing Agagkantor's face. Perhaps the encroachment of winter is getting to them both. Yes, that is what it is – and when spring is coming, he will right himself, like the rest of the Dark Forest.

For a while, they work together in companionable silence. Sýstir wonders how much he remembers of last year, or whether the days have blended together for him, the way they have for her. Maybe for trolls, a year is barely a second in their eyes, with every event compressed in between just as insignificant. He took her in without question, after all, and although she's spent hours wondering why, she's never been able to voice it, for fear of the answer.

Someone else might have told her that she should be grateful to be pitied, or at least seen as so insignificant as to not matter in the grand scheme of a troll's life. Sýstir glances at Agagkantor, shadowed against the firelight, and he meets her gaze.

"Are you warm enough?" he asks.

She nods. The tips of her fingers and toes are still unusually sensitive to temperature, and the recent downward plummet has left them burning painfully in the cold.

"I have a gift for you," he says gruffly.

She blinks at him, surprised. "A gift?"

He pulls out several objects from underneath a fur and hands them to her. New boots of roe deer hide, lined with fur and oiled for waterproofing. Sýstir slips her feet into them, relishing their softness. Her last winter boots were hand-me-downs from Ada, who in turn had received them from someone else in the village. They were left in the cottage, along with everything else.

Without thinking, Sýstir flings her arms around Agagkantor in a hug. After a frozen second, he pulls her in tightly.

"It is no great thing," he says, but she can tell he's pleased. "You will have to tell me how they fit."

Sýstir beams up at him. "They're perfect."

There are other gifts besides, it turns out. A thick bracelet for her upper arm – and in her size – to match Agagkantor's, with the runes for Little Bird hammered into the warm gold. Supple leather gloves for her hands. Iridescent beetle shells, polished to a high shine, from the woodland gnomes, to adorn her clothes as she wishes. Fine silk thread from the spinn faeries, alongside dainty buttons carved from acorn caps.

Agagkantor doesn't mention an occasion, but Sýstir's chest glows with warmth. *He remembers*, she thinks.

After the gift-giving, Agagkantor starts to sing his song of protection, low and thronged with the warmth that she's come to recognise as magic. The language isn't one that Sýstir understands, but she feels its power settle on her like a shroud. Like standing under Nattaskur, or touching the bottom of the river. *Home*.

After a while, she joins in with him, adding harmony to his melody. Her voice rises higher than his, and for a moment, the hart is filled with nothing but music.

"What was that for?" she asks, smiling, as they finish.

"You could call it a replenishing of the heart," he says.

Later, they break crusty bread slathered in butter over thick stew. And although the meal is no finer than any other, to Sýstir, it feels like a feast.

• • •

That night, Sýstir waits until Agagkantor's soft snores emanate from the other side of the hart. Fenrir curls up at the foot of her bed, ears twitching as he dreams. Then she pulls on her old slippers, wraps her cloak tightly around her, and slips outside.

Though it hasn't snowed yet, she can taste it on the air, and the wind is knife-sharp against her face. She pulls her cloak closer to herself, the memory of last year's winter slicing through every defence she's erected against the slippery terror beneath. For a moment, she stands frozen at the edge of the cave, fighting the panic that threatens to submerge her.

Maybe it'll always be this way, come winter. Maybe some memories are too deep to uproot.

That's why she's out tonight, after all.

The fear never quite subsides, but the panic does, and she gathers her courage, holding it tight to her chest. She walks purposely through the forest, guided by the thin light of the waxing crescent moon. Her eyes have long adjusted to the forest's deep darkness, so much thicker than that of the village, but even if she struggled, there are other markers she would recognise. The trees rustle as she passes underneath them, their branches a black lace against the sky.

The path she takes leads to a part of the forest that she hasn't been in for a while, away from the rush of the river. The trees aren't unfamiliar to her, but nevertheless she feels their careful gaze on her as she steps off the path, into the undergrowth where so few Väsen venture.

It's taken her an entire year to find the hollow that she'd nearly died in. The hollow that had come so close to becoming a grave. But even in the dark, she catches sight of the blackened shell of tree trunk and recognises it instantly.

How strange, she thinks, that she knows exactly where she is now. That she would never get lost in this part of the Dark Forest, or that even if she did – the trees playing trickery, the snow reshaping the landscape – she could call on the woodland gnomes or the róut faeries to help guide her way. That it was truly a miracle Agagkantor found her on that icy, bloodless night because she knows now how little he strays from the well-trod boundaries of his home when he's not travelling wider.

It's only been a year, but she's already almost too large to fit into the hollow now, having grown taller. And she's not sure she could bear the thought of climbing back in, to feel the cold clenching around her heart. Instead, she kneels and places a small stub of candle in the centre. It takes a few tries for it to light – Sýstir can't tell if it's nerves or the wind fighting her efforts – but then it catches, illuminating the hollow in a weak glow.

Sýstir steps back and takes a breath.

She has thought about what she might say for a long time. She has, in fanciful moments, pretended to do away with her humanity altogether, and exist wholly as a creature of the Dark Forest. But even though she is Väsen, there is too much inside of her to forget. Too much human blood runs through her veins, so that when she smiles, it's with her mother's bowed lips, or when she braids her hair every morning, it's with the ghost of Ada's fingers working alongside her own. There is the part of her that still can't sleep properly unless she's on a mattress, with a roof over her head and a fire in the hearth.

The human part is still hungry. It still wants the human things. No matter how deeply it hurts.

Sýstir waits until the flame steadies.

"This is for my mother," she says. "I mourn you."

Even though the wind is brutal, the candlelight lingers stubbornly. For a startling second, the flame twines and flickers, looking for all the world like her mother dancing in their kitchen. Then the wind gutters, and it steadies again.

"This is for my sister," she says, but the rest of the words stick in her throat.

There is technically no sister to mourn because she isn't dead. Sýstir would know it in her bones, in the very fire of her soul. And she has tried, over this year, to make peace with the decisions they have made. It should be enough to know that Ada is most likely safe with their cousins, carving out the life she should have had, if only Sýstir hadn't been in the way.

The candle flickers, fragile.

What would she tell Ada, if she was standing here?

"I miss you," she confesses.

She misses the way her sister would tease her. She misses the confident way Ada's hands would pull her hair back from her face, the way she'd once fought a boy for Sýstir, so that she was never teased by him again. She misses her sister wholly and entirely; how she wishes she didn't know just how impossible it is to compile an entire person in a handful of words. All the world's volumes wouldn't be enough for Ada, and Sýstir would still be a better sister if she had even that.

"It was my fault," she says, hoarse.

And this is the terrible, terrible truth.

Her mother had been Vala, already disliked and somewhat feared. But if Sýstir had been better at disguising herself – never singing with the thrum of magic, never running gracefully through the fields like she so clearly belonged to another world – they might have maintained their precarious position in the village, or saved enough coin to leave. Even if the villagers didn't know what to call Sýstir precisely, they could guess at what she was not: *human*. A vala with a human daughter was one thing; a vala with a Väsen child was another.

Her mother had spent decades walking a tightrope of suspicion and necessity. And how much harder it must have been with the added burden of a huldra daughter.

How much easier it must have been to fall.

Despite all the promises she made to herself, a tear falls, then another. She takes a hiccupping breath, trying to steady herself.

The trees whisper to her before she hears them. She has just enough time to blow out the candle and climb into their boughs. She waits as a group of skóug trolls pass through, lantern swinging in the darkness.

She's grateful for the trees' early warning. Though they wouldn't harm her, she doesn't want the trolls to see her like this, all her human flaws exposed like a raw nerve ending. Not tonight. As they pass underneath, she notices the branches held reverently between them. An entire family, ready to pledge themselves to the Dark Forest – and each other. While she is still here, trapped between both worlds.

At last, she lowers herself back down to the ground. She stares after them, tears shining on her face. The longing hurts like a wound that can't be healed, like it's the world itself crushing her.

Something shifts in the dark, and she jumps. A hand comes down on her shoulder, steadying her.

"I'm here, Little Bird."

Sýstir turns into Agagkantor's shoulder and sobs.

...

The walk back to the cave is long, the crescent moon pricking a path for them through the undergrowth. Sýstir's teeth chatter, but she can't tell if it's from exhaustion or grief, or the decision that has been slowly coalescing in the back of her mind for months now. She has been so afraid to give voice to it, but the time for fear is past.

She waits until they're back in the hart, cloaks shucked and drying.

"I'm going back," she says.

Agagkantor cocks his head, the way he does when she's said something too human or otherwise inexplicable. "It's late now, but we can return tomorrow—"

"No," she says, her voice shaking. "I would like to leave the Dark Forest."

Silence.

Agagkantor looks at her, still as rock, and not for the first time, she wonders what he must be thinking. Whether he is deliberately impassive, or whether his expression is simply not for her to understand, the gap of translation suddenly a gulf. But she is certain he can read everything written on her own face, including the guilt vast enough to swallow her.

Because the truth is, she doesn't want to leave the Dark Forest. Queen Hilda's Rise may not care for her, but she has Agagkantor. She has a bed moulded by the soft memory of her body. A pot filled with warm soup or filling stew. A hearth to always come home to.

An entire world with a huldra-shaped space made just for her.

What does she have if she leaves? Nothing but ghosts.

That is, except for Ada. Flesh and blood and sinew Ada. Ada a year taller, a year wiser – and an entire year without Sýstir.

Sýstir has no way of knowing whether their separation was of Ada's design, or if it was Sýstir's fault for straying from the path. And truthfully, she has been too much of a coward to find out. Last winter, she had been too weak to go looking for Ada, so she had stayed to gain strength. In spring, she had told herself she would not be another burden, so she had stayed to learn how to fend for herself. In summer, she had wanted to know more of her Väsen side – to better hide it, perhaps – so she had stayed to grapple with her huldra nature.

But now she is strong, she can fend for herself, and she leaves her tail loose. There are no excuses left. She must return.

It might be that Ada will fling open the door and welcome her with outstretched arms, to be sisters again. If that means Sýstir hiding away her tail once more, swallowing her singing, living amongst those who would kill her if they knew of her huldra nature – well, her family have paid worse prices for her.

And if the door is hesitantly cast open, Ada's arms folded across her chest?

She just wants to make sure Ada is happy. To get one more glimpse of her sister. That would be enough, she thinks desperately. It would have to be enough.

Agagkantor breaks the silence with a heavy sigh. "I have always told you it would be your right to leave. But maybe it would have been better if you'd left straight away."

Sýstir looks at him, puzzled.

"The Dark Forest is for us. For Väsen," he continues. "You have always known this."

"I – I wouldn't ask Ada to come here," she says.

The words sound hollow, stupid, even to her. She has conjured entire daydreams of Ada finding her way here, of stumbling across Agagkantor's home because the Dark Forest wills it. She's imagined showing Ada every delight, the world opening up the way it had for her: the tjärn faeries skimming the surface of a still lake, the hills carving wide vistas across the forest, the sheer wonder of Nattaskur.

A jewel in a treasure box that she has saved for no one but Ada.

"I would come back," she says, her voice small. "I just want to make sure that she's well."

Agagkantor shakes his head. "You may want to return. But wanting is not enough. Not for the Dark Forest."

Sýstir blinks at him, feeling slow. "What do you mean?"

"You are always free to leave, Sýstir," he says. "There are no caged birds here. But the Dark Forest only extends its hand to those who need it once. If you leave, you cannot return."

Sýstir's ears are ringing. *If you leave, you cannot return.*

"She's my sister," she says. "I have to."

Even if it means giving up all that she loves. Ada has already done that and more.

"Do you really think you'll find your sister out there?" Agagkantor says quietly. "What happens if she does not wish to see you?"

His eyes have a strange gleam to them, and Sýstir shrinks from his gaze. All of a sudden, he is wearing that stranger's face, with a stranger's words pouring from him.

He pauses. "Do you know how I found you, Little Bird?"

Sýstir has always believed it a stroke of fate, come too late to save her mother or sister. But she has wondered, nevertheless.

"I saw your sister first, on the border of the Dark Forest."

Sýstir sucks in a breath. "You didn't tell me that."

"She did not look for you. She did not call your name. She saw you, Sýstir, and she turned away."

"Agagkantor..." she whispers, pressing one hand to her mouth.

"You were betrayed before you ever suspected it," Agagkantor says, slipping into a soothing tone entirely at odds with his words. "She did not care whether you yet lived or died. She might have even preferred death, knowing how much trouble a half-Väsen would bring to her human world."

Every insidious worry, every terror that she has quietly imagined in the privacy of her own head, slips out of Agagkantor's lips with ease. She chokes on a sob.

The truth sinks into her. Of course Ada wasn't looking for her. Of course she doesn't remember their shared life the way Sýstir does. Because for Sýstir, every memory was a stolen joy, whereas for Ada... it would be a joy stolen from her.

Sýstir has always known, deep down, that her sister begrudged her for herself. Now, at last, there is proof.

"The Dark Forest chose you for a reason," Agagkantor says. "Would you prove it wrong?"

A cold numbness settles inside of her. Sýstir has never been chosen by anything, or anyone. A curse bestowed on her mother, a burden on her sister, a plague to the world from which she escaped. Agagkantor is right. But if he is right, then why does her heart still hurt?

Why does she still miss what she has already left behind?

Agagkantor guides her back to her bed, his hand resting on her shoulder. His eyes glint red in the firelight.

"You're already home, Little Bird. Where else would you ever need to be?"

· TEN ·

A year slips by. Two years. Like a breath held in, and then exhaled.

Sýstir comes to know the changing seasons of Trollheim – the trolls' own name for the Dark Forest – by the way the light shifts, always drowsy and soft, yet endless in summer when the midnight sun steals the night from them, or barely a glow on the horizon when polar nights sink the forest into perpetual twilight. Her favourite season is early autumn, honey-drenched and rich with the gathering promise of quieter months. Of the sweet-spiced smell of jam-making to preserve the sweet berries she picks, of the quiet snap of pine needles under her feet, the forest ablaze with orange and red.

She tries not to think about what Ada would be doing at this time of year. Whether she might also be making jam from their mother's treasured recipe, so that their cousins' house is filled with the same scent.

She tries not to think about Ada much these days.

Sýstir sings as she hangs her wet laundry outside, rigged up with homemade rope and strung between two saplings, golden but still full-leaved. The colours on her clothing have faded over the years so that everything is the mottled colours of the forest, all warm browns and softened greens. Agagkantor has managed to keep her well-fed and warm, but his interpretation of clothing is so vastly different to her own that she's found herself scrambling for some form of presentability. She'd kept patching her original dress, the hem let out, and then let out again, until finally she was forced to trade it for one of Agagkantor's pelts, stretched and cleaned and made supple for wear. She'd stitched a patch of the original fabric into her new clothes, so that she'd always be able to carry it with her.

She supposes that she must look like one of those wildwomen the villagers always warned their children about: strange, and perhaps a little beautiful, for that was how the wildwomen whisked away their children and husbands in the stories. Now Sýstir wonders how much of the myth originated from Väsen, creeping through human settlements to safer pastures. But even though her clothing is wild by human terms, it's not crude. Her dress is threaded through with silk from the spinn faeries, and decorated with hand-carved beads from Agagkantor and herself, runes weaving her tale so that anyone with a keen eye might catch a glimpse of her history. There are pockets with an abundance of tools: fine bone needles, the witch-stones with the holes bored through, a small knife to pare fruit and trim small branches.

Sturdy clothing. Useful.

She's just wringing the last of the water from her clothes when a low singing startles her. It's neither the skóug trolls nor Agagkantor's rumbling melody. Years gone by, the singing would have frightened her, but now she waits, unbothered, for the bearers to walk past.

Two woodland gnomes come into view through the trees. Their packs are laden with pots and pans strung up on the sides, copper winking at her.

They look at Sýstir curiously. Even though she's grown familiar with the Dark Forest – and itself with her, as Agagkantor's ward – she still stands out as a huldra. Not for the reasons she'd originally suspected; rather, that she's anyone's ward at all. She's seen only one other huldra since her first, and she'd moved with the unsurpassed grace of a solitary creature.

"We wish to speak with the skóug troll Agagkantor," one of the woodland gnomes says.

Sýstir glances behind her to the cave entrance. "He isn't home."

There's a pattern to Agagkantor's travels, she's noticed. First, he starts to busy himself in the hart with no particular purpose, so that for several weeks, Sýstir is on the constant edge of irritation. Then he leaves his pack out and the walking stick she'd carved for him. Finally, days, weeks – once an entire two months – later, he tells her that he's leaving. Only for a week here and there, but enough to fill the cave with Sýstir's loneliness in the meanwhile. If trolls are slow to anything, she's long realised, it's in making decisions. Or perhaps it's just Agagkantor, along with his irritable mood swings and deepening temper. They are familiar enough by now, she supposes, to be annoyed by one another occasionally, or show flashes of their less agreeable sides – and isn't that part of being a family, anyway?

"We can wait until he returns," the other says.

"You might be waiting a while. He's gone to visit one of the giants, and he won't be back until tomorrow." She pauses. "We've met before, haven't we? At Nattaskur's blooming."

The woodland gnomes look at her, and then smiles crease their faces.

"Indeed we have. But you've grown since then, huldra."

The woodland gnomes make their introductions, any trace of wariness gone at the revelation of her identity. The shorter one reveals himself as Korí, while the taller one is his wife, Hallr. They unshoulder their packs on the ground in a cacophony of clanging.

"You may come inside if you wish," Sýstir says.

Hallr shrugs. "The nights aren't too cool yet, so we'll enjoy the stars while we can. Might you join us instead?"

Sýstir glances up at the sky, perfect and cloudless. She hasn't slept under the stars for a while. She goes back inside and returns with blankets, fresh crusty bread, newly chopped logs for the fire – little bits and pieces for a more comfortable evening.

"Where have you travelled from?" she asks.

"From the edge of the eastern mountains," Korí says. "It's a long journey to leave so late in the year, but we've had plenty of business to attend to."

"Agagkantor is our last stop," Hallr says, reaching for a slice of bread. "And then home again."

For a while, they talk companionably, each taking turns to stoke the fire and cook. From within their packs, the woodland gnomes pull out dried fish, a weighty salt rock, spices and herbs. As the evening wears on, they bring out different kinds of objects: beads carved from seashells, cured gut for stringed instruments and fishing, blocks of half-carved wood in the shape of animals, each no bigger than Sýstir's finger. Between bites of food, they explain that they are musicians, often travelling between dwellings to perform and teach, trading on the way. Sýstir tries to conceal her surprise; while woodland gnomes are appreciative of music, she knows none who would profess to create it.

"We came here a few years ago for several days, when Korí put in the skylight. Most odd thing, for a troll. Normally they use moss to plug the holes in a cave, but he'd insisted on glass."

"He said he wanted to always have the light with him," Korí says, a peculiar note in his voice. "For another Väsen, I would understand that, but…"

He trails off. Sýstir shrugs; even though she knows little about the other trolls, Agagkantor has always struck her as eccentric. If any troll wanted a skylight in his hart, it would inevitably be him.

"Do you play?" Hallr asks suddenly.

Her head tilts towards the lute resting next to Korí's pack.

"No, but I sing. And the flute, sometimes," Sýstir says.

"Then, perhaps as payment for your hospitality, we might offer you a song?" she suggests.

Sýstir smiles. "I would more than accept."

Korí picks up the lute and begins tuning it. The wood grain of its body is striking, polished to a high shine. His fingers pluck a soft tune across the strings.

"Once there was a daughter of gods," Hallr begins, her voice a rich warble. "And how she loved the trees."

It's a folk ballad Sýstir is familiar with, if only because she's heard its telling in so many different variants from travelling musicians who had visited her village in Midgård. Gromildr, Goddess of Hope, who had helped both human and Väsen escape the clutches of her terrifying brother, Oden, and the world he sought to remake in his cruel image. Sometimes Gromildr escapes with her people into the wilderness; sometimes she's caught at the very last moment, Oden's spear catching her fingertip to cause a wound that never heals. In one version of the ballad, a sapling grows from her bloodshed, the first of an endless forest. The Väsen, however, sing of it as history, not folklore, without the variations she recalls.

It's been a long time since she's woken from a nightmare about Oden's men, but she still feels a pang of sympathy for Gromildr. If the men are pale imitations of his terror, she dreads to think what Oden in truth might have done.

For most of the evening, the woodland gnomes exchange music with Sýstir. They explain a little more about their unusual musical origins; they had both learnt to play from an elderly sprýg gnome, who had been keen to share her knowledge. In turn, Sýstir passes on every song she can remember: stories about immortal wanderers, ill-fated lovers, hopeful lullabies that infuse dreams with a sweeter tomorrow. She doesn't remember falling asleep, but when she wakes, dawn is just peeking over the horizon.

The next day, as promised, Agagkantor returns early in the morning. He looks deep in thought as he comes into view, but his expression changes to one of welcome surprise when he sees the woodland gnomes.

Sýstir gives him a cheerful wave and leaves them to it. Agagkantor doesn't often entertain visitors, but she's noticed that he appreciates the privacy. So she retreats to the river, taking the route along the bank, slippery with spray, to watch the salmon run.

It's a spectacular view: hundreds of fish struggling upstream, leaping over rocks and flashing silver bellies. Half of the forest are probably upstream trying to catch them for supper, but Sýstir either goes in the predawn glow to fish, or else well after dusk, when fewer Väsen are around to notice her. Instead, during the day, she contents herself with watching the stragglers make their way against the current.

Halfway downstream, she realises that her hair has come loose. Using the river as a makeshift mirror, she leans over the water to pull it back into its serviceable braid. A rippled image of Ada stares back up at her.

Their features have never quite matched up, with two different fathers between them. But this older version of Sýstir is an uncanny silhouette of her sister as she remembers her. Though Ada may well look different again, the last years of childhood having sloughed off her some time ago.

Despite all the promises to herself, her thoughts wander.

Sýstir turned sixteen at the cusp between summer and autumn, so Ada will be very nearly nineteen, her birthday just around the corner. At nineteen, she'll have surely married by now, with perhaps a child on the way, if not already in her arms. That was the fate of all the village girls, with the exception of Sýstir, who didn't qualify. It hadn't stopped them from whispering about Ada's future husband late at night, giggling over who it might be.

The baker's son, a snot-nosed boy a year older than Ada, with greasy hair and a tendency to shy from baths. Or one of the twins at the tavern, both handsome enough – if you could tell them apart – but prone to flirting with anyone in the vicinity.

The last time they had spoken about beaus, Ada had turned her head to the wall, as though Sýstir hadn't already seen her red as a poppy.

"Who is it?" she demanded.

"No one," Ada mumbled back, waving her hand.

But Sýstir had caught Ada kissing the farrier's apprentice two days before, and seen her making eyes at him weeks before that. It had unnerved her, watching Ada slip away from childhood. Perhaps more unnerving was that Sýstir herself had started to see hints of it in her own reflection, like a rose primed to unfurl from its bud. Others, too, had noticed in the village, with glances that lingered, and strange, uncertain expressions, as though they could not decide whether she'd become beautiful or monstrous. But she had still believed, even then, that it would always be the three of them in the cottage, the two sisters forever on the precipice – but never tipping over – the brink of bloom.

"Don't make that face at your sister," their mother had said when Sýstir complained. "She's allowed to fall in love with whoever she wants. Except the baker's son." She wrinkled her nose and then smiled. "I must insist on a son-in-law who bathes."

The farrier's apprentice was a nice boy who was good with horses and didn't stare at Sýstir or call her ugly things when no one else was around. But she resented him anyway because it promised a day when he would pluck a bouquet of flowers and walk down to their cottage and propose to Ada with his cap in hand – and she would say yes. Ada was *her* sister. Ada wasn't for anyone else's taking because Sýstir had already chosen her.

A child's foolishness, really. But she'd truly believed that she could stop Ada from marrying. That their lives would be preserved in amber, the sisters forever children and their mother forever youthful, with only a single grey hair shining amongst the gold.

She hopes Ada is happy, wherever she is. That the price she has paid on Sýstir's behalf has, at last, reaped its rewards of a normal life. A human life. And if Sýstir grieves for all that they have lost between them – well, that is her own price to forever pay.

She saw you, Sýstir, and she turned away.

Just like that, she slips the memory into her pocket and walks on, where it sits smooth and quiet in the back of her mind.

• • •

As daylight shrinks, Sýstir spends much of her free time outdoors, eager to take in as much of the Dark Forest as possible before snow makes all but the most obvious paths impassable. By now, the walk over the burial hills feels second nature to her. Though many of the trolls' names are lost to memory, she has a fondness for each boulder. There's one twice as tall as Agagkantor, almost worn entirely smooth by time and weather. Another is squat and round, a cluster of lines suggesting a frown. One particular rock she has taken to calling the Lady because there's just enough space to place a flower in a hollowed nook. And there's always something there: lily of the valley in spring, lady's slipper orchid in summer, rose hip in autumn, dried heather and sprigs of pine in winter.

Today, the flower in Lady's nook is withered, so Sýstir swaps it out with a bouquet of crisp golden and flame-red leaves she'd picked on her way, before continuing downhill to Nattaskur. Her heartbeat increases as she gets closer, as though she's crossing some forbidden boundary, even though by the Dark Forest's own rules, she has just as much a right to be there as anyone else. Her tail twitches in anticipation.

There are a few good hiding spots near Nattaskur, but Sýstir's favourite is a cluster of bushes, twined in a thick grove of trees. She settles in, ignoring the branches that prick at her skin. It's always hard to get comfortable at first, but then the faint strain of music starts and she forgets about everything else.

A family of sprýg gnomes have come to Nattaskur with their youngest to place a wreath on their branch. The young sprýg gnome is far too small to reach even the lowest branches, but he makes quick work of climbing upwards. His wreath is clutched tightly in his fist, and he's soon lost to view, swallowed by Nattaskur's brilliant foliage.

Sýstir waits for him to descend, falling into his family's arms. There's singing and merrymaking, and their lanterns stay lit well into the night. She knows they'll sleep under the safety of

Nattaskur's shadow and make the return journey tomorrow. They've probably walked for days, or even weeks to get here. Because it's worth it, if it means joining Nattaskur's legacy.

Something painful twists under her ribcage. She's come here at least twice a week for months now, but she hasn't really let herself think about why. It's a familiar walk, she's told herself. She likes the burial hills, she tells herself. She likes the scent off Nattaskur, and the steady hum of its heartbeat.

But there's the image of the gnome tumbling into his parents' outstretched arms, rolling over and over in her mind.

Why are you really here, Sýstir? What are you doing?

Wishing for things that she can't have. But then, she thought she could never be free to leave her tail untethered, to sing without concern, or befriend others without deception. And now she has all of those things, wished for and received. Agagkantor has told her for years that she belongs to the Dark Forest – that she is there precisely *because* she belongs.

She has spent so long holding on to the past, dreaming of Ada's return, whatever she might have told Agagkantor and herself. But Ada is happy where she is, and truthfully, Sýstir is, too. Perhaps now it's time to turn to her future.

That night, she can't seem to sit still. She almost overturns the pot on the hearth twice, sending embers skittering across the floor. She drops her spoon enough times that Agagkantor plucks it out of her fingers with a weary sigh, before returning to his mending. He knows her well enough by now, she thinks ruefully.

"Little Bird, you can ask me what is so clearly on your mind," he says.

"Agagkantor," she begins.

She means for it to sound casual, but it comes out too sharp and uneasy. Agagkantor puts down his mending and looks at her questioningly. She takes a deep breath to steady herself.

"I've been here for some time now," she says, twisting her hands together.

Agagkantor raises an eyebrow. "Are you not happy?"

She almost laughs. "No, I mean – yes, I'm happy. Happier than I ever thought I could be. But I'm – I would like—"

She stops and takes another deep breath. *Why are you really here, Sýstir?* she thinks again.

"I would like to graft my branch to Nattaskur."

The words come out breathlessly, tumbling over one another. But they're out in the open. She digs her nails into the soft flesh of her hands.

"I know I don't have a family tree, as such – and I suppose you don't either. And I don't really have, well – but I could find a tree and ask it... to be..."

She trails off uncertainly. Agagkantor just looks at her, his black eyes unfathomable. Even though the hart isn't any warmer than it usually is, sweat trickles down the back of her neck.

She rallies herself. "I've followed all your lessons – I know so much more about the Dark Forest than I did when I arrived—"

He cuts her off. "No."

The syllable stuns her into silence. Agagkantor so rarely denies her anything, and never without an explanation. Never just like... *this*.

"Why?" she persists. "Is it because I'm... half?"

Half human, half Väsen. But not the sum of her parts, or even a sum of one of her halves.

His gaze slides away from her, towards the fire. "I will not discuss this with you further, Sýstir."

"I just – the other Väsen have done it, and you've always said that I'm of the Dark Forest, and if the trolls at Queen Hilda's Rise can—"

Agagkantor's stool clatters on the floor as he stands up, tall enough that his head brushes the ceiling. His eyes glint red-gold in the firelight.

"I said no!" His voice cracks like a thunderstorm.

Sýstir flinches and shrinks away from him. Tears gather in an unshed ache at the back of her throat.

Then Agagkantor's frightening expression eases. He sighs heavily, folding back into his hunch. He presses his hands to his forehead before linking his long, tapered fingers together in weary contemplation.

"Forgive me, Little Bird," he says, closing his eyes. "I did not mean to scare you. But my answer remains the same."

Sýstir presses her lips together to stop them from trembling. She's not a child anymore; she won't cry just because she's been told no. But her heart thrums with longing.

"I just want to belong," she whispers.

Agagkantor's gaze softens. "You already belong."

But late that night, Sýstir still can't sleep. She tosses and turns, every inch of her bed too soft and hard all at once. In her first year, she'd rigged up a pair of curtains, as they'd done in the cottage, and although Agagkantor hadn't said anything, he'd huffed and muttered his usual annoyance at human trivialities. Most nights she leaves them open, but tonight she pulls them shut, cocooning her in the dark. Fenrir curls up against her, but even his low purr can only bring so much comfort.

The rite of Nattaskur is for all. Every Väsen in the Dark Forest.

But not for Sýstir – never for Sýstir. She has let go of her old home, her old self, and now her sister. How much more must she prove herself before she's deemed worthy?

She glances upwards through her skylight, but although she searches until her eyes finally slip shut, the stars never come out.

· ELEVEN ·

It takes a few flurries and retreats of snow for winter to truly sink its fingers into the earth. But the snow, as it always does, eventually catches and sticks, along with a harder, crisper cold. The glassy lakes turn opaque and glittering, as ice scores deep furrows into their depths. Tjärn faeries draw ferned patterns in the frost, so that the rocks and trees take on fantastical whorls and eddies. The wolves, never far away, grow bolder with hunger, and Sýstir often comes across their prints scattered across the snow, or catches a flash of amber eyes in the trees. Though they don't particularly bother her, she keeps Fenrir close to her side when they go out hunting, lest their appetite be stronger than their caution.

And she goes out a lot – more than she would enjoy, truth be told. She and Agagkantor have not spoken of their argument over Nattaskur, and the cave feels... tighter than it normally does, like an ill-fitting stocking. If either of them were less stubborn – and Sýstir knows well enough by now just how stubborn Agagkantor can be – they might have already moved on. But the hurt still sits like a knotty fist under her breastbone. It's simply easier to go outside than contend with the silence.

Winter Solstice is often the time for exchanging gifts, for eating the last and most treasured of the preserves. Even Agagkantor softens at the presence of a hearty meal and candlelit decorations. Last year, Sýstir had spent weeks knitting him a blanket, dyed a warm, lustrous green with the help of the Sprýg Gnomes, and embroidered with the story of their meeting.

He will thaw, she thinks, and she'll leave the topic of Nattaskur alone for a time. And everything will be just as it was.

This morning, she lies in her bed a little later than usual, still wrapped in that hazy warmth, dreaming up the kind of present he might like. A new knife, perhaps, from Hallr and Korí, slimmer and more deft for carving. Or she might go to the sprýg gnomes to request a new story – that is often the best gift of all.

Agagkantor's voice rumbles through the cave, interrupting her thoughts. "I must travel to visit the giants."

Sýstir sits up. "What, again?"

Agagkantor's long ears twitch, as though hearing something beyond the cave. "I will likely be some time, so we will not be able to celebrate the Solstice together."

Sýstir's stomach lurches unpleasantly. All of her plans dissolve instantly. No Solstice dinner. No exchanging of gifts. No stories by the hearth.

No thread to stitch them back together.

"Do you have to go?" she says, and she hates how fragile she sounds.

He hesitates, and for a minute, she catches the old Agagkantor she recalls and loves best of all. The one who had enough patience for her, even when she tested it. The one who had time for her, always.

"It is important, Little Bird, else I would not be going so late in the year," he says gently.

Sýstir watches him carefully that evening as they sing together, a wave of protective magic washing over them both. His gaze is shadowed in the firelight, and even though he says nothing unusual – even though, to all intents and purposes, this is a night like every other night – she catches glimpses of something distant and uneasy written across his face.

Sýstir falls asleep to troubled thoughts, and when she awakens, the hearth is mere embers. Agagkantor's pack and walking stick are gone. She rouses, groggy, and trails outside to the wet chill of the corridor, icy stone pricking at her bare feet. He must have left at some point during the night; his footsteps are already fading, mussed by wind and other animals. Sýstir stands in the corridor for longer than strictly necessary, her skin pimpling from the cold. But she doesn't leave.

The usual tight knot of anxiety winds around her, familiar and constant as a shadow. He's left her before, but not so soon after an argument – and they've argued plenty, she thinks ruefully – and not without making up in some way or another. She forces herself to take a deep breath, and then another one.

She is fine. Agagkantor is fine. And when he returns – they will be *fine*.

Only then does she turn around and go inside.

She busies herself the way she always does when her mind starts to wander into traitorous territory – chores. She sweeps the hart from top to bottom, dusting places a cave would surely never think itself to be dusted. She seasons the new pot the woodland gnomes had exchanged with Agagkantor, slicking it with hot oil over the hearth until the metal gives up rainbows. She restuffs her mattress, which has grown saggy and thin from use. She evicts spiders with a gentle but firm hand, reorganises the pantry, bakes bread.

But the hart is a small cave to tidy – and neither of them are creatures of clutter.

Sometimes she wishes she was still the little girl Agagkantor had rescued, who had been exhausted after a few chores.

Outside, snow falls steadily.

...

It snows for two days straight, so that the world outside turns a muted, crisp white, unbroken except for the faintest of knytt footsteps. The creak and distant boom of snow slipping off the top of the cave outside, or the treetops, echoes throughout the day. When Sýstir finally emerges, Fenrir's tracks are scuffled all around the entrance, amongst others.

She retrieves the two stones threaded together from her pocket and clicks them together twice. Moments later, Fenrir slinks through the trees towards her, sleek and fluffy with his thick winter coat. She rewards him with a strip of dried venison and he nuzzles at her calf. Something in her unwinds a little.

It takes her a little while to make sure she has everything she needs: hunting bow with the string recently waxed, arrows painstakingly fletched by herself, her bone skates. Then she sets off through the trees, humming to herself as she does so. The sky is heaving with the weight of an oncoming storm, the sun drawn behind dark clouded curtains.

At the edge of the river, Sýstir stops to tie her skates to the bottom of her boots, fumbling with the leather straps. She made them herself, polishing the bone blades until they were flat and smooth. Then she kneels and feels for a particularly hefty stone. She hurls it far across the river. The thud as it strikes the ice echoes satisfyingly across the open space. For good measure, Sýstir throws another one, landing several measures further than the first. This time she hears a splinter, more delicate and dangerous.

Well, she won't be going that far out, she thinks.

It's still early enough in winter that sometimes the ice doesn't shoot deep through the water. Every year in the village, someone foolish or drunk or just plain unlucky had strayed too far and fallen into the river. Most of the time they managed to climb out themselves, or were pulled to safety. But sometimes the river claimed them, and then their bones would wash up on shore come spring with the tattered remnants of winter boots and fur cloak.

Towards the end of one winter – surprisingly warm, the sun always shining – a deer had gone through the ice. Sýstir had been walking with Ada, and they'd both run towards the sound, mistaking the bellows for a person. Sýstir had wanted to go after the deer, but Ada had stopped her.

"If you go under, I can't promise I can get you out," she warned.

Sýstir flinched at the sound of the deer, lunging at thin ice. "We can't leave it."

"Wait here," Ada commanded.

And because Sýstir was obedient, she'd waited, twisting her cloak worriedly in her hands. The deer's eyes rolled in its head, fur dark and sodden. But when Ada returned, Sýstir's stomach swooped unpleasantly. A bow and arrow in her sister's hands, with her sister's practised eye.

"It will be a kindness," Ada said softly.

Sýstir had hunted before – and would do so again and again, of course – but always with the animal as her equal, the chase fair and paid for in gratitude. To kill for the sake of killing, even for mercy's sake, sent revulsion shuddering through her. Then she imagined the alternative. Not one where the deer climbed back out of the river, shook itself off and bounded into the forest. No, it would be one drawn-out moment of paddling in the freezing water, panicked cries unanswered, until either the cold or exhaustion pulled it beneath the surface.

"Do it," Sýstir said.

She squeezed her eyes shut. The arrow whistled through the air, a sharp cry – and then nothing. Ada had been right; it was a clean, quick death. But that night Sýstir had been chased by its sinuous ghost through her dreams, white bone luminous in sickled moonlight. She had wondered afterwards if it had been a nightmare sitting on her chest, drinking from her fear, so vivid was the dream.

Now, Sýstir eyes the second rock cautiously. No, she won't be that deer.

Behind her, Fenrir meows mournfully. Sýstir glances back and flashes him a reassuring smile.

"Not coming, Fen?" she says.

He gives her another look and turns back into the forest. He's starting to test the boundaries of his own independence, choosing to walk alone, or split from Sýstir at an unseen opportunity for solitary adventure. He is a creature of the forest before he's her friend, and although that old panic rouses within her, she does her best to tamp it down. Even now that he's grown, he's not what she would consider entirely safe – but then neither is she, by that same measure.

She considers this minor dilemma as she slips on to the ice, testing the glide of her skates. Something delightful flickers within her.

Sýstir gives one more experimental tug on her skates, before pushing off – and then she's flying, fast as any horse and a hundred times as smooth. She shakes off the bite of winter, wind teasing wisps from her hair. *Faster*, her feet urge her, and she obliges. She throws out her arms wide, feeling the wind glide beneath them, testing her balance. A tjärn faerie trails her, dancing along the faint scores her skates have left behind.

She turns, and the skates obey her with precision, her tail adding surety to her balance. Cold air hits the back of her throat. She's often wondered what it must be like to fly as a bird, soaring unimpeded through the air, or as the faeries, dancing where the whims of the wind take them. If this is the closest she'll ever get, then she'll consider herself satisfied.

As she travels downstream, the river hums with activity. Several trolls sit near a hole carved for fishing. Sýstir thinks of that rock, the bright sound it had made, then glances at the trolls. They're awfully close to the centre, where the river rushes fiercest and freezes most reluctantly. If they were other Väsen or Agagkantor, then perhaps she might have called out a warning. But when their gazes meet hers, annoyance evident in every line of their bodies, she skates on. Most likely they would snipe at her for talking to them at all, especially of things they already know.

She veers off at a well-used trail, where the deer nose through the snow to the hardy shrubs underneath, and pauses to take off her skates. She slips her bow from over her head and tests the tension in the string: perfect. Her tail flicks out behind her, silent.

But her mind keeps straying from the hunt back to Agagkantor, and she can't keep her bow steady. The deer flee, scattering powder under their hooves. Sighing, she steps through the hip-high snow drifts to try and retrieve her arrows. Overhead, the dark clouds close in; tomorrow she'll be forced back into the cave, unless she fancies slipping through the Dark Forest in a storm. Though she does love the Dark Forest in all its forms: trees whipping with the wind, the rain singing on its downward journey. All the places she loves best, transformed into their more elusive selves. Maybe the time away from the cave will be good for them both.

Sýstir is skating back when she hears it: the sound that sends her stomach into free fall. A crash of ice – and a scream. She puts on a burst of speed, then another, feeling the ache of her calves. She wishes fervently for that winged feeling.

She should have told the trolls about the ice.

It doesn't take long for her to find the victim. A skóug troll thrashes in the water, trying to grip the ice. Chunks of ice float in the water around her, useless. Frantically, Sýstir looks for the other trolls, but there's no one else to be seen. She's on her own.

Hot panic washes over Sýstir. She thinks of the deer, the black of its eyes. One hand touches the bow strapped to her back. The soft whistle of an arrow. The stillness afterwards.

No, she thinks – and the force of the thought surprises her.

"I'm coming!" she shouts.

Think. Think.

But she is not strong enough to pull a troll from the water, and there is no one else around to help. Her breath hitches in her lungs.

Then Sýstir's gaze snags on a slither of rope on the thinning ice. The troll must have brought it with her for fishing. She grabs the closest end, and ice pops and cracks underneath her. Quickly, she loops it into a firm knot around her knife handle and stakes the knife deep into the sturdier ice as a hold. When she tugs on it, the knife doesn't shift.

It will hold, she tells herself fervently. It has to.

She throws it to the troll, landing shy of the water. The troll snatches for it, but the current underneath is too fierce. Already exhaustion is written across her face.

Sýstir drops to her knees, shucking her bow and arrow. Carefully, she starfishes out on to the ice, careful to spread as much of her weight as possible. Inch by agonising inch, she pulls herself forward, the rope clutched in one freezing hand.

But she is running out of time. As she gets closer, water slops over the edge of the hole, fearsome in its chill.

"Take the rope!" she shouts, whipping it back out.

The troll reaches for the rope twice, but it slips through her fingers. On the third try, Sýstir pulls the rope back and shuffles forward, determined to get as much leeway as possible. The ice creaks beneath her. She tries to flatten herself out further. *It'll hold*, she thinks again, willing it to be so. In her mind, the deer's eyes roll in panic.

She flings the rope towards the troll one more time, just as a crack fissures underneath her.

The ice gives way.

Sýstir goes under.

There is a moment when the world goes black with fear. Sýstir's lungs seize in her chest. She's in the small space of the hollow; she's curled up in the bushes, Oden's men inches from her. The water burns like flame. It's been seconds; it's been hours. She can't breathe, she can't—

She claws her way up to the surface and breaks free. Her lungs burn. She sputters water. The cold is like a vice, squeezing her chest. She lunges for the ice, but she can't grab hold. The current drags at her, tugging her away. Her limbs are leaden with cold, and even staying afloat is near impossible. If she goes under again, she won't be able to surface.

She is going to drown and no one will know until spring, if they know at all. Agagkantor will think she ran away, and she'll never be able to make up with him. She'll never—

A hand grasps her. The other holds tightly to the rope. The troll.

She's still in the water, but she must have grabbed the rope when Sýstir went under.

"H – hold on," the troll says through chattering teeth.

Sýstir grabs at her belt and holds on with the last shreds of her strength, as the troll uses both hands to tug at the rope. Handful by handful, she drags them both through the water, waves rippling in their wake. The rope strains against the knife's handle, the sound ricocheting off the ice – but it holds. It *holds*.

Then, all at once, they are free.

Together, they crawl on to the bank, exhausted and freezing. Sýstir gasps in lungfuls of air, her breath clouding in front of her. Her cloak clings to her, sodden and so heavy it hurts her shoulders. As one huge shiver racks her, then another, her thoughts sluggishly relay what comes next. Cold synonymous with pain. Then that terrifying, dream-like state beyond the cold, where it stops burning.

Then the soft, blanketing mirage of warmth. Then nothing.

"Wait... here," the troll says.

As if Sýstir can do much else. Her tunic, she can't do anything about, but with frozen fingers, she peels her cloak from her skin, fumbling at the heavy fabric. She pinches her skin, bright and pink, to stay alert, but she can't tell whether she's too weak to grip or whether she's already too numb, because she feels nothing.

Wearily, she rests her head on her knees and closes her eyes. Just for a second, just to rest. Now she's alone, the adrenaline is starting to dissolve, leaving only more exhaustion in its wake. Every limb feels like lead.

She must have only closed her eyes for a minute, but something nuzzles at her face. She blinks sleepily at Fenrir, who clambers into her lap – and firmly bites her. He must have heard her shouts and come to investigate.

"Ow," she mumbles. "Not now, Fen."

But the distant, worried voice in her head that had receded with the cold starts to come back to her. She can't fall asleep. With effort, she forces herself to try and wring out as much water from her clothes as possible.

Moments later, the troll returns with an entire log of firewood and kindling. Sýstir is too exhausted to move, so she watches as the troll builds a fire, carving a space in the snow. From Agagkantor, she's gleaned that they tolerate the cold better than herself. But even so, the troll has to stop and recover her strength, and it takes several tries before a spark catches the kindling.

For a long while, there's nothing but the sound of Sýstir and the troll breathing, the fire crackling between them. Sýstir moves as close to it as she can without burning herself. Her mind starts to return to her as she warms, the shivers receding, and she studies the troll quietly. Her eyes are soft, a deep obsidian green that reminds Sýstir of a still lake. Gold bracelets clink softly on her wrists. It's the same skóug troll she'd encountered at Nattaskur, years before.

"I'm Sýstir," she says, then curses inwardly.

Of course she would know who Sýstir is. Sýstir, the unwanted huldra. Sýstir, half human, half Väsen and entirely other. But the troll only gives her a smile that, if Sýstir is not mistaken, is grateful.

"Well met, Sýstir," she says. "I am Fulgir. Thank you for saving my life."

"Where did the others go?" Sýstir asks, thinking of the trolls who had been with her.

"They gave up." Fulgir opens up her sodden pack to reveal several large fish. "I did not."

Sýstir looks at her – and then begins to laugh helplessly. After a beat, the troll starts to laugh, too, a low, welcoming rumble.

She saved a troll. She went under the ice, and came back up. She's alive.

She's *alive.*

· TWELVE ·

Sýstir manages to make it home, where she spends the better part of the afternoon simply sleeping. Her dreams are full of cries, the low resonance of ice, a nameless dread that's slow to dissipate when she wakes. The cold takes time to seep from her bones, and she piles every blanket in the hart over her bed.

But in the morning, she wakes clear-headed and full of a strange, rousing emotion that takes her a moment to identify as joy. The last time she had been truly in danger like that, it had been inside the hollow, waiting for the cold to take her. But this time, she fought back.

It's not necessarily true that she forgets what brought her into the water, or its knife-sharp cold, but it falls to the back of her mind. There are chores to be done, bruises to heal.

Two days later, though, it all comes rushing back to her. When she steps outside, a bouquet of dried rose hips, obviously preserved from the summer, wait for her. She picks it up and turns it between her hands, puzzling at the gift. Rose hip tea will be good for Agagkantor's joints, always stiff when the weather turns, and to stave off the illnesses that sometimes plague winter. She glances around to see who left it, but there's no one there.

. . .

After her scare on the river, Sýstir decides to set aside skating until her bruises heal, choosing instead to move through the forest with her trusted boots. On her next visit to the clearing, she passes by a cluster of skóug trolls and freezes, wishing herself to be just another tree in the background. But instead of ignoring her or shooting her dark looks, they each nod at her.

Too surprised to nod back, she simply stares. Next to her, Fenrir looks just as puzzled as she feels.

The next day, another gift arrives: a thick gold bangle, furled so that it resembles a fern leaf. Far too small for Agagkantor, but just right for Sýstir. She tilts it up to the light and squints at the delicate rune etchings.

As she's examining it, the feeling of being watched ripples through her, and she glances up. A troll stands at the end of the pathway to Agagkantor's cave. Fulgir.

They look at each other, breaths held.

"Do the gifts suit?" Fulgir says, breaking the silence.

Her ears flick back, and Sýstir realises that she's *nervous*. A troll, nervous of her. Sýstir almost bursts out laughing for the sheer absurdity of it.

"We have not dealt with a huldra in some years," Fulgir adds.

Even though Sýstir has long stopped considering herself wholly human – except when it's imposed upon her – she still struggles to conceive of herself as wholly huldra. She doubts very much that huldras live as she does, but the rest is a mystery. Agagkantor hasn't been particularly forthcoming with how he might have handled a true huldra, should one have appeared on his doorstep instead of her.

Belatedly, Sýstir realises that Fulgir is still waiting for an answer.

"The gifts are lovely," she says hastily. "But... I don't understand why."

Fulgir looks at her as though the answer is so obvious as to be irrelevant. "We owe you a life debt, Sýstir." She spreads her hands. "We wish to thank you. *I* wish to thank you. So we invite you to join us, at our Rise."

Sýstir blinks.

"What – what time? I mean, when?"

Fulgir touches her own brow with her forefinger, then traces her hand upwards, to where the sun is slowly sinking. "When the crescent moon touches the face of Nivir."

Nightfall, then.

"Be well, Sýstir," Fulgir says.

She heads back into the forest, but Sýstir stares at Fulgir's retreating figure. An invitation… from Queen Hilda's Rise.

She's passed their cave often enough on her way through the forest, and felt the casual pangs of loneliness at seeing other Rises of trolls go past, happily engaged in conversation. But she'd long ago accepted that Queen Hilda's Rise was off limits; it's never even occurred to her that one day she might see the inside of their cave, or the knife-edge of what that might mean.

She could be walking into the welcome that Fulgir has implied. She could also be walking into a confrontation, and it's just her foolishness that's made her believe otherwise.

What would Agagkantor do?

Agagkantor would turn them down without question – and with good reason. Sýstir still cringes when she recalls the Skóug Trolls at the celebration of spring under Nattaskur. How quickly and easily they had turned on her. And even though the wound is mostly healed over, years old at this point, she has no desire to break it open again and be left bleeding in front of strangers. Maybe that slow nod between them instead of a scowl is enough for Sýstir. It *should* be enough.

A voice, much quieter than Agagkantor's, rises in the back of her mind. Soft and sweet, with the barest hint of charcoal because that's how Sýstir will always remember her now, willingly or not. *What would Mother do?*

Sýstir tries not to think about her mother in those last moments, or in the weeks leading up to them, unspooling the many reasons that led them all down that singular path. It's better to not think about it, because then Sýstir has to remember it all: the breathtaking cruelty, the helplessness that had tugged at her, sorrow warring with fury and then guilt. And above it all, that all-consuming terror.

But her mother was the first one out of the door when someone called for a midwife – even if it was for a neighbour who had spat at them in the street with a hissed *Vala*, or sold them the worst of the harvest at an extortionate price – and the last to leave when the birth was slipping sideways, every second spun out like precious silk. She housed travellers who were thin on coin and food, simply for the price of a story, and sent them on their way well fed. She picked up endless stray cats and nursed their litters, even though their fickle natures meant they often escaped as soon as they could.

And when Sýstir was teary over the village children who ignored her, her mother would bring her close and whisper, *You have to keep choosing hope, even when it hurts.*

How it had hurt, in the end.

But today, the sky is that crisp winter blue, and sunlight filters gently through the trees, and it occurs to Sýstir that it might be a perfect day to try to choose hope.

When she comes out of Agagkantor's cave at dusk, Fulgir is waiting for her. The fabric draped over her shoulders is laced to look like moss, over a much warmer cloak of wool. Even though trolls don't suffer the cold in the same way, it's clear that Fulgir has not quickly forgotten the chill of the water, either.

"Well met, Sýstir," she says and smiles. "Shall we?"

Sýstir awkwardly walks alongside Fulgir, aware of the silence strung between them. But Fulgir doesn't seem to mind it. The pathways are quiet at this time of night, though Sýstir catches the bellow of moose in the distance, and the accompanying howl of wolves. The snow crunches underfoot, glittering in the crescent moonlight.

Sýstir has only ever seen the Rise's cave from a distance, carefully concealed in the trees. But as they approach the entrance, she feels something close to awe. The boulders are so much larger up close, almost mountainous, blanketed with grey-green moss and sprawling roots from the trees that have made their home above.

Outside of the entrance, a skóug troll stokes an earthen furnace, a blaze glowing within. Another troll sits nearby, a long-handled hammer resting in her hands. They both raise a hand in greeting to Fulgir, and if their gaze catches on Sýstir, it's at least with more curiosity than hostility.

A sudden, panicked thought occurs to Sýstir. "Did you tell them I was coming?"

Much as she dislikes Queen Hilda, the last thing Sýstir wants is to further offend her, or any of the other trolls.

Fulgir pats her on the hand. "You need not be afraid here."

Sýstir takes a deep breath. She's faced down Oden's men, pitiless cold, and clawing hunger. She has lost everything – even the things she didn't know were possible to lose – and she is still here. A few trolls cannot scare her now, she decides.

Fulgir slips underneath the boulders, into a crack that's barely visible from where Sýstir is standing. After a beat, she follows, twisting her shoulders to get in. Despite the trolls' larger size, it's still a squeeze, and she finds herself holding her breath, straining for footholds. The air cools and thickens with a pleasant, earthy scent, not entirely unlike Agagkantor's cave. But instead of the corridor opening into a single room, Sýstir steps through to a huge atrium. Trolls cluster inside, in varying sizes and shapes – and so many more than she could have imagined.

There's little furniture compared to Agagkantor's, who is already frugal with his own belongings and chides Sýstir for her attempts to pad out her nest. But what is present is beautifully crafted: pots with runes etched along their bottoms; stools inlaid with gold that sparkles in the firelight, surrounding a central cauldron; and runes carved all across the walls and ceilings, detailing the grand history of the Rise itself in wondrous poetry.

Greetings ring out as Fulgir passes the trolls, with more than a few lingering looks at Sýstir. Most of them, she realises, she's seen before. Either when she's hiding to watch the rite of Nattaskur, or at the river in the summer, or on the spring pathways opened up by the thawing snow. It's an odd kind of comfort to know that if she's not amongst friends, well, she's not amongst strangers, either.

Another troll passes them, almost twice as tall as anyone else in the cave. Instinctively, Sýstir takes a step backwards.

"Well met, Grendel," Fulgir says.

Sýstir glances up to the troll and has to resist the urge to flinch. It's several years past, but she still recalls the troll who had shamed her at the gathering under Nattaskur. He must remember her – Agagkantor's scrawny ward, hiding her tail, eyes wide as anything – but he only gives her a short nod.

They are not enemies, she tells herself, trying to quell her uneasiness. *They have invited you here for a reason.*

It might just be Sýstir's imagination, but she's almost certain that Fulgir rolls her eyes after him.

"The tallest trees are rarely the strongest," she says, by way of explanation.

Sýstir smiles tentatively. She's heard Agagkantor use that phrase more than once – usually when talking about Queen Hilda's Rise.

"Come, the Echo awaits," Fulgir adds with a grin.

Sýstir follows her down the tunnels, which snake deeper into the earth. The air takes on a chill, then turns warm, carrying the scent of charcoal. As they move further in, a deep glow permeates the tunnel, casting shadows on the walls.

Sýstir hears it before she sees it: a roar of crackling flame, the clang of hammers ringing out, a low rumble of song. Fulgir slows down so they can both peer around the corner.

The heat is intense, and the two trolls inside are stripped to their waists, their hair laced with gold. Even though the hammers must easily be twice the weight of a grown man, and at least as tall, they wield them comfortably, pounding a bar of metal laid out on an anvil. Behind them, another troll, smaller than the two, feeds the furnace, charcoal dusted on their cheeks.

It feels as though she's stumbled upon some mythic image of old, straight from the stories her mother would tell her.

Neither of them look up from their work, but their ears twitch towards the entryway. Fulgir pulls her away, pressing a finger to her lips.

"Best we leave them undisturbed," she whispers.

Sýstir glances back one more time as they leave, but her attention is quickly captured by the tunnel ahead, swathed in darkness. Fulgir picks up a lantern and kindles it, leaving just enough light for them to see by. It's unquestionably for Sýstir's benefit; even though she has excellent night vision, nothing compares to the trolls' eyesight, attuned to the pitch-black of the deepest caves.

"What's the Echo?" she asks.

Fulgir answers with a backwards glance and a smile. "You will see."

She turns a corner into another of the cave's atriums – and Sýstir almost bumps into her, arrested by the sight laid out before them.

Gold glints at her from every angle, heaped in haphazard piles, or organised neatly on recesses. And in every possible shape and size – from thick bangles and scattered beads, to an entire sheet that shimmers Sýstir's distorted reflection back at her. All of it inscribed with runes – the Rise's stories, recipes, tales between friends noted down. A few stools are lined up against one wall, a chisel left behind on a half-finished torque.

Sýstir reaches out, then draws back, tempted to touch something just to make sure it's real, and terrified at the same time.

"Humans... do not have this?" Fulgir says curiously.

Sýstir shakes her head. "Gold is too precious."

Outside of the Dark Forest, she's only ever seen gold once, when the nobleman had passed through the village. Just one ring, but how proudly he'd worn it – and how little gold it took to demonstrate his power. A king's entire ransom would not amount to this.

"Those few who can write use vellum," she explains. "And ink. Paper, sometimes, if it's available. Mostly we just remember, as best as we can, through story or song."

Fulgir shakes her head as if to decry human foolishness, and Sýstir stifles an answering smile. Of course, paper wouldn't survive a year down here, and vellum not much better. Where the paper would deteriorate with damp, the vellum would prove attractive to all kinds of forest insects. By that point, there would be nothing else to do *but* remember.

Gold, however, lasts forever.

Sýstir follows Fulgir back out of the tunnels, past the smithy and up to the hart. A delicious smell pulls them forward; Sýstir's stomach rumbles. Even Agagkantor, who is so quick to criticise the Rises, has spoken fondly of their shared meals with an uncharacteristic nostalgia.

By the time they emerge, every troll has gathered around the hearth in the centre of the hart – even the soot-stained ones from the smithy.

But Sýstir stiffens, her easy joy fading. Because in front of them all is Queen Hilda. Sýstir only ever sees her from afar – much in the way of the Rise's cave – but she hasn't forgotten that first meeting, when Queen Hilda had all but implored Agagkantor to cast her back into the cold. It's because of Queen Hilda that the Rise has remained a mystery, that the Skóug Trolls have shunned her, that Sýstir has never been able to fully set aside her human self. How can she, when no one else will?

Sýstir is about to back away, to protest that she is quite full, actually. But Fulgir draws her close, right next to the empty space between another troll and Queen Hilda.

"Sit," Fulgir says firmly.

Sýstir glances at the entrance longingly, but there's not much else she can do. Hesitantly, she sits cross-legged next to the queen. Someone passes a bronze cup brimming with liquid to Queen Hilda, who raises it. The entire hart falls silent.

"It is a great honour to sit amongst the hero of our winter," she says. "So we honour you in turn. Be welcome, Sýstir."

Queen Hilda drinks from the bronze cup, then passes it to Sýstir. She takes a tentative sip: spiced honey mead. Out of the corner of her eye, Fulgir motions for her to pass it forward, and she hands it off quickly, before she can spill anything. Slowly, the conversation starts up, as bowls are ladled with stew and cups are filled with a watered-down version of the mead. The nearby trolls introduce themselves, and Fulgir offers a quick sketch of context, so that Sýstir is not entirely in the dark. Her gaze particularly lingers on Fundin, a shorter, comparatively slender troll, who sits even more quietly than his companions.

"The son of our queen," Fulgir whispers.

Sýstir cannot remember the last time she shared a meal like this. But the feeling strikes her as familiar, if dusty with disuse. When she finishes her bowl, someone hands her another, adding crusty bread to an already hearty meal.

"How fares Agagkantor?" Queen Hilda asks.

Sýstir hesitates, wary. "Well enough."

Agagkantor has never told her the purpose of his long visits to the giants or the wyrms, or even further elsewhere. She imagines that he would probably be displeased if she mentioned them to Queen Hilda, so she lets her answer end at that.

"And has he been teaching you much of our Dark Forest?"

It doesn't escape Sýstir's notice the way Queen Hilda clings to that possessive *our*, or how little room it leaves for Sýstir. She straightens her shoulders, just a little.

"I've learnt Elfdalian, and I'm familiar with the ancient pathways. I know of Gromildr and Oden in verse and prose. I've – I've learnt a lot."

Pride prickles sharply underneath her words. Even beyond what Agagkantor has taught her, she has learnt to fend for herself, to walk as one with the Dark Forest. She's tamed a lynx, survived a fall through the ice, conversed with the trees. Would a human be capable of that?

"And of Nivir?"

Here it is – the trap laid for her.

"Like I said, I've learnt a lot," she says, just a little too sharply.

Queen Hilda must sense it because she turns away, as though Sýstir has said something distasteful. But her tone is gentle when she responds, "May we all be so knowledgeable in our lifetimes."

The conversation shifts, settles to more mundane matters. Sýstir listens to it all, though she never quite loses track of Queen Hilda. If she wants to needle Sýstir, well – she'll have to be better at it because Sýstir is determined to enjoy this evening.

Yet she can't help but notice that as the meal progresses, several trolls approach Queen Hilda quietly to ask for advice, or to request assistance. Each time, Queen Hilda listens before replying – usually a few careful words of encouragement, or a promise of help. Sýstir would grit her teeth at the interruptions, but she has to admit that the troll queen never replies with anything but gentle patience.

A flicker of uncertainty whispers through Sýstir. This version of the troll queen is so vastly different from the one that Agagkantor described, which has never left room for kindness or warmth. Then she remembers the way Queen Hilda had looked at her – *through* her – on their very first meeting, imploring Agagkantor to cast her out, and she steadies. Yes, Queen Hilda may be kind to her trolls, may even shine benevolence upon them as she sees fit. But this is not the truth of her, and Sýstir will never forget that.

After dinner, someone brings out a bone flute, polished so that it gleams in the firelight. Another starts to sing, their voice reminiscent of the echo deep below the mountains. Someone else takes up the verse half a step after the first singer, and soon the entire hart reverberates in a harmonious round. Magic resonates underneath like a second echo, a quiet, calm healing that soothes the aches of the day.

Sýstir finds herself humming the melody, her sweet voice an octave higher than the trolls'. The song is familiar, she realises – a variant on one of Agagkantor's, but with a fullness that their own two voices have never been able to fulfil.

A sudden lump comes into her throat, tears pricking at the corners of her eyes. She and Agagkantor often sing together, but not like this, with harmony woven like an unbroken chain. It's been so long since she's been amongst so many beings, part of the communal choir instead of listening to it wistfully from outside.

Not since long before she left the village, when she was small enough that the world still fit in the palm of her hand.

She glances at Fulgir, singing beside her. For a sweeping second, it's Ada, her voice a little rougher than Sýstir's, but still cherished, still loved. Then she blinks, and the hart returns to view.

When the round eventually concludes, Sýstir takes a few steadying breaths to quell the tears at the back of her throat. Fulgir gestures to the entrance of the cave; her time is up, for now.

"I will lead you home," Fulgir says.

"I can go by myself," Sýstir says, but Fulgir is already walking to the entrance with her.

She smiles at Sýstir. "We do not have to walk alone just because we can."

The quiet on the way back feels companionable rather than awkward. And Fulgir is right; although Sýstir is more than capable of going home by herself, how much nicer it is to go with someone. Fulgir drops her off at the pathway up to the cave, darkness swathing the forest.

At the entrance to the cave, Sýstir pauses.

"Hello?" she calls out.

Even though she knows Agagkantor isn't back, from the banked embers in the hearth, she still waits half a beat for the reply. But the resounding silence is all that greets her. And even though the Rise's cave is enormous compared to her cosy one-roomed cave, how empty it seems in here.

She stokes the hearth half-heartedly, wishing the crackle of the fire could fill the cave as beautifully as singing.

· THIRTEEN ·

Sýstir wakes up the next morning, still caught in the afterglow of her visit to the Rise. Even though it was only the night before, the memory has the shape of a lovely dream, perfect and impossible, and even more impossible to encounter again.

And that's fine, she tells herself. Even if it only happened once. Even if it means that Agagkantor's cave feels a little bit colder, a little less bright. The Skóug Trolls, at least, are less likely to throw hostile glances her way when they cross paths in the forest. And she can still sing, even if the only voice is hers.

Sýstir manages to, if not quite believe this lie, then repeat it to herself with increasing conviction. But two days later, she arrives at the edge of the river to find Fulgir waiting for her, and the lie crumbles in her hands.

She freezes, wondering if she's made a wrong turn somewhere, or if she has somehow managed to insult the trolls again, after all. But Fulgir only smiles at her, somewhat sheepishly. A rod and net are slung over her shoulder, a long knife for shearing through ice loose in her hand.

"I have been here a while. But I would confess to some nerves," she says, glancing out over the crystalline river.

Sýstir has every intent of getting out of this as quickly as possible, to make her excuses and leave before the tide can turn against her once more. She has her bow and arrows with her to hunt deer – this time for their hide as much as their meat; she's grown again and her winter shoes are starting to pinch. And she already has plenty of salted fish to last the next few weeks.

But instead, she finds herself saying, "I can come with you."

Fulgir seems delighted by Sýstir's skates as she straps them to her winter shoes. Trolls' feet are wide enough to support them on the ice without slipping, but she watches as Sýstir loops around her, getting used to the switch between ground and ice.

They fish for several hours, and by the time they're done, Fulgir has more than enough for them to carry. Sýstir catches herself walking with Fulgir comfortably, a haul of fish in her hands – and stops. They're close to the entrance of her Rise's cave, and she'd barely even realised. She's being too bold, too careless.

Fulgir pauses with Sýstir. "Do you not wish to come?"

Sýstir stammers out a response – something about the smell of the fish, as if trolls cared about such things, and the chill outside – that she's entirely sure makes no sense whatsoever. It hadn't occurred to her that she would be welcome again.

Fulgir smiles, secretive and full of humour. "It is warmer inside. Enter and be well, Sýstir."

...

Sýstir is nervous those first few times with the Rise, passing skóug trolls who might have given her a hard look at another time. Even though she finds herself disappearing into the shadows at the back of the hart, or sticking close to Fulgir's solid frame, she stands out all the same, shorter and lithe by comparison.

Often, she lingers by the quieter smithy, watching the trolls hammer out sheets of gold to use in the Echo or other metals to make the round-bellied pots used for cooking or storing salt and other herbs. Their larger hands wield tools with a fine dexterity to add embellishments, and it doesn't take long for Sýstir to be able to tell the difference between each troll's work. And if they shift slightly, so that she's better able to see their craft, no one mentions it.

When she's not in the smithy, she spends time sifting through the Echo with Fulgir. More than one of the stories are familiar to her, from Agagkantor's own recounting. But in the mouth of another person, they slip slantwise, much like how the legends from Sýstir's own childhood took different paths depending on the teller.

They never manage to stay for quite long enough, though, because there's always one troll or another who comes to invite them to dinner, or with a request for help. Sometimes it's just to talk – though so much is done through expression and gesture alone that Sýstir has a hard time keeping up.

It strikes her how different these skóug trolls are to Agagkantor, in so many small ways – and then it strikes her again, with a little more pride, that only a few years ago, she wouldn't have noticed at all. Every time she thinks she's reached a comprehensive understanding of the Dark Forest, one more layer peels away.

Often she asks Fulgir to come with her instead, elsewhere in the forest, where it's easier to shake off the vestiges of awkwardness that still linger around the other trolls. Fulgir's longer strides clear land at twice the pace of Sýstir's, but she makes up for it with the loping gait that she recalls from that long-ago spied huldra.

Fulgir blinks, surprised, when Fenrir slinks out of the forest, alert to the sound of Sýstir's stones clacking. Sýstir turns to hide her smile. It isn't often that she gets the chance to surprise anyone, much less the trolls. They had met briefly after the near-calamity on the river, but he'd snuck off soon after, perhaps a little cowed by a stranger. Even if Fulgir had assumed a familiarity with the lynx on Sýstir's part, she probably hadn't anticipated Sýstir's method of calling him. It's a kind of magic, after all, to be able to call a lynx from the forest just like that.

Though with Fen, Sýstir considers, it's always a request. She would never *command*.

Fenrir has grown in his lustrous winter coat, dusted with snow, so that she's tempted to cuddle him for as long as he'll tolerate. But she reluctantly extricates herself so that Fulgir can run a cautious hand over his fur.

"This is Fen." Sýstir kneels down to hug him. "We're friends."

...

As spring starts to rouse itself, Agagkantor is nowhere to be seen. It's often the way for him, with journeys taking longer than anticipated, but it doesn't stop Sýstir from listening out for his returning footsteps each evening. In the meantime, Fulgir shows her all the best places to find wildflowers, how to coax out fish hiding amongst the river's eddies, and where to climb the tallest of the glacial boulders to see the Dark Forest spread below them. The latter becomes what Sýstir considers their spot – a meeting place to talk, to sing when words won't suffice, or to sit in companionable silence. Having a friend, she's discovered, is like tugging down an old, heavy curtain to discover warm sunshine outside.

As they watch the clouds scud past, Sýstir spies another huldra – a flash of movement between the trees. She glances at Fulgir, whose expression suggests that she's already seen the whip of motion. Sýstir can't tell whether or not the huldra is the one she'd seen years before as a child.

It's said that all Huldra are half-siblings, born from the same father. Sýstir had asked her mother once, long ago, why she and Ada shared some features but not others. Her mother was cooking, and the spoon slipped from her fingers, splattering soup on the floor.

"Your father was Väsen," she said, after a long pause. "He... is the reason you are Väsen, too." She closed her eyes briefly. "You must never tell anyone, understand? If someone found out, it would be very dangerous for us. But even more so for you. You must promise me, Sýstir, that you will not tell even your closest friend."

Sýstir's brow knitted with worry, though she had no reason to worry, having no friends to tell anything to, never mind a family secret. Ada and her mother and the animals outside – that was all she needed. And there were no secrets between them in the first place.

"I promise," she'd said.

"Good." Then her mother had ruffled Sýstir's hair, breaking the spell of tension. "And how glad I am to have my little spark of magic with me."

But Sýstir remembered the look on her mother's face, and she never asked again.

Agagkantor shed a little more light on the subject a year ago, when they'd been out together in the forest, tracking deer near one of the lakes. Sýstir had been about to skip stones when they caught a glimpse of silky hair, slicked on the water's surface. Agagkantor placed a hand on her shoulder.

"Näcken, sire of all huldras," he said. "Take great care, Sýstir, that you do not disturb the water."

Sýstir wonders what her huldra half-sisters think of their parentage. Each of them carries the same mix of human and

Väsen blood, yet they've probably never agonised over their half-human origins – if they stop to consider it at all.

Fulgir is still watching the space where the huldra had appeared. But she bites her lip, a sign that Sýstir's come to learn as a desire to ask a question, with the uncertainty of the fragile boundaries between them. Truthfully, she doesn't mind the questions, though she often finds herself having to explain the intricacies of human interaction, most of which seems inexplicable to Fulgir.

Sýstir closes her eyes, listening to the song of the breeze. "You can ask."

"So how did you come to live with Agagkantor?" Fulgir asks.

Sýstir hesitates. Though there's no secret to her origins, or the human blood that runs alongside her Väsen self, she has never told her story to anyone but Agagkantor and Queen Hilda during those early weeks in the Dark Forest – and even then, only the slim, hard facts. She long ago learnt that Agagkantor doesn't care for her stories about the village, even if they're harmless.

But she tries to explain it anyway. She starts with her mother, the vala. The years of mistrust. The unravelling in those last few weeks, irreparable. When she gets to Ada, though, the words stick in her throat. In Fulgir's company, it has been so easy to forget about the permanent bruise of her elder sister, unsoftened even by the years since Agagkantor's revelation. That pebble, small but persistent, digging a blister into her flesh.

Fulgir waits patiently while Sýstir takes a few deep breaths, pressing the heels of her hands against her eyes. When she lowers her hands, she's calm again.

"I apologise," Fulgir says, her eyebrows knit with worry.

But Sýstir waves it away. "It's fine. It hurts, but..." She trails off, begins again. "Ada was mostly serious."

And it's true; for as long as Sýstir can stretch her memory, Ada was the responsible one. The first to see the light changing on the horizon and turn for home; the first to de-escalate a fight where another might have flung words like daggers; the first to offer her shoulder for some new burden of responsibility. Grating on Sýstir's nerves about what *should* be done, how they *should* behave.

Looking back, though, it's easy to see how much of this incessant nitpicking had been fuelled by fear. All the *shoulds*, because to stray from them was to court danger.

"She could be fun," Sýstir adds, drawing further on the well of her memory. "And she was clever. Brave, too."

And stubborn, though that was a dangerous combination with bravery. Like the time she'd prevented some of the older village boys from drowning a cat they'd found, after they'd ignored Sýstir's attempts to stop them. Or the time that she'd stood up to the owner of the tavern after a disagreement, utterly fearless. She was deft with her words more than her fists, and perhaps that's where her power lay.

By contrast, Sýstir was the one who was quick to anger, quick to cry, quick to wound. A wild thing, her mother had often said, with varying levels of exasperation. No wonder Ada had been so eager to leave Sýstir behind. She swallows the knot in her throat.

"Do you have any siblings?" she asks.

Fulgir takes the change of topic gracefully. "No, I am not blessed as such. But in the Rise, we are all kindred." She pauses at Sýstir's incomprehension. "We are... bound to look after each other."

"It was like that, too, in the village," Sýstir says quietly. "Or it was supposed to be."

Briefly, she tries to imagine what it might have been like. To sing in harmony, to claim all as kin, to not leave anyone out in the cold just because they couldn't buy their way into a bed. Before the Dark Forest, it would have struck her as an impossible fantasy.

She exhales and smiles. "I think I prefer your way."

• • •

Fulgir leaves her at the pathway to the cave. Sýstir tries not to mind the long walk back, or the empty cave with the cooling ashes of the fire. Just as she has tried not to notice when Fenrir slinks off into the Dark Forest, gone two or three days, or that the scent of charcoal is starting to creep back into her dreams.

She's dozing off by the hearth when heavy footsteps sound along the corridor. Sýstir springs from her stool, her heart racing. And then—

"Little Bird?"

Agagkantor's weary figure appears in the hart. He stoops underneath the doorway, his eyes red-rimmed and the lines across his face more pronounced with exhaustion.

"You're back!" Sýstir exclaims.

She throws her arms around him, too pleased to stop herself. But instead of returning her embrace, he stiffens under her touch. She pulls back, a frown knitting her forehead.

"What's wrong?"

Suddenly, she hesitates; she's forgotten all about their fight. Surely he can't still be angry with her?

He looks as though he wants to say something, but instead he sighs. "It was a long journey," he says, easing slowly on to his stool. "With no easy answers."

She takes his cloak from him, and his walking stick, lending an arm to rest upon as he makes his way to his stool. She has always known that Agagkantor is old, even by Skóug Trolls' standards. But tonight, she finds that the creases in his face are deeper than usual, his weariness born from something other than travel.

"If I'd known you were coming, I would have brought in more firewood – cooked something proper, at least—"

He raises a hand. "Peace, Little Bird." Then he smiles at her, and her stomach unknots. "I am glad to be home."

While he rests, she stokes the fire in the hearth, makes dough for bread, adds more ingredients to the stew already cooking. Agagkantor talks gently to her as she works and the tight anxiety that's wound itself around her for weeks starts to unravel. She has missed this – just the two of them, the cave a perfect size once more.

He tells her of meeting Korí and Hallr at the crossing beyond Nivir, of the giant Ólaug he had conversed with – so large that her very voice shook the earth – and the faeries who had accompanied him for several nights, drawn to the fire he'd made. The night that Tor, God of Thunder, crackled over his head, but without a single drop of rain. The morning when he'd seen a huldra loping through the trees and thought of her. His tales start to take that spun- thread shape of fairytales, and despite every intention, Sýstir finds herself nodding off.

"And what has befallen you while I have been gone?" he asks, corralling her focus.

She blinks back her own exhaustion. Her stories are not the same as his – not of big adventures – but she tells them anyway. Hoping that he'll be tempted this time to stay longer, or better yet, bring her next time. She might not be able to cover such long distances without rest, but if it's winter again, and she brings her skates...

Her thoughts turn back to the slip of ice.

"And Fulgir said—"

Agagkantor interrupts. "Fulgir?"

Inwardly, Sýstir cringes. She hadn't meant for Fulgir's name to slip out; she'd meant to ease him into the idea slowly. But her mind, it seems, has other plans.

She takes a deep breath. "Of Queen Hilda's Rise."

As quickly as she can, she outlines the chance encounter. The ice breaking, the frantic cry for help. The ache in her calves as she'd skated harder than she'd ever done before to reach Fulgir in time.

"They wanted to thank me, I suppose," she says. "For saving her."

Agagkantor's expression darkens. Sýstir's hands twist together nervously, her mind racing. She supposes it would have all come out eventually, and perhaps it's better this way – for Sýstir to present this new friendship to him in a straightforward fashion, rather than for him to believe that she's hiding a secret.

"Queen Hilda and her trolls are not to be trusted," he says.

"They're – they're not all bad," Sýstir says uncertainly.

Maybe Grendel still frightens her a little, but she's seen the unflinching kindness of the other trolls, the same way most beings in the Dark Forest have extended a generous hand. Maybe some of them still harbour Queen Hilda's inexplicable dislike, but if they do, then they've chosen to remain quiet for now. And she'll make sure she gives them no reason to change their minds.

"I much mislike this, Little Bird," he says darkly.

Sýstir hesitates. "Maybe if you saw that they've changed – maybe if you come back to the Rise's cave—"

"Don't presume to tell me what will certainly be false," he snaps.

She flinches. Agagkantor has barely been home for an hour and already they're fighting again.

"I – I'm sorry." Then she rallies. "But it can hardly be a bad thing, can it? To have the trolls a little less watchful?"

She waits, trying not to watch Agagkantor's face crease with worry or anger. He can't ban her from seeing the trolls – and she supposes she cannot cure his inexplicable hatred of them. But she and Agagkantor – *they* can coexist together, can't they? He doesn't have to know how much she likes spending time with Fulgir wandering the Dark Forest, or how often she loves to sing with the other trolls. He doesn't have to know that leaving the Rise is hard, and returning is so easy, like she was always meant to do it.

He doesn't have to know that there is a sliver inside her that stands amongst the Rise and feels at peace.

"Mark me," Agagkantor says, foreboding. "This will not last."

· FOURTEEN ·

Agagkantor has rarely been proven wrong, but Sýstir is grateful to see that his warning is unfounded. Because a year passes by, then another, and the Rise welcomes her still. She celebrates with them at the Solstices, at the coming of spring under Nattaskur. When she sings with them, she feels the swell of their song, the quiet cling of healing magic around her. It becomes second nature to call upon Fulgir, to share the first taste of wild strawberries with her or the first summer swim.

Agagkantor grumbles when she comes home late, and mutters that she doesn't seem like herself. But the truth is, she feels more herself than ever: both the old self – first to crack a joke, first to laugh amongst family – and the new self, who no longer needs to worry about seeming too Väsen. So she cheerfully ignores his complaints, hoping that he'll eventually learn to live with these two halves of herself, the way he has already managed between her human and Väsen sides.

Tonight, the Rise is thick with the drowsy, earthy scent of late summer. Sýstir should be heading home, but instead she traces runes in the dirt floor for the youngest trolls, while Fulgir carves the feathered outlines of ferns on a new bone flute. More than once, she's caught herself with the unexpected wish to stay overnight, and all the other nights thereafter, before the guilty image of Agagkantor alone in the cave flashes in her mind.

The troll children complain when she finally stands up, brushing her skirt free from dust.

"I can't stay, little ones," she says softly.

Not yet, anyway.

She bids goodbye to the children and to Fulgir, who clasps her hands in farewell. As she leaves, she notices someone watching her.

Sýstir meets Queen Hilda's eye, unafraid.

...

Sýstir has long since lost track of individual days, but her birthday is always within that cusp of summer and autumn. And as the season turns, she finds herself counting down regardless.

Eighteen. A woman, by human standards. At eighteen, Sýstir would have been courting in the village, or maybe engaged or married – perhaps even with a baby of her own. If she was human. But even before she really understood the depth of what she would give up, she had already resigned herself to spinsterhood by the time Oden's men had chased her from the village. She'd decided to be content with helping Ada and her mother, to making her life as small as it needed to be. Whatever it took to survive.

Her mother had been saving jewellery for Ada's eighteenth. Nothing grand – a copper band with a lily engraved around its edge, and an amber pendant flecked with honeyed stripes. Sýstir had always wondered what would be left over for her own birthday. But the chance to ask that question came and went years ago, taking the answers with it.

She doesn't know what it means to be an adult in the Dark Forest. The Skóug Trolls live on a different timeline entirely, in the same landscape as trees and mountains. For the older trolls, she's not even sure if they can truly understand the experience of *child*. For them, their birth is just rock and deep and earth, and then *troll*, awakened from its boulder shape, at once millennia old and hours young. As Agagkantor told her, the first babies came later, their childhoods a patchwork of haphazard if well-meaning guesswork as to what they might need. And some of the faeries, whose lives span fleeting days, or even hours, probably can't conceive of a helpless infant self. She's seen sprýg gnomes celebrate their thousandth favour at all years of age. Where does adulthood rest in that?

Maybe adulthood is just a foolish, human thing – something

else to be discarded. Agagkantor pays little attention to the idea of a birthday, claiming that her entry into the Dark Forest is the only time worth celebrating. So Sýstir tries to put the human rite out of her mind, and consider eighteen a year just like any other.

One clear morning, she makes her way to a place the river splits in two, chasing downstream in smaller tributaries, a humped bank of earth between them. She stretches out her arms, feels the breeze wash over her. The air smells like pine and warm earth, like the year turning over in its bed.

She might already be eighteen – she has no way of knowing which precise day, anymore – but today, she's decided to be seventeen for a little longer, just to hold on to that last childish impulse. There's a cluster of boulders that fords the river, and according to Hallr, a deep cave within that remains curiously dry, said to be the lost hoard of an ancient lindworm.

She'd said this to Sýstir with a smile and a wink that had made it clear where the truth of the story lies. But Sýstir still feels that childlike pang of adventure. In the weeks to come, she'll have to set that aside, the urge to explore anew.

At the edge of the treeline, she pulls out the rocks that Agagkantor gave her long ago and snaps them together. But Fenrir doesn't appear. She isn't entirely surprised, though a faint pang of disappointment shoots through her anyway. She knows that Fenrir has caught the attentions lately of another lynx, and if she's not mistaken, there will be kits later in the season. *He is a wild thing*, Agagkantor had said, and she has long made her peace with that.

Fulgir is waiting for her by the river. There's unexpected energy in her today; she moves with a lightness that makes Sýstir smile.

They spend the day exploring the cave within the boulders as promised, and though the lost hoard is nowhere to be seen, Sýstir can't help but feel that she's received a treasure of sorts anyway. Time, stretching glorious and golden in front of her. Besides, the cave is full of treasures of its own: stalactites clustered on the ceiling like teeth in the jaws of some ancient monster; damp earth that is neither sand nor soil, with a scent that eludes Sýstir's knowledge; even tighter spaces that only the smallest of Väsen might pass through. They emerge to late afternoon, the river whispering of its journey further uphill.

It's starting to be too cold for a swim, but she dips a toe in, gasping at the chill. She's tempted to go in anyway, for as long as she can bear it, but Fulgir stops her with a pointed shake of the head.

"What's wrong?" Sýstir asks.

But Fulgir gently sits her down on the ground. Her fingers, deft even for a troll, comb out the day's knots in her hair, and start to draw it back into a braid. This, too, Sýstir has missed. It feels like the ghost of another lifetime, resting its hands on her shoulders. How many times had Ada or her mother done this, in the easy companionship of womanhood?

When she's finished, Fulgir places something on Sýstir's head. A wreath, twined with pine and ferns and braided birch bark.

"What's this for?" Sýstir says, surprised.

Fulgir just smiles and leads her forward, away from the river towards the trees.

The forest is alive with soft light, flung from lanterns bearing Eld. Spinn faeries dart over her head, placing berries delicately in her hair. The Sprýg Gnomes have come out alongside Fenrir, a chain of wildflowers around his neck. There must be some kind of festivity, Sýstir thinks, though she can't place one on any calendar of the Dark Forest that she knows of.

To add to the number of surprises, Hallr and Korí are here, instruments slung over their backs. She grins at them, so thoroughly delighted that she's briefly lost for words. She'd thought she'd seen the last of them for the year when they'd arrived in mid summer with news for Agagkantor and a new song for her.

"We may have received a missive some weeks back," Hallr says, winking at her. "We thought it might be best to stick around for a time."

Sýstir turns to Fulgir, astonished. "What is this?"

Fulgir smiles. "It is your season of birth, is it not?"

Sýstir had mentioned it some time ago, not more than an afterthought. She had never expected anyone to remember, much less think it worth commemorating.

"You did all of this... for me?" she says.

Fulgir nods. "We are bound to look after each other."

Kindred.

Before she can say so much as a word of thanks, Fulgir is pulling her further into the fray. Korí and Hallr start to tune their instruments, the sound carrying across the trees.

Thróttr is waiting for her amidst a cluster of other sprýg gnomes. If she's not mistaken, he has speared a feather through his luva to mark the occasion.

"We are honoured to celebrate with you," he says.

The Sprýg Gnomes gift her all sorts of useful objects: a collection of pine needles with which to make salves and medicinal tea; lustrous beads of milky grey and deep green carved from moss agate, like the forest itself captured in a gem; several spindles of silk collected from the spinn faeries and dyed in autumn colours. They gift her a harp, too, while Kori and Hallr present a knife with a fine bone handle, etched with runic writing. And there's a feast waiting for her: all the bounty of the Dark Forest, laid out to share.

There are a few trolls missing – Queen Hilda, Grendel, and one or two of the youngest children – but most of the Rise have ventured out to celebrate. Sýstir finds herself being greeted by so many familiar faces it takes her a moment to recall their names. She didn't realise that it was possible to know so many beings – that somewhere in these years she's found wayward friendships.

Korí and Hallr strike up a merry reel, and although Sýstir is rusty, she soon finds herself picked up by one of the trolls and pulled into the dance with them. Tjärn faeries, attracted by the music, twirl above them, bright against the shadow of the trees. Sýstir dances until she's giddy with joy, her breath curling in the chilly night air.

The crescent moon is high above their heads by the time the festivities wrap up. Quietly, the forest is restored to itself, so that no one would ever know that a celebration took place here. Everyone says their sleepy goodbyes to one another, trudging back to their homes.

"Thank you," she says, pulling Fulgir into a tight hug. "Truly... thank you."

As Fulgir turns to follow the trolls back to the rest of the Rise, Sýstir pauses. And there is a second – perfect and singular – when she sees herself follow in turn.

Then she shakes her head, and starts down the path to Agagkantor's cave. On the way back along the river's edge, she catches a glimpse of her reflection – and for the first time, her mind doesn't immediately turn to Ada or her mother. Instead, she is reminded of the huldra she'd seen as a child, and the beauty that had so captivated her, now mirrored in her own face. Perhaps this is what those in the village had lingered upon, even if they couldn't put a name to it: the inherent huldra-ness of herself.

But more than that, she looks flushed with happiness, unable to keep a smile from her face. A huldra belongs in the Dark Forest, after all, and isn't today the very proof of that?

As the cave comes into view, Sýstir takes off the wreath and shakes the berries from her hair, trying to ignore the faint pang of sadness. If she lets on what happened, Agagkantor will have questions for her, and she has no desire to further spark his ire over the Skóug Trolls. He would have hated the celebrations, and it doesn't matter that it was for her, or that no one came with anything other than joy in their hearts; he would have found fault all the same.

He wouldn't have wanted to be there, she reasons, before a second, shocking thought slips through. *You did not want him there.*

She is being disloyal, she tells herself sternly. Agagkantor saved her when Queen Hilda would not, took her in, taught her how to be Väsen. He's given her everything, and then more again. There can simply be no room for resentment or ingratitude. But she can't shake the warm glow from her chest, or the thought that has chased her for the last few weeks. The Rise. *Home.*

Agagkantor is mending his belt by the glow of the fire, the needle deftly dipping in and out of the leather. There's a slight tremor to his hands, she notices. Perhaps reconnecting with the Rise will be good for them both, she thinks. Much as he's grumbled about receiving any kind of gifts from the trolls – or worse yet, using them – he still drinks the rose hip tea, with only a whisper of complaint, that Fulgir continues to bring, sleeping well afterwards.

He has taken care of her for so many years; it feels good to give back to him. Maybe then, a small voice in the back of her head whispers, the guilt won't feel so profound.

"You look... happy," he says.

Sýstir smiles, trying to pick the remnants of birch bark from her hair inconspicuously. "It was a good day."

And how easy it is to see all the good days yet to come: more birthdays, more time spent with the Rise, with those who might one day see her and call her kin.

"I'd like to do it," she says suddenly. "I'd like to complete the rite of Nattaskur. I know it's—"

"We have already discussed this," he says shortly, cutting her off. "My answer does not change."

"I was a child then," she says. "I didn't know what I was asking. I know now."

It is a half-truth; Sýstir has always known what she asks for. But it's true that her understanding has grown richer, her feelings more certain. She is of the Dark Forest. Why wait any longer to tie herself to it?

"I need not explain myself to you," Agagkantor snaps. "And I will not bend to your whims."

"Why?" she demands, annoyance prickling her. "This is no whim."

Agagkantor shakes his head at her, as though she's a child again, asking questions with obvious answers. "Must there be a reason? Must you demonstrate your mistrust of me at every turn?"

Sýstir sighs, trying not to let her exasperation show. "I trust you. I've always trusted you. It's not about that."

"What do you think you will earn?" Agagkantor presses her. "The Dark Forest has already claimed you for its own. You have no need of a meaningless rite."

Sýstir bites her lip, tasting blood. No, she doesn't *need* the rite of Nattaskur in the same way that she needs food in her stomach, a hearth to sleep beside. But a world where *need* is synonymous with *survival* does not leave much room for living. And if the hollow in her heart cannot be mended with *need* alone, then perhaps it's all the same anyway.

In her head, the trolls' choir echoes like a bell. The children lingering by her side, reluctant to let her go. How easy it might have been to give into them and stay. They are all the family she has, now.

She straightens her shoulders, stands firm. "I would like to know, Agagkantor."

He scowls at her, fire reflecting in his gaze, and she flinches, despite herself. Then something shifts behind his eyes.

"I did not wish to tell you, but you force my hand, Little Bird." He pauses. "The rite is minded by the Rise, especially when it comes to you."

Sýstir brushes away her unease. "I know."

"Queen Hilda chose to put the decision to the entire Rise," he says.

Fulgir has never mentioned anything about the rite of Nattaskur as it concerns Sýstir; none of them have. But Sýstir knows that the Skóug Trolls often sing in rounds to discuss communal matters, and consensus is rarely reached through one voice. There are very few decisions made that do not involve the entire Rise.

Decisions like those around the rite of Nattaskur.

"They chose to withhold it from you."

Ice slips down Sýstir's spine. "What?"

"If it was my decision alone, then we would be at Nattaskur already, years past," Agagkantor says. "I know you have set aside your humanity. I know you will not fall to that weakness. But they are not convinced. They still fear the girl who entered the Dark Forest, not the huldra who lives within it."

Sýstir shakes her head, horror sweeping over her. It can't be true. There *must* be some other reason why they would vote against her – some kind of misunderstanding, or—

"I know how much you wish to graft your branch to Nattaskur," Agagkantor continues, relentless. "But the Rise is riddled with falsehood. They extend friendship with one hand, concealing the dagger in another. They hide cruelty in their kindness."

"I – I don't believe you," Sýstir says, stumbling over her words. "Then why—"

Agagkantor shrugs helplessly. "It is not for us to comprehend their reasons. I am their kin, Little Bird. Yet where have I chosen to live?"

Out here, away from the Rise.

Sýstir is too old for tears, but they spring to her eyes anyway. She stares hard at the ceiling, blinking them away furiously.

"I am most sorry, Little Bird."

Sýstir doesn't trust herself to look at Agagkantor. "I'm going out for a while."

Even though she's only just taken off her shoes, she puts them back on again, pulling her cloak over her shoulders. The crisp night air hits her like a blow.

She yanks the last remaining pieces of wreath from her hair, wiping away her tears. Foolish, foolish. What is she but an oddity, a pet at best? She thinks of all the times that Fulgir had asked her careful questions about life in the village, all the answers Sýstir had been willing to spill because that's what she believed friendship to be: that push and pull of understanding. It was never supposed to be a *test*.

Of course the Rise was never going to let her complete the Rite of Nattaskur and belong to the Dark Forest. She is an outlier, dangerous by the very definition of herself. It was just that... she'd hoped. To be like every Väsen born underneath the Dark Forest's canopy. To belong to Nattaskur. To belong to the Rise. And like a fool, she'd carved the dagger into her own flesh. They hadn't even had to raise the blade.

When she finally returns to the cave, she's red-eyed but otherwise spent of tears. Agagkantor is pretending to sleep, and she pretends not to see him doing so. The next morning, he greets her with his usual nod, and she returns it before starting the day. If the cave is a little quieter, well, then they pretend, too, that the silence has been there all along.

· FIFTEEN ·

The days grow shorter, the nights long and bitter with cold.

Sýstir pads through the Dark Forest, Fenrir beside her. He chuffs at her heels, as if he can sense her disquiet. He probably can, she thinks. They know each other too well.

She no longer ventures into the Rise's cave. No longer stops by the river with Fulgir, or visits their viewing spot. No longer sings in an endless round, or traces runes on the floor for children, or listens to the murmur of dozens of trolls at once, at peace in their presence.

Instead, it is just her and Agagkantor, silence wound tight between them. Because anything she says – even a sigh that is just a little too loud in its loneliness – is an opportunity for him to needle her further about her choices, and where, exactly, they have led her. Some days, he doesn't even need to say *I told you so* for her to feel its lingering hand on her shoulder. The cave is stuffy with the pressure of all their unspoken grievances.

In the back of her head, a worrying whisper nags at her: *he is not himself.*

Most likely, Agagkantor is simply expressing his annoyance with her at its fullest because she went against him, wilfully spending her time with the skóug trolls he'd warned her about. And even though he was right – as he is again and again, it seems – she can't quite bring herself to concede her mistake. Given that, it is unsurprising that he might snipe at her over the littlest of things.

Maybe it's that he isn't leaving the cave as much. Where he might once have taken Sýstir, he now sends her out alone. And when he does leave, it's always at dusk, with barely a word as to where he's going. His moods were already mercurial, but lately they've felt... erratic. Harsh.

A deep foreboding washes over Sýstir. She's heard rumours, carried by Korí and Hallr's travels, of an illness sweeping the edge of the Dark Forest. But Agagkantor has never been ill, to her knowledge – she's not even sure if trolls *can* become ill – and they're so far away from the borders of the Dark Forest that it might as well be another realm. No, it's a foolish thought.

Maybe if she apologised, she could smooth things over, and life would go back to its easy routine. After all, he has been right twice over – first with Ada, and then with the Skóug Trolls. But every time, she finds it sticking in her throat, unwilling to move past her teeth. *Human stubbornness*, Agagkantor calls it. *Human weakness*.

"I haven't done anything wrong," she tells Fenrir, sounding more confident than she feels.

So she leaves the cave at early light instead, and returns home at dusk when Agagkantor is more likely to be out. She's aware they can't go on like this, circling one another with the wariness of strangers and the resentment of bitter enemies. It's just... she doesn't know what to do.

Fulgir would, though.

Fulgir came to see her a few times, but her company had felt like something worse than bitter consolation. Like pity. And in that light – because how could Fulgir not know of Sýstir's fate? – the hand of friendship had been a cloying ghost, taunting her with all that she was never meant to have. Even the festivities on her birthday are a hard thing to recall, a cruel joke made at her expense, with Fulgir, unwitting or not, at its centre.

It was easier to let her go – to let all of it go, even if she can't entirely pretend that it never happened to begin with. The one quiet mercy is Agagkantor, who, while barbed and sharp with her, has not said a word about her dwindling visits to the Rise.

Instead, he'd sung that song of protection over her, even if it didn't quite have the same resonance of the Rise's own chant. Though she's long since recognised the thrum of magic that Agagkantor weaves into it, she's never been able to work out its intention, except that it envelops her in a warmth akin to sinking into a hot bath. The ache of the hollow in her back eases, along with any lingering fatigue. Even her mind calms, so that she's able to think more clearly, if not without grief or anger. It is one of the few lingering elements, perhaps, that suggests Agagkantor cannot truly extricate himself from his origins.

But if he, who has sworn himself to voluntary exile from the Rise, cannot rid himself of the trolls' ways, then what hope does she have?

Today, her mind and feet seem to be working against her because she finds herself passing by the Rise. Ever since her birthday festivities and Agagkantor's revelation, she's steered clear enough that these days she runs into few of the skóug trolls. But she still sees them, even if they can no longer catch her in the humiliating act of longing, the way they used to. After all these years, it turns out that Sýstir is still at her most skilled when she's hiding.

She watches the children venture outside, warming themselves by the furnace, the older trolls minding them while they work. From outside, she can't hear their singing, but she fancies she senses it nevertheless: a hum that pulls at her bones, tantalising and excruciating all at once.

Sýstir watches for a few minutes, maybe more, caught between that mesmerising longing to join them, and the increasing certainty that she cannot stay. Then her gaze snags on two new figures ducking out of the corridor's overhang.

Grendel and Queen Hilda, deep in discussion.

Their voices are too low for Sýstir to catch any meaning, but there's nothing they could say that would interest her particularly. It's just... that casual *luxury*. Neither of them have ever had to justify their place, or endure a vote that would strip them of their right to belong. Her fist clenches; her foot shifts.

Queen Hilda glances up – straight at Sýstir.

Sýstir ducks, hot shame creeping up her neck, followed by a quick surge of anger. It's not enough that Queen Hilda marked Sýstir as an outcast from the very beginning, or that she stoked the Skóug Trolls' dislike of her. No, she would not be satisfied until she was certain that Sýstir would be exiled by all, denied the only thing she's longed for.

As tempting as it is to look back, Sýstir doesn't want to give

Queen Hilda the satisfaction of knowing that Sýstir is back in her place – outside of the Rise. Instead she turns away, towards the rest of the forest. But the awful, bitter feeling lingers.

Choose hope, her mother had urged her – but look at where that hope has led. To nowhere, and nowhere again. To worse than nowhere, perhaps, because now all she can think of is the warmth of the hart, the glitter of the Echo, the laughter and casual camaraderie around the hearth.

Fenrir, close to her side, noses at her hand, and then very gently bites it. She sighs. Fenrir had liked Fulgir, even if he hadn't enjoyed the noise of the Rise itself.

"I know," she says. "Come on."

She stops briefly at the nearby dwelling to drop off a few particularly lovely stones she'd found. The sprýg gnomes are busy at work, tilling earth. There, their children will grow underneath the earth for four seasons, safe and tended to by their parents. Even Thróttr has his own patch of dark soil, half hidden under ferns and moss, having reached adulthood some time ago.

A few sprýg gnomes wave their hands as she passes, but she shrinks back, suddenly uncertain. This feels... special – not meant for an outsider's eyes. Or maybe it's the pang of heartache that seems to permanently live within her these days, seeing other families. Quickly, before she can attract too much attention or be drawn into discussion, she moves on, taking Fenrir with her.

She pushes deeper into the Dark Forest, beyond the paths that she knows so well. The one silver lining – and how slim it is, weighed up against recent events – is that Sýstir's knowledge of the Dark Forest has stretched with her new boundaries. Here, there are lakes that wash their shorelines in red, from iron ore buried below their surface. Rocks worn so smooth as to look like beds for giants – and who is to say that they haven't been, at one time or another? Occasionally, she hears a cry that is neither bird nor creature, and wonders if perhaps a lindworm or crown dragon is rousing from its long slumber. The trees cluster tightly together, weak light filtering through their branches.

She knows there are other Revels and Rises – lilvätt and eldar and knytt and more – beyond her small boundaries. So many, that to hold the vastness of the Dark Forest would be like cupping a river in her hands. She's once or twice considered trying to find her other huldra brethren, to see if they might teach her more of herself. But that would require a longer journey, and more knowledge, and Agagkantor's blessing.

So Sýstir must content herself with the trees' whispering in Elfdalian of far-off news from distant Väsen, the huff of Fenrir beside her, the firm wood of her bow slung over her shoulder, hand carved years past now. She stops to splash her face with water from the iron lake, noting the scuff of deer hooves in the shoreline mud. Careful not to disturb the tracks, she walks along the shoreline, following the deer.

The iron lake filters off into a river, gathering pace as it heads downstream. Sýstir follows until the forest is heady with dusk. But there's no sign of the deer, and little else to hold her interest. She's about to turn back when she sees a log, recently fallen across a creek.

The creek isn't deep – there's no reason she couldn't ford it – but the banks on either side are steep, and probably mud for most of the year. Sýstir's passed through once or twice, and each time has considered what lies on the other side. The trees on the other side prickle the sky, just as they do on this side. But Sýstir wonders at their sparse, feathery branches, and the curious stillness within them. There's little sign of other creatures.

She steps onto the log tentatively, and it's sturdy underneath her feet. The wood is oddly warm, pulsing through her soles.

"What do you think, Fen?" she asks. "Shall we go on an adventure?"

But he nudges her hip with his head, pushing her away. He looks up at her with his baleful gaze, and she relents. He's probably hungry, and she could do with a hunt to shake some of this energy from her limbs. The hoof prints have long gone from the earth, and there are better places to track down deer anyway.

Truthfully, she doesn't mind turning back. The cool silence of the forest beyond unnerves her. Even in winter, there is always the suggestion of hush, not the quiet of a void.

She's searching for the path back to more familiar ground when a growl ripples through Fenrir. A warning.

Sýstir stops, letting her senses take over the way Agagkantor had taught her. The way she's honed after years of sharing the Dark Forest. The air is still, the trees silent. No movement at all – and yet Fenrir's fur starts to bristle, his back arched. Carefully, she unslings the bow from her back.

She scans the forest around them. Green, grey, green again – all the colours that have become so familiar to her over the years.

A flash of amber.

Wolf.

She barely has time to move before the wolf surges out of the forest behind her, fierce strength rippling through its body. She flings herself to one side, bow in one hand, as the wolf leaps for her. It rushes past – a feint – turning back. Testing for weakness.

"Fen, stay!" she shouts.

She rolls upright, making as much noise as she can. She might not have seen the wolf before its advance – and how odd, for she usually spots them well before they reach her – but enough sound will scare it off. At least this explains the absence of the deer. She won't make easy quarry; he'll give up soon enough.

Next to her, Fenrir growls. But they've done this routine enough times to be well trained. She stamps her feet and waves her hands in the air.

"Go on, be off with you!" she shouts.

The wolf snarls, teeth glinting. It pushes off the ground, barrelling towards her. It's coming back, Sýstir thinks, dazed.

She forgets to move, the bow loose in her hand. The wolf should have been frightened off. It should be loping back into the forest to chase rabbits and other small creatures.

Instead, it charges.

Sýstir realises, too late, that she should have nocked an arrow seconds before. She is entirely vulnerable. She is *prey.*

Something crashes into the wolf. *Fen.* There is a flash of fur and hissing as the lynx wrestles with the wolf. Fangs and claws blurring as one.

Sýstir reaches for her arrows frantically, feeling them slip against her fingers. Her hands are trembling too much; she needs to focus. She grabs one just as the wolf rears its head.

A high, agonised yelp; Fenrir falls. She fumbles the arrow once, twice, before it hooks correctly on the bow.

The wolf lunges at Fenrir – a killing blow.

"Fen!" Sýstir cries.

She lets the arrow fly, notched feather skating between her fingers. It skims the wolf's flank, but it's enough to make it turn. She reaches for another one, but the wolf is already pressing in on her, too close to shoot.

It leaps, and this time there's nothing she can do to stop it.

The wolf collides with her, sending her crashing to the ground. Her teeth rattle in her skull, pain blooming everywhere. She flings her arms upwards, still clutching the bow. The arrow dangles uselessly, then falls.

The wolf snaps at her, pushing against the weight of the bow. Under her fingers, the wood splinters. It's impossibly strong – and she is already too weak, already tired.

There's something wrong with it, she thinks wildly.

Wolves hunt in packs, but this one is alone. And its eyes are deeper than amber, red-rimmed and full of malice. Its breath washes over her, hot and rank. Teeth like jagged stones at the bottom of a waterfall, ready to tear through her.

Desperately, her fingers scrabble for her knife in her belt. *Almost – just a little further—*

Got it.

Without thinking, she plunges the knife into the wolf's flank. Warm blood spills over her hand, but she pulls out the knife and stabs twice, three times.

Finally, the wolf slumps over to the side, dead.

Sýstir lays there, breathless, her head spinning. Her entire body judders with adrenaline. Then she staggers to her feet, away from the carcass. She's killed before – wrung chickens' necks, loosed arrows at deer, snared rabbits in traps – but not like this. Not life against life, raw terror scraping her bloody.

Next to her, something keens. *Fen.*

Sýstir rushes to him, her hands fluttering over his wounds. His fur is matted with blood, the skin underneath slashed to ribbons by the wolf's powerful claws. She tries to sing like the trolls, willing herself to find that scrap of power deep down inside. But her throat is too dry, her voice wavering. Without the community of the trolls and the serenity of the Rise, the song is just that, the magic wilting in her mouth.

"Fenrir! Fen," she urges. "You have to get up. You have to move."

He lies there, whimpering through each ragged breath.

Old childhood terror submerges her. Charcoal, fire. Her mother.

No.

She will not lose him.

Gathering what remains of her strength, she heaves him into her arms. He screams, his claws digging deep into her skin. After years in the Dark Forest, Sýstir is strong. But Fenrir is heavy, limp in her arms but for that unbearable keening sound. Every time she adjusts him, he cries out.

There is so much blood.

She flies through the forest, wishing to be even faster, stronger. Back on to the pathways she knows, familiar dirt beneath her feet. She thinks about the Rise for an instant, then dismisses it just as quickly. No, there's only one place to go.

She stumbles into Thróttr's dwelling, searching wildly for someone, anyone. They must have heard her coming – heard the panicked flutter of her heart, Fenrir's laboured breathing – because Thróttr is already waiting for her at the threshold. His eyes widen in alarm.

"Bring him here," he says.

They make space for him, clearing away ferns so that his bed is of soft moss. Red spackled amongst the green-grey.

"I would ask a favour," she stammers. "Please, Thróttr – I just—"

She's never been good at stitching up her own wounds, never mind someone else's. Agagkantor will most likely be out with the dusk, and even if he was in, he has no experience in this. Worse yet, he might tell her to let Fenrir go. He'd told her as much all those years ago, and he would be more than ready to be proven right again.

Thróttr looks at Fenrir with his careful gaze. "This is beyond me."

Sýstir feels as though she's been shot through with one of her own arrows. She sinks to her knees.

"No," she gasps. "Please."

She knows that Fenrir was never meant to be hers, that he was always the forest's before he was his own. That she knew they would always part in some way because Fenrir has already been too lucky, and death has just been biding its time.

But she had never imagined it quite like this. This ending feels... wrong. Unjust. Nausea rises in her throat.

"Call upon our cousins, the woodland gnomes, Stiga," Thróttr says to another sprýg gnome. "They will know what to do."

Stiga needs no further instructions. She leaps on to the back of a squirrel, whispers something in its ear, and disappears through the ferns.

"She is fleet-footed, Sýstir," Thróttr tells her gently. "We will do what we can in the meanwhile."

The Sprýg Gnomes make Fenrir as comfortable as they can, staunching his wounds with moss and wiping away the blood from his fur. They have always been cautious around him, but now he is so weak that they don't need to worry. And that, in turn, sends fear spiking through her heart.

She crouches down so she's eye level with Thróttr. If she looks at Fenrir now, she knows she'll be undone entirely.

"What can I do to help?" she asks instead.

She has never felt so entirely useless.

Thróttr considers her. "Stand watch over the fire. And..." He pauses. "Hope that help arrives quickly."

· SIXTEEN ·

Sýstir stays out all night with the Revel.

It's cold, but she barely feels it. She keeps the fire bright, though she recognises that it's more to keep her out of the way, her hands occupied. Because in saving Fenrir, she is utterly helpless.

Four woodland gnomes arrive breathless and alert; they'd clearly run all the way here, sped on by Stiga. They barely glance at Sýstir before they turn to Fenrir, conferring in a hush that sets her already frayed nerves on even further edge.

Agagkantor will be wondering about her, she thinks distantly. He might be angry or worried, out searching, though he knows well enough that she can look after herself. It would be a kindness if she went home to let him know where she was. But all she can think of is that if she leaves now and something happens—

Sýstir bites hard on her lip until she realises she's tasting blood.

Thróttr comes to find her just as dawn is breaking. Sýstir forces herself to look at him, terrified of what she might find.

"Is… he—"

She can barely get the words out. But Thróttr must know what she means because he gives her a cautious nod.

"The woodland gnomes have done their best. They have cleaned and stitched the wounds. But I must warn you that they were… unusual."

Sýstir frowns. "What do you mean?"

He hesitates. "The wounds were beginning to fester already, with a rootlike structure we cannot identify. But our cousins are very skilled, Sýstir. They have managed to quell them for now, though it may take some time to see how they fare."

"So Fen will live?" she asks.

"Your lynx is most likely to survive, but I cannot say whether he will be well. He is very feverish, Sýstir," Thróttr says, looking as weary as she feels. "We would suggest he stay here for a time, to be watched over. His wounds will need a close eye upon them."

Sýstir doesn't trust herself to speak, so she just nods. Fenrir will *live*.

"Would you like to see him?"

She nods again, tears burning bright in the corners of her eyes. Thróttr leads her into the centre of the Revel, where a clearing has been made to accommodate Fenrir. He is still matted in blood – whether his own or the wolf's, she can't tell – but his wounds are covered in what looks like a poultice made from ferns and other plants.

Fenrir is breathing heavily, but he's no longer making that awful noise of pain. Sýstir can't tell whether it's a good thing or a bad thing, and she's too afraid to ask. She kneels down next to him, and places her forehead on his, as she did when she was younger. Past the metallic scent of blood and fear, he smells the way he always does. A slight rumble goes through him.

"You know why I named you?" she whispers, tears soaking his fur. "Because I knew you would need the strength of the god-wolf itself. And so you are just as strong. That means you can't be conquered by another, understand? That means you have to live. Otherwise that will have been the biggest wolf – and – and—" She swallows. "That simply isn't true."

His raspy tongue licks the tears off her chin, and despite herself, she laughs weakly. He will be alright, she tells herself. The wounds will heal, the blood will be washed off.

In her mind, the wolf rears up, teeth dripping with saliva. She shudders.

"Thank you," she says, turning to Thróttr. "I – I am in your debt forever."

Thróttr taps the side of his luva. "It is just a favour, Sýstir." He nudges her gently with his hands. "Now go home. Be at ease."

He is right. But Sýstir glances back at Fenrir, the soft rise and fall of his chest.

Thróttr nudges her again, more firmly. "We will send for you should anything go amiss. On my life, Sýstir, he will be safe with us. We will care for him as kin."

Sýstir thanks him again, though she barely feels the words leaving her mouth. She still smells like blood, like the wolf's overpowering scent. Her arms are bruised and scored deeply with scratches; her cloak reeks of charcoal from manning the fire all night. She needs a bed and something to eat, probably – and then she'll feel like some semblance of herself.

But despite all of this, she finds herself taking the long way back to the cave, each footstep wearier than the next.

What will Agagkantor say? He might very well blame her for wandering into unknown territory, for not minding the signs of a wolf pack – though there was only one – or for simply not protecting Fenrir. After all, it's because of her that they'd even been that far out in the Dark Forest in the first place.

And then she would have to explain why she's strayed so far of late. Why she hesitates coming back each night, to a place that feels less and less like home with every tense silence or sharp spat.

This is all my fault, she thinks wretchedly.

She rounds the corner – and nearly bumps into someone.

"Fulgir," she says, startled.

The skóug troll looks at her, surprise washing over her expression. Compared to Agagkantor, Fulgir has always been an easy read, and Sýstir catches all the emotions playing across her face: curiosity, regret, pity. It's been a while since they've seen each other; the last time, Sýstir had barely done more than nod in passing. She was too angry, then, but now...

"Well met, Sýstir."

Sýstir is aware that she's staring, but she can't seem to stop herself. Belatedly, she remembers that she's supposed to reply, and she stammers out a greeting. Her thoughts are still tumbling over one another, most of them back at the dwelling.

Fulgir cocks her head. "What ails you?"

Sýstir stiffens. "I'm fine."

Fulgir just looks at her, as though Sýstir is made of ice, utterly transparent. Her gaze strays to the blood spattered across Sýstir's clothes, the slight tremble of her hands. The absence of a second shadow alongside her own.

"Where is Fenrir?" she asks softly.

"He – he is—"

Something unravels inside Sýstir.

"Oh, Sýstir," Fulgir says.

Sýstir falls to her knees, puts her head in her hands and sobs. All the fear that has pent up within her, all the grief she has cradled so carefully, spills over her in an unstoppable tide. She cries for Fenrir limp and bloody, for the terror that had choked her when the wolf had been inches from her face, for the dread of returning to Agagkantor and yet more fighting. For the knowledge that she's losing everything she held dear, the Rise forever out of reach, even though it was never truly closer than arm's length to begin with.

Without a word, Fulgir puts her arms around Sýstir, warm and familiar. After a beat, a soothing rumble surges through Sýstir, and she realises that Fulgir is humming a tune that they'd often sung together with the Rise.

Oh, how she's missed this. A lump rises in her throat, even though she's cried enough to feel the first faint throbs of a headache.

Eventually, Sýstir forces herself to disentangle from Fulgir, who is distinctly damper than before. She takes a few deep shuddering breaths.

"I'm sorry," she says, wiping her eyes. "It's just that – it's been so long – and Fen..."

Her poor, brave lynx warrior. She will never forgive herself if the unthinkable happens.

"We may yet be able to help."

Sýstir shakes her head, tears gathering again. "No one would help me."

"*I* would help you," Fulgir says firmly. "You are always welcome at the Rise."

"But I'm not."

Sýstir says it without meaning to, and from the look on Fulgir's face, she wishes she could take it back. Even though Fulgir must know – they must all know, if they voted her request down – it feels like shame upon shame to admit it out loud.

"I welcome you," Fulgir says. "And am I not a troll of the Rise? Am I not kin to Queen Hilda and those who came before? Is my voice not enough?"

Sýstir bites her lip. "You don't know what happened."

"Then speak, Sýstir."

It comes tumbling out without her meaning to, a waterfall of words. Returning home after her birthday, wreath still half snarled in her hair. Pleading with Agagkantor to finally bear a branch to Nattaskur. The awful truth that he had finally revealed to her.

"I know of no such vote," Fulgir says uncertainly.

"But it must have happened," Sýstir says. "Otherwise I would be allowed."

Fulgir clasps her hands over Sýstir's, warm and steady. "Petition Queen Hilda. She has never turned a being away, no matter their plight. She will listen to you."

Sýstir shakes her head. Fulgir wasn't there for that first visit, when Queen Hilda had all but implored Agagkantor to cast Sýstir back out into the cold. She hadn't felt the barbed sting of an insult wrapped in honeyed concern. Sýstir would be dead if Queen Hilda had had her way.

"She cast out Agagkantor," she says. "What's to say she won't do the same to me?"

Again, she adds silently.

Fulgir hesitates. "And that is what you believe?"

"It's the truth."

Sýstir digs her nails into her palms, unable to meet Fulgir's prying gaze. It is the truth, yes, and what a damning truth it is.

"May I offer you counsel?" Fulgir asks.

Her hands tighten on Sýstir's, her long ears ruffling in the breeze. A fist of heartache closes over Sýstir's chest. It's been so long since someone has touched her.

"It is in our nature – troll nature – to dislike incomplete truths, or truth that can never be caught in its entirety. Like water through our hands," she says, spreading her fingers out to demonstrate. "Perhaps, however, that leads to a desire to set down a... kind of truth in stone, and forget the water altogether."

Sýstir's brow knits together. "I'm not sure what you mean."

But even as she says it, she catches a glimmer of understanding. Agagkantor's unwillingness to hold the two truths of the Rise in each hand: the Rise that had sworn against him and his half-human ward, and the Rise that had welcomed Sýstir to a place at their meals – or at least, appeared to do so. Even Fulgir herself has presented a contradiction of friend and stranger.

"He was once akin to Queen Hilda," she says. "I would tell the rest of the story, should you wish to hear it."

Without quite meaning to, Sýstir sits on a mossy hump alongside Fulgir. It's her exhaustion catching up from her terrible night, she tells herself. But there's something inside her that aches at this familiarity, that would give five more minutes to pretend that all is as it was.

"I'll listen," she says.

The story unspools slowly, with all the strangeness of a myth. Agagkantor, young and proud and brave, a hero to the trolls through his connection to the Goddess of Hope. But with heroism comes power, and with power comes the need to clutch ever more of it. Agagkantor, less young, but no less proud or brave, became king of the Rise.

"That's impossible," Sýstir can't help blurt out.

Fulgir raises an eyebrow at her and she flushes. It's terribly graceless to interrupt a troll's story. It's just... *Agagkantor.* As *king.*

"I'm sorry," she says sincerely, and Fulgir continues.

He was king, for a time. Good and fair, in the way that Sýstir would have expected from Agagkantor. And he might have stayed like that, if he had not been called to travel far afield from the Rise one tumultuous season. When he returned, he would not say where he had been, or with whom he had conversed. He was, however... different.

"He was not well, Sýstir," she says. "And we did not notice, at first."

But they picked up on the quick turn of temper, the rage that seemed to simmer underneath even innocuous comments. The erratic behaviour, the distancing of friends, the threatening of allies. Sýstir thinks of Agagkantor's inconsolable irritability these last few seasons, and a shiver crawls up her spine.

"When he realised what he was becoming, he handed over the throne to Queen Hilda, then a young troll herself. Willingly," Fulgir adds, "but not without grief."

They had continued to be allies, as though all remained well, even if there was one less voice in the harmony of the Rise. But even allyships sour, and Agagkantor – brave, stubborn, proud – perhaps did not consider himself easily ruled. Their friendship eroded over many seasons, crumbling entirely in just one.

"So we stand upon its ruins," Fulgir concludes. "And maybe it is that you are a casualty of its rubble. But I could not tell you upon which side."

"It is impossible," Sýstir says again.

Agagkantor... king. Agagkantor friends with Queen Hilda. If the occasion weren't so serious – her thoughts drift back to Fenrir – she might have even laughed. Sýstir cannot imagine Agagkantor young, never mind the rest of it. And although his temper has quickened in the intervening years, he has not suffered with cough or cold. He is what she might call difficult, but that is not illness.

"Speak with him," Fulgir says. "And to Queen Hilda. She may yet have good reason to hesitate over the gift of Nattaskur. If that is what has happened. I have never doubted her, Sýstir, and would I not doubt someone who spurns my friend, or causes needless hurt?"

"Thank you," Sýstir says, meaning it.

Even if the story is nothing but a fable meant to comfort the trolls with their decision to exile Agagkantor and therefore herself, it was still worth sitting down to hear it. And be in Fulgir's company for the time.

Fulgir raises her hand in parting. "Fare well, so that we may better meet again."

Sýstir mulls over Fulgir's words as she takes the long way home to the cave. She's never asked Agagkantor about his past, so obviously painful. And in exchange, he's been gentle with hers, not picking open old wounds for curiosity's sake. It's been a kindness, on both their parts.

Now, though, she considers what Fulgir said. It's possible that she's lying – but possible in the way that a snow flurry might occur during summer, or a thunderstorm on a cloudless blue day. And Sýstir would see it on her face, as she does with every emotion. However implausible the story, it's clear that Fulgir believes it.

She doesn't need to speak with Agagkantor, she tells herself. If she asks him to shed blood of his own volition, will he not ask her to do so in return? They have lived long enough in each other's company without the answer to these questions, and she's never yet been dissatisfied. But she watches the early dawn light shine on the river and thinks, *what if Fulgir is right?*

It would explain Agagkantor's animosity with the Rise, his hatred of Queen Hilda. The way they had squared up to one another during Sýstir's earliest weeks in the Dark Forest. Perhaps if she had known, or been watching more closely, she might have glimpsed a king within the troll. But even her memories fault her; she had simply been in awe of the trolls as they were. It's hard to say if there was kingliness in that.

When she arrives home, Agagkantor is contemplating the fire, the way he seems to do with frequency these days. In his hands is the harp gifted by the Sprýg Gnomes, the strings made of silk rope from the Spinn Faeries and newly waxed. The birch wood gleams with polish, and he's carved a new rune into the pillar: Freja.

Light. Hope.

Despite herself – and all that has happened over the last few months – Sýstir's heart squeezes with fondness. He is still trying. They have not entirely shattered what they have so delicately put together over these years.

"You have returned," he says, and she can hear the relief in his voice.

"I'm sorry – I know it is late. I was... distracted."

He sighs. "I considered that you might have made other plans. After all, you have long been free to go where you wish."

It takes her half a moment to understand what he means. *He thought I might have moved away*, she thinks, surprised. Even though there is nowhere for her to move but the Rise, which would require her to go against everything he has taught her, and everything she has learnt of them since.

"Agagkantor," she begins, unease stirring within her. "You belonged to the Rise once, didn't you?"

Agagkantor glances up sharply. His ears flatten, a frown knotting between his brow as he finally takes in her bloodied clothes, her haunted expression.

"Where have you been?" he demands.

Sýstir ignores him; she can't let herself get distracted by Fenrir. If she thinks of him now, she'll cry all over again – and she's not sure she'll be able to stop.

Instead, she tries to clear the knot from her throat. "What happened, when you left the Rise? Was it... hard?"

She tries to frame it in such a way that it sounds like she's speaking of herself. But Agagkantor's expression shutters.

"What did they tell you? Who have you been listening to?"

Sýstir shrugs, even though her heart is beating rabbit-quick. "Nothing – no one. I just... I was curious, that's all. Because..." She hesitates. "It's been hard for me."

It's not a lie; he can't have failed to notice her unhappiness. Agagkantor doesn't quite look at ease, but he leans back on his stool a little.

"There are times in one's life that require sacrifices, Little Bird. The mother evicts the ailing fledgling. The tree excises a limb to save the trunk. We may think piteously of the fledgling, the branch, and consider it justice ill done." His tone hardens. "But do we ever consider the choice the tree must make? The mother? What is considered ill justice for one may mean survival for the rest. The Rise was weak. Therefore I had to exemplify strength."

Sýstir tries to hide her sharp intake of breath. "You were powerful once? Like Queen Hilda?"

He looks at her sharply, and she worries, for a second, that she's overplayed her hand. He must know that someone has said something to her. He must know what she's really asking.

"I am weary," he says curtly. "And the past matters not. Let us speak no more on this."

She doesn't push him. But she notices that he does not ask about Fenrir or her state again.

"I'm going to wash," she says, just to see if he'll pursue the line of thought.

But he doesn't. Outside, in the chill, she wipes Fenrir's blood from her as best as she can. The icy sting of water is not quite enough to lift the fog of exhaustion or the grief worrying at her, but it clears her head a little. She scrubs until she can no longer smell the wolf on her, until her skin is pink and raw, her own bruises surfacing with the dirt. And her mind works carefully, methodically, piecing together all that she has learnt in the last few hours.

Agagkantor has always spoken of his own separation from the Rise as a choice, with the Skóug Trolls too foolish or unkind to bridge the gap between them. At worst, Sýstir has always believed it to be self-imposed exile, borne from a rift that neither could mend. She has never suspected that there might be another reason for his exile.

Agagkantor is hiding something.

· SEVENTEEN ·

Sýstir sleeps until well into the afternoon, finally succumbing to her exhaustion. When she opens her eyes to early dusk, Agagkantor is watching her. She avoids his gaze as she stirs herself, trying to clear the last vestiges of sleep.

Overnight, her suspicion has hardened into distrust – a foreign feeling to her. She *knows* Agagkantor. He is the family she's chosen, time and again.

But he has given her so many reasons to doubt him, of late. His insistence that she stay away from the Rise, that the rites of the Dark Forest were made to strangle rather than celebrate. It had made sense when all she knew of the Rise was Queen Hilda. But now...

A dark thought has been needling at her, spurred by Fulgir's suggestion: what if they voted against Sýstir *because* of Agagkantor? She has always considered herself the mistake, the problem to be dealt with. Now, with this new history between them, she's not so sure.

She needs answers. Even though the light is fading fast, she pulls on her boots and reaches for her belt.

"Where are you going?" Agagkantor asks.

Sýstir pauses. It's an innocuous question, one that they have both asked of each other without thinking. Because the truth has always been straightforward and insignificant. *I'm going to the river to fish. I'm going to the clearing to search for lingonberries. I'm going for a walk with Fen.*

Lately, though, the truth feels like a precious thing to come by.

"I won't be long," she says.

Agagkantor looks at her as though he has something more to say, but instead he settles back on his stool. Even though the fire is dim, he leans away from it, as though it pains him. She pauses to look at him – trying to see him anew, given everything that Fulgir claims. He is nothing like the human kings of old fairytales, who are all, inevitably, lovely of face and fair of temper. But with his head bowed, his hands clasped together, there is something... more, perhaps, within him. For a second, she can almost see it: a younger Agagkantor, sword in his hand, command in his fist.

A kind of king, but one that sends a quick shiver down her spine.

"Do not wander far," he says, and she jumps, startled. "The wolves are passing close by."

She glances at him one more time before she leaves, and something worrisome stirs within her.

First, she stops by the Revel to check on Fenrir. Thróttr guides her gently to him, where he sleeps aided by some sedative. His eyes flutter in the throes of some dream, and his breaths are shallow. Too shallow for her liking.

"He's getting better, isn't he?" she asks anxiously.

Thróttr glances at her, uneasy. "He is sleeping well. But Sýstir..."

Sýstir shakes her head. "No, he will be fine. He has to be."

"I will continue to watch over him myself," Thróttr says, not quite conceding. "And he is fighting – that much is clear." He frowns. "What was the creature again?"

"A wolf," Sýstir says distantly.

"An odd wolf to make such wounds," Thróttr mutters.

She kneels by Fenrir, stroking his fur. She sings to him again, and this time she feels the shape of the magic inside her mouth. It's the same round from the Rise, the same one Agagkantor has sung over her every year, in honour of the night they'd met.

She searches within herself, the way Agagkantor has taught her, for healing, calm, serenity. And it's hard to say how much of a difference it makes – she is still so careful about that thin line between help and harm when it comes to magic – but Fenrir's breathing seems easier. The flickering behind his eyelids stops.

"That should help," she says.

Please let it help. Thróttr checks Fenrir and nods, apparently satisfied. He clasps his hands over her own, his palm barely big enough to cover a finger. But she appreciates the gesture nevertheless.

"I will send for you if he gets worse," he says. "We have seen these knife-edge struggles before, and he may yet come through." He hesitates. "But it may be time for the Dark Forest to call him home, as it will to us all one day."

Sýstir's stomach clenches. "I'll be back soon. I promise."

With the greatest reluctance, she leaves Fenrir, taking him in for as long as she can. He'll live, she thinks again, trying to make it so through sheer force of will. She would know if it was his time. Otherwise she would not be turning away, down the path to the Rise.

She hasn't been to the Rise's cave in some time, but the beauty of it is that it's largely unchanged. The same boulders, dressed by the same moss, with the same trolls busying themselves outside; only a fallen tree suggests that time is still holding court. A pang of nostalgia washes over her, painful as a blade pointed at her heart. If Queen Hilda hadn't so roundly rejected her, she might have had all of this, not just for a scant time, but for years past – and years to come.

The trolls watch her, expressionless, as she stands in front of the entrance. As she walks in, she can feel their gazes burning between her shoulder blades, and she forces herself to stand a little taller. They don't stop her as she enters.

The hart is full of its usual sounds: chatter, a snatch of song, the busy clatter of activity. Queen Hilda is at the other end, conferring with her son, Fundin. As soon as Sýstir enters, their gazes catch. Queen Hilda excuses herself from her son and beckons Sýstir with one slow finger. Sýstir tries not to bristle; she's here as a guest, and if that means capitulating to Queen Hilda's authority, then she will do what she needs to.

"Well met, Sýstir," Queen Hilda says.

It doesn't feel like a good meeting. This last day has felt like a nightmare from which she is unable to wake. But if she can understand why she's been barred from Nattaskur – in Queen Hilda's words, not Agagkantor's – then perhaps she can still salvage something between them. Perhaps she can have the friendship of the Rise once more.

"We have not seen you in some time," Queen Hilda says.

"I – I know. I heard... That is, there was..." She hesitates. "Is it true? That Agagkantor was once king?"

Queen Hilda frowns. "It has been a long time since he was called as such, and few memories stretch that far now. But yes, Sýstir, he was king."

So it's true, then. Fulgir was not lying – and Agagkantor was evading. Her stomach tightens.

Queen Hilda's frown deepens. "What is it that you would ask of me?"

She's trusted Fulgir this far. And although Sýstir has never told anyone else of her deepest wish, besides Agagkantor, she has yet to ask in person. Maybe this is where it has all gone wrong: Agagkantor, goading the trolls, reminding them of their shared fractured history, and throwing away any chance Sýstir might have had to prove her worth. But she is no longer a child, no longer Agagkantor's echo; she can speak for herself.

Sýstir locks her fingers together to stop them from trembling. "I would like to graft my branch to Nattaskur."

She has no tree to call her own, no family to help her climb into Nattaskur's lowest branches. But the Dark Forest is her home.

Queen Hilda looks at her for a long moment, a myriad of expressions flickering across her face, each one indecipherable. Sýstir wishes, for a moment, that she'd never come here at all. It reminds her too much of the look the villagers had given her, after they'd learnt of the wayward power in her voice – like she was a weapon of someone else's making, to be used without her own knowledge.

"I have had to make many difficult decisions in my time. I must do what is right for the Dark Forest and those of my Rise. And I worry about you, Sýstir."

Sýstir tries not to flinch. Her hands twist tighter around themselves.

"You, who will not drink of Nivir, who came to us well beyond infancy. Who has been shaped by human cruelty, much as you have been tempered by the Dark Forest. Who walks alongside Agagkantor and his poisoned tales and has recently rejected the hand of peace we had outstretched, though I cannot claim to know why."

Sýstir does, though. Because Agagkantor had told her to.

"No, Sýstir, if it was my choice, you would not join yourself to Nattaskur."

Sýstir's shoulders slump, her heart sinking. It shouldn't surprise her that this is the outcome – this has *always* been the outcome, inevitable and immovable. Agagkantor had told her himself. And yet.

"But I was overruled," Queen Hilda continues.

Sýstir stares at her. "What?"

"The Rise believes you worthy," Queen Hilda says. "They reminded me that we are all Väsen, no matter our origins, or how far we have strayed from the Dark Forest. They reminded me that we are allowed a second chance to grow into what we may become."

Queen Hilda's tone sounds pitying, as though Sýstir has failed at this, in the same way that she has failed to be fully Väsen.

"I confess, I do not know why you have come today," Queen Hilda says. "Our decision was made long ago."

Sýstir frowns at her, uncomprehending.

"You are free to affix your branch to Nattaskur," Queen Hilda says. "You have been since your first year here."

Sýstir's mind goes blank. White-cold. This cannot be true.

Agagkantor lied.

Queen Hilda is trying to save face through dishonesty. If she claims that Sýstir has been allowed for *years* to graft a branch to Nattaskur, that couldn't possibly be right. Because she's been told time and again that she's not allowed – never allowed. No, this is because Sýstir has finally confronted her, and there is nothing worse than hearing your own words flung back at you. So she is consoling herself with falsehoods instead. She must be.

Agagkantor lied.

Sýstir has always been prone to misunderstanding when it comes to the words and intent of other Väsen. Queen Hilda said it herself: Sýstir has not had the education of a life in the Dark Forest – just a handful of years and an errant tutor.

And anyway, Agagkantor is not himself. She's seen the way he stares at the fire wearily, the curious aversion to sunlight, the way he tends to anger where he might have met her younger self with patience. How easy it might have been for meaning to be swallowed by his mercurial temper; hasn't she, too, said things she doesn't mean in the heat of an argument?

Agagkantor lied.

It's as though someone has split a fissure through ice, and now the entire sheet is shattering underneath her.

"Sýstir, do you fare well?" Queen Hilda asks, breaking the silence.

Sýstir glances up, startled. She'd somehow forgotten in that instant that Queen Hilda is still opposite her, that the roof of the cave hangs high above her head. She tries to return to herself, to grab on to the solidity of the here and now.

"If Agagkantor wishes not to accompany you, we may send another in his stead," Queen Hilda says gently.

She reaches for Sýstir's hand, as if she knows anything about what Sýstir is feeling. As if she *cares*.

Fury spools through Sýstir, molten-quick. She jerks away.

"I don't need your pity," she hisses.

The troll queen's expression doesn't change, but Sýstir can sense the interest of the hart changing. Close by, her son watches, careful. Sýstir forces herself to take a deep breath, but she can't quite seem to take in enough air.

"It is good, then, that you have no need of it," Queen Hilda says, colder. "When you are ready, Nattaskur awaits. It is the wish of the Rise."

But not the wish of the queen. And... not the wish of Agagkantor.

"I – I have to go," she says, not waiting for the reply.

Sýstir stumbles out of the Rise, breaking into a run as she exits. Her chest feels too tight; her thoughts are a blur – except for that one repeating line: *Agagkantor lied.* And not just one lie, wrested from the heat of the moment and regretted ever after. No, this is a lie that he's spun from the moment they met, every word calculated to make her believe she was unworthy.

Every kindness, every softening, every moment that he'd given her grace—

What did he intend? Did he think she would stay with him, biddable and compliant, for the rest of her life?

At the entrance to the cave, she stops. How cold and lonely it looks, without a cluster of skóug trolls or an outside furnace glowing steadily. How little like a home. How desperately she doesn't want to go inside. But she must.

She enters – how ordinary it feels to perform this little action, how horrifying – and readies herself for war.

"Agagkantor," she says.

He sits hunched in the darkness, his hands curled around themselves. He looks up at her, the firelight catching red in his gaze.

"Little Bird," he says. "The hour is grown late."

She'd meant to start with a steady calm. But as soon as she meets his gaze, she realises just how useless all that pacing was. Something hot burns through her.

"Why didn't you tell me?" she asks, and now she can't keep the anger out of her voice. "About Nattaskur?"

Agagkantor's expression shifts to one of impatience. "We have already discussed this—"

"I've just been to see Queen Hilda," she says.

He waves his hand. "I do not wish to hear about your excursions. You know where this all leads, and has already led." He shifts away from her. "I do not wish to see you hurt yourself yet again."

Days ago – *hours* ago – she would have cut herself off, because she would have rather preserved their fragile peace than argue further.

"They voted on it," Sýstir says, shaking with anger. "They voted *yes*."

Agagkantor's hands tighten on his staff. "Hilda is a liar, and you are a fool if you believe otherwise."

Sýstir wants to laugh at the absurdity. "*She* is not the liar."

Agagkantor has been in her life for so long that she almost forgets what it was before him. But now, standing here, the fire between them, she sees a stranger.

"I know about your history," she says, the words rolling too quickly for her to stop. "I know that you were the ruler before Queen Hilda. I know that something happened, that you were—"

"Enough!"

Agagkantor stands, and Sýstir is abruptly reminded that he is twice her size, three times as broad, infinitely stronger. For the first time, a faint flicker of fear crawls up her spine. She knows no songs that carry protection against an enemy.

But then, she's never had to worry about Agagkantor.

"Am I not allowed to protect my ward?" He turns away from her. "I did what was necessary."

"You – you let me believe I was..."

Unwanted. Alone.

Beneath her fury, her heart is breaking, breaking. Such a cruel lie. And for what? So that she would stay with him a little longer? Because he wished for someone to be beholden to him, the way the other trolls had once been?

"I taught you the voice of the Dark Forest, did I not?" Agagkantor insists. "I sang over you as if you were my own kin."

His arguments continue, but Sýstir tunes them out. If this is a lie, then what else has he engineered? What other falsehoods has she swallowed willingly, even happily?

"You are my *ward*," Agagkantor says. "We are kin."

Kin. There was a time when that had meant something different: not the scent of damp earth, or Agagkantor's gravelled tone, but the light laughter of her sister's voice, so hauntingly close to her own.

A sister who had turned away from her, and who she had turned from in kind. Because Agagkantor had told her to do so. Because she had believed him. The way she had believed him about the trolls, about Nattaskur—

A cold horror drops through her.

She looks up at him. "Tell me this: did you truly see Ada that day?"

She waits for him to tell her that he did. She waits for him to tell her that Ada had turned away, just as he'd said, without calling her name over and over.

His eyes, red-rimmed, flare in the darkness.

"You do not belong in that world," he says. "You would not have been happy with her."

She closes her eyes. "You let me abandon her."

"And you did it easily enough," he says, his tone biting. "Did you not wait a year to make your decision? You did not truly wish to go."

Sýstir imagines herself bursting out of her own skin with scales and claws, as the monster that she was once promised to be. But not all wounds are delivered with daggers. She levels her gaze at him.

"We are not kin," she says quietly.

Agagkantor shudders as though she's struck him. But she's only voicing the truth now. No, he isn't a friend and he isn't a parent, and the time for her to be foolish enough to pretend either of those things has long gone.

"There are no ties between us, blood or otherwise. You used me, Agagkantor." She pauses, letting each word find its mark. "You told me long ago that creatures of the Dark Forest were not made for keeping. And yet how diligently you've built my cage."

Agagkantor's shoulders sag, just a little, and she knows that she's hit a wound. The childish part of her screams that she should stop now, that she is breaking something beyond repair. But the rest of her keeps going because this is already broken, already irreparable.

She laughs, but it doesn't sound like her own. "I let myself believe you. All these years, I could have been at the Rise. I could have—" she chokes "—I could have brought my sister here."

All the friendships she's forsaken. The family. Fulgir. *Ada*.

"If I left the Dark Forest, would I be barred forever? Or did you say that just so you could hold on to me for longer?"

His silence tells her everything she needs to know. Betrayal upon betrayal. She can hardly breathe for it.

"I sang protection over you," he says, but it sounds weak to her ears. "I kept you safe."

"I was not safe with you," she says. "Goodbye, Agagkantor."

She turns to leave, her mind whirring frantically with a plan. She'll find Ada, she thinks, and bring her to the Dark Forest, as she should have done years ago. It won't take long; Sýstir still knows Ada like she knows her own reflection, like she knows the sound of her own heartbeat pulsing beneath her chest. Their cousins' home is but a day's walk from her childhood village. Then she'll gather up Fenrir, claim Nattaskur for her own. Perhaps even drink from Nivir, if that is what it takes to earn the Rise's trust.

She's done being at Agagkantor's mercy.

"You may have been accepted by those who would think best of you," Agagkantor snarls, as she gathers her things, "but heed me: a tree always takes root in the likeness of its parent." He pauses. "Human."

Sýstir reels back, as Agagkantor's bladed words lance through her. *Human*. Even though Agagkantor was the one who'd told her to see herself as Väsen, who had shared with her the Dark Forest's innermost secrets. Who had laid her out like an uncharted map and cleared the dust away to make her navigable for the first time in her life.

"I – I'm not—" she starts, before she gathers herself. "I know what I am. And I know what the Rise will make of me."

Sýstir snatches her cloak, glancing back one last time at the home she made for herself. The home Agagkantor has destroyed.

"You will be alone, Sýstir!" he shouts after her. "There is no home for the likes of you and me!"

· EIGHTEEN ·

The wind feels like a howl in Sýstir's ear, even though there's only a light breeze. A howl of grief. A howl of rage.

A howl that screams *Ada*.

Sýstir has spent five years mourning her sister. Wondering who she's become, and what else she's cast aside. All because Agagkantor had told her that Ada did not want her own flesh and blood – that she was happier without her Väsen sister.

And Sýstir had let herself believe it.

But she can't lay all the blame at Agagkantor's feet. She had chosen to believe that it was better – not easier – to let Ada go. She had never questioned why Agagkantor might tell her this, even though Ada had pushed Sýstir to run with her, instead of leaving her to the mob. Even though she had said *don't go far*, when it would have been easiest for her to say nothing at all and let the forest take Sýstir, as it so nearly had.

But she and Ada are two halves of the same whole. And it is time to fix what she should have done long ago.

She takes a step towards the path that will lead her along to the river's end and out of the Dark Forest. Then she stops, Agagkantor's warning ringing in her ears.

There are no caged birds here. But the Dark Forest only extends its hand to those who need it once. If you leave, you cannot return.

Despite herself – despite everything she's promised, everything she believes in – she hesitates. She might have come from the outside world, but the Dark Forest is her home. She presses her forehead to the trunk of the nearest tree, feeling the coarse grit of bark, the pulse of life both within and sustained by it. She closes her eyes and imagines the branches soaring upwards, the roots searching below. Intrinsically linked to the Dark Forest because it *is* the Dark Forest. Just like her.

If she has learnt anything in her years in Trollheim, it's that she cannot leave any part of herself behind, no matter how hard she tries.

She will not lose herself to this.

She walks through the trees, determination clenched in her grip. The undergrowth thins, the ground becoming firm and packed under her feet. The trees' whispers quieten. Then she glances up, and the pale full moon looks back at her.

In the next step, she slips out of the trees altogether, on to a hard dirt road. Fields ribbon across cleared land, and the horizon is speckled with the sturdy lines of cottage roofs, smoke coiling above them.

She's back.

Sýstir rummages inside herself for that burst of nostalgia, or the longing ache inside of her that she's certain she remembers having. But the hollow beneath her ribs feels... empty. She glances back one more time at the trees behind her, dark and solid and reassuring.

Then, before she can change her mind, she steps out of their protective shadow, on to the road.

Most likely, Ada has gone to their cousins' village, so there is, strictly speaking, no need for Sýstir to venture past their old home. But the road goes straight through their old village, and truthfully, she would like to know what has become of it.

Anxiously, she thinks of Fenrir. She'd checked on him once more before she left, but he was resting peacefully, and although Thróttr had not been completely at ease with Fenrir's condition, he'd lost the panicked, helpless look that had so frightened her before. It might be that she finds Ada within a day's walk; it might be longer, with a hard conversation at their reunion. But she has already failed her sister once – she cannot do it again. And Fenrir is in good care.

Angrily, she considers Agagkantor's hand in all of this. If she had known earlier, she might have sidestepped this heartache entirely.

The packed earth of the road feels different beneath her feet, testing her balance with every footstep. Tucked away, her tail aches, the persistent and unyielding pain at the forefront of her mind. She considers every movement, the slight way she presses forward to accommodate the extra length of her tail, and tries to adjust her gait so that it feels more human – or what she remembers as being human. The road is lined with trees grown for timber, uniform, but the night sky seems to swallow their shadows, leaving her feeling as exposed as if she was naked.

Had she really thought she could live like this? To stay silent and demure by a fireside because she cannot sing, or court a lover, or take any friendship as true? To let the summer sun beat down on her, unrelenting, instead of diving into the river, and to forever walk stilted instead of run? To exist in the world as its willing prisoner, fashioning every bar of her cage herself, because any slip-up – even the hint of suspicion – would be fatal?

Even then, they would have come for her. And burning might have been a kindness in comparison to the other methods they could inflict. Punished for simply being who she is, instead of what they wished her to be.

Moonlight pours across the road, the village coming closer with every step. And Ada. Sýstir's heart thuds, and she can't tell if it's anticipation or fear.

She walks until she hits the first field spread out before her, tidy and oddly lifeless compared to the wild sprawl of the Dark Forest. In spring and summer, wildflowers grow on either side in small fragile clusters between the edge of the field and the road. Now it's simply weeds. It seems strange to think that this had once felt plentiful to her. That she had dreamt of tending her own patch of greenery, and might have considered herself satisfied.

The orchards come into view, apples still clinging to the trees. She tries to remember the name of the farmer, but it eludes her. The hollow in her back throbs.

As she walks along the road to the village, the sound of voices startles her. The words sound wrong, until she realises that it's because they sound like her own, with none of the lyricism of the trolls, or the careful intonations of the woodland gnomes. That rolling accent of the Dark Forest.

A group of men pass her, broad and overloud in beer-fuelled cheer, with two lamps carried between them against the evening. Sýstir pulls her hood just a little closer over her face, hoping they won't see her. But there's nowhere to hide on this plain road, and the men slow, curious.

"Are you lost, maiden?" one of them asks.

They are just trying to be kind, Sýstir thinks. But the lantern light hits her face and she sees their expressions change, surprise melting away to something she doesn't like the look of.

"Too pretty to be out on the road this late," another one says.

For a few panicked seconds, she freezes. A child again, with no recourse except to go unnoticed for as long as possible, or to hope they lose interest. That cage, those bars.

But she isn't a child anymore, and these men have no power over her.

She pushes her hood back, and she sees the men appraise her anew, greed lighting their faces. The rose, unfurled at last, with all the shock of a huldra's full-grown beauty. A beauty that is as much a weapon to wield as a knife.

It is also a distraction.

She sings, low and full of intention. In the Dark Forest, her song is just another magic, one note in a hundred-voice harmony. But in the village, she is so much more than herself. So much more than the men in front of her.

The closest one approaches her, but whatever his intentions, they fall to the wayside as her song washes over him. His pupils dilate and his mouth curves into a lazy smile. The men behind mimic him, rolling to a stop.

"What might we do for you, maiden?" he asks, and she can't tell if his words are slurred from drink or from the power held in her own fist.

She considers him, a wild, dangerous excitement thrumming through her. She could make him do anything: jump into the river, or walk until he meets the horizon – or at least, walk until the song's power fades. Climb the scaffold and place the noose around his neck willingly, happily—

The thought sucks the air from her.

"Go home to your wives and daughters," she commands. "Go in silence. Forget you saw me."

The men slope back down the road, the only sound their footsteps. Sýstir watches them, feeling something predatory rise within her. Like Fenrir stalking his prey, the absolute stillness before he pounces. Then she lets out a shaky breath.

This place is doing something to her, she thinks. It's the press of angry memories, that charcoal scent, her mother's hand slipping into hers as they walk down this road again and again—

She slips her hood back over her head. She'll find Ada and then she'll go home. And hope that no one pays attention to her in the meantime.

She thought her heart might settle as she reaches Midgård, but instead it flutters against her ribcage like a bird straining to be free. There's the tavern, where wealthier merchants could buy a room for a night, and poorer ones could spend a coin to share the stables. There's the fence she and Ada used to climb over to take the shortcut leading to the river.

Like a rebellious creature, her mind drifts.

There's the post where she'd once seen a man whipped for theft. The cemetery which had swelled one winter, when illness and hunger had prowled through the village. The square which had once held a pyre—

Sýstir clutches her head. *Think of the Dark Forest. Think of Fen. Think of the moss-clad canopy folding over you and the waxing crescent moon and the sweet breeze.*

She deliberately doesn't think of Agagkantor or the choices facing her when she returns, but they dance at the edges of her thoughts nevertheless. It doesn't matter; when she finds Ada, all will be well.

Sýstir is so deep in thought that she barely notices when her feet start to lead her of their own accord, turning away from the main road into a small lane. The grass grows long and the trees above dapple shadows on the dirt. By the time she does notice where she is, her feet have come to a halt. Because though her mind is elsewhere, and even though it's been years, her body remembers.

Standing in front of her is their home.

She's tried not to wonder what became of it. Whether they might have scoured the land clean, or whether they might have given the cottage to a more worthy family, cottages being hard to come by. But they must think the vala's land cursed because the cottage is empty, the garden abandoned to the wild.

Or perhaps it's their own deeds that they've deemed cursed. Perhaps no one could bring themselves to live in the cottage that they'd killed for.

Sýstir glances behind her, but there's no one around to see her.

Carefully, she steps over the broken fencing, into the brambled thicket that used to be the path winding up to their door. From here, she can see that the roof hasn't survived the intervening years; branches twine upwards, pushing aside what remains of the rushes in their search for sunlight.

With every footstep, tears gather behind her eyes. What did she think she'd find here? Did she think that Ada would simply be waiting for her in the doorway, hands on her hips, wearing the exasperated smile of her mother when she'd stayed out too late?

Yes, she thinks, and the pain is a fierce knot in her stomach. Yes, and she is more the fool for returning to a place that so obviously only exists now in her memories.

No. Of course Ada would not be here.

Sýstir rallies herself. It's only a matter of time before she and Ada are reunited – hours if she walks fast, and if the wind is with her. Then she can finally, *finally* stop chasing ghosts.

As she turns to leave, her gaze snags on the apple tree at the back of the garden. Their mother had planted it when she'd first arrived in the village, and by the time Sýstir was old enough to stand underneath its branches, it had felt taller than the world. No apples had tasted sweeter than those it bore, and no tree was so perfectly suited for climbing, with plenty of low branches for young hands and feet.

Using her knife, she carefully saws a branch from it, the sap oozing from the cut. It feels... right in her hands. A fitting way to complete the rite of Nattaskur. Perhaps, she thinks, brightening, she and Ada can even graft the branch together. A new family, unsullied by Agagkantor's lies or Queen Hilda's condemnation.

As she climbs back out of the garden, she realises she hasn't gone unnoticed. Someone has come to investigate. An old woman, her arms folded in tight suspicion.

"You have no business being here," she snaps.

Sýstir shoves the branch into her belt, where it can't be seen. "My apologies."

The woman peers at her. "You look... familiar."

An old memory nudges the back of Sýstir's mind, but there are too many of them pressing for space. She glances back at the cottage.

"Just passing through," she says, which is hardly a lie. Then, because she is feeling bold, she asks, "What happened here?"

The woman spits on the dirt. "Vala's ground. Oh, years back now. But we do not cross cursed land."

Not a memorial, then, but a warning. Anger stirs under her skin. Even after all this time, they still fear what they cannot understand, or ever hope to be. In this, perhaps Queen Hilda is right.

The humans will never learn.

"What about the vala's daughters?" Sýstir says.

In her mind, she sees them now: Ada, still growing into womanhood; her dark hair braided neatly and bound with a ribbon; her hands deftly mending something or other. And Sýstir behind her, clumsy because she doesn't yet know what it is to walk as herself; hair already loosening from the braid that won't stay in; half a dozen stones in one pocket and a fledgling in the other. Their mother behind them, a silhouette that feels more like a half-forgotten memory with every passing day.

They were just living. That's all.

The neighbour narrows her eyes at her suspiciously. "You said you weren't from around here."

"There were two of them, weren't there?" Sýstir says. "An older daughter and a younger one. Just little girls, really."

A deep, satisfied thrill runs through her as the neighbour flinches.

"They – they ran."

"And how far do you think two girls could run?"

Not far enough, Sýstir knows.

The neighbour folds her arms. "It was over and done with long ago," she says tightly. "The older one was caught and the young one never came out of the forest."

Sýstir's breath catches in her throat. "Caught?"

"And hung. We don't hold with any kin of a vala."

Ada is—

"You would do that to a sixteen-year-old girl?" Sýstir asks distantly, barely listening to the response.

The world recedes to a pin-sharp memory, clear as the moonlight wreathed around them. Ada holding Sýstir's hand, pulling her away so she wouldn't see more than a glimpse of flame. Whispering *run* into her ear to cover the sounds behind them. Ada, brave and stubborn, choosing to fight for them both instead of surrender.

"It was not the pyre. It was a mercy," the woman says uncertainly.

Her beautiful, clever sister. A mercy to give her a criminal's fate, a thief's fate, instead of a vala's. But what had she stolen, except the chance to live?

Sýstir's hands reach for a handle in her belt because she always carries a knife. Because there are bigger and stranger creatures in the Dark Forest. Because she never knows when she might have to fend off a wolf.

"You're missing one more part of the story, Elise."

Now the neighbour flinches again, more visibly – because it is Elise, after all these years; Elise with grey threaded through her hair and lines woven through her face. Because Elise has been allowed to grow old, to see the seasons keep turning. It's because of Elise that Sýstir's mother is still young in her dreams.

It's because of Elise that Ada is—

Something hot steals over her. A stranger, slipping into her body like a glove – and how well it fits.

"The final part of the story is this," she says, feeling the handle of her knife between her fingers. "The young one does return from the forest. Because she remembers."

Elise gasps and turns. But the ground is still glassy with ice, and she slips. She tumbles to the ground with a hard thud and cries out. She tries to get up again, but there is that luxury of growing old, growing fragile. And how easy it is to break an ankle.

How difficult it is to heal, without a vala.

"*What are you?*" she hisses.

"I am what you made of me," Sýstir says softly, pulling her tail free.

That handle, so smooth between her fingers.

The world flashes white, then red.

· NINETEEN ·

When Sýstir comes to, she's running.

She leaves the village behind, past the cottages with their unnatural uniformity, the fields with their toothy fences like a cage. She pushes south towards the river, instead of north, even though every footstep takes her further from the forest she once got lost in. Every rational thought is shunted aside in favour of the overwhelming urge to flee – by any means necessary.

What have you done?

She reaches the river and wades in, pushing through the current, barely feeling the shock of the cold as the water sluices around her waist. Something is twining through her bones, burning as though she's swallowed a mouthful of embers.

She should never have come back to the village.

She should have stayed in the Dark Forest. She would have lived in ignorance forever and been happy with the toothache gnaw of her sister's absence – not this vast plain of emotion, as though the sky itself is too small to contain what she cannot name. Now, she does not even know if her home will hold her. Not after what she's done.

But there is nowhere else to turn. Not anymore.

By her memory, the river winds its way down flat grassland, through a series of villages, before spilling out into arterial tributaries. No forest in which to hide, the full moon shining too bright upon her, even through the clouds. But Sýstir's body has already picked up what she now hears: the quiet but steady pulse of a familiar chorus in the crackling language of the trees, beckoning her further.

Her head is bowed as she moves upstream, so she doesn't see the flat banks become choked with low ferns, or the branches overhead that suddenly appear from a forest that should not be present. She doesn't stop, even as the shadows turn dappled and soft, mist blanketing the ground in a silver haze. When she looks up, the clouds have shifted, and the moon has re-emerged with the knife-shine of a sickle, its waxing crescent familiar.

The Dark Forest closes over her, answering the cry of her desperation, and it should be comforting that she is home. It *should* be a relief. But all she can think of is the tackiness of her palms, the too loud, too brash men in the village. The scream still rattling through her skull.

Her hands are streaked red. Why are her hands red? Blood in the creases of her palms, underneath her nails, tacky on her wrists where the river has failed to carry it away.

She'll go home to wash it off properly, and—

Something shudders through her. She can't go home. There is no home to go back to – only Agagkantor and the conniving gleam in his eyes, and the lies that he has spread so effectively between them.

She bites her lip and tastes coin-sharp blood.

Her hands...

She should be crying, she thinks. She should be breaking down in the forest. Her sister is dead. Ada, who had placed all her trust in Sýstir's otherworldly skills to find food, who had sat down for just a moment while Sýstir slipped away. Who might have waited and waited for Sýstir to return, until the sun rose and Oden's men returned to finish what they'd so enthusiastically started.

Guilt engulfs her. Agagkantor was wrong: grief isn't a rock; it's a tide. And how fast it comes in now. She gasps a breath, and then another. But there isn't enough air in her lungs.

Ada is supposed to be at home, loved by the cousins who wouldn't have taken a huldra in, but would have accepted their true kin. She is supposed to fall in love, to marry and bear children, and live the life that Sýstir might have snatched from her had they stayed together.

And you should have stayed, a voice hisses. If Sýstir had not ventured off to look for mushrooms, or if she'd turned back to look for Ada earlier, or if she'd told Agagkantor on that long ago winter night that she was leaving the Dark Forest no matter what he said—

Sometimes Oden's men held prisoners for a while. A year, two years. To drag out the punishment, because death is too easy, too quick. All the while she was living easy in the Dark Forest, Ada might have been languishing, waiting for Sýstir to rescue her, the way Ada had rescued her from the village. Instead, Sýstir is here, and her beloved sister is in the ground, lifeless and alone.

She gasps. She didn't ask about the grave. She didn't ask about the *grave.*

They scatter a vala's ashes at the four corners of a crossroads and leave no gravestone behind, so the spirit can't find its way back to the village to take revenge. But for Ada, there would have been a body, a shroud. A place to lay wildflowers: willowherb and forget-me-nots and cornflower.

Her sister should have flowers every day of the year.

She stumbles and nearly falls, scattering the spinn faeries hovering above her anxiously. She turns and the shadows clutch at her. Her thoughts keep fragmenting, splitting under the weight of trying to remember.

Something digs into her side. The branch from the old apple tree, oozing sap. It's odd; she keeps forgetting it, but each time she touches it, a thought comes back to her. Nattaskur. They say that all Väsen are reborn under the rite of Nattaskur.

The rite.

That's what she'll do. She might not be able to put flowers on a grave to mourn her sister, but she can at least make sure that their home is remembered. Even when Sýstir is gone, Nattaskur will hold her memories. In that way, Ada will live forever, woven through every winding root, until the earth itself is suffused with the sound of her laughter, her quiet, clever smile, the steel heart buried under her skin.

New resolve runs through Sýstir. In the moonlight, her hands flash red and she shudders. But the knowledge of what happened to make them so is spilling away from her, like water through her fingers. The echo of a song circles in the back of her head.

She reaches the Rise still humming it softly. But a figure blocks the entryway. Queen Hilda.

"What did you do?" she asks quietly.

Sýstir doesn't answer. Her hands shake. The branch from her home has already shed most of its leaves, and those that remain are tipped in arterial red.

"I wish to claim my right," she says, and the words sound like a stranger's.

Queen Hilda's gaze strays from Sýstir's face to her hands, to the red streaked across her skin. Her expression shifts; her eyes grow wide with horror.

"What have you wrought upon us?"

Sýstir can't seem to shake the right words from her throat. She needs to do this for... With great effort, she wrenches her thoughts back to the present.

"I – my right – Nattaskur—"

Queen Hilda shakes her head, severe. "No, Sýstir. You will not sully our rite with your hands."

Hatred spills hot and heavy over her. And what a relief it is, to finally acknowledge what's eaten at her this whole time. She doesn't have to pretend anymore to acquiesce to Queen Hilda's indifference, to try and shape herself into some impossible creature worth her respect.

At last, there is no hiding the true measure of one another.

"You can't stop me," she snarls.

Other trolls are coming out of the Rise now, drawn by the sound of their raised voices. But Queen Hilda flings a hand out, preventing them from approaching further. She looks every inch the ruler, command absolute.

Sýstir takes another step forward, into the moonlight. Even though it's a weak thing, it feels harsh against her skin.

"I will not let you destroy what we are charged to protect," Queen Hilda says. "You must leave, Sýstir. I withdraw our invitation. I cast you out of the Rise. May we not meet again under these stars."

Sýstir glances away – and catches a familiar gaze instead. Fulgir. Fulgir, whose face never lies, is creased with horror... and hurt. Then her eyes drift downwards, to Sýstir's hands.

I have done something unforgivable, a voice whispers weakly in the back of her mind.

She flees.

The Dark Forest seems to make space for her as she passes, easing her way. With her skirts hiked up above her knees, her sleeves ripped, hair snarled, she is beyond herself.

The voice in her head that's been a whisper all night finally reaches a crescendo. *They killed Ada.* And she wasn't there to protect her.

What did you do in return? it asks, insistent. *How did you honour your mother, seek justice for your sister? What would they think of you now?*

A quiet, human fragment of herself turns inward, curling into the space between her heart and her ribs.

The rest of her flows through the Dark Forest, fleet-footed the way her body has always known to be. Silent, the way Fenrir taught her. She winds through the pathways she knows so instinctively that she no longer needs moonlight to guide her. She keeps going past the turn-off to Agagkantor's cave, to the Revel of the sprýg gnomes.

There is unfinished business, she thinks. And she holds on to that feeling, pushing the other one – the terrible one – away from her.

The Revel is humming with anxiety when she approaches, firelight throwing shadows up the trees. Somewhere within, there's a low animal keening. Fenrir.

Thróttr sees her face, then her hands, and blanches.

"Sýstir—"

"Where is he?"

Thróttr twists his hands. "Fenrir is... He took a turn while you were gone. We are making his hour peaceful. Please, Sýstir. There is little else to be done."

Sýstir sweeps past him. The echo of song she'd wielded in the village is still flowing in her, power bruising her fingertips. She has spent so much time clinging to the vestiges of humanity, because in the back of her mind, there was always that hope that she would see Ada again, and be as they were. But that was a child's dream, and she is done with those.

Fenrir's breathing is laboured, his chest moving faintly. Though stitched by the delicate hands of the woodland gnomes, the wounds radiate red underneath his fur, hot to touch. He can barely raise his head to look at her.

She kneels down by his side, and there's that old, familiar panic stirring within her. But for some reason, it can't touch her. It's as if everything has been locked behind a glass pane, distant and unreachable. It is better, she thinks, to be this way; her thoughts are clear, her focus unwavering.

"It is not too late for you," she says, placing her bloodied fingers over his wounds. "I won't leave you behind."

She reaches for that well of power deep within her again and sings, feeling the magic reverberate in her melody. Her mouth shapes the wordless song of the Skóug Trolls, the one that they had used during her very first visit to heal her suffering, calm her sorrows. Pain blooms behind her eyes, but she dismisses it forcefully. The Dark Forest has gifted her this magic, this song; what else is she to do but use it?

Fenrir whimpers, then yowls. Sýstir pushes deeper, harder. She doesn't need the trolls to sing alongside her, to amplify meagre power – not when she has her own to wield. How foolish that she had set aside so much of herself. That she'd thought being a huldra meant extra balance, perhaps a fine singing voice, when it means so much *more*.

"Something is wrong," Thróttr whispers.

Sýstir stands. "I have healed him."

Fenrir rises with her, clumsy at first, like a marionette. His wounds are still there, but a new strength is flowing into him – strength that she has bestowed. Some part of her recoils a little in horror, but it is the self locked behind that pane of glass, growing fainter with each moment.

"Not with him," Thróttr says. "With *you*."

She looks down at her hands, and something seems to catch at her. The angled blade, the power in her mouth, in her own bare-fisted strength. But her mind is drawing curtains over the memory again.

"I am well," she says, and she is.

Fenrir growls, a low rumble deep within his chest. He is still limping from his injury as he walks beside her, but his movement grows more assured with each footstep. Thróttr backs away. More sprýg gnomes are coming to investigate now, their expressions fearful as they cluster together.

"You should not be able to do this – no väsen should hold such power," Thróttr says, shaking his head. "This – this was a mistake."

You are a mistake. The lance should reach the furthest part of her, but it bounces off, harmless. Instead, there is that pure, clean anger thrumming inside of her, and hollow relief that she is finally no longer crying. Tears have got her nowhere, but anger gives her strength. Purpose.

"Very well," she says calmly.

She turns away from the Revel, Fenrir walking at her heels. Every now and then his head jerks, as though he is trying to rid himself of some sound. But the forest is quiet tonight, with little else but the rustling of wind.

Forget Queen Hilda. Forget Agagkantor. Forget them all.

Forget her red-stained hands, and the village, and the way the old woman had looked at her when she'd reached for the most eternal of songs.

Forget Ada, and her clever mind, and her kindness, and—

Her mind shutters. The Dark Forest clips past her. Wind slips down the single line of her spine.

She can't say for certain when she stops, or why. Just that the ground is harder on her feet, the rush of water replacing the wind. Something in her – the creature that is shrinking, shrinking – recognises where she is.

It's the creek with the fallen log.

She steps onto it deftly, that odd warmth pulsing through her feet. She turned back here, once, though she can't quite remember why. But the forest beyond looks untouched.

Something chuffs at her other hand: Fenrir. He looks at her, red tinged at the edge of his eyes. Everything is painted in red, it seems.

Do I stay? Do I go?

There is supposed to be an answering echo in her head – there always has been. But the voice that might sound like her mother, her sister, even Agagkantor, lies unresponsive.

"Where I walk, you walk," she commands, and Fenrir snarls in response.

She will carve a new home within the Dark Forest for herself – one that does not subscribe to other Väsen's whims. One that is entirely her own. And from there, how much easier it will be to watch over her precious trees, her rippling lakes and glacier-carved hills. To place the memory of Ada into the heart of the forest, so that every creature, Väsen and otherwise, might sing her name.

That is what's left now. That is *all* that's left.

Sýstir does not once look back as she crosses the creek to the other side.

II

· THE HULDRA ·

· TWENTY ·

Time passes.

It is a curious thing, this slip of the seasons. Humans are so very diligent about keeping track of time, down to the day, the hour. Väsen, on the other hand, feel for the change of the winds, the light turning from gold to blue, the hibernation of one plant and the emergence of another.

Across the creek, time in the Dark Forest feels especially elusive. Here, the light struggles through the trees, with midday never a sure thing. The trees that blossom do so just ahead or behind the forest on the other side of the creek, with twisting branches that ooze warm sap. The wind is forever whispering of winter. And the creatures tread with care – if they tread at all.

The forest is particularly still around a cave set some ways from the creek. There are signs that suggest it might have once been occupied by skóug trolls, similar to those of Queen Hilda's Rise. Now, however, Väsen speak of a vengeful ghost, of something ancient and cursed that has filled the empty space left behind.

Dusk creeps over the horizon. And Sýstir emerges from the cave.

She pushes her hair back from her face and breathes in the wet, earthy scent, burnished with a sweetness that makes her think of rot. If she looked at her reflection in the water, she would find herself a little taller, with the willowy form of someone who has shed the final shroud of youth and come into the beauty of adulthood, perpetually suspended like droplets on spinn faerie silk. But she would find herself wearing the rags of someone who has long since lost interest in their appearance, her hair long and loose to her waist. When the wind blows a certain way, or the sunlight hits her shoulders, the hollow in her back aches with a pain so fierce it bites. So she sticks to the shadows, daring the sun only when she must.

It's an overcast evening, so the light from the crescent moon doesn't sting the way it normally does. The air is cool, but she barely feels the temperature. She cocks her head to one side, as though she can hear something calling her, though the forest is quiet.

The Dark Forest thrums through her as her attention is drawn towards the faint sound of singing. The voice is sweeter than any troll's, a siren call that pulls at some deep knot in her chest. But it is not enough to stand here and admire from afar. Not enough to feel the moss beneath her feet, the wind rippling through her clothes. She needs to be closer. Sýstir shucks off her dress and steps out of it, leaving it in the shadow of her cave. She takes a deep breath, relief flooding through her as moonlight meets skin. Her heart pulses in time with the song, with the Dark Forest itself.

She takes a few steps forward, and then she is running through the forest, slipping through the trees. She touches each of them briefly as she goes. Rough bark against her palms, soft moss and damp dirt beneath her feet, the unyielding smoothness of stone as she climbs a boulder and descends. She twists towards the song, longing and curiosity pulling her forward relentlessly. Rain starts to fall, slick against her bare skin.

The song takes her along the river and she wades in, the water folding over her soundlessly. There is barely a ripple as she swims downstream, using her tail to steer. Mist clings to the surface of the river, thickening on its banks.

The song fades as Sýstir approaches its source. A huldra, crouched at the edge of the water. Naked in the moonlight, silken hair spilling over one shoulder, it is easy for Sýstir to see the hole in the huldra's back: a concave gap of mottled, grey flesh where the rot that afflicts them all has set in. Sýstir's own back twinges in response, pain forever tangled with hurt or shame or fury. It's the price for their beauty and their power, for standing in between the worlds of human and Väsen. The price for daring to be born at all.

But tonight, there is no lovelier vision. The huldra sings again, a wordless tune that spills over with power and sweetness. The same one that resonates in Sýstir's heart.

She climbs out of the water and this time, when the huldra sings, it's Sýstir who answers in harmony. The power of their collective song sinks into her bones, filling her fingertip to fingertip with magic. Though Sýstir is still wet from the river, warmth courses through her. For a moment, there is nothing but this night stretched out in front of her, beautiful and endless.

The huldra meets Sýstir's own gaze, startled, long lashes framing wide-set eyes. It is the one she met years ago, she realises, when she was just a girl-thing. But instead of joy meeting joy, the huldra recoils. Her brow creases – and Sýstir is shocked to catch fear on her face.

"Too much magic," the huldra whispers, her voice lilting. "Too much power."

Between one breath and another, the huldra flees, slipping into the depths of the forest.

Sýstir lifts her head and sings the last notes of the song. Only silence answers. Well, it is one thing to look upon a girl-thing and another entirely to face one another as equals.

When no one else appears, she pads back towards her home. If another Väsen saw her from afar, they might catch a glimpse of the sleek silhouette, the curve of her tail, the maw of her back.

Huldra.

Yes, Sýstir is still herself. But she is something else, now, too.

• • •

Sýstir can't say when she began to prefer the evening to the day, but she finds herself gravitating towards it, like some strange, nocturnal thing. She slings her bow over her shoulder, her quiver full of arrows. Fenrir slinks out after her, his eyes red – a quirk of the magic still propelling him – and cast low to the ground. He's had his fair share of fights over the years, and the skin underneath his ragged fur is a battleground that shines silver where it catches the moonlight.

"Ready, Fen?" Sýstir asks, voice husky with disuse.

In response, Fenrir growls and snaps at the air, though there's nothing to be seen or heard. It used to be that she could ruffle his head without a second thought, but now he snarls at anything that comes too near, and she's not too shy to admit that she'd rather hold on to her fingers.

She glances across the path, and for a moment, a thought slips across her mind like quicksilver, there and gone too quickly for her to grasp anything but the disquiet it leaves in its wake. It's not an unfamiliar feeling, but it unsettles her nevertheless. A forgotten thing – but not entirely so – raising its head from the depths of hibernation before sleep and willpower drag it down again.

She has forgotten much, she considers, some of which she'd fought to remember and lost. But her mind is not entirely her own these days. Some evenings, the shadows play tricks on her, so that the cave is awash with ghosts from her past lives: villagers and family and enemies, and those she had known but whose names she cannot recall – only the feelings with which they had left her.

Sometimes, she reaches for her name, and finds that it feels like a question mark on her tongue, as though she has gone by many, and this last one was but a fleeting whim. When all else fails, she feels the slight ache of the hollow in her back, the elongation of her spine through to her tail, and holds on to that reassurance tightly. Even if she has no name, she is Huldra, and that has always been true.

You are diminishing, a small, timid part of her whispers. But there is another part of her, seductive and powerful, that suggests *you are transforming.*

As far as she's aware, there are few, if any Väsen who grace the land over the creek that Sýstir has claimed for herself. She recalls her own hesitation – and perhaps there was good reason for it. The forest is thin here, and the only animals that prowl are scavengers. When the trees speak to her, it's with a pained, arthritic hush, as if even the barest rustle of branches exacts a great price.

The other Väsen hiss *Scar of Rotinn.*

When Sýstir recalls its name, she worries that perhaps she has chosen poorly in her home. It's true that she spends longer trying to source her meals, even though hunger rarely pinches her. Fenrir is a capable hunter, and he often brings back food to share between them, even when prey is scarce. Whether he crosses the creek or not is a question that she long ago decided not to concern herself with.

There's little to hunt around the cave itself, so Sýstir walks along the marshes around the mirror-black lakes. The land here is treacherous; one wrong step and the ground gives way to water, from which there is little chance of return. But she is careful, and the path stays firm underneath her feet, even though this, too, is prone to shifting.

"To me, Fen," she commands, and he bares his teeth in response before following her.

She walks past the mossy boulders that are all that remains of the trolls who once lived here. Maybe berga trolls on their way up to the mountains, gathering the last of their strength before the final length of the journey ahead of them – only to never complete it. There are clusters of such rocky outcrops deep in the marshes, where a wrong foot or missed turn ensnared them. Entire families, swallowed by the Dark Forest.

The hunt is relatively successful – a roe deer that had become stranded on this side of the creek. It strikes Sýstir that the deer looks sickly, too thin and bearing older wounds that haven't healed. But then many of the animals who find themselves here do not last long; drowning in the marshes is only one of many ways to die.

After Fenrir takes his share, she drags the carcass back to the cave, where she'll dress it later. Her head is still reeling with that lingering unease, the hollow in her back throbbing. At moments like these, she doesn't quite trust herself with a knife; what her memory hides, her hands betray, weighed down by the ghosts of past actions. She has blacked out and come to, bloody and exhausted, on more than one occasion. Sometimes she stumbles across the bodies of her unwitting prey afterwards: small creatures like birds or voles, as though a cat has been slinking through her home. Other times, it is just the echo of that night in the village, her body replaying the action while her mind lies dormant.

She heads back out into the forest, where night has truly fallen. Fenrir lopes behind her for a section of the path, before diverting into the bushes. He might return to the cave to sleep, but she suspects that's the last she'll see of him for a while. After all, wild things make for poor pets.

Amongst the mossy glacial rocks to the north of her cave, there is a sparse tree that marks a secret she's certain even the trolls didn't stumble upon. She slips between the boulders, twisting her body away from the pallid moonlight, until she comes through to an underground cave. Here in the cool dark, water drips endlessly from somewhere above, leaving a quiet black pool below. Sýstir eases in, letting the chill wash over her until it becomes bearable.

Several springs past, she had stumbled upon this secret of hers, desperate to escape the midday sun. She has never seen another creature here, Väsen or otherwise, and there is a magnitude of luxury in being able to swim in the dark on her own. Even Fenrir, for all that he acts as her second shadow, cannot quite fit through the gaps – or else is reluctant to try.

It's here that her mind feels at its clearest, able to recall the parts of herself that are furthest away. The anger that propelled her returns, sharp and clear, shaping her thoughts. So, too, does the grief, the regret, the terrible shame thrust upon her.

But tonight, she wants to remember. These last few days feel important, though with no clear reason, as is so often the case. Though her mind forgets, her body remembers, and often the only sign that something is significant or amiss is a course of emotion running through her.

She lets the water pull her in, relishing the sting. It is the cusp of the season, summer giving way to autumn. And – ah, that's it: her birthday. Or season of birth, since the days have long since run into each other. The vice-like squeeze in her chest starts to ease. It would explain that expectancy that she's felt over the last few days, the restless energy that's been building with the season's turning, as though her body has been counting down to some explosive moment.

Something else starts to surface in her mind – the rockfall rumble of laughter; someone tuning an instrument; berries in her hair – but with effort, she pushes it away. She does not need to remember the finer points of the last birthday she'd celebrated with Fulgir and the others. All she needed to recall was the significance of this time, and she has done so. Of course, her season of birth means little to her now, given the intervening years; she knows she is older than her youth suggests, and yet she does not feel old. Why would she choose to tally her life in such a meaningless way?

Satisfied with her answer, she emerges from the pool, soaking wet and shivering with the fierce cold. She wrings her hair out carelessly, then slips back into her clothes. For a while, her thoughts will stay as crisp and clear as they are when she swims those long lengths.

And you will know how much you regret everything, how you

wronged and were wronged in turn. That your hands will always be red because blood leaves a stain.

You killed her. This is your fault.

"No," Sýstir says hastily – and aloud, she realises.

This gut-clenching nausea, this... this *fear* is why she doesn't swim so often. It brings her too close to those early years here, when she'd scraped through the first winters, half mad with something she could not name.

It is easier to let her memories erode, lest she fall upon their blade.

...

Sýstir is hunting once more with Fenrir when she senses an unfamiliar rustle in the trees. Quietly, she diverts to the path along the edge of the river, skirting the treacherous marshlands towards the log over the creek. For an absurd moment, she thinks of Agagkantor, though there is no reason for their paths to ever cross again. And she has no desire to see him. Not even to hear an apology – which he would never lower himself to offer, anyway – or a beg for forgiveness, which she would never be able to give.

But there *is* someone on the other side of the creek.

She gathers her song to her, readying her power – always a quicker instinct these days – before she realises that she recognises the Väsen on the other side, like a memory stepping from dream to reality. Fulgir. Her gold beads, strung through her braids, wink painfully in the light.

Sýstir stops. She has seen Fulgir only a few times since that unspeakable night, and always at a distance from across the river. The trolls have no reason to come this way, but Fulgir must have found one excuse or another. Trust her to keep interfering, picking at old wounds.

"Well met, Sýstir," she says. "It has been some time."

She offers a smile, but Sýstir doesn't smile back.

"Has Queen Hilda missed my presence so much that she's sent you?" Sýstir asks, sarcasm bleeding through.

It wouldn't surprise her if Queen Hilda was keeping an eye on Sýstir, to ensure that she is suffering appropriately. No crumb of happiness, no moment of fleeting joy permitted, without Queen Hilda to crush it.

"I came alone." Fulgir pauses. "To see you."

And what does she see, Sýstir wonders. Neither of them are young anymore; though trolls bear the weight of age differently, it does not escape Sýstir's notice that Fulgir carries herself with a newfound steadiness. There are additional gold beads in her hair and a second torque on her upper arm in the shape of a twisting oak leaf. Perhaps merely jewellery; perhaps some ritual of adulthood that has slipped past Sýstir.

"Look as long as you like," she says, in that same sardonic tone. "The view does not change."

Fulgir hesitates. "I only wished to see if you were... happy here."

Sýstir snorts. "Is this what you've come for? To play at sympathy? Of course I am happy; I have my own home, my own kin." She pats the top of Fenrir's head. "I have no need of anything, or *anyone* else."

But Fulgir's gaze slides over Sýstir, like she's looking through glass.

"You are ailing, Sýstir," she says.

Sýstir folds her arms. "I'm fine."

She is *well*. Better than she has ever been before, even. She has carved out this new home for herself, has she not? *Transformation*, she thinks again.

Except for those moments when her mind isn't her own, when fathomless rage sloshes up her insides. The way even clouded daylight prickles her skin. That there are times, in that haze between sleeping and waking , when she feels as though a stranger has slipped into her skin, winding its tendrils around her bones. And though it may wear Sýstir's face and speak to her with her own voice, its words are ones she does not recognise.

Next to her, Fenrir snarls and snaps at air. Fulgir recoils and takes a step backwards. Sýstir smiles thinly; of course, there are only monsters on this side of the creek.

"I do not wish to see you in this way," Fulgir says. "This land is not safe."

"And whose fault is that?" she snaps, before she can stop herself.

Fulgir gives her a long piercing look. "We must all walk the road of our choices."

Except it seems as though time and again, Sýstir is walking the road of another's choice. It was the villagers who hounded her out of her home, Queen Hilda who denied her the rite of Nattaskur, Agagkantor who lied to her again and again.

And if she made one mistake? If she was driven to act through unimaginable grief? Surely this road should not be so cruel.

She is being punished for *their* mistakes. Her hands are red because of *them*.

"Drink from Nivir," Fulgir urges. "Atone. Rejoin us, and we will seek a cure for this ailment together."

Sýstir laughs, hollow. "And would your queen welcome me with open arms? Would the Rise call me kindred at last? Would I be trusted?"

Fulgir falls silent.

"I see," Sýstir says.

She tries to sound sharp, but even she can hear the resignation in her voice. Even if all was well, Queen Hilda would never let her be at peace. And without Queen Hilda's approval, the trolls will never truly accept her. Not as she was before – and certainly not now.

Sýstir sighs, and for a moment she feels the weight of her old self settling on her shoulders. The one who might have crossed the creek with Fulgir, who might fall again and again on the sword of her regrets despite the pain. Who would not listen to the stranger's voice in her mind.

"You should give up this folly," Sýstir says.

Let Sýstir become the wraith that she seems destined to be now. There is no other future for her – not anymore.

Fulgir gives her a small sad smile. "I do not give up, Sýstir."

· TWENTY-ONE ·

For three days, Fulgir's voice echoes in Sýstir's mind. *I do not give up.*

It does not matter, she tells herself. Fulgir's pity is misplaced.

But it is Sýstir who has given up, who has let her fate be dictated by those like Queen Hilda, who would rather she hadn't lived long enough to see through this fate at all.

It's not often, these days, that sleep comes to her willingly, and when it does, it's much too fragmented for dreams. She suspects that it's something to do with the land itself; even the Mares, who would favour this perpetual gloom, do not cross her path. There's always something pricking at her senses: the stab of dim light, the whisper of the Dark Forest, the rumble of Fenrir close by. And underneath, that steady thrum of unease.

Tonight, though, she falls into the dark abyss of uninterrupted sleep. For the first time since she crossed the creek, she dreams.

She dreams of her mother, a silhouette of flame, pulling her into a burning embrace. She dreams of her sister, sixteen years old and so painfully beautiful it hurts to look at her, aglow with a light from within. But when Sýstir reaches for her, she turns to ash under her fingertips.

And... she dreams of her old life. Her other self.

There is Sýstir, thirteen and young and still brimming with hope. She looks like she has just brushed her fingertips over the edge of her future, and how it glitters, like sunlight striking snow. Her sister, her mother behind her, and her friends at her side.

And in front of her, a great tree, brilliant green.

Heart and soul of the Dark Forest.

She wakes in one terrible gasp. For a second, she doesn't recognise the cave around her, and something traitorous in her says, *this is not Agagkantor's cave.* Then her home returns to her, shattering the remnants of the dream.

Next to her, Fenrir growls. At some point, he must have returned from his hunt, to settle at the foot of her bed. He is old, she thinks, with sudden clarity. Much older than he has any right to be.

By the time Sýstir shakes off the vestiges of sleep, the dream has slipped away, faster than meltwater and just as futile to hold. But the feeling stays within her, impossible to shake. The shadows seem to cling to her.

She looks around her cave, grounding herself. But she can't help but recoil a little, as she usually does when she wakes. What a small, ill-fitting home she has carved for herself. There are few of the comforts she's enjoyed in the past: no stool to sit upon; no pillow upon which to rest her head; no stores of preserves to make the colder seasons more comfortable. In fact, taking stock of her belongings, she is not quite sure how she has survived this long.

The only item of note is the dusty apple tree branch, dragged with her from her previous life into this one. She picks it up with a kind of reverence, cradling it in her hands. When she brings it to her nose to inhale, there's that sickly sweet scent that dapples the land around this part of the Dark Forest.

She had saved this for a reason, she thinks. Old desires, old dreams, flare within her, bright and sharp.

Nattaskur.

For as long as she's been in the Dark Forest – since that first awful, wonderful year – she has only ever wanted to belong in entirety. She has the branch; she has the means to graft it to Nattaskur. But for some reason, she has left this dream alongside everything else, back on the other side of the creek.

She has let Queen Hilda walk away from the ashes of Sýstir's life, triumphant, and has lingered here, wrapped in her grief. It was easier than putting up a fight to claim what should rightfully be hers. What is the point, when Ada is worse than gone, Agagkantor worse than a stranger?

Fenrir nudges her, but she ignores him.

That night, she slips into the dark pool and lingers for hours, swimming back and forth in the quiet. She was a fool to let so much of herself be lost, to let grief and anger be her master. To let herself exist as little more than a ghost in her own body.

What are you going to do? she asks herself, over and over again. In the quiet of her mind, out loud in the silence of the pool, her teeth chattering as the words slip between her lips.

When she finally emerges, her body is numb with cold, but her mind feels clearer. At the cave, she picks up the branch, weighing it in her hands. She had set her feet on this path the moment she had spied the apple tree – and before, if she is truthful. Back to the first time she'd started the long climb up to the burial hills, and all that awaited there.

I am going to Nattaskur. I am going to finish this.

Sýstir ignores the sting of the last of the day's sun as she walks through the Dark Forest. To an untrained eye, it would look the same as it always had. But everywhere she walks, she notes the changes that have occurred in her absence. There are new pathways forged by the woodland gnomes, long-standing trees that have at last succumbed to time and fallen, and the soft footsteps of another huldra, now that Sýstir is no longer around to contest their solitude.

She hums as she walks, spinn faeries gathering behind her to listen. She has missed this, she thinks with a start. The way the light comes down through the trees, pollen drifting in its soft haze. The whisper of Elfdalian as the trees pass messages to one another from across the forest, like a chorus with no end. The faintest strains of music, no doubt from a nearby Revel of sprýg gnomes. Everything perfectly attuned, like one chord plucked from a dozen strings.

When she reaches a fork in the path, she pauses. One way leads back down to Agagkantor's cave, and to the Rise further on, threading between familiar haunts until it reaches the river. Her feet even tilt in that direction, curious. If much has changed here, what else has changed in the place she once called home?

The other path leads upwards, to the burial hills and to Nattaskur. To a future sealed by the Dark Forest.

The branch throbs in her palm, wet sap clinging to her fingers even though by all logic it should be dead. She has spent too long in the past, and would linger there longer if she let herself.

Nattaskur is what's important; the *future* is all that matters now. Decisively, she turns away from the Rise.

For hours, she climbs, until she reaches the burial hills. Up here, it's easy to see so much of the Dark Forest spread before her, lush and alive and twined with mist. She had forgotten what it was like to inhale air and taste green untainted by marshlands.

And there it is. Nattaskur.

The great tree stands proudly in the centre of the clearing, branches swaying gently in the breeze. As she makes her way down the hills into the cupped valley, she notes the impressions of footsteps on either side of her. A family of sprýg gnomes, perhaps, come to celebrate their latest young ones. Come to enjoy what they already have, not even realising just how special it is to have it at all.

Sýstir's jaw tightens, the ache in her back throbbing.

By the time she reaches the foot of Nattaskur, night has well and truly arrived. Sýstir glances around her, waiting for Queen Hilda or another skóug troll to step out and stop her. But the clearing is silent. All those who might have celebrated the rite have long returned home.

Sýstir presses her hands to the trunk of Nattaskur, feeling the texture of its bark below her fingers, and underneath that, the pulse of the Dark Forest itself. Gromildr's heart and soul, sacrificed to create this sanctuary for Väsen with nowhere left to turn, vast and ever-moving and alive. *This* is her home.

She's heard the words the other Väsen use to start the rite, each one picking a different element to focus on: good health to the Dark Forest and their kin; faith in the everlasting cycle of growth and rot, despite the inevitable grief it brings; courage for the darkest nights of their lives and good humour for the dawn. But none of them seem quite suitable for her. She tries an amalgamation of them, waiting for the words to fit in her mouth, as she once thought they might.

"Nattaskur, I come to join myself to you, and my subsequent kin, should there be any to follow in my steps." Her voice rings loud in the quiet, too stiff and formal.

There was a time when she'd imagined this ritual very differently, surrounded by her most cherished ones the way most Väsen seem to celebrate. But tonight she is alone, with no friends or family to celebrate. Just Fenrir, who seems more interested in hunting than in the solemnity of the occasion.

Underneath her fingers, the apple tree branch quivers, pulsing with a strange, quick energy of its own.

"I wished to bring my sister here, once upon a time," she admits. "But the best I can do is give you my memories of her in her absence."

What pitiful, fragmented memories she has left. Ada braiding crowns – or was that Fulgir? – to place in her hair. The fierce clasp of her hand as she hauled Sýstir upright yet again, smoke and flame and men urging them onwards. The faint smile she had offered up before they were separated forever, even though neither of them had known it at the time. And the memories of what Sýstir herself has done in Ada's name.

I am what you made of me.

Her vision bleeds red. The ache of the hollow in her back is a roar.

Sýstir stumbles away from Nattaskur, her heart pounding. For a moment, she sees neither its trunk nor the clearing – but a wash of images that flickers through her mind, uncontrollable.

She shakes her head fiercely. Once she grafts her branch to Nattaskur, all will be well. These feelings will fade. The trolls will no longer deny that she belongs in the Dark Forest. And then she'll be able to remember Ada as she should, with none of the guilt she can't bear to look at.

Her breathing steadies, even though the hollow in her back is still painful. At last, the right words come to her. She looks up at Nattaskur, holding the memories of her sister – *only* her sister – close to her.

"Please, remember us when I cannot," she says.

Then she starts to climb. She has never been this close to Nattaskur before, never felt the roughness of its bark against the soft soles of her feet, or seen the thin veins of its leaves translucent in the moonlight. From here, it's easier to note where other branches have been grafted to its trunk, old scars revealing the joints, or new growth that cannot quite mimic Nattaskur itself.

She removes the branch from her belt and holds it up. This will do, she thinks. High enough that the trolls would be hard pressed to remove it. High enough to soar with the birds and to move with the breeze. High enough to catch a glimpse of the starlight on cloudless nights.

The sap oozes thickly, carrying that peculiar sweet smell

with it. Curious, since it has lain dormant – even dead – in Sýstir's cave for so long. But this reawakening is surely confirmation that this is meant to be, that she is only doing what she should have done years ago. She shuttles the thought to the back of her mind, where it cannot disturb her, that its scent reminds her too strongly of other dead and dying things.

Something quivers within Nattaskur, alert. Sýstir reaches for her knife and pries away a section of bark. It seems like a clumsy tool to wield, but she has never seen the grafting itself performed. And, she supposes, there is no gain without bloodshed.

"I'm sorry," she whispers nevertheless, as she cuts deeper.

It is much easier to trim the apple tree branch, the wood strangely soft and giving beneath the blade. Using some twine, she fastens the branch to Nattaskur securely. In the thin moonlight, the joint looks red and angry, like a wound.

She climbs down slowly, relying on the extra balance from her tail, until she lands lightly in the grass at Nattaskur's base. She dusts her hands off and looks back up at her handiwork. The sap is still oozing from the joinery, looking more like blood than anything else.

Sýstir closes her eyes and waits to feel changed. For the Dark Forest to open itself up to her wholly, as she has opened herself to it. But all she feels is the itch of bark dust on her skin, the uncomfortable prickle of moonlight, the grass underneath her feet. When she opens her eyes, a tjärn faerie drifts past her, uninterested in the significance of what's just occurred.

It is as though nothing has changed.

Fenrir finally gives up chasing whatever he has found and returns to her. He allows a quick ruffle of his head, before snapping his teeth at her and bounding off again. He has not been particularly affectionate since his injuries, and lately it seems that he is crossing into a new phase of unsettlement. Underneath his fur, amidst the old scar tissue, there is a fine network of webbing, as though a plant has taken root within his skin. It is barely noticeable to the touch, and yet she is certain it had not been there months earlier.

"Well, time to return again," she tells him, and he growls in response.

As she walks away from Nattaskur, the breeze tastes unusually sweet, like the cloying scent in the Scar of Rotinn.

She lopes through the forest now, eager to be back across the creek before the other Väsen wake. A quick smile steals over her face. Queen Hilda might have done her best to prevent Sýstir from joining the Dark Forest, but she has failed. The graft's join will heal quickly, and by the time the trolls discover her branch affixed to Nattaskur, it will be too late to do anything but watch it grow.

Queen Hilda has taken everything from Sýstir; it is nice, for a change, to take from her in return, though it's only her pride.

Yet even as Sýstir settles back into her cave – even when sleep is folding over her as dawn arrives – she cannot quite lose the feeling that something is awry.

· TWENTY-TWO ·

Sýstir sleeps in her cave for several days, energy spent. This is how it goes these days: too much excitement, and her body betrays her. It is not so much the exertion of walking – and she would laugh if anyone suggested it – but the overwhelming experience of seeing so much of her old home, with the accompanying memories to assault her. And, she adds to herself, achieving what she once thought impossible.

When she finally wakes, moonlight gilds the entrance of her cave. She stays where she is for a moment, feeling out the minutiae of her limbs. There is still the same ache at the hollow in her back – a near constant low hum of pain that ebbs and flows with the daylight – and the same flick of her tail. The same sadness that clings to her. When she gets up and her feet hit the ground, it is still soft dirt and nothing more. No familiarity of connection. No twinned heartbeat, aligning her with the rest of the world.

Maybe the truth is that Sýstir already possessed the magic of the Dark Forest. But that can't be right; otherwise she would never have felt that compulsion, like a taut thread jumping every time she moved. And Queen Hilda would not have done everything in her power to prevent it.

It doesn't matter whether she feels it or not. It is done; she is one with the Dark Forest, wholly and inexplicably.

But that foreboding eats at her. When she emerges from her cave, she realises why. There is a faint keening on the wind that reminds her too much of a child's crying. And it's coming from the trees. Even Fenrir seems more uneasy than usual, his teeth bared in a grimace. He prowls towards the creek, as though stalking something familiar.

It's been a long time since she's crossed the creek, over the river, and now she has done so twice in several days. Too close to be coincidence, she thinks. Fenrir follows her quietly, his ears pricking.

The moss is soft and spongy underneath Sýstir's feet, the air sweet with the scent of dark earth. Above, the trees confer in a hushed murmur that sets her nerves on edge. They are nervous, she thinks – and this in turn makes her uneasy. The trees are the heartbeat of the Dark Forest; they are the first to know if something is amiss.

As Sýstir walks towards the burial hills, her pace quickens. The trees urge her onwards, the breeze an insistent push between her shoulders. Above, the crescent moon filters through gathered clouds. She is halfway up the path to Nattaskur when she realises she's not alone. A sprýg gnome veers out of the bushes, urging their mount – a sleek squirrel – onwards.

By the time she reaches the burial hills, it is clear just how many have been called by this singular wrongness. All of the Dark Forest, it seems, if such a thing could be possible. The ground quakes with the footsteps of giants, the faintest beat of spinn faerie wings, the methodical trudge of skóug trolls from beyond the cradle of the forest that Sýstir had once called home. And there's that undercurrent of fear, stretched taut between them all.

It's been a lifetime since she's been amongst so many other Väsen. An old memory flickers weakly of the first time she had come to spring's awakening; she had been surprised, then, by the sheer number of beings, all weaving between one another. But tonight, they seem oddly reluctant to cross from their own species, their expressions a mix of uncertainty and worry. Amongst them, she spies hasl trolls, sprýg gnomes, giants, mares and more. Even Näcken has joined, a solitary figure in the shadow of the trees. Every Väsen is represented.

Nervous, Sýstir slips into a group of huldras.

Unlike herself, the huldras wear no clothes, uncaring of the night's biting chill – a trait that they largely seem to share. Although she, too, feels the cold less acutely these days, Sýstir has tried and failed to divest herself of the too human comfort of clothing. Another weakness, Agagkantor would say. She glances at one of the huldras, waiting for surprise to cross her face. But the huldra isn't interested in Sýstir at all; in fact, no one is.

Instead, every gaze is focused on Nattaskur.

From here, it's impossible to see her branch, but she knows it's there; she can feel it. Then she catches that sickly sweet smell again, the one that reminds her of damp and decay. Of grief and rage, too close to that unthinkable night she refuses to remember and can't forget.

It smells of... death.

"Rotinn," someone murmurs, and a new shiver of fear runs through the group.

Sýstir knows of the Scar of Rotinn, but it's only of late that she's come to understand that the name bears another meaning. A whisper of a far-off rot that creeps over its victims, silent and relentless. A change in temperament: a quickening of anger, an aversion to the day, the constant flush of fever. Perhaps a worse fate awaits beyond. But she'd long ago dismissed it as too far-fetched, even for the Dark Forest.

"It is a myth," a hasl troll says, loud enough to be heard by the huldras. "We have heard of no such thing."

The other huldras simply blink at the conversation, as though it is all beneath them. But Sýstir shivers.

Another hasl troll scuffs at the ground, clearly nervous. "I have heard it is a sickness."

"A darkness," a huldra corrects, her gaze still trained on the clearing below.

"A sickness, a darkness – does it matter, when it is nothing but fancy?" the hasl troll says.

"It may be fairytale," a woodland gnome says, half-clinging to his own group but his words clearly directed at the hasl trolls. "Yet the Skóug Trolls must have a reason, surely?"

With a shock, Sýstir realises that the Skóug Trolls are here, too, close enough to Nattaskur to stand within its shadow. There are so many trolls that she recognises: Grendel, even taller and broader than she recalls; Fundin, slighter than the rest of his kin; and... Fulgir. Her heart twists.

And there, alone at the base of Nattaskur, is Queen Hilda.

Queen Hilda's gaze is creased in deep sorrow, her expression weighted with something Sýstir cannot name. The Skóug Trolls are singing, she realises, and though she doesn't recognise the song, it has the lilting rise and fall of devastation, a round that seems to pick up extra voices with every repetition, until the entire valley echoes. The sound strikes her squarely in the heart, and it's all she can do not to sink to her knees in aching, wounded grief.

It is a song... of mourning.

But they are not up on the burial hills with the other Väsen to commemorate whoever they have lost. Sýstir tries to catch Fulgir's gaze, but she looks steadily onwards at Queen Hilda, as though there is no one else to behold.

"What are they doing?" Sýstir whispers.

She's so quiet she's certain no one hears her. But an older huldra turns to face her. Not quite mirror image, but with those same wide eyes, set slightly too far apart to hold the pretence of humanity convincingly.

"They are waiting," the huldra says.

For what? Sýstir wants to ask. But the song is already diminishing to a handful of voices, audible only as a burr that nevertheless pulls at her grief. To the left of her, a woodland gnome is weeping silently, tears streaming down her face.

"Väsen of the Dark Forest!" Queen Hilda calls.

The crowd turn to her as one, like flowers after the light. Then there is a collective recoil, as they see what she is holding. The handle of an axe is curled in her fist, the blade shining in the weak moonlight. Sýstir's stomach lurches. So this is what they're here for.

The trolls have discovered her secret. They have come to excise her branch from Nattaskur like cauterising a wound. Like the mistake that it is. As far as she knows, no Väsen has ever had their branch removed from Nattaskur. To take an axe to it, just because they dislike Sýstir – no wonder the trees are upset.

Now she knows, at least, why she could not rest. Because even if her mind was lulled into a false sense of assurance, her heart knew.

"We call you here not because we wish to, but because we must."

Sýstir glances to either side of her, recalculating the crowd's appearance. She had not been called here by the trolls, of course – they will not cross the creek, even when a hunt strays into her territory – but by the very trees themselves.

"You have heard of the evil that creeps across the Dark Forest. The plague to which we can find no answer."

The darkness that whispers to Sýstir at night, its quiet,

seductive voice twining around her thoughts. So eager to paint everything in red.

No, Sýstir is well. She has always been well.

Queen Hilda looks weary with resignation. "Now, it is here. At the very heart of Nattaskur."

A collective gasp ripples through the Väsen.

"That's a lie," Sýstir says, but her voice is lost underneath the susurration of the crowd.

She was at Nattaskur only a few days ago. And there was no sign of this... plague – why would there be? But now she sees that sap weeps through its bark, wet and red. Like blood.

"We have one who has studied much of its effects, and he confirms it is true," Queen Hilda says.

A skóug troll steps through the crowd. His ears are flat with solemnity, hair ribboned with gold beads, arms braceleted with gold bangles that Sýstir would recognise anywhere.

Agagkantor.

Sýstir cannot believe it. Agagkantor, siding with Queen Hilda's Rise, even after their soured history. Agagkantor pushing his own lies, with them – *through* them. Fury washes her vision. Maybe Queen Hilda is allowing herself to be manipulated – or maybe they have always been united, and Sýstir is the fool for not seeing it until now. But one thing is clear: whatever they've planned, she must stop them.

No one else knows them as she does. No one else has pieced together the lies, the manipulations they have wrought between them.

Queen Hilda places one hand on Agagkantor's shoulder, and he nods.

"The Rotinn must go no further," she says.

She places her free hand on the trunk of the tree, and presses her forehead to it. The song of the skóug trolls grows louder, unmistakably threaded through with pain.

"Nattaskur, heart of my heart, soul akin to my own. My kin have lived generations under your care," Queen Hilda says.

Sýstir tries to push through the crowd. She is too far from Nattaskur.

Queen Hilda steps back from the trunk. Her hand tightens around the handle of the axe. And Sýstir knows, just before it happens, what the axe is really meant for.

"But I must do what is right," she says.

The axe lifts, shining, cruel. An aberration.

A ripple of shock goes through the other Väsen. Someone is weeping. But no one will stop Queen Hilda. No one is moving.

Sýstir is more forceful now, elbowing her way through. If no one will stand up to the Rise, then she will do it. She has done it before. But her legs are moving in that dreamlike state, too slow and unwilling. She urges herself to move faster, faster, wishing for flight itself—

Queen Hilda pulls back. And swings.

A scream ripples through the Dark Forest.

The axe bites deep into Nattaskur's trunk. The sound echoes in the clearing.

Sýstir stops. She sinks to the ground, her heart pulsing loud in her ears. This cannot be happening. This is not real.

Queen Hilda raises her arm again, and swings. Again.

. . .

It takes all night for Queen Hilda to carve her wound into Nattaskur's trunk, and well past dawn. There are times when she has to pause, or lean upon the handle of her axe. Even from here, her arms shudder with exhaustion.

Nattaskur is a great tree – it is *the* great tree. But it has no protection against this act of war. Sýstir can only watch as the axe devours a little more with every swing. Her hands are clenched so tightly into fists that her nails draw blood from her palms. The trees keen, the pain such a chorus that she knows not where theirs end and hers begins.

There is a collective ripple of breath as one of the Skóug Trolls – so old her skin resembles mountain crags – lets out a mournful sob. Sýstir has never seen a troll cry, and did not believe they could, but there's an unmistakable trace of a single tear glistening down her face. At her feet sits an emerald, perfectly preserved in teardrop form.

The Skóug Trolls look uneasy now, their gazes shifting from the emerald to one another. *Good*, Sýstir thinks viciously, and then with a piercing grief. They will know what they have done – and how they will regret it. But how the other Väsen will regret, too.

When the axe has eaten through almost half of the trunk, Queen

Hilda sets it to the ground and wipes her brow. The expression on her face veers between exhaustion and determination, as though she truly believes that she has done the right thing. But there is nothing right about this.

She straightens up to look at the Väsen. "To exist... is not easy. And darkness takes from us more than we wish to give."

Queen Hilda glances up – and meets Sýstir's gaze. Sýstir reels back. Even though it is surely impossible, Sýstir knows with absolute certainty that Queen Hilda knows about the branch. What Sýstir has done.

Her gaze flickers to the sap bleeding from the axe's wound. Red and oozing, like the sap from the apple tree branch. A putrefaction – a corruption. And she had brought it there.

I have killed Nattaskur.

For a second, Sýstir feels as though the land itself has been pulled from under her. *She* is the reason Nattaskur is infected. *She* is all that is wrong.

It wasn't her fault – it *can't* be her fault—

Panic claws its way up her throat. Then it occurs to her: it would mean that she's already infected with this same darkness, and that can't be true. She would know if she was a poison to the Dark Forest – and the second she did, she would root herself out. Her heartbeat steadies; her anger settles back into her bones. She would never commit even the smallest of crimes against the trees.

She would know... wouldn't she?

Queen Hilda continues, "Nattaskur has long been the heart and soul of this forest – the very memory of Gromildr and her act of hope that we continue to need for the world." She sighs. "Now it will be up to you. Up to you to connect with one another, to listen to one another, to love one another."

She bends to grasp the hilt of her axe once more. Nattaskur looks like a prisoner on their knees, like the death blow is only a hurrying of what has already been set in motion. The axe swings one final time.

"Stand back," Queen Hilda calls.

A splintering sound cracks through the clearing like thunder. A flurry of leaves scatters in the air like unseasonable snow.

Nattaskur – beautiful, great, the home of homes, heart and soul and everything in between, and even Sýstir in her ignorance had recognised it all those years ago – falls.

The silence is breathless.

Then the axe shatters in Queen Hilda's hands. She flinches as the shards fall harmlessly to the ground.

"It is done," she says.

As one, the Skóug Trolls leave the clearing, their heads bowed. A giant is crying now in earnest, tears falling to the ground. Someone else screams, piercing, but no one shushes them. Two dwarves next to her start to argue, their voices so loud that no one can make out what they're saying. All around her, the Väsen fissure into a chaos of anger and confusion.

Sýstir's ears are ringing.

Nattaskur is gone.

· TWENTY-THREE ·

Sýstir stands watch at the top of the burial hills, numb.

In her head, the silver of the axe rises and falls, rises again. The trees scream, or perhaps it is the Väsen weeping, or perhaps the very gods themselves.

Nattaskur is gone.

It is so wholly unthinkable. This is no act of mercy or protection. This is punishment, devised to strike at her heart. Who will carry her memories now?

The Skóug Trolls had returned shortly, each one holding an axe of their own. They had cut Nattaskur into further pieces, as if Queen Hilda's singular act of brutality wasn't enough, until all that remained of Nattaskur was kindling. Even gentle Fulgir had wielded an axe.

Then they had built pyres. And Sýstir knows well enough of the kind of creatures committed to such desecration.

All that remains now is a stump, scorched clean by flames to ensure that no living thing will ever grow from it. The grass around it is grey with ash, scoured of every leaf, every twig that might have carried Nattaskur within it still. Obliteration, in every way imaginable. Even Sýstir cannot bring herself to go near it. But she stands vigil until her head spins with exhaustion, hunger cramping her stomach. Only when Fenrir comes to find her does she finally relent.

But she doesn't go home. What is home to her now? And there is all of that rage inside of her, surging through her limbs. So much power – and nowhere to put it.

...

In the days afterwards, a thick fog settles on the ground and refuses to lift. It rains endlessly, as though the entire world weeps for Nattaskur's devastation.

Like many others, Sýstir returns to its stump again and again. She allows herself to cry just once – quietly and alone, with no one in earshot. If she could grieve truly, she would howl into the very dirt, burying herself until no one would recognise limb from root or branch. But even that, she realises, would not be enough to scour this loss from her.

Every time she crests the hill, she thinks that she must be mistaken, and she'll see the crown of foliage slide into view, the image preserved. Her resolve to protect the Dark Forest – to punish those responsible for Nattaskur – is still there, but how can she, when the crime is so vast, the perpetrators so protected?

Someone sits down next to her, and she's shocked to realise that she recognises them. Hallr and Korí, their instruments on their backs. The wood of their fiddles is scuffed and in need of a polish, their strings slack and untuned.

The woodland gnomes exchange a glance. "Queen Hilda is nowhere to be found," Korí says.

Hallr shrugs. "It is said that she has fled into exile. To meditate on her actions, and to grieve for the Dark Forest."

Korí seems less convinced. "To hide from her guilt."

Sýstir doesn't say anything, but she watches the way the two woodland gnomes size each other up, as though this is an argument they've long held between them. They have been married for as long as she's known them and generous with their affection, but the energy between them feels off-kilter. Tense.

How many other Väsen must be this way? There must be dozens of similar conversations between lovers, friends – even enemies who find themselves cautious allies when it comes to who is to blame over Nattaskur. A thin but uncrossable line drawn between sides.

"It seems to me," she says carefully, "that a time of change is coming."

"Yes," Korí says darkly. "Change is coming."

...

Sýstir has not walked across the Dark Forest regularly for aeons. But now she moves through it as though she never left, picking up the old ties she thought she'd left behind. There are some friendships, of course, that have been severed forever – Fulgir, she thinks painfully, and Thróttr, who would not leave his Revel to meet with her – but others have more flexibility. And there are, it turns out, a fair few Väsen willing to meet with the huldra who defied Queen Hilda and the skóug trolls.

She spends more time in the dark pool, even though the warmth of the season is loosening its grip, and the water's chill is giving way to an intolerable bite. She waits until she's numb with cold, until her lungs start to seize. When she finds that she can barely gasp for breath, she dives, reaching for the silty bottom.

There is so much she has forgotten wilfully, and more that has slipped haphazardly from her mind. But now, she needs to remember, to draw upon the parts of herself that she had once spurned. She must be sharp as a blade, if she is to do what must be done.

She meets with the woodland gnomes who had been ready to graft a branch to Nattaskur, and are now forever thwarted. Sprýg gnomes from a Revel that had never been entirely comfortable with the trolls' proximity to their delicate structures welcome her gladly. She gifts as she did of old, with rare feathers and glimmering stones, or flowers pressed and dried into fragile beauties. She travels several days to meet with the nearest giant, who can barely speak for his anger.

I'm just stopping for a visit. I only wished to say hello.

All the while, she sits and listens, and says very little. There is power, she realises, in silence. Often, the Väsen just wish for someone to vent their frustrations to. But no one is listening to each other anymore; they are each too wrapped in their grief.

It is that quiet, secretive instinct that prompts Sýstir to ask a question at the right time, or to break the silence at a key moment. To offer a small smile of sympathy. And there is that inevitable lull in the conversation, where all that can be said has been spoken, and what is left is the question of what to do now.

At this point, Sýstir schools her expression into one of thoughtfulness, as though this idea has only just occurred to her. "Well, if you wish to speak again, you are always welcome to visit me." A gesture, sometimes, such as a hand on the shoulder, but often it is just a nod, or a tilt of the head. "I am always here for you."

She watches as they smile weakly back, or shake their heads as if to say *no, we will not be joining you*, or wipe away their tears. And days later, she is just as kind when they cross the creek to the Scar of Rotinn, hesitant and afraid, but with the same firm goal in their minds: to see justice be done.

It's true that not all of them join. Some she reaches too late; they are tethered to their kin, who have already decided that Queen Hilda's actions serve them all. There are those who would rather ignore the oncoming storm. And there are others who have heard about Sýstir – and fear her.

She's aware of the whispered rumours around herself. The most beautiful huldra of all, said to kill you with a mere look, should you dare to meet her gaze. It is said, too, that she walks with the ethereal footsteps of moonlight, that one strand of her hair makes a harp sing in perfect tune. That you would sell your soul for one of her songs, and be lost forever, dying in exquisite rapture while your body wastes away.

It is all nonsense, of course. But it doesn't hurt for the other Väsen to believe her capable of such force. They come to her, alone or in twos and threes, awed and furious in their sorrow over Nattaskur. And perhaps they harbour their own personal resentments of the skóug trolls, or wish to wrest some power of their own. Sýstir takes them all in.

At night, the Scar of Rotinn is alive with the light from campfires – more activity than this part of the Dark Forest has seen in years. It is... a different kind of Dark Forest than the one she is used to. But that is the nature of this migration, she thinks. Soon, the Väsen will find their proper homes: caves and trees and clearings, and all will be as it should. Though, she thinks, hesitating, it might be considerably more challenging in this part of the Dark Forest, where the land is less merciful by its nature. And there is no substitute for Nattaskur's presence, or the grief fisted in her heart.

Yet with every Väsen who crosses over, who offers a friendly hand or a shy smile, whose gaze darkens at the mention of that unspeakable day, something within her, so long dormant she thought it had died, stirs. It is not quite hope – for there is no fixing the past – and it is not quite satisfaction, for there is little by which to be satisfied, but it yawns and shakes out its limbs nevertheless.

Purpose, she thinks unexpectedly one day, and the answering glow within her confirms it.

It is a misty, damp day when Korí shows up on the other side of the creek, his pack shouldered wearily. His mouth is pinched in unhappiness, but also determination. He is not, Sýstir notes, with Hallr.

"She would not come. Agagkantor dissuaded her. She said she would not take part in this... foolishness," Korí says when she asks. "Though I am hopeful that she will come to understand, in time."

Agagkantor. Sýstir's stomach twists with anger.

But she gives Korí a sympathetic smile. "You are always welcome with me."

...

She deliberately waits a while before returning to the problem of the trolls. Give them enough time for their doubts and worries to fester, to consider their absent queen and all the difficult questions she has so easily avoided by virtue of her self-imposed disappearance. Enough time for those doubts to become cracks in their armour, and for Sýstir to slip in.

On a chilled evening, Sýstir stands outside the Rise's cave, her gaze sweeping over its well-worn boulders, dappled in mossy greens and greys. Though little has changed, the ground beneath her feet feels different – at once both softer and firmer. It takes her a moment to realise that the last time she was here, she'd worn shoes, the forest floor muffled beneath the layers of leather. Now, she cannot remember the last time she'd felt the need to separate herself from the earth in this way. Such needless, foolish armour.

It's hard to believe that she spent so much time agonising over belonging here – as though there was ever really any question of whether Queen Hilda would let her in. There are no trolls outside today; perhaps they've made themselves scarce, knowing in their deepest of hearts that they are irrevocably guilty.

Without anyone to stop her, she makes her way inside, invitation or not. Immediately, the scent and sounds catch her: warm and earthy, good cooking, and the faint hum of music that is forever breaking her heart—

She stops herself, waiting until the memories settle. They are just another distraction.

By the time she enters the corridor towards the hart, the trolls must know she's coming. It's grown too quiet, too solemn. But no one stops her.

The fire is crackling in the centre of the hart, and the trolls are about their day, as though everything is normal, save for that uncanny hush. It sounds like grief, stuffed into too small a space. Their heads turn as she enters.

"Well met," she says. "It has been too long."

The trolls look at her, their expressions caught between worry and fear, as though Sýstir is anything to be afraid of. It is an expression that she's rarely seen on any singular troll, and now here they are, with too many questions and so few answers. The faces she recognises, however, are tight with tension: Grendel and Fundin, in conversation seconds earlier at the hearth. She's seen so little of Queen Hilda's son that she'd nearly forgotten he existed. He must be akin in age to Grendel and Fulgir, but whereas Grendel possesses broad physical strength and Fulgir inner calm, Fundin is nothing but a vessel into which another might place their ideas for him to call his own.

Sýstir glances around the hart, hoping for a glimpse of Fulgir, but she's nowhere in sight. Perhaps she has decided to leave the Rise, unable to live with the knowledge of what they have done. Perhaps she has heard the rumours of the Väsen who have come together to right this dreadful wrong. Perhaps she is making her way to the creek at this moment, and—

Sýstir takes another step forward – and Grendel pushes his way between her and the rest of the Rise, barring further entry. His bulk casts a strong shadow against the firelight, and he seems almost molten within.

"If you come for Queen Hilda, she is not here," he says curtly. "Leave us, huldra."

"I am not here for revenge," Sýstir says, the lie working against her teeth. "And if I was, I would be misguided. For you are not to blame."

"Why have you come, then, if not to cast blame and seek revenge?" Grendel demands.

Fundin places a hand on Grendel's arm and they exchange a wordless glance. Then he sighs and steps back. Without meaning to, Sýstir's eyebrows raise. Despite Queen Hilda's absence, it seems that some hierarchies haven't entirely fallen.

"In truth, I cannot say well met," Fundin says, just loud enough that the observers can hear the cadence of their conversation. "But it is good to see you, nevertheless."

Sýstir says nothing. She is good at this part: the waiting, the confession of grief and guilt, the admittance that perhaps Queen Hilda – their most beloved, their guiding star – has led them so far astray that they no longer know the way back. And it is her who will say, gently, *let me show you.*

But Fundin holds his gaze steady, no such confusion written across his expression, and he fills the silence easily enough. "As Grendel said, our queen is elsewhere, so I speak in her stead. What have you come for?"

Sýstir pauses, picking her next words carefully. "I did not come for revenge, true. But there are others who would extend their anger towards you all, in her name. So it is in all of our interests, then, to find Queen Hilda and have her explain more fully."

Something hot sings in her at the thought of finding the queen. What satisfaction it would be to see her, a prisoner in the forest she failed to protect. But Sýstir keeps her expression calm, her tone mild.

Fundin's expression remains unchanged, though she catches a certain hardness in his eyes. "Even if we could inform you of her whereabouts, do not ask us to abandon our queen."

"Just as she has not abandoned you?" Sýstir says, raising an eyebrow.

"She was forced to make a terrible sacrifice."

"She has sacrificed all of us for her own follies, whatever they may be," Sýstir says, unable to curb her impatience. "She cut down Nattaskur!"

The hart grows even quieter, as though saying the very name is sacrilege. There is an intake of breath, a dry sob – and oh, how still they are. They know what Queen Hilda has done. They know that it is irreversible.

"Why would you suffer a queen who would cut out the very essence of our home?"

"The huldra has not drunk of Nivir," Grendel says to the trolls, cutting through her thoughts. "Of course she cannot understand the meaning of sacrifice."

Sýstir didn't think herself capable of getting riled by Grendel; he is a *knott*, to be swatted away without a second thought. But she finds herself clenching her fist, and has to unclench it deliberately.

"Whereas, Grendel, you would bend and bow and scrape quite happily in the name of your laws. Never mind that Nattaskur is dead. Never mind that your queen cannot even face what she has wrought."

Now it's Grendel's turn to flush with anger. He pushes forward, but it is too late to cut her off. If he'd wanted to stop her, he should have barred her entry into the cave and banned her from the Rise. He'd assumed she was weak.

He'd assumed wrong.

If she cannot convince Fundin of the truth, then there are other ways to persuade. She reaches for that deep wellspring of magic, pulling it over her teeth, her tongue. There is a wordless song that makes her think of the trees calling out to one another, following the sweet warmth of sunlight after a hard winter. Notes that sound like green, growing things, like the crisp of early spring frost. Several trolls look to her instinctively, their faces creased between yearning and pain.

They will follow her, she thinks. They will be trees amongst sunlight, honed to justice for Nattaskur—

A voice drowns her out, then another. Fundin and Grendel, singing in strong, purposeful harmony. In fits and starts, the Rise joins them in a round – no beginning and no end. Unbreakable.

Sýstir's magic snaps like a thread pulled too taut.

"You will not compel us," Fundin says, and there is no trace left of mild politeness. "I do not call you enemy, but neither are you friend. It is time, I think, for you to leave."

Sýstir laughs bitterly. "No, I would not be your enemy." She raises her voice, so that the trolls at the back of the hart might hear her. "You have been told that what is good for one is good for all. You have been told that the laws of Nivir would promise you security, happiness and the continued protection of the Dark Forest." She pauses. "You have been deceived."

Out of the corner of her eye, she catches trolls shaking their heads, as though she is sullying the Rise itself simply with her presence. But there are others who are listening intently, she realises, grief etched in the slump of their shoulders, the weariness of their gazes. Who can still hear her sunlit song and taste spring dew on their lips.

"I am not an enemy, though some of you no doubt have been

told this. I have always wished to protect the Dark Forest. Yet I am but one Väsen. And it will take more of us to achieve what one alone cannot."

A snort from Grendel. Well, he is still free to believe that she is more human than Väsen. But she does not doubt that anyone here would look at her and see her for anything other than what she is: a creature of the Dark Forest.

"I ask for your help. We must find a way to right this wrong, so that we may face this threat together. You know where to find me."

Grendel is incandescent. "You would fracture our Rise—"

She lowers her voice, her gaze on Grendel. "And I know where to find you, lest you forget. Those who ally with Queen Hilda – well, I cannot promise other Väsen will feel so merciful."

She smiles beatifically, like she is kindness itself. And for a moment, she is, with nothing but the desire for clean, pure justice. How clear it is now, how much the Dark Forest needs her. And how much work there is left to do.

"I'm sure I will be seeing you soon," she says.

Then, leaving silence in her wake, she sweeps out of the cave.

· TWENTY-FOUR ·

After Sýstir's speech at the Rise, the trolls do not immediately come to her. But then, she wouldn't expect that. They will take their time. They will talk amongst themselves. And the word will spill from Rise to Rise, far more effectively than anything Sýstir could ever accomplish on her own.

In the meantime, Sýstir gathers her allies. There are more Väsen making the pilgrimage to cross the creek every day, in all shapes and sizes – including those for which she has no name. Some come to argue, of course, or to try and lure back their family. More often than not, it is easy to persuade them to cross, using carefully minded words – or, failing that, a song, soft and seductive as the warmth of a fire.

The first troll comes almost an entire season after she visited the Rise, their footsteps heavy. They carry little on their back: a stool, a cauldron for cooking, a knife and some rope. Others have come bearing much more, and Sýstir is not shy about ensuring that they bring their fair share to provide for the camp. But this one she lets through without a word.

He is a younger skóug troll from Hilda's Rise, she notes. Good. It will be the young ones first, she thinks, who have yet to calcify into Queen Hilda's image of all that a troll should be and value.

"What about food?" another Väsen says, whose origins elude Sýstir. "We cannot go hungry at their whims."

Sýstir gives her a sharp glance, and she silences. Although she cannot quite call herself leader yet, she won't have her decisions questioned. Not when the mood is so crucial, delicate as a spinn faerie's silk thread.

"He will provide," Sýstir says firmly, once the troll is out of earshot. "Do not fear; I will ensure that all is well."

He will, of course, be valuable in other ways. But there is no point in telling her Väsen; they can only see one season ahead, if that. They are too concerned with news from their families and loved ones – whether they have decided to make the sometimes arduous journey to the Scar of Rotinn, or whether they continue to hide behind the pretence that everything is as it was. Whether there are other reasons for the enduring silence.

Now that there is no one to temper them, darker creatures are beginning to emerge and give into impulses that might have been curbed by Queen Hilda – though Sýstir would never admit this aloud. Nevertheless, when she treads the Dark Forest at night, it is with Fenrir at her side, and more caution than she's ever recalled feeling before.

The next troll comes. And the next. A slow-moving exodus, but one with a steady purpose. Each one a crack that sends further fissures through Queen Hilda's Rise.

Sýstir is just about to retire for the evening when Kori ducks into her cave apologetically. She is still getting used to the lack of solitude after so long being alone, whether she wished for it or not. Irritation rises through her, hot and quick, and she whirls around. But the expression on Korí's face stills any sharp words.

He is afraid. He is not supposed to be afraid of her.

She massages her temples, trying to quell her annoyance. "Forgive me. It has been a long day."

"Another troll," Korí says, with some unease. "This one wishes to speak with you first."

Sýstir sighs. The hollow in her back aches from the tip of her shoulder blades all the way down to where her tail meets her spine. And there's that anger still plucking at her nerves. But she won't miss an opportunity to bring another troll to her side.

"They await you at the crossing place," he adds.

Only when she's no longer visible from the cave does she let her shoulders slump. She doesn't even realise her fists are clenched until she relaxes them. The small voice that is not entirely her own whispers of all that she might do to satisfy her anger. But she shoves it back down, waiting until her body returns to herself.

She has always been hot-headed, from the time she was barely more than an infant. It was Ada who spoke with level-headed reason, who could defuse an argument about to spiral into blows, or who would see clearly where others were clouded with anger. Though it's a wound years past the making, Sýstir sucks in a sharp breath before banishing the image of her quick, clever, dead sister.

But this furious storm inside her is new, always one wrong word away from release. Perhaps this is Agagkantor's legacy, a groundwater poison that has wicked through her bones. He has already imprinted so much of himself upon her that it only falls to reason his mercurial temper is amongst his "gifts".

She very carefully avoids the thought that it could be something else entirely.

As promised, the troll is waiting for her across the creek. Sýstir almost doesn't recognise her, but then Fulgir puts one hand up cautiously in greeting, and her body unwinds. She has looked for Fulgir more than she would care to admit to, whether on her long walks through the Dark Forest, or amongst the few trolls that have come in a group. And now, as if through will alone, she is here.

Sýstir waits for her to cross, but she stays where she is. That is understandable; more than one troll has hesitated or even sought to turn back before they step across. But Sýstir has never yet failed to persuade them, and she doubts Fulgir will need even that.

Sýstir cannot keep the smile out of her words as she crosses the creek, too impatient to wait. "Have you come to join us at last?"

She could use Fulgir, more than she let on at the Rise. Sýstir might have lived in the Dark Forest for decades, but Agagkantor had sheltered her from more than she realised, and there are ancient feuds and familial grudges that must be settled, not to mention rivalries over the pettiest of things – barely half of which she understands. And that is all before they consider her own background: half human; outsider; a strange, solitary creature.

Fulgir would have sway with the other trolls, who have not quite settled their grievances with the Mares. She would reassure the Woodland and sprýg gnomes that there is a place for them in the Scar of Rotinn. And she would be a sign to all that justice has only one side.

Sýstir does not trust anyone to be her right hand – not even Korí, who still watches the camp for signs of Hallr. But Fulgir is an open book, trustworthy, kind and firm all at once.

What a pleasure it will be to have a true friend standing by Sýstir's side.

"There is much to discuss," Sýstir says. "And now that you're here, the other trolls will..."

Fulgir shakes her head. "I have not come to forsake my kin."

Sýstir stops. Her imaginings drain away like water. It's not that Sýstir had thought Fulgir would come straight away, or that she wouldn't have to quell misgivings. But she'd thought – she'd hoped—

"I have come to beseech you: do not split us Väsen further," Fulgir continues. "There is good reason—"

A flash of anger runs through Sýstir. "*I* am not the reason why Väsen come to the creek nightly and contemplate its crossing. *I* am not the reason why Queen Hilda has fled. And *I* am certainly not the reason why we have had trolls from your Rise join us of late."

"It was Rotinn, Sýstir," Fulgir says patiently. "We have already let it ravage our friendships, our kinships. We should not give it cause to further part us."

Sýstir stops paying attention, still caught on that word ringing through the air. *Rotinn.* Underneath, she hears a damning voice that sounds suspiciously like Agagkantor, as though he is standing behind her, whispering lies into her ear. *You bestowed Rotinn upon Nattaskur. This is your fault.*

She shakes the imaginary voice from her head. Even though it's been years since she's spoken to him, he still seems to ensnare her thoughts at the worst times. Like poison, she thinks.

"Nattaskur is incorruptible," she says, dismissing the thought. "It would have taken a great evil to overcome it."

And it *would* be a great evil. Sýstir is not evil, or even malicious. She has never failed to extend the hand of kindness. Has she not saved Väsen, taking them under her wing? Has she not stood up for justice at great cost to herself? Is she not now standing here, trying to persuade her friend to join her?

"We cannot say how it came to be corrupted with Rotinn," Fulgir says. "But it sickened so quickly, there was little choice."

And so Queen Hilda took it upon herself to fell it. A familiar pulse of anger runs through Sýstir. This has nothing to do with her imaginary Agagkantor, or anything she might have thought he would say to her. This is Queen Hilda's doing – no one else.

Fulgir continues, "Nattaskur would poison the Dark Forest,

and we would wither for all that was our heart and soul." She sighs. "There was no lesser sacrifice to be made in its stead."

"Presumably that is what your queen told you."

A long pause. "It is."

Sýstir raises an eyebrow. "And you would believe her over me?"

"I do not wish the Dark Forest to fall into further harm. And these – these Väsen that you gather... To what end do you feed them your anger?"

Sýstir cocks her head to one side. "I am hardly feeding them anything. Perhaps they are simply in need of someone who will listen to them. Who will understand their fears and grievances. Who will help them feel protected, should someone think that they can be cast aside just as easily as Nattaskur. They are always welcome to come to me."

Kori's face, afraid, flashes in her mind. She shakes it away.

"Besides, have we brought violence upon you? Have we declared war?"

Fulgir's shoulders slump. "No, Sýstir, you have not yet cried war."

Sýstir's eyes narrow. "Why have you come, then?" she says, and this time there is no mistaking the iron in her voice. "Speak or leave."

Fulgir sighs. "I come bearing a proposal that might bestow upon us all what we seek. We offer peace, Sýstir."

Peace. What a tempting thought – and yet the trolls would poison the word before the Dark Forest ever knew its true meaning.

"Let me guess," Sýstir says, sarcasm biting in her tone. "You would save Queen Hilda, and thus save the trolls, with the Dark Forest to be preserved in your own image?"

"I would save you from yourself," Fulgir says quietly.

Sýstir laughs; an absurd notion. "I think you and I must have a different understanding of the situation at hand, Fulgir. It is not I that needs saving."

But Fulgir's expression suggests otherwise. Despite Sýstir's insistence to herself that she would not get angry, it stirs within her. Where was Fulgir when the Rise spurned her, again and again? Where was her friendship during those long years on the other side of the creek? Where is she now? Not stood by her side, but opposite her.

If there was a time when Sýstir needed saving, it has long passed – and the only saviour is Sýstir herself.

"State your proposal," she says sharply. "Let's get it over with."

"I would ask that we drink from Nivir together."

"Still?" Sýstir demands. "You have already asked once; did anything in my answer invite uncertainty?"

Nivir. Unbidden, Sýstir's imagination spools out the future: journeying to its banks, where the waterfall cascades into the pool below, even during deepest winter. Cupping her hands to hold its water to her lips. Drinking and becoming one with the trolls' laws.

Shackled to them.

Had she drunk from Nivir as a child, it would have promised nothing, save to curtail her nature. She would have still been rejected from the Rise, still borne the shame of Queen Hilda's disapproval. Except with the forbiddance of drawing blood, she would have been entirely defenceless alongside her vulnerabilities. Agagkantor was a traitor, but in this, he was correct: it is folly to believe there will never be a reason to fight.

"As allies," Fulgir insists. "With Fundin's blessing and the goodwill of the Rise."

"I see this benefitting no one except yourself," she says.

"We would rewrite the laws together," Fulgir says. "With all of the Dark Forest. No voice would go unaccounted for."

Sýstir considers this. It is not the worst plan she has heard of, though it seems full of potential for needless confusion, with months, or even years, of haggling and compromise. It would be a miracle if Nivir did not run red with blood spilt over the proceedings – on one side, of course.

But it would be a chance to unite the Dark Forest. There would be no more sides drawn. And with Sýstir there, a guarantee that the disaster of Nattaskur could never be repeated.

"That seems... of a fairness to me," Sýstir says cautiously.

As reluctant as she is to adhere to any Väsen-made law, she must consider what is best for the Dark Forest before her own interests. She has sworn to protect it by any means; if that means setting aside her own distrust and pained, bloody history, then she will do so without a second thought. But it must be wholly protected.

Justice must be done.

Fulgir pauses. "In return, we would beseech Queen Hilda to return to us and rule once more."

The window of possibility slams shut.

"You would bring back Hilda?" Sýstir says, her voice silky with withheld anger. "You would let Nattaskur's devastator walk free?"

Sýstir has dreamt of the punishments that might be inflicted upon Hilda, should she return. She knows it should be a chance for collective justice, with all to weigh in. But in Sýstir's dreams, it is herself and Queen Hilda, alone in a dark cave with the silvery glint of a blade.

"I have tried to understand," she says tightly. "But I cannot."

Fulgir looks at her, anguish clear. "Do you not recall her words? We must do our best to heal, not dig at each other's wounds when we are both already scarred. On this, she is right." She places a fist over her heart. "And I grieve, Sýstir. I *mourn*. Do not make another wound of me, I beg you."

For all her anger, Sýstir hesitates. She has never seen Fulgir look so lost. She bites her lip, considering. Perhaps she is making a mistake, or perhaps there is another path forward—

Fulgir sighs. "She remains our queen, Sýstir."

"She was never my queen."

And she never will be. If they intend to bring back Hilda as their queen, there will only be more devastation, more grief. And Sýstir will have failed to protect the Dark Forest.

Sýstir swallows the knot in her throat. After all of this is over, perhaps then there will be time to grieve. But nothing can stand in the way of her purpose. Not even the oldest, most cherished of friends.

"Return to your false prince," she says shortly.

"Sýstir—"

"Tell Fundin that there will be no peace. Not until justice is exacted."

It is not quite the same as declaring war. But the trees rustle with it nevertheless.

· TWENTY-FIVE ·

The news spreads slowly. A whisper here, a rumour there. That the skóug trolls of Queen Hilda's Rise do not wish for forgiveness – or even consider themselves in need of it. That they mock the other Väsen for their complacency and weakness. That they are already rallying themselves to bring Queen Hilda back and restore the Dark Forest to her rulership.

It did not take too much effort on Sýstir's part. Just a few passing comments to those already loyal to her, and a snatch of song for the wary. The lightest tap of persuasive magic to see her vision through. Anyway, it is only giving voice to what the trolls have surely thought to themselves over the last few seasons. As though the other Väsen are fools to be puppeteered at will.

The second rumour spreads quickly on the back of the first, and without any magical intervention to prompt it: Sýstir's gathering of Väsen is hungry for action. And the laws of Nivir, which have always held sway, now tremble, just a little.

"We must protect what is ours," she says to those that come to her. "By whatever means necessary. If you wish to be faithful, you must break your ties to the trolls entirely. They hold sway over you – and you do not even know it." She leans close. "Stop drinking from Nivir and remember who you are. Not a Väsen of Queen Hilda's trolls, lesser to their needs. You are a Väsen of the Dark Forest. *You* are your own law."

After everything they have endured, it is not so difficult to turn them away from Nivir. It is easy to drink from other water sources.

But Sýstir does not fail to notice a new... violence within her Väsen. Perhaps it is that justice, denied to them for so long, has provoked a response too overwhelming to be denied. Perhaps they have always held a secret desire for stronger action, and Sýstir is their excuse. The camp hums with simmering anger; now it overspills.

Alongside Sýstir, Korí watches a group of Väsen return from the other side of the creek, their hands bruised around the knuckles. Although not one of them sports obvious wounds, their arms are spattered with blood.

Korí's mouth is pinched with worry. "What have they done, Sýstir? What are we permitting?"

"I cannot wonder at their judgement," Sýstir says. "I trust them."

Korí hesitates. "Queen Hilda would have wondered."

Rage courses through her like lightning. "Do not speak her name!"

Silence folds over them.

Korí looks at her, and not for the first time, she is aware of how little she truly knows about his thoughts. Does he measure her against Queen Hilda? Does he forget who has cost them peace, and who will bring it once again?

"I apologise, Sýstir," he says, though she has the odd feeling that he is not particularly sorry at all.

She takes a deep breath, steadying herself. She cannot be so quick to anger, not with so much still left to be done.

"The Dark Forest allows it, so it must be allowed. I will not be Hilda in another guise, to impose my will as I see fit."

But her gaze lingers on the glint of blood, wet and red, and something deep within her thrills with satisfaction.

...

Sýstir sleeps lighter these days. Dreams more often. Of a child's irrepressible laughter, the glean of water on a river she has never swam in by daylight, the thick scent of her mother's honey mead. So she tries to stay awake, dozing in fits and starts in the shelter of her cave.

But sleep reaches in anyway and plucks at the strings of memory, of pain.

You cannot escape yourself, Sýstir.

She bolts upright and for a second, she is not here at all, but at the fringe of a pyre. It is her mother screaming, Ada reaching for the fire. She turns, and there is her not-self, watching the flames lick higher. She smiles, and her teeth are slicked in blood.

Panic clutches at her throat, the world awash in heat. She blinks once, twice, forcing herself to take deep breaths until she remembers where she is. Oden's men cannot come for her now. What has happened has already come to pass, and she is still here, unbroken. She is *safe*.

She emerges from her cave, shaking off the last vestiges of sleep. Perhaps a long walk in the cold predawn air will set her mind at rest. But she stops at the entrance of her cave, surprised to see a figure sitting by the dying embers of the campfire outside.

Korí cradles his nyckelharpa in his hands, thumbing at the scuffs it has accumulated. There is beeswax for polishing at his side, but he makes no motion to use it. There are dark circles under his eyes, and for the first time, Sýstir considers that she is not the only one wrestling with the past.

"Winter makes poor company of our instruments," he says, glancing up at her.

Sýstir could leave him to it – the warmth of the fire no longer entices her the way it once had – but she finds herself sitting down opposite him anyway. It has been so long since she has spoken to Korí as a friend instead of ally. So long since they have spoken at all, she realises, instead of in quick instructions passed back and forth.

"How so?" she asks.

"The wood shrinks and cracks. The strings slacken and twist against the bow. It takes a practised hand to coax a tune."

Sýstir looks at the instrument again, thinking. When was the last time she heard it played? Sweet and full, jubilant, or even in mournful solemnity? The strings hang limp on the nyckelharpa, and even more so on the bow.

"Hallr called them our unruly children." He closes his eyes. "I miss her smile, Sýstir."

Sýstir sighs with sudden understanding. So this is the cause of his dark circles, the constantly furrowed brow.

"We travelled afar during the blooming of Nattaskur. *Next time we will attend*, we consoled ourselves. Next time, we will rejoin our kin. For what is endless in the world except the forest, the stars, and Nattaskur?" He looks at her bleakly. "I will never listen to my wife sing under its blossom again."

And that is why he is here, she thinks. Because Nattaskur is gone, and there is nothing certain in this world – not even the stars.

"She will always be welcome with us," Sýstir says, and means it. "She will come, given time."

But he shakes his head. "I could not even tell you where she is, never mind where she may be, given time."

Sýstir's heart aches at the despair in his voice and how it hums against her own. In the back of her mind, she sees Fulgir's expression of anguish. *Do not make another wound of me.* Yet Queen Hilda has made wounds of them all.

"This storm will pass, Korí, and we will see blue skies again. You will reunite with her once we are freed from Queen Hilda's trolls." She smiles, just a little. "Play your music, and you will hear hers answer."

Korí smiles back, weary but with genuine warmth. "It shall be done."

They speak for a little longer, and although Korí doesn't play, he polishes his nyckelharpa so that it no longer looks so lonesome. It is not quite their easy friendship of old, but it is nice, at least, to be warmed by its remnants.

As the predawn light shifts from blue to rose, a young lilvätt arrives on her toad, a little breathless.

"A messenger from the skóug trolls of the Rise," she says. "They wish to see you at the crossing place."

Sýstir considers this, still tired from her broken sleep. For a fleeting moment, she wishes that she had never started any of this in the first place. That she could curl up, a creature of hibernation, and be done with it all. Then she sighs and rallies herself. She is doing this for a reason: to avenge Nattaskur, and to ensure Queen Hilda never again holds the Väsen in her fist. To let Korí sing once more with Hallr in harmony. That is worth a few nights of broken sleep and bloodshed.

"Very well," she says, biting back her weariness.

But she doesn't go immediately to the creek, letting the troll wait for a time. It is helpful to remind them who, exactly, is in command. By the time she arrives, with Korí by her side, the troll's face is pinched with annoyance. It's one she doesn't recognise, but he holds himself tall. A twinge of worry runs through her; perhaps they have sought to renew their numbers in some other way.

"Not Fulgir this time?" she says, raising an eyebrow.

The troll's annoyance shifts. He is nervous, she realises. And not without reason. For the first time in the Dark Forest's memory, the trolls are vulnerable. How satisfying to know that she does not even have to lift a finger to inspire respect, when years previously, she would barely been gifted with civility.

"We invite you to the Rise," he says. "Tomorrow, when the last of the sunlight strikes the river."

Dusk: an unusual time to conduct a moot for the trolls. But Sýstir cannot tolerate daylight these days. And she doesn't need to ask to know who told them that.

...

Sýstir brings Korí with her, along with a few other trusted Väsen. No trolls; she won't have them swayed by nostalgia – or worse, familial obligation. As agreed, she heads to the Rise at dusk, trying not to wince as the last of the sunlight glints through the trees. When she enters the corridor to the hart, it is to an almost empty cave.

There are a fair few trolls who have walked across the logs bridging the creek – for there are now several ways of crossing – and remain in her camp even now. But there are others who are neither here nor counted amongst Sýstir's Väsen. Either they have been hidden away... or they have decided to take their chances elsewhere. Instead, there are just a few that she recognises by face if not by name. Seated in the centre are Fundin, Grendel – looking furious as ever – and Fulgir.

This will be painful, Sýstir thinks, but not for her.

On Fundin's right, Grendel remains stoic. It's probably taking everything he has within himself to do so. What a game it will be, Sýstir thinks, to see how long he might last before he breaks. Her smile widens just a little as their gazes meet, and he stiffens.

Fulgir is on the left, placid as usual. Her ears twitch; the only sign that she must be a touch annoyed by Sýstir's silent needling. Sýstir's smile fades. She had hoped, somehow, that there would remain a crack of doubt for her to breach, or some new persuasive argument that would win Fulgir over to her side. But now, seeing the three of them side by side, it's quite clear that there is no room for Sýstir's efforts.

"Well met, Fundin," she says.

Fundin wearily returns the greeting. "Please, sit with us," he says.

Sýstir glances at her Väsen. "They will stand. But I accept your offer."

Just because the laws of Nivir prevent the trolls from bloodshed doesn't mean that they are entirely powerless. And she would rather not discover if they, too, have learnt how to play this game of makeshift war.

She settles herself opposite Fundin, who sits where Queen Hilda once did. With so few trolls in the Rise, the hart is more cavernous than usual, every noise ricocheting off stone.

"Where are your kindred?" she asks.

Fundin looks unhappy at the question. "Those that decided against this summit were free to make their home elsewhere."

So Fundin is too weak to convince the others of his decisions, or to hold fast to their loyalty. Well, Sýstir had known that from long before he had called this gathering. He is too honest, too willing to give himself away.

Sýstir shrugs. "I am here. For what did you call me away from my home?"

"I wish for this conflict to cease," he says wearily. "I wish for the remaining trolls to live in peace, be it within this Rise or elsewhere."

Sýstir lets the words linger in the air, pretending to mull them over. She waits just long enough for the silence to become uncomfortable, and for her own Väsen to rest their hands pointedly on their weapons. Fundin shifts on the ground.

"How would you pursue this peace of yours?" she asks mockingly.

"We will allow you to pursue your interests, and we will no longer try to subject you or your followers to the laws of Nivir as we are bound. In return, you will allow us to live without fear, underneath our queen, who will return from exile."

Fulgir and Grendel exchange a glance, as though this is a plan long-since crafted between them. But it is a desperate move, by a desperate king.

"You wish for peace," she says. "But I see no peace offered here."

Queen Hilda, yet again. She is a ghost, a draugr, a haunting that Sýstir should not even have to put a thought to. But there she is, tenacious even in the silhouette she has left behind.

Fundin spreads his hands. With the right troll, it is the gesture of a curious king, willing to indulge a subject. But Fundin makes it look like a plea, like he is already begging for mercy underneath the death stroke.

"Then what would you suggest?"

Sýstir smiles again, more thinly. "Actually, I have devised a treaty of my own making. One that I think will bestow upon you a peace that suits us both."

She nods to Korí, who unfurls the map they'd hastily made the night before. It is a crude thing with vast swathes of empty space – as if the Dark Forest could be mapped even in partiality, and pinned to vellum like a butterfly – but it has the key landmarks for their plan. Sýstir traces her finger across the river, and through the clearing where Nattaskur once stood. Her hand smudges the charcoal drawing, smearing a line.

Fundin frowns. "I do not understand."

But when Sýstir looks up, she sees that Fulgir does.

"You wish to rule, and I cannot stop you." *Yet*, Sýstir thinks. "So I, too, wish to lead the beings that have entrusted me with their care." She spreads her hands out in a conciliatory gesture. "It is fair, no?"

Let the trolls see the result of their version of fairness. Let them struggle to reason with it. For there is only one true fair being, and it is the Dark Forest itself.

She turns her attention back to the thin line on the map. There is Nattaskur down the centre, and the river rolling through the line. Everything else is on either side: the Rise on one; the burial hills, Nivir and the Scar of Rotinn on the other. The rest of the Dark Forest sprawls unmapped – and unmappable – past them, spilling over the edges of the vellum.

"We will have one half of the Dark Forest," she says, regaining her patience. "And you will have the other, to do with as you will. Those who follow me will not have to subject themselves to your laws."

She waits for Fundin's reply, but even before he speaks, she already knows the scope of what he'll say. She knows what a hunted animal looks like; that precise moment when its gaze meets hers, resigned to its fate.

"And Queen Hilda?" he asks.

"I will not brook her presence in the Dark Forest, when she has dealt such irreparable harm."

Grendel surges forward, fury written across his expression. "How dare you."

Sýstir's guards tense, but she holds up one hand. "You have a choice."

Fundin's gaze moves from her poised hand to her Väsen, tension coiled tight in their limbs. He must know that her Väsen are no longer drinking from Nivir – that they are more than capable of fighting for what they believe in. Whatever it takes, to secure their vision.

"Excuse us for a moment," he says.

He gets to his feet, along with the other trolls, and Sýstir reaches for her magic, a song poised on her lips. But he only gathers Fulgir and Grendel to him in quiet conversation. Worry crosses over their faces, but their voices are too low for her to make out. Despite herself, Sýstir's heart pangs. She has never once relied on another to make her decisions for her, or to help shoulder the weight of her worries.

Then she rallies herself. It is better, of course, to stand alone. A strong leader needs no one. And isn't she strong? Would a weak leader be capable of all that she has achieved?

She glances at Fulgir, and something in her aches.

Fundin sits back down, exhaustion written in every movement. Fulgir touches his shoulder gently, and he sighs.

"This is not fair, Sýstir. I will not pretend, even for your sake. But I will do what I must for peace – and make no mistake, it *is* peace I wish for the Dark Forest." He looks at her bleakly. "We must accept these terms."

"Then it is settled," Sýstir says, feeling every inch of her new power. "Inform your Rise. Do not cross our boundary, for there will be consequences."

She rises, victory sweet on her tongue. But before she can leave, Fulgir stops her with a heavy hand. There is a rare expression of anger across her face.

"You have no right," she says quietly.

Sýstir wrests her arm away. "I have every right."

"You would divide the Dark Forest? Who are you to demand such a burden from it? To split kin from kin?"

Sýstir narrows her eyes. "I am *serving* the Dark Forest."

I belong to it. Even here, in the cave, she can close her eyes and feel the earth beneath her feet, the roots sunk deep around them in a protective shell. She has never felt so in tune with it before, pain twinned to pain. What is that, if not belonging?

Fulgir shakes her head. "You command, Sýstir. It is not the same."

...

On the way back to the Scar of Rotinn, the wind howls, the season turning to the sharp bite of winter. Sýstir inhales, relishing the crisp chill. Korí, however, seems uneasy, pulling his cloak closer to him. The Väsen guards have gone on ahead, to relay early news of their victory.

"We did well today," she says.

"But... half?"

Sýstir shrugs. "For now, let them contend with their half. The Dark Forest will be reunited again."

What remains of the Rise's fragile power will come apart eventually. She hadn't missed the way the other trolls had shifted from foot to foot, indecisive and angry. The trolls have never liked questions with no clear answer. Today, she has given them something to wonder about, to sit with them as they sleep and eat and mutter amongst themselves. Fundin has already sowed doubt over his leadership abilities; all she's doing is reminding them of it.

"What about those on the other side?" he says anxiously.

She catches the meaning of his tone. *Hallr.*

"We will have the entire Dark Forest eventually. As it was meant to be, not as the trolls have constructed it," she says. "And then all will be well."

Nestled in the crook of her ribs, there is an echoing purr of anger, sharpening its claws.

...

Korí makes his excuses and leaves her to walk back to the creek alone. She suspects he will try to find Hallr again, maybe persuade her to stay on their side of the Dark Forest, if she still refuses to join them. Sýstir cannot imagine to whom she would be as loyal. Agagkantor, once, perhaps, when she was still young and foolish enough to swallow the vast landscape of his lies.

She is near the creek, still pondering this, when she notices someone standing at its edge. For a foolish moment, she thinks that it must be Fulgir, come to apologise. But the hooded silhouette is not that of troll nor dwarf nor gnome. Yet it looks oddly... familiar – a woman.

A *human*. In the Dark Forest.

Sýstir can barely breathe for the shock of it.

The woman doesn't appear to notice Sýstir's approach, so she slows her pace to a light-footed walk. She waits until she is close to draw her knife – her song could draw the attention of another Väsen. Humans should not be able to enter the Dark Forest; if this one has slipped through, then it's an error Sýstir is only too happy to rectify.

But before she can spear her prey, the woman turns, her hood falling, and catches her gaze. She looks, if not entirely pleased, then... excited. Anticipatory.

Sýstir clutches her knife tighter. Anger courses through her.

"You have no business here, *human*," she snarls.

The woman looks at her, wide-eyed. "Ah, my apologies, I heard there was a huldra here and..." She trails off, and her mouth makes an "oh" of surprise. "It's you, isn't it?"

Sýstir doesn't wait. In one expert motion, she presses her knife to the woman's throat, relishing her wince as blade meets flesh. Even at the height of a hunt, with an animal's pulse under her thumb, Sýstir is merciful: a quick, clean stroke or shot to the heart. But she is not feeling merciful today.

A hand on hers. Something about the touch, the *familiarity*—

"Sýstir, it's okay," the woman says, and her voice, too, is familiar.

Sýstir eases the pressure on the knife, and the woman swallows. Her other hand reaches out to spool a thread of Sýstir's hair between her fingers.

"I could never get your hair to stay braided properly," she says faintly.

A memory lances through Sýstir, like lightning aimed at her heart. A cottage, a warm hearth, a rasping song that had met her own in lovely, imperfect harmony.

The knife slackens in her hand. "Who are you?"

The woman takes the opportunity to slip from the knife's reach. She pulls back before Sýstir can ensnare her, standing tall and proud in the faint light of the crescent moon.

"It's me," she says.

Breathlessly. Hopefully. A feeling that echoes like a fantasy.

The woman looks at her steadily, dark eyes ablaze. "Ada."

· TWENTY-SIX ·

Ada.

How long has she been desperate to hear those words? Dreamt of them even in the coldest abyss of her life?

But it can't be true. Because her sister is dead.

Any other sisters would be huldras by necessity, and therefore not sisters at all, in the true, familial meaning of the word. And they would look much as Sýstir does. This woman, this... Ada, shares little resemblance to Sýstir, with her glossy dark hair and deep eyes, the warm hue of her skin. Yet there is something about the way she bites her lip, the soft divot between her brows, that puts her in mind of a sixteen-year-old girl who still haunts her memories.

"Surely you'd have at least half a welcome for your sister." Ada hesitates. "Even though it has been a long time."

Wind races through the trees, tugging on Sýstir's clothes. Though the cold doesn't bother her – not really, not in the way that it once might have, like so much else – she shivers.

Another cold evening. Another girl, hand in hers, pulling her up. Running through the fields, always just ahead of her, always moving just out of sight.

This is why you are forever stained by blood. This is why you live here. Think of all you've done in her name – how ashamed of you she would be—

The memory snaps into place, like a dislocated bone popping back into its socket.

"My sister is dead," Sýstir snarls.

Ada shakes her head fiercely. "They hanged some other poor girl in my name. But I lived, Sýstir."

Genuine sorrow crosses her face before she wipes it away. It reminds Sýstir of Fulgir, all honesty, whether there is joy or pain to be shared. It's one of the things Sýstir had so liked about her troll friend; her openness reminded her of her sister. As does this woman in front of her. Ada.

"I travelled to our cousins, but they refused me. I figured out you'd been claimed by the Dark Forest, but of course, by then, it was too late. And I tried to return – you would laugh if you saw the months of research, the years of travel. But the Dark Forest doesn't open for just anyone." She exhales. "You have no idea what I've done to find you."

Sýstir stares at her. If this woman is truly Ada, then surely Sýstir would not feel this way: as though someone has pressed a knife to her own throat and is waiting for her to lean towards the blade and draw blood.

"Prove it," she says suddenly. "Prove that you are my sister."

Sýstir has blithely swallowed too many lies for her to believe this one, even though it's the most tempting of all. And there was no lie in the desolation of her old home, the malice in her neighbour's voice as she'd spoken victoriously of the vala's demise.

Ada gives her a look that reminds her so painfully of her mother that Sýstir has to look away. But instead of protesting, Ada rolls up her sleeve, to show a puckered twist of scarring dappled all the way down her arm to the palm of her hand. It is clearly an old burn, the skin taut and pink. In the gathered moonlight, it looks like feathers, or fingerprints.

"I tried to pull her out of the pyre," she says. "Before they came for us. Before we had to run."

"So?" Sýstir's grip tightens on the knife. "A scar could be from any wound. If you think that I—"

Ada cuts her off. "I made her a promise. You were there – you saw it happen."

Sýstir might have seen it happen. She might have seen her mother in her early death throes. Might have seen her sister reach through the flames, because, even at the end, when there was not even the most pitiful of hopes left, she'd still tried.

"Look at me," Ada says quietly.

And for a second, Sýstir *does*. She sees the woman, Ada, *really* sees her this time. She takes in the long dark hair that has been braided with the hands that had once braided her own hair. She sees the slight elongation of Ada's face, the fingers of adulthood plucking at childish features. Her posture, so like that of their mother.

She just wishes – she so badly wants to *believe—*

She sucks in a quick breath. "Perhaps I would be convinced if I had been told that my sister is alive and well."

Ada tilts her head, as though she is considering this. Though her gaze is on the knife in Sýstir's hand, there is no fear in her eyes, and she doesn't cede ground.

"Walk with me, then," Ada says, "and I will tell you a story."

"Along the river," Sýstir commands.

In the cusp between autumn and winter, the river is quick and unpredictable, the calm water deceptive to the current underneath. Bitterly cold. Fatal, most likely, to a human, were they to slip and fall in.

It is a challenge – and Ada's expression says as much. But she simply nods.

Sýstir cannot help but look at the way Ada walks, with powerful, confident strides, along the slippery riverbank. There is a chip of a scar on the edge of her jaw, stark in its newness – and that is not all that is new. The Ada she remembers dressed like any other village girl, and it would be hard to pinpoint her as anyone even slightly extraordinary, never mind the daughter of a vala. But this Ada is clad in thick wool and scuffed boots that look like they've seen far more than village roads. Her belt is laden with the tools of a traveller, and she shoulders her belongings easily. She adjusts her cloak, and Sýstir catches at least a dozen patches in its lining.

They meet each other's gaze, and Sýstir has to resist the peculiar urge to look away.

"Your tail is free," Ada says.

Sýstir gives her a sharp look, waiting for the slip of human ignorance. How wild she must look, barefooted and ill-clad, with only a patchwork shift of woven flax and moss – as though she's transformed from tree to Väsen, and is only waiting for the opportunity to change back. How monstrous she must seem.

But all Ada says is, "You walk easier with it." Her expression softens, just a little. "You've grown up."

You were always grown up to me, Sýstir thinks. It was only later, when she herself turned sixteen, that she'd realised how young Ada truly was, to be in sole responsibility of her sister. Put like that, their escape was always destined to fail.

"You said you wished to talk," Sýstir says curtly. "So talk."

"There is a story our mother used to tell us," Ada begins slowly. "About two sister stars, who were joined at the hip, practically. Just a fraction of the sky between them. And where one sister went, the other followed. But as the years turned, they started to drift away from one another, pulled apart by the forces that had once birthed them. The fraction became a distance, and the distance became a gulf."

And the gulf became an abyss. The words come to Sýstir so easily, without even realising. Because she knows how this story goes.

"They travelled across the sky until they could no longer see each other – not even the afterglow of their brilliance. And when they rose in the night sky, they looked across different lands. Each sister longed to tell the other of all she experienced, all she endured, and wept alone to know that it would not be possible."

A sad story, Sýstir thinks, of a whole that was never meant to be fractured.

"But," Ada says, holding a finger up, "the world keeps turning, doesn't it? And what leaves must always return. So even though they can't see each other now, and perhaps not for a millennia more—"

"They'll find their way back to one another one day," Sýstir whispers.

Sýstir has never told anyone the story of the star sisters and their plight. Not even Agagkantor, to whom she has told too much. It had been too painful to talk about the way their mother had dragged them close – usually after an argument, or just as they were setting up to start one – to recount it. But sometimes there was no reason at all for its telling; sometimes Sýstir just wished to hear it one more time. Particularly in that final year, when her sister's gaze strayed towards the horizon, towards her human future, and Sýstir knew she would not be able to follow.

But she knows it by heart. They both did.

"I looked for you, Sýstir," Ada says, thick with unspent tears. "I loved you. I still love you. You are my sister."

Sýstir looks at her in the half-light, and she finally cannot deny it.

"Ada," she says.

There is a beat – and then Ada flings her arms around Sýstir. After another beat, she returns the embrace, resting her head on Ada's shoulder. She closes her eyes, feeling the solid weight of a second body around her. This is no dream, nor nightmare, nor wistful imagining. *This is real.*

Though Sýstir has not cried in years, she presses her head against Ada and sobs.

...

There is so much to discuss. And so much *time*.

They walk down the river to a more sheltered part of the forest, where Ada gets a fire going against the dark. Sýstir cannot help but marvel at all the ways her sister has changed. If Sýstir has adapted to a life in the forest, then so has Ada, in her own way. From her bag – the straps mended, and then mended again – she pulls out a box that is half iron and half wood.

Sýstir cannot quite catch what she does with it, but there is a spark, and a fire. Even when Ada hands it to her, she cannot make sense of its mechanism.

"I traded with a skóug troll close to the foothills for it," Ada explains. "You should see the lakes there. So wide and deep, they look like... well, what I have always imagined an ocean to look like." She spreads her arms wide to demonstrate. "The flowers are so spectacular in spring that they hold a festival entirely dedicated to bees – can you imagine such a thing? I had so many questions that I fair suspect they stuffed me with honey to keep me quiet."

Sýstir finds herself smiling without realising. This is the Ada she remembers: clever, quick, always curious to a fault. The Ada who had collected dried flowers and herbs for difficult poultices, or who could spend an afternoon walking along the river's edge to unravel its history.

"You really have travelled across the Dark Forest," Sýstir says, somewhere between awe and unease.

Ada's smile fades a little. "I looked everywhere for you, Sýstir, and the Dark Forest is vast. The road here was not an easy one."

Sýstir has always known her fragment of the Dark Forest is just that – a piece of something much greater. But she has never quite considered what that might mean. Now, hearing Ada describe unfamiliar landscapes, unfamiliar Väsen, she has to contend with just how little she truly knows.

"There is so much I wish I could show you." Ada claps her hands together, and it is as though they are two young girls again, sat beside their mother's hearth. "We can go together. Just think – the both of us on adventures, like old times. If you move fast, we could leave tonight. Do you have a sleeping pack?"

Ada starts to count off the supplies for the journey, as though they've already begun it. Something in Sýstir bristles, and she leans away from the fire. This Ada, too, she remembers: the eldest sister who confidently forged ahead, whether or not Sýstir wished for it. Forever the eldest; Sýstir forever the youngest. Then she takes a deep breath. Ada is here, *alive* – and Sýstir is quibbling over this?

"The paths will be closed soon with snowfall. Maybe in the spring," she says.

And she has yet to fully deal with her problem of Hilda's Rise, she thinks uncomfortably. If she left with Ada now, she would be abandoning her Väsen at a critical time, when their loyalty may wane along with their appetite for justice. They already have their half of the Dark Forest, they may reason – what more could they want?

Sýstir glances at Ada again. It is like looking at a ghost. A ghost that she has mourned twice over, that she has dreamt about so often that even now she thinks this may all vanish in the dawn. She had buried her memories of Ada in Nattaskur, so that she would at least live on in the slow eternity of its roots. But there is no need for the trees to remember a dead girl when the living woman sits across from her.

Would it not be understandable if she set down the burden of Nattaskur? Could she not... choose Ada?

For the first time since Sýstir crossed the creek, the furnace of anger stays quiet.

"Tell me about your life, Sýstir," Ada says, breaking the quiet. "I wish to know... everything. You did not grow up like this overnight."

Sýstir shrugs. "It is a long story. A skóug troll took me in and – and here I am, really."

"A long story?" Ada asks. "We have time for that."

But there is no easy way to explain all that has happened. For to explain why she is not living near the Rise still, she would have to explain Agagkantor's lies, their argument. And that would unravel into the fight with Queen Hilda, the decision to go back to the village...

The actions she has taken, in the name of her dead sister.

"As I said," she says, attempting a smile. "A long story."

Ada gives her a long look. It is the exactly the kind of expression that would make her confess to eating the last of jam, or chipping a favourite mug. But this is no chipped mug, and Sýstir is no longer a child. That awful, bristling feeling returns.

"Then let me tell you one of my own," Ada says, with a tone that brooks no argument. "Do you know what else I found, creeping towards the border of those lakes with their beautiful flowers and bee festivals? A darkness, Sýstir – a kind of evil, if evil could be considered its own essence. Rotinn."

The word rings between them both.

"I know you are sick," she says, pressing harder. "I see you flinch from the fire. I saw you quick to anger. You are too comfortable in this night."

Sýstir bites her lip. She has insisted to everyone – to herself – that she is well, that she knows every ounce of her fury and claims it for her own. That she does not feel even the weakest of sunlight searing across her skin, that the darkness doesn't whisper to her. That the hollow of her back flares bright pain at its own whims, and not when she is caught between herself and her anger. It would be so easy to say it again, to let the lie rise over her lips.

But this is *Ada*. She has never lied to her sister before – not when it mattered.

"I don't know what to do," she says helplessly.

Ada takes her hand, her gaze urgent. "Come with me. If we go now, we'll miss the snow. There are others looking for a solution – and they may be able to help. It might not be too late for you, Sýstir. But we have to go while we can."

But her Väsen. But her plans.

And even if she was healed from Rotinn – it is Rotinn; she cannot deny it – she would not be healed of all. She would not be able to change what she has done.

She pulls away from Ada. "I – I can't—"

"You must," Ada says fiercely. "There is no other way."

"It's just that I have responsibilities and—"

"Sýstir, you have always been a stubborn thing. Don't be stubborn with this."

Sýstir glares at her. "I have my reasons. Am I not fully grown to make my own choices?"

"Then why must you persist in making such foolhardy ones?" Ada snaps.

They look at each other before Ada rubs one hand over her face and sighs. For a sliver of a moment, she looks... weary. As though there is more than a pack of curious trinkets weighing between her shoulders.

"Forgive me, I thought—" She breaks off and attempts a wan smile. "It seems to me that I came here looking for a slip of a girl. And instead I have found a woman."

A Väsen, Sýstir thinks, with unexpected sorrow. How they have both changed.

"But I would have you humour my worry," she continues. "I know you are not bound by the laws of Nivir. I know you are free to do as you wish. But I've seen what Rotinn does – you cannot take the risk."

Sýstir's heart seems to stop. "Who told you this?"

But she already knows.

"I've travelled far, Sýstir – and I'm not the first to hear of the war that plagues this stretch of the Dark Forest. I've met a lot of Väsen." Ada pauses. "Including Queen Hilda."

No. It cannot be true.

"She told me how you have suffered, and of her own regrets, that she should have intervened earlier," Ada says, the words spilling out in a rush. "I would not have found you without her help. If I had not come now, but later, you would be no more than a vengeance of yourself."

But Sýstir barely hears her. She is caught on those two words: *Queen Hilda*. Even in the depths of her exile, even though Sýstir has done everything to undo her influence, here she is again, striving for power.

"Where did you find her?" Sýstir says.

Ada must notice the change in her voice. "Sýstir..."

"She is the cause of this devastation," Sýstir says, anger winding its way through her. "She has bled the Dark Forest of its life and freedom. She cut down Nattaskur. She stole everything from me!"

"I'm sure she did what she must," Ada says. "I know it was a hard decision. But there was never any hope of saving Nattaskur. *You* are still alive – you must think of yourself."

Sýstir stares at Ada, disbelieving. "Nattaskur *is* myself."

A flicker of impatience ripples across Ada's face. "As I said, it is a great loss, but—"

"You are not Väsen. You cannot understand this."

The realisation strikes Sýstir like a bolt of lightning. *You will never understand this.*

This is no sister who has come back from the grave to reunite with her family. This is a woman who has come to deliver a message. An arrow, shot by an unseen archer.

Ada reaches across to place her hand over Sýstir's once more, but Sýstir snatches it away.

"Don't touch me!" she snaps, a pathetic edge of fear creeping into her voice. "Is this why you came? To spy on me for Queen Hilda?"

Sýstir feels for her knife again, its weight reassuring in her hands. Just when she thought Queen Hilda was done with her poison, here it is, bottled in the worst vessel imaginable and presented like a gift. Her *sister.*

She will never forgive Queen Hilda for this.

"Sýstir, I beg of you to stop this fight," Ada pleads. "It will consume you whole – and take the Dark Forest with it."

"You need to leave," she snarls.

"You will hurt others," Ada insists. "You're already hurting *yourself.*"

Sýstir cannot take more of this. She whistles, long and loud. A beat later, a dozen whistles echo her own.

For the first time, Ada's expression flickers with panic. "Who is that?"

"My family," Sýstir says.

Two dozen Väsen seem to spring out of nowhere: woodland gnomes, mares, a troll, and so many more. They bare their teeth their very presence thrumming with power and all its implications. Something rushes through her, and though she cannot mistake it for love, it sits there nevertheless. They have come for her.

"I said, you need to leave," Sýstir says. "They will make you, if I cannot."

Ada glances between them, her expression wary. "I am her sister," she says loudly.

Sýstir thrusts her knife towards Ada, firelight glinting off its blade. "You are no sister of mine."

Not while she is under Queen Hilda's thrall.

Ada pauses, as though she could say any number of things. More accusations of Sýstir's misdeeds. More pleading to bend to Queen Hilda's rule, even from afar. The Väsen shift around her, coiled with the longing for violence.

But then she climbs to her feet. Tears glimmer at the corners of her eyes, but her voice is steady. "I do not want to leave you again. But I will not fight against the family that you have chosen."

Without warning, she grabs Sýstir's hand and pulls it towards her, angling the knife at her own heart. Sýstir's pulse races in her throat. The blade is so sharp – and Ada is right there—

"If you cannot find a way out for yourself, then I will forge one for you. You *are* my sister, whether you wish me well or ill." The blade pricks at her skin, just once, and a bead of blood wells up. "You will always be my sister, and so I will always come for you. Remember that."

Sýstir watches as Ada re-shoulders her pack, the Väsen clustered around her with eyes narrowed. Everything in her is urging Ada to stay; everything in her is fighting to keep the blade from reaching its target. The pain in the hollow of her back flares and she gasps. Then Ada goes, leaving Sýstir with her knife aimed at nothing but the darkness.

...

The fire wanes, then ebbs, then dies. Rain starts up, first as a drizzle and then in earnest.

Sýstir sits in the darkness, her Väsen departed back to camp. The cold does not bother her. The wind does not make her shiver. The rain does not have her seeking shelter. The dark does not compel her to start another fire.

Ada is gone, she thinks, over and over. Ada is gone.

Just before dawn strikes, she climbs to her feet. For the first time, she feels no sorrow, no joy – not even shame.

Why would she, when anger blazes so brightly within?

III

· A VENGEANCE ·

· TWENTY-SEVEN ·

Time plies its fickle trade again.

The seasons turn, rolling from one to another, but to Sýstir it is all a flat grey. She cannot tolerate the daylight of spring and summer. She cannot feel the chill of autumn, nor the bite of winter. No flower smells delicate, and no food holds flavour. The only scent that lingers is that of a sweet rot, its origin unidentifiable.

She burns from within.

Queen Hilda has done the unthinkable. She has turned Ada against her, and made their reunion worse than their parting. In the name of herself, and her trolls.

Because of Queen Hilda, Ada is gone.

Sýstir has held off on the last part of her plan – to rid the Dark Forest entirely of Queen Hilda's influence – and now, too late, she understands what a terrible mistake she has made.

It is not too late to rectify it, though. Her Väsen, once a frightened collective, are now daring rebels, ready to protect the Dark Forest from further harm. Ready to reclaim their home as theirs, instead of a territory guarded jealously by the Skóug Trolls. They shiver with pent-up energy. It is a fierce kind of hope, but hope nevertheless.

The only one who pushes back at her is Korí.

"This is not like you. And this – this is not like us," he says. "We asked for justice – not war."

"Through war comes justice," she says.

Korí shakes his head. "Hallr would disagree, I know it."

"And where is she?" Sýstir snaps. "She made her choice; you made yours."

Korí flinches at her tone, but she ignores it. She cannot afford to be soft, to let anyone think they might escape the throes of war.

That evening, she gathers her Väsen to her. They have been waiting for this moment, she knows. This long winter has starved them of much, but finally they can act. Finally, they can be free.

Sýstir surveys her Väsen. They are from all corners of the Dark Forest: giants, mares – even a few huldras, though they spend much of their time outside the camp. Here is her weapon of choice, honed and polished like a blade.

Fenrir slinks next to her, with the limp that has never quite healed. He snaps at any Väsen who gets too close, his teeth bared in perpetual grimace.

"It will not be easy," she begins. "You must be vigilant. The trolls have drunk from Nivir, so there is little opportunity for bloodshed on their side. But that will only make them more devious," she says.

"Do – do we really have to hurt them?" someone says.

"And kill, though it pains me to say this."

Truthfully, it does. There are only a few trolls who are obstacles to be removed: Fundin, Grendel… and Fulgir. She's given the other trolls of the Rise chances to surrender themselves, or escape altogether. She would rather that, than spill blood needlessly. But now the time has come for it to be needful. If she leaves the remainder of the Rise to their own devices, who else will they corrupt? Who else will they whisper the sweet, empty promises of Queen Hilda to – and the tale of her monstrous foe, the Huldra?

This is for Ada. This is for Nattaskur.

"We will be swift," she says. "It will be a mercy."

…

The camp is a riot of activity as they prepare themselves for a one-sided battle. They are grim-faced, pre-emptive grief already etched in their expressions. This is no easy quest for them, even if they ache to see justice done. The skóug trolls have ripped the Dark Forest asunder, splitting friends and family. For some there will never be a path back to what they were, before.

Sýstir watches them with an emotion that would sit somewhere between pleasure and satisfaction, were she to still feel such things. It is good, at last, to put action to her anger once more.

They have fashioned a crown for her in the form of a wreath, with leaves dipped in gold to hide their frailty. Sýstir holds it in her hands for a long time, but doesn't put it on.

"I am not a queen," she snaps. Then she looks around; there is someone missing from her usual trusted Väsen. "Where is Korí?"

She finds out the reason for his absence from two woodland gnomes, each trembling with the anticipation of her anger.

"He – he said he wished to find his wife," one says, shaking so hard she can barely speak. "He said – he – he—"

The other woodland gnome intervenes. "He could not fight against the Rise, he said. He would not risk bloodshed."

So Korí is gone. She had known he would be upset by the turn of events, and perhaps that he might argue with her yet again for more diplomatic means. But she had never considered he might leave. He has stuck with her through the felling of Nattaskur, the first early days of carving out her new world, her negotiations with the Rise. So why not this?

Now all she has left of her faithful group is Fenrir. He bounds through the marshlands, half terrorising everyone. When he comes up to her, it is with a wild anger that even she cannot quell.

"Fenrir," she says, lacing her words with the power of song. "To me."

But he snaps at her, fangs bared. There are tufts missing from his fur, and where it thins, the skin underneath is razed with painful-looking boils, some of which are already starting to burst. He is beginning to look like a corpse in truth. Like the wolf who almost killed them both, that day in the forest. She swallows, and there, at last, is something that is not quite anger: dread, curling around her stomach.

No matter. She will attend to him after this battle, she thinks. There will be some poultice, some medicine to ease his pain and make him whole again.

But a worrying thought nags at her, even after she tries to dismiss it. *There is no poultice that can save him from this.*

• • •

As dusk falls, the Väsen march through the Dark Forest as one, an overloud collective that flows across oh-so familiar pathways. Unbidden, Sýstir thinks of the men of Oden, who had ridden noisily across the landscape on their horses. But this is no invading force; this is the Dark Forest, striking back.

Just before they come to the fork in the path to the Rise, she raises her hand and the Väsen stop. Smoke drifts on the air, incongruous with the sharp scent of snow. Carefully, they approach as one.

The trolls are waiting for them. Someone – perhaps Korí, and won't he pay for his treachery – must have alerted them because they have dug a trench around the entrance to their cave. Fires flicker from every possible vantage point, the light so painful her skin burns. From here, it looks wrong, too human, antithetical to nature in every way. A sacrilege of the Dark Forest.

Her resolve tightens.

The Skóug Trolls do not plead with her, or hurl insults. Instead, they stand in front of their cave, unarmed and unyielding. Their only defences are simple wooden shields, the edges rounded so that they can do little more than bruise their opponent. No bloodshed.

This will be too easy.

Sýstir stops before the trench. The air hits clean and cold in her lungs. Fenrir paces next to her, as though he, too, cannot tolerate the light. He had appeared just before they all set out, and although Sýstir cannot touch him, she is grateful he is here.

Her Väsen's expressions flicker in the light: pained and afraid and determined. They have risked so much to be here. It would be easier, she thinks, if they had come for cruelty's sake.

She straightens her shoulders, and lets the trolls see the glint of her sword. "Will you surrender?"

Silence.

"Then we will do what we must." She takes a deep breath. "Onwards!"

The Väsen behind her burst into frenetic movement. They surge forward, pressing against the trolls, who have no choice but to pull their shields close to their bodies. There is the snarl of teeth and the clash of steel against wood.

It is brutal. It is breathtaking.

Sýstir spots a break in the defence and leaves her Väsen, flowing through to the corridor of the cave. She sings in bursts of power, incapacitating those who would fell her. But she doesn't stay to see if they live or die by her song; her Väsen will make sure they cannot interfere. She has bigger enemies to face.

Behind her, the sounds of fighting grow near, chasing her into the hart. She glances towards the noise, and for a moment, she cannot tell who is ally or foe. Just a mass of teeth and claws, an angry tide seething towards her.

A movement catches the corner of her eye, and she whirls around. Then she sees her – Fulgir.

Fulgir stumbles and falls to her feet. Blood flows freely from a wound; her face is spattered with it. If she had anything to defend herself with, it is gone, lost in the chaos. She looks up at Sýstir, her eyes wide and... afraid.

This is her chance; Sýstir should take it. She does not feel anything, after all. No shame, no regret, no mercy. She has promised herself she would not feel this. She feels the song that summons death pressed between her teeth, eager to escape and be heard.

You must do this. For the Dark Forest. For Nattaskur. For Ada. For—

But this is *Fulgir*. Unbidden, Sýstir pictures large warm hands placing a wreath on her head, crowning her. Not gold and a lifetime, but wood and a scant few hours. Because it was her birthday, and wasn't that something to celebrate in better times?

A smile, a quiet laugh. *Kindred*.

"Go," she hisses.

Fulgir hesitates. All around them, the battle rages: Väsen clashing with Väsen. Magic and blood and the cries of the injured. No one is paying attention to them.

Sýstir pushes her with her foot, hard. "Please!"

Fulgir scrambles up, quick for a troll. She looks desperately between Sýstir and the battle one last time before diving into a small hallway. Gone.

Sýstir is still looking at the empty space where Fulgir had been when another skóug troll appears to take her place. She reels with shock. Agagkantor stands in front of her, a bow in his hands.

Agagkantor, who had vowed never to rejoin the Rise. Who would die before drinking from Nivir, and die again at defending Queen Hilda's legacy.

Agagkantor, who poisons everything he touches.

"Sýstir!" he shouts.

A warning – or a claim.

Sýstir's mouth twists. She moves towards him, every line of her body intent on vengeance. She has no such divided loyalty towards him.

He raises his bow and takes aim. Fine, they are mutually agreed, then. She feels the rage bubble up within her and the surge of magic that comes with it. She will need no weapon beyond herself for this. He could shoot an arrow straight through her heart and it would not hurt. He has already made his worst wounds.

She just needs a breath to ready herself. To sever this last thread of her old life.

Agagkantor meets her gaze – and angles his bow away. Sýstir turns as his arrow flies towards Fenrir.

A cry.

"Fenrir!"

She reaches him as he falls to the ground. When she looks up, Agagkantor is gone.

Fenrir snarls weakly as she gathers his body into her arms. There is not a great deal of blood, but it is a true shot, the arrow buried deep. She tries to sing over him, reaching for that well of power that comes so easily to her these days. But it refuses to take. He is slipping away, his breathing faint and unsteady. His eyes, red-rimmed and filled with fear, flicker and roll.

Whatever thin thread of magic she'd given him years ago... snaps.

His body slumps.

Sýstir clutches him to her chest and howls.

...

It is all over quickly, just as Sýstir designed it. The Rise reeks of blood and death, and it does not feel merciful or gentle. It feels like vengeance. It feels like guilt.

For a while, Sýstir's Väsen move the trolls' bodies in twos and threes. Those that have been slain are already changing, returning to the stone from which they came. They will be left outside, a reminder to their kin of what happens to those still yoked to Queen Hilda.

Sýstir stays with Fenrir's body as her Väsen flow around her. He has run warm since the wolf's attack, but now he is stiff and cold. She strokes him anyway, in the way that she hasn't been able to in years. Despite all he has been through, he's still soft as a kit.

She could run her fingers through his fur for hours, listening to the rumbling purr underneath.

How far they have come. And now, no further.

Someone touches her on the shoulder gently. A troll; she forgets his name. She looks up, dry-eyed.

"Where is Agagkantor?" she asks hoarsely.

"Gone. As is Fundin and the others." He glances at Fenrir and his gaze turns complicated. "I am so terribly sorry, Sýstir. But..."

"It was his time," she says, the words sounding foreign on her tongue.

Absently, she touches her cheek. But there are still no tears.

As if from a distance, she watches the troll take Fenrir's body gently from her. There's a flicker of fear in his eyes, but she doesn't stop him.

"What would you have me do with him?" he asks.

Sýstir considers the question, while the rest of her mind homes in on the limp body, the matted blood, the slight loll of jaw. Lynxes really are such beautiful creatures, she thinks. Even after the injury, when his body rippled with scar tissue and old aches plagued him in the cold, he moved with leonine grace.

If this was another animal, any parts not worth eating – and lynx do not make for satisfying meals – would be left outside for the Dark Forest's scavengers. Especially in this weather, when everything that moves hungers.

But he was so beautiful, and this is not just another animal.

"He was a warrior, was he not?" she says. "He should be treated as the Väsen. Buried, or – or whatever they may choose." Väsen handle their dead differently, depending on custom, but Sýstir knows that there are some who bury them. To return to the earth, to live on in the roots of the trees, in the memory of bark and branch again. Growth and rot working in harmony.

"The ground is frozen solid," the troll says, nervously.

"Then he will have a hero's shroud," she says. "He will burn."

...

That night, the Scar of Rotinn is brighter than ever before. There are not many pyres – not compared to the trolls, who have need of none, anyway – but each one is attended by mourners. Fallen loved ones, fallen comrades; it is all grief to Sýstir.

She forces herself to stay and watch, embers flickering into the air. She could not keep Fenrir forever. She knew this from the moment that she'd plucked him from Thróttr, and pressed his small, soft face to hers. A favour, after all, is a fleeting thing.

She inhales. Charcoal and smoke; her mother flickers in the back of her mind, a burning silhouette. But the only cries this time are that of the mourners, and the dead are blissfully so.

After the mourning finishes, the pyres nothing but charred heaps of embers and ashes, the wake begins – an odd clash of celebration and sorrow. Though Sýstir no longer particularly enjoys listening to others sing, she stays to watch the Väsen bring out their instruments and coax tunes from their stiff joints. Some still hold onto one another, crying quietly on each other's shoulders. A sprýg gnome gathers her children close to her, hugging them tightly, while another stares at the embers, alone.

So much has been lost this night, even with everything they've gained.

An eldar dances in the last of the embers, kicking grit from the pyres, before someone swats them away, though it's too cold for the ashes to start another fire elsewhere. Once, there was a time when Sýstir might have enjoyed seeing the fire faeries indulge themselves in the flames, but now her gaze washes over them, unseeing.

Even though this celebration is at her own hands, and at least partially in her honour, she can't bring herself to join in. She walks through the camp, nodding to groups of Väsen nursing their own campfires, recounting tales of their heroism or bravery. They part for her, like a river's ebbing tide, but after she moves through, the crowd closes again. The laughter is always louder behind her.

Absently, her hand reaches down, expecting fur, a wet nose – and stops.

Sýstir feels a sudden urge to return to her cave, to pile her blankets on top of one another and climb underneath, lulled to sleep by a roaring fire. To let the fog wash over her once more.

Wearily, she rubs her eyes, careful to shield her face from the others. They must not see her tired. They must not see her weak.

Anyway, her cave is no longer her own, either. There will be someone waiting at the entrance with a question – or more likely, a problem that only she can solve. A dispute, a request for justice, a plea for more food – always more food – or some other minor quibble for which she must dole out her limited patience.

She turns away, willing her mind elsewhere. It is nearly over. She cannot give up now, not when she is so close.

At the edge of the camp, a woodland gnome and a giant are standing watch. More out of habit than necessity, now that Hilda's Rise has been vanquished. Evidently someone has been brewing mead, for there is a cup for the gnome and a bowl for the giant. Though they should be merry on this night – victory in their hands at last – they are solemn.

"Lady Huldra," the gnome says, toasting her with the cup. "Would you like to join us?"

"What I wish is to be left alone."

Obediently, the gnome bows her head and they both retreat. Sýstir walks along the edge of the bank, watching snow drift across the frozen creek underneath. Let them have this night, she thinks.

Laughter, at last, drifts over the camp, caught between the faint strains of music. They are celebrating their victory, even if it comes on the heels of great sorrow. As their leader, Sýstir should be celebrating with them; it doesn't suit to be off elsewhere, sulking and morose, and leave them questioning the truth of this night. But they will not miss her for a time, she thinks. Let them be their own heroes. Let them hold on to the glow of their bravery for a little longer.

The moonlight shines thinly on the ground.

Yes, they have something to celebrate while she has little. Because although she can claim the battle as hers, she still lost today. She is still weak, still prone to those human frailties of the heart.

She should have killed Fulgir. Even now, she can't remember the feeling that had caused her to stay her hand. But somehow, it had not seemed... right, there. To see Fulgir frightened because of her.

To see those hands that had once crowned her with joy so shaken.

Who knows where Fulgir will end up now? The skóug trolls may consider regrouping – what's left of them – but the Rise is no more. Not as it was under Hilda.

Yet, because of her weakness, Fenrir is dead.

Maybe it's a small mercy, but there's no rush of grief like the one that had so engulfed her the first time he had put his life on the line for her. Just a sorrowful emptiness that sits somewhere behind her ribcage, where the rest of those difficult feelings seem to lay. But the truth remains, hard and unyielding: he was loyal – perhaps the most loyal – and she betrayed that loyalty. Worse, betrayed it for a troll who has in turn betrayed her, time and again. She should not have needed that extra scant time to ready herself. She should have been ready from the beginning.

She will honour Fenrir's memory, she thinks fiercely. She cannot undo her own lapse of judgement, but she can remove those who had sought his end. Her mind turns across the creek, to the small cave near the river where she had once called home.

Agagkantor has shot his arrow.

It is time to shoot hers.

· TWENTY-EIGHT ·

While the others in her camp celebrate, their hunt already at an end, Sýstir begins one of her own. She pads through the darkness, wending her way back across the paths her Väsen had moved through only hours before. Her feet whisper across the snow like a ghost, her body soundless as it lopes through the Dark Forest.

Agagkantor knew what he was doing when he loosed his arrow. He'd known, too, what he was doing when he'd appeared next to Queen Hilda at Nattaskur's felling. He'd known what he was doing when he had lied to Sýstir.

This entire time, she has had her eye on Queen Hilda. Perhaps she should have been keeping her eye on an enemy closer to home.

The crescent moon is high in the night sky when she stands in front of Agagkantor's cave. The garden she had cultivated in her youth has almost entirely vanished under a sprawl of ferns. There are no signs of the long sticks she used to hang her washing, or the bucket in which she kept water.

How small it seems, now. How pathetic.

It might be that Agagkantor has escaped forever, abandoning his cave to join the few left from the Rise. But she does not think so. She can easily imagine him retreating somewhere familiar, that in his arrogance he would not believe her capable of returning to the home they had once shared. And there is a thick path cutting through the snow.

When she enters the dark narrow corridor, it's as though she's being pulled back through time. This, too, is smaller than she remembers. But when she once dreamt of Agagkantor's cave – reluctantly, desperately – it was as her younger self, when everything felt enormous.

Quietly, she steps underneath the low doorway that leads into the cave. It's so dark that she can barely see anything; the hearth is but a few embers flickering weakly, with barely enough warmth to chase away the pervasive chill.

"Who goes there?" A gruff voice in the darkness.

Agagkantor is sat on his stool, as far away from the hearth as possible, as though he cannot bear the light that emanates from it.

He looks older than she remembers. Or perhaps he has always been old to begin with, and only now does she realise the vastness of his age, the weakness that comes with it. He would not have made a good king, she thinks; weakness has no place in a king's grasp.

"Agagkantor," she says.

Agagkantor looks up at her. He has not escaped the battle unscathed; his arms are scratched bloody, one eye swollen shut. His shoulders slump, like rubble after rockfall. When he shifts in his chair, a hiss of pain escapes him.

"Little Bird," he says, with effort. "How far you have fallen from your nest."

Sýstir has thought of all she might say to Agagkantor in this moment. She has envisioned apologies, more fighting, stubborn silence. How desperately she has tried to unfurl their calamitous relationship, as though by doing so she could come to understand the reasoning behind it. But her thoughts keep slipping back to Agagkantor's unflinching gaze, the flight of the arrow.

"Why did you do it?" she asks.

He doesn't answer her. Instead, he tilts his head to the side and exhales. His eyes briefly flutter shut, and she notes all the new creases in his face, all the lines of stress and age.

"I told you Fenrir was not made for keeping. I told you he was a wild thing."

"So you saw fit to kill him."

The only friend who has stayed loyal to Sýstir. The only one from whom unconditional love was a given. Of course Agagkantor would want to take that from her. He has already taken everything else—

"I saw an animal in pain," he says wearily. "I sought to do right by him."

She flinches. It is a barely noticeable gesture, but Agagkantor's gaze tracks back to hers. Even after all these years, they still know so much of one another's reactions.

Fenrir had not been... himself, it is true. But there had always been flashes where he seemed like his kit self, and the world regained a little of its colour. How could she possibly have taken him deep into the forest and let him go, one way or another? How would the world have looked to her, then, walking back alone?

She cannot let Agagkantor get under her skin. *She* is the one directing the conversation; *she* is the one who will get answers.

"Did you think you would be safe here?" she says with a scornful laugh. "Did you think I would be too afraid to come? You should have left with the others."

Agagkantor heaves a breath, and this time she can hear the strain in his lungs. There is blood, she notices, gathered thick against his tunic.

"I wished to return home," he says.

"The Rise isn't your home?" she asks sardonically.

Once, the betrayal might have stung. Agagkantor was the one who had dissuaded her from meeting with the Rise, who had fuelled the divide between them. The arguments they'd had over her visits to the trolls, the nights where she'd wipe away angry tears because it seemed so impossible to hold both friendships in her hands. A younger Sýstir might have openly wept for knowing that he would spurn her yet again to join them.

Then again, a younger Sýstir would not be where she is now. Agagkantor is not the only one who has changed.

"They asked for my help. And I did not have to trust them to recognise the need for it." He peers at her, squinting in the dim firelight. "You are not well."

Sýstir shakes her head. "You are mistaken; I am well," she says curtly.

Agagkantor shifts in his chair with the weary groan of arthritic pain. "That is often what those corrupted by Rotinn say, until it is too late to reverse its progress."

"I know what Rotinn is," she snaps, remembering too late that she is supposed to stay calm.

How quickly they slip into these old patterns, she thinks. Agagkantor the wise, ever-knowing parent – and Sýstir, the wayward, ill-behaved, ill-gotten child.

"I bestowed my protection upon you as best I could," he says, though his voice is distant, as though he is elsewhere. "Meanwhile, I spent half a season at a time seeking its end."

The travel. The long weeks away. Consulting with giants and wyrms of old, and other trolls in remote Rises. She had known, even then, that he was not quite right. That his mood swings were more than that of a mercurial temper. But she had not suspected what the travel was for, or what knowledge Agagkantor might have sought.

"I would not have wished this upon you, Sýstir," he says.

He lapses into silence, and Sýstir takes the opportunity to study him. His eyes are red-rimmed, his body braced against the firelight. Illness – no, *Rotinn* – taking advantage of his weakened body.

Yet he is too calm, she thinks, as though he is untouchable. *He* is the one who can barely move for his injuries, who has been abandoned by the fleeing remnants of the Rise, who will be alone forever. And still he dares to pity her. Her anger surges; the hollow in her back twinges with pain.

"Why did you do it?" she demands. "Nattaskur? The Rise? *What did you do?*"

"I believe the question is, what did *you* do?" he says quietly. "Did you think I wouldn't catch your footprints in the clearing? Did you think that I could not see the marks of your knife, or the wisps of your hair caught in Nattaskur's branches? I know my own."

"I am not yours," she hisses.

"Nevertheless," he says, as though she has not spoken at all. "You inflicted Rotinn upon Nattaskur. This is your responsibility to bear."

She recalls her wish to Nattaskur, the desire to preserve all her memories within it, all the way from the slenderest of branches above to the deepest of roots below. Never mind that she was bestowing everything: not just the warm smiles and the laughter and the sunny days of her life, but the fear and terror of her early days in the Dark Forest. Her resentment of Agagkantor's disdain. Her hatred, pure and unyielding, for Queen Hilda.

She shakes away the thought. This is not about who poisoned Nattaskur.

"Did I raise the axe? Did I whisper treachery into another's ear? Did I betray my kin?" she asks.

He sighs wearily. "And I will carry this burden beyond the end of my days. But the Dark Forest cannot become as we are." He shakes his head. "I am sorry."

Sýstir laughs scornfully. "Sorry for what, exactly?"

He closes his eyes, every line stark on his face. "I should have left you in the hollow. I should not have tampered with your fate."

Sýstir reels back as though she's been slapped, and this time there's no hiding her shock. He is saying this to hurt her. He does not mean this.

Agagkantor is a liar. He has always been a liar.

"I see it now," he says distantly. "I could not see it then. But Hilda spoke true. The Dark Forest wished to take you, but we considered ourselves above its command, to our fault. And so I brought you upon us all."

Molten rage courses through Sýstir. In a few strides, she is closer to him than she has been in years. But he seems unbothered by the anger that radiates from her.

"You will not foist your regrets on me," she says. "I did not kill Nattaskur."

"I wished to do right by you, Little Bird, even if it meant defying your fate," he says quietly. "I wished... for a great deal. And how we have suffered for it."

Sýstir wants to laugh at the absurdity of it. *He* has suffered? After everything she has endured at his hands. Everything she has faced. A slick, icy calmness washes over her.

She levels her gaze at him. "Then let me end your suffering."

She reaches for that power within her – so easy, these days – and begins to sing. It is an old ballad, of loved ones drowning. It sounds like dead branches shifting in midwinter, like the roll of a deer's eye before it plunges through ice.

She has sung it before, just once.

Agagkantor gasps, but there is no air for him to take. Sýstir keeps singing, letting the melody ring through the cave. This is what it was always going to come down to, she realises, though perhaps she had known it from the moment they'd parted. He knows too many of her weaknesses, what few remain.

She will be done with him. She will excise this poison from her veins. He is false family. And after this, he will mean nothing to her.

He mouths her name. Searing pain races across her back, but she ignores it. She is doing this for the good of the Dark Forest.

For the good of Väsen everywhere. For herself, and all that she has lost in his name.

There is one last, shuddering breath.

Something pushes back on Sýstir's power, like a string being pulled taut. Magic, from deep within Agagkantor. And then it snaps.

Sýstir exhales raggedly. She waits for his chest to rise again, for him to have the last word, as he had so often loved. She waits for that one final whisper of *Little Bird*, like a curse he has bestowed upon himself. But there is no response.

He is... gone.

Sýstir feels the sudden urge to laugh. Agagkantor is dead, and she is free.

She turns around – and her gaze catches on her old sleeping corner. She had mistaken the shadow for a sack, but as her eyes adjust to the darkness, it becomes clear that it's her old mattress, soft and thin with age. Her bedding is there, too, folded up neatly at the foot of the mattress, along with the slippers she'd outgrown the season before she'd left. Her curtains are still hung up, parted to one side.

Curious, she takes a closer look. All of her belongings that she'd left behind are still there: her childhood collection of feathers and rocks, layered now so thickly in dust that it's hard to tell what colour they once were; her first frayed pieces of rope, made with inexpert fingers; the abandoned attempt at a scarf for Agagkantor, interrupted when she'd asked Queen Hilda for the truth.

It is like the ghost of her childhood self is still roaming the cave, like she might appear in the entrance any moment, dragging a small Fenrir with her. But there is so much care here, too.

Like he was waiting for her to come back.

She turns back to him. His eyes are closed, but she touches his hand. His skin is cool to the touch, as cold and hard as the walls of the cave. He is already transforming into what he once was.

A sudden dizziness washes over her. She will never be able to take this back.

But she did what was necessary. He committed a crime, and so justice had to be done.

Besides, he was already wounded and ill. Unable to follow the scattered Rise. Winter is already a long, hard endeavour; without anyone to help him, he may very well have ended his days here regardless of Sýstir's intervention. In another's eyes, it might even seem a mercy.

She snatches her hand back. She does not have to justify herself to anyone, least of all herself. He deserved this fate.

"You mean nothing to me, Agagkantor," she says, her voice echoing in the cave. "You have always meant nothing to me."

She waits for her rage to agree with her, for warmth to kindle her bones once more. She should be ablaze with victory.

But even as she leaves, all she feels is the lingering cold of Agagkantor's hand.

· TWENTY-NINE ·

Sýstir has barely returned from Agagkantor's cave when a sprýg gnome comes running full pelt towards her. He sports a black eye and a nasty cut on one arm – some of the Väsen had been less than discriminate about who they'd hurt in battle – but otherwise seems in good spirits.

"There are trolls on the other side of the creek," he says breathlessly. "A delegation."

By the time Sýstir reaches the crossing place, the word has spread, and a gathering of Väsen trail behind her. Curious, no doubt, to see the exhibition ahead.

"Are they here to fight?" someone asks.

A troll – one who had defected from the Rise before the winter – shakes his head. "I do not think so." He hesitates, then glances at Sýstir. "Will you kill them?"

There had been those who had disliked the bloodshed, or who had slunk away in the thick of the night, too cowardly to fight for their home. Korí, she thinks, and tries to remember that she is supposed to be angry. A few had even argued that to go against those that have drunk from Nivir was to engage in slaughter. As though Sýstir herself had relished the prospect. As though she had enjoyed it.

Sýstir had made a careful note of the absences, to deal with in the future. Her law is fragile, despite their recent victory; she can tolerate no disloyalty.

The way you were disloyal to them when you refused to kill Fulgir?

"No," she says decisively. "We let them go."

There's no point in risking ire through needless bloodshed. And even if Sýstir wanted to, she cannot disrupt her own plans now.

As she suspected, there are only two trolls waiting on the other side of the creek. Fulgir and Grendel, on behalf of their sham of a prince. Fulgir's face is set like stone: angry, and trying not to show it. Grendel looks humbled by the force on Sýstir's side of the creek. A spark of satisfaction warms Sýstir, and it is a relief to feel something; at last, they know who they're dealing with. At last, they have found the true measure of her.

"Lay down your weapons," she commands. "Otherwise there will be no audience."

"We bear no weapons," Fulgir says in her clear voice.

And it's true; there's no glint of blades on their belts, no thread of magic tuned to Sýstir's own. From here, they look like the trolls out of a fairytale – and just as easily brushed away.

Sýstir waits until she's halfway across the creek before stopping. She tips her cloak so that she can see she carries no weapons with her. She has no need of them, after all, when her voice lends her such power. The only object she carries now is a long-tipped tooth from Fenrir. A sprýg gnome had given it to her after the pyre, the sole part of him that wouldn't burn.

"Where are the rest of your kin?" she asks.

Grendel's expression twists into one of fury. It's an odd expression on a troll, but Grendel's face wears it well. Fulgir lays a hand on him, and he breathes out deeply.

"You slew them, as I recall," he says through gritted teeth.

"Our remaining kindred beg their absence," Fulgir says, more placidly.

She is not telling Sýstir the full truth, or even half of it. But Sýstir's scouts have seen the exodus of the skóug trolls across the Dark Forest, choosing to stay with other Rises, or find a new home of their own. There will be casualties – not everyone is built with the required fortitude – but they will be mourned as Väsen who furthered the cause. The war truly is won; the Rise is broken.

"I look forward to seeing them grace our presence again," Sýstir lies.

The trolls look at each other, uncertainty between them. Fulgir's gaze flickers to Fenrir's tooth.

"My apologies for your loss," she says.

Sýstir stiffens. "We give our all to the cause."

"May what is gone rise again," Fulgir says, and although it doesn't sound like a threat, Sýstir hears the echo of Queen Hilda in it all the same.

"The dead do not return," she says bluntly.

They stand in uneasy silence. Perhaps the trolls had decided between them who should speak; she notes the way that Fulgir glances at Grendel, as if he is supposed to offer more than insincere platitudes before she steps in.

"What will you have us do now?" Fulgir asks wearily.

Sýstir folds her arms as if contemplating, though she'd decided on this plan last night.

"You may surrender and subject yourself to our laws," she says.

"That is treason," Grendel hisses.

She shrugs. "That is the only acceptable outcome. Your queen has fled; your Rise scattered. There is nowhere left for you to run."

She watches carefully as Grendel and Fulgir glance at one another, fury and resignation in one.

"But it is no small thing I ask of you," she continues. "So I will give you grace. Make your decision by the time the sun strikes the horizon."

"And if we do not?" Grendel asks, a dangerous tone in his voice.

Sýstir levels her gaze at him. "Then may you enjoy the last of your days."

...

The news comes in the form of a missive: Fundin, Queen Hilda's ill-fated son, and the remaining skóug trolls of the Rise surrender. At sunrise, they will wait at the stump of Nattaskur to hand over what remains of their power.

The Dark Forest falls to Sýstir.

It is exactly what she wanted. And it tastes like ash in her mouth.

The cave is too busy, as is the marshland around it, Sýstir's Väsen celebrating their victory – the true return of their homes. She has never felt entirely synchronous with them, except for their mutual goal to free the Dark Forest, but now she searches their faces and sees only strangers. What victory are they celebrating, truly? If there is any victory to be had, it's hers alone; *she* is the one who stood up to Queen Hilda. *She* is the one who was ready to give her life in service to the Dark Forest.

They barely notice when she crosses the creek and makes her way into the rest of the forest. The path to the Rise's cave is quieter than she's ever seen it, with not even a spinn faerie to cross her way. The trees are unusually silent. Then again, they have been of late; she has not heard so much of a murmur in their language of crackling twigs and rustling leaves and bending branches. It is as though they have all buried deep within themselves to hibernate away the sorrow of Nattaskur's loss.

When you wake again, it will be to spring, she pledges.

The ground around the cave is still scarred with the remnants of their battle, scorched where the fire had caught the grass ordinarily buried deep beneath the snow. Dark blood – mostly troll – spatters the ground. But it is already snowing again, and soon all evidence will vanish under its blanket.

Tomorrow, this will be hers. She can choose to sit at the hearth where Queen Hilda had once passed judgement, or wander in the echo where she and Fulgir had read to one another. She might stand in the centre of the hart, where they had sung so freely, gentle magic layered until the entire Rise was suffused with its warm resonance.

And yet.

She keeps walking, along the river where she had rescued Fulgir from the ice, to the clearing where Agagkantor had taught her the first words of Elfdalian. Icicles hang from the trees, silent around her. She sits in the centre, closes her eyes and listens, breathing in that quiet, deep way she's mastered. What does she hear?

The crunch of snow under her body, ever present. The wind, rifling through the trees. The sound of her heartbeat, jumping behind her ribcage.

But no spinn faeries hovering playfully to snarl her hair, or the distant song of the trolls. No Fenrir, curled up next to her, one ear out for any disturbance.

She gets to her feet, anger and irritation striking one after the other – with foolishness below that. Because that is what this exercise is.

Even Thróttr's Revel has vanished, packed up and moved to different ground in the Dark Forest. Their homes, nestled cleverly in the trees, are dark and empty. Most have suffered in this war with the Rise, and she's heard of sprýg gnomes gathering under larger Revels to survive, where they refuse to join her.

She walks steadily through the night, trying to shake this restless energy from her limbs. Tomorrow, she must be focused on her victory. But the unsettled feeling doesn't dissipate; instead, the longer she walks, the deeper her unease grows.

Finally, she finds herself at a place that haunts her dreams.

It has been years since she looked upon the hollow that might have been her grave, that had been saviour and deathbed all at once. Far too small for an adult, but just big enough to accommodate a small girl seeking shelter. Looking at it now, it's hard to imagine how anyone might have had the luck to stumble across it.

Perhaps there is some truth to Agagkantor's words. She has wondered, time and again, what would have happened had he not found her. Would she have been discovered by some other Väsen? Would she have recovered from her illness and scraped a life in the forest on her own, like some wayward child from myth?

No. She was already dying when they met, and he had stolen her death from the Dark Forest.

Maybe it would have been different if Ada had been there with her, the two carrying one another. Perhaps they might have died in each other's arms, ill and hungry, to become a tragic ballad, a warning to desperate young girls. Perhaps Agagkantor would have swept past them both, unwilling to take in a human. Perhaps they would have staggered out of the Dark Forest hand in hand, to face whatever awaited them there: the men of Oden; the wrathful villagers; the wide, terrifying world of the humans.

It might have been a short, brutal life. Or a long one, forever an outcast, chasing a family who would never have her – and thus never have *them*. Perhaps the future was written in the stars too long ago for Sýstir to ever change it, her fate sealed by those determined to let her walk this ill path.

But it was not meant to be like this, she thinks.

She looks up at the sky, seeking the stars. Her mother had once told her that the stars were like freckles across the sky's face, with every constellation a different tale of Väsen and gods and humans: stories to come, and stories yet to pass. And she searches for one of the star sisters, ever familiar.

Tonight, though, the sky is a flat black, blanketed by snow-laden clouds, and there are no stories to tell, past or future.

· THIRTY ·

Hours before dawn, Sýstir stands at the crossing between the Scar of Rotinn and the rest of the forest. Her Väsen have come to send her off: giants and huldras and mare and woodland gnome – and yet more. Every size, every shape, every nature, rallied under her banner of protection.

This is what she has achieved. *This* is what it means to be connected to the Dark Forest. They are practically family now.

Though she prefers to let her closest leaders speak on her behalf, today is too important for her to leave in silence. She has spent so long thinking about what she might say at this moment – the gravity of all they have achieved in the face of such hardship and loss. But now that the hour has come, all that matters is what's in front of them. A future without Queen Hilda's Rise, or the stranglehold of Nivir.

"You have endured much, for which I am grateful." Then she pauses. "The Dark Forest is grateful."

She does not mention that the trees have stopped talking to her. But that is okay, too, for all will be well again soon.

"Victory is already had," she says. "Now, I'm simply collecting what is owed."

And cleaning up after herself, though she doesn't tell the others that. This weight she'll carry on her shoulders alone. It doesn't give her pleasure to think of what lies ahead.

There is no room in her Dark Forest for its betrayers – not even those she had considered friends.

"Let us accompany you," one of them urges.

She might have entertained this suggestion from Korí, or at least enticed Fenrir to accompany her. But Korí has left her and Fenrir is dead.

She brushes them away. "No. I shall end this as I started it."

She crosses the creek to the sound of their cheering, the flicker of flame behind her.

The walk to Nattaskur is long and quiet – too quiet. The forest around her has the washed-out appearance of something dead.

Briefly, Sýstir wonders if Ada has left the Dark Forest, or whether she is still within it, trying to scrape a living like the Väsen who have chosen no sides. Once her business here is done, Sýstir will search for Ada – and they will be reunited properly this time, with no ill deed between them.

Atop the burial hills, she stops to catch her breath. Though her memory is pockmarked with holes, this recollection stands out clear and crisp: Sýstir, struggling to keep up with Agagkantor's long steps while he explained the history of each troll who had died and been carried here.

Looking back, it had amused him that she believed the burial hills were a site of some disastrous warfare, not a place of sanctity. But now that she's seen battle, this is a battleground of its own kind, she thinks, made manifest by Queen Hilda. The recently fallen trolls will have no home here, marked as it is within Sýstir's own territory.

She lingers on familiar landmarks, greeting each like an old friend. The Lady still stands, though the boulder's edges are soft with snow. There are no flowers in the nook – for no flowers bloom in winter – but also no pine or dried heather, or anything else that she might have been gifted in harsher seasons. Sýstir fumbles in her pockets before remembering that she carries very little with her these days.

She is about to move on when her gaze snags on a new boulder. Even though he has returned to stone in the way of all trolls, just another formless rock in the landscape, she recognises him.

Agagkantor.

Another skóug troll must have broken the laws to creep across the boundary and return him here. It must have been the day before, but snow has fallen so steadily that he is all but buried by it. The journey to carry him here would have been arduous, exhausting.

She should be burning with fury that one of her rules has been broken, and for her greatest enemy. And later, she will apprehend those who have defied her – for that is the hard responsibility of a leader. But for now, she can't bring herself to care. It is right, she thinks, that Agagkantor's final resting place is here, at his greatest betrayal, and what will soon be her greatest triumph. He can spend eternity watching over his irrevocable mistake.

"Am I still your Little Bird?" she asks quietly.

The air rings with silence.

She reaches out to brush the snow off him, out of habit more than anything. In winters past, as a girl-thing, she would have done much the same. There is a version of Agagkantor, she supposes, who would have been proud of her as she is now. After all, she has rescued the Dark Forest from its captors, restored the true law of the land itself, and eradicated Queen Hilda's rule. She has done everything he could not.

Yet the Dark Forest is silent around her. It has been a long time, she realises, since she heard its casual joy. The fading crescent moon above shines with the slippery silver of tears.

No matter. It will come again.

"You said you regretted me," she says to him, the wind snatching at her voice, "but I will make it so that no one even remembers you to wonder of your regret."

With that, she leaves him behind. Let the snow and time bury him.

Fulgir is waiting for her in the thin group of trees around another boulder known as the Gatherer, for the way that flowers grow around it in summer.

"Well met, Sýstir."

Fulgir glances at her with those deep moss eyes, always with so much to give away. But for once, there is nothing Sýstir can glean.

"Have you come to rescue me from myself?" Sýstir asks lightly.

Fulgir looks at her for a long time, assessing with that cool gaze. She tilts her head, and it is nearly the same pose as in the battle against the Rise. The moment that Sýstir faltered.

Sýstir blinks, startled. She has the peculiar feeling of watching herself outside of her own head, as though a stranger inhabits her body. She flexes her fingers, feeling the tactile rub of skin.

"Your strength precedes you, Sýstir," Fulgir says eventually. "But I have always thought you strong."

In someone else's mouth, it would sound like a compliment.

Fulgir glances at the sky, burnishing lighter with the arrival of dawn. "We should be moving."

For a while, they walk in silence amongst the dead, save for the crunch of snow underfoot. Sýstir brushes an icicle from a nearby boulder, barely feeling its deep chill.

"Does the cold still bother you?" Fulgir asks.

Sýstir glances at her suspiciously. But there is no malice on Fulgir's face. Just calm and polite curiosity.

"No," Sýstir says curtly. "Does it bother your pretender prince?"

Now that he has no hart in which to lay his head, no Rise to swaddle him with ridiculous notions of kingship.

Fulgir glances upwards at the sky. "He is no pretender. We chose him in Queen Hilda's stead, not because he is her son, but because he has always had our trust, as did she. You underestimate him. I would follow him to wherever he led us."

Sýstir clenches her fists. "And so you have."

They are nearly at the top when Fulgir stretches, shaking off a dusting of snow that has gathered on her shoulders. She sighs with an ease that belies their situation. She has no idea, Sýstir thinks, of what is to come for her.

It is an agonising thought. But she cannot risk the trolls attempting to dismantle her rule or stir up rebellion in the Dark Forest. A leader must do the hard things, make the difficult choices, so that others may not have to choose at all.

Fulgir pauses, her gaze on the horizon. "After this, will you be at peace, Sýstir?"

Sýstir blinks, surprised. "Peace?"

"When your war is won, and your enemies no longer your enemies, and the Dark Forest entirely your own... Will you be at peace?"

Peace. It is a preposterous word, one that has slipped from Sýstir's lexicon entirely. She has never been at peace; there is always an enemy to fight, always a new battle on the horizon. Even when she rests in her own camp, it's with one eye open and both ears listening. There are whispers of ambition from the other Väsen, who have certain... *ideas* about who should hold power in the Dark Forest.

But Sýstir has always known: it is the trees, and only the trees, who deserve to stand above all. It is the Dark Forest itself that welcomed her when she had nowhere left to turn. The Dark Forest that has given her a home and a purpose. That has shown her kindness under its gentle canopy, even when no one else would.

It is the Dark Forest that the skóug trolls betrayed when they cut down Nattaskur and proclaimed themselves to know better than the land. "I am a leader," she says stiffly. "What is peace to me?"

"There was peace in the Rise," Fulgir says, then sighs. "What singing we had."

She hums a snatch under her breath, and Sýstir reaches for her knife instinctively; singing is a weapon. But no air is crushed from her lungs, no dreamlike state comes over her. She recognises the tune as the one she would sing with the Rise. Dozens of voices lifted in chorus, beautiful and comforting. A quiet longing stirs within her.

"Stop," she snaps.

Fulgir looks at her with that infuriating calm. "As you wish, Sýstir."

The heavy silence resumes. But Sýstir cannot shake the melody from her head, as though it is trying to chase her thoughts away.

"What *is* that wretched song, anyway?" she asks, though there's not enough sting in her words to show true anger.

Agagkantor had called it a song of protection, while the trolls had used it for healing, a swell that had filled the Rise. But it was layered with magic that she could never quite pick apart, though she'd often tried.

"It is the oldest song we know," Fulgir says. "Passed on from generation to generation, parent to child. A protection spell, though I confess I could not interpret the specifics." She pauses, and there is that quick mind underneath the calm. "It is not told to anyone else, even outsiders."

Sýstir snorts. "But Agagkantor—"

"Only parent to child," Fulgir says again.

Sýstir shakes her head. "I was not his child."

She was only ever a means to an end – to further his needling of Queen Hilda, or to fulfil his own selfish interests. But reluctantly her thoughts drift back to his cave, and to the collection of her old belongings, left as though she had only stepped out for an errand. He could have thrown them away, and resumed his life as it had been before she'd ever stepped into it. Yet he had chosen to keep them.

"I have a question for you, Sýstir," Fulgir says.

Sýstir glances at her sidelong. "You may ask."

"Is it you who slew Agagkantor?"

Sýstir presses her lips together. She has nothing left to say of Agagkantor; anything of interest vanished with his last breath. And so, too, should have any evidence suggesting the manner of his demise at her hand. She had not even laid a finger upon him.

She does not know how Fulgir might have gleaned that there was something more to his death than his battle wounds. She should lie, she thinks, and let the matter be. But looking at Fulgir, she cannot quite bring herself to do it.

"He is dead, and there is one less betrayer of the Dark Forest to contend with," she says eventually. "Does it matter how he passed?"

Fulgir looks at her, as though she is trying to see her through a pane of glass. But Sýstir is not glass; she is earth and rock and ice, and all that Fulgir will see is her resolve. Something inside her bristles.

"Let me guess," Sýstir says, and she cannot keep the taunt from her voice. "You would have had us fall into each other's arms, repentant, so that we may have both returned to the Rise under your watchful eye. Such goodness. Such nobility."

She expects Fulgir to protest with some earnest sermon of forgiveness and second chances, or perhaps of kin being about more than blood. But instead Fulgir only looks away, back to the flat grey of winter storm clouds. And for the first time, Sýstir has no idea what she is thinking.

Fulgir's gaze is steady on the horizon. "No, Sýstir, I cannot save you from what you have wrought."

Then she stops abruptly as they reach the burial hills' crest. Below them, the valley of Nattaskur slopes downwards. Sýstir wrenches her thoughts away from Fulgir, Agagkantor and the past. She must look towards the future now.

It is time.

· THIRTY-ONE ·

The obliteration of Nattaskur still takes Sýstir by surprise, a relentless gut punch. The clearing is stark, and the landscape seems too empty, as though some god of old has carved out a hollow where Nattaskur should be.

Fulgir says nothing, but the grim line of her mouth is word enough. Even she cannot stand the sight. But what Sýstir cannot understand – even now, after everything – is why Fulgir stood by and let her own world unravel.

"You could have stopped this," she says suddenly. "This is your doing as much as it is Queen Hilda's."

Fulgir shrugs, as though they're talking about nothing more than the weather. "It is done, Sýstir. We have made our choices."

Sýstir considers pushing further, to demand an explanation that would make sense. Especially knowing that soon there will be no more chances left to ask. But despite all she said on their walk over, she finds that she can't muster the anger needed to sustain an argument.

I am so tired, she thinks. She has carried the weight of the Dark Forest on her shoulders for so many years. But it is nearly over now; soon, they will all be free from the last of the skóug trolls' control. The last of Queen Hilda's influence, however faintly it may claim its hold.

As they descend, two more figures come into view. Fundin, the usurper-king, and Grendel behind him, mountainous and stoic with helpless anger. His gaze skims to the absence where Fenrir should be, and his mouth twists in something like a smirk. He looks pointedly at Sýstir, to make it clear that he is well aware of his action. Another version of herself might have sworn fury at him, but she simply levels her own gaze until he has to look away.

It will be quick, she decides, for Fundin and Fulgir. She has already meted out what she can stomach. But Grendel, she thinks, will not go so easy. Maybe he is overdue for a taste of his own cruelty.

"Well met," she says sedately.

Grendel scowls. But Fundin merely clasps his hands in front of him, as though this is another audience between two equal leaders.

"Well met, Sýstir."

He looks tired and bruised, half-healed wounds dappling his arms. Well, he will rest soon, Sýstir thinks. She inclines her head at him in greeting.

"We would settle this at the stump of Nattaskur, if you would be so willing." He smiles wanly. "It is custom."

She can indulge in this kindness, as a small mercy. What harm will it do to let them believe themselves honoured in their last moments? She has the words ready in her mouth anyway: a potent song of slumber and death that she has perfected in the confines of the forest, not unlike the one she used on Agagkantor.

But she has to stifle her shock as she moves into the clearing proper. Nattaskur's absence is a wound on the land. Red tendrils spread from the stump like poisoned arteries. As she gets closer, she catches a sickly sweet smell rising from them – the telltale sign of Rotinn. Despite Queen Hilda's efforts, it seems as though it is determined to slither over the land, unstoppable.

Despite herself, Sýstir's stomach twists. But it is only for a second. She cannot be swayed by doubts now.

"You must come a little closer, if you can bear it," Fundin says.

His voice is steady, but his hands shake at his side. Perhaps he knows what is coming to them all. Perhaps he is simply trying to delay the inevitable. She takes another step forward, then another, filling her lungs to sing those fatal words, and—

Underneath the corrupted scent of Nattaskur, she catches a half-familiar feeling – like the hum threaded through the song of the Rise.

Magic. A *trap*.

She whirls around. "You lied to me."

She reaches for the power of song, but Grendel and Fundin sing as one, their harmony pushing back on hers. They are trying to drown her out, she realises. Their magic barely skims the surface of her own – even between the two of them – and she rallies herself.

But out of the shadows, another voice joins them. Then another, with the unmistakable gravel of a troll. Not just skóug trolls, but every single iteration. Craggy and mountainous with heft, or longer limbed and nearly delicate-looking next to their counterparts.

They cannot stop me, Sýstir thinks furiously. She pulls every ounce of power from deep inside herself, pouring it into her own song.

The chorus becomes stronger, as other Väsen join, clinging to the edges of the trees. The ones who had spurned her, who had turned away from her new vision. The boom of a giant's low bass tones; the high reed of a lilvätt; the raspy warmth of a woodland gnome – they are all here. And where they cannot sing, there is the pluck of a harp or trill of a wood flute. The trees rustle with them, their whisper carried on the height of the song. And how cruelly beautiful it sounds, a harmony that cannot be unravelled.

Sýstir takes an unnerved step back. Her voice falters. They are all singing as one, pure and unbreakable.

You underestimate him, Sýstir. She should have been paying more attention to Fundin.

Then she clenches her jaw. If she cannot be heard, she cannot march them to their own deaths.

Very well; there are other ways to die.

She reaches for her knife – and Fulgir's hand comes down on hers. Painfully. There is still that same calm behind her eyes, but none of that mild warmth. The conversation at the burial hills, her attempt to sway Sýstir into peace – it was all a ruse, Sýstir thinks.

Her mouth twists into a snarl. "You've changed."

Fulgir is unmoved. "Perhaps you know me less well."

Fulgir pushes her forward, towards the stump. Sýstir cannot see behind her, but she knows instinctively that whatever happens, she does not want to find out what awaits her. For the first time in years, panic cleaves its way through her, hot and immediate.

She wishes herself bear, moose, wolf. She is larger than herself, than the trolls. Whatever it takes to escape.

Desperately, she shoves at Fulgir, but it is like shoving a boulder, immovable.

"I warned you," Fulgir says. "I tried."

The trolls' song changes, rising like a bell struck over the forest – blanketing Sýstir's own frantic heartbeat. She slows instantly, her limbs like slurry. Her eyelids grow heavy; her shoulders relax of their own accord. The urge to lay down and sleep falls on her like a hammer blow – and how long it has been since she has had true rest.

It is a fight that lasts a lifetime. It is a fight that lasts seconds.

And Sýstir is losing.

She slumps on to Fulgir's shoulder, dead weight. Fulgir is singing, too, she realises distantly, weaving in and out of the other trolls' harmony. The part of her that worries over where she is going – surely towards her own end – fades to a burr. Her mind floats on reluctant tranquillity; she can barely feel the ground beneath her feet.

Fulgir drags her towards Nattaskur's stump and faintly, she notes that it has been carved out into a hollowed abyss. It is a prison, she thinks, each word rolling slowly through her mind. Made for her.

Why not... let it all go?

And then what? a furious voice demands. Sýstir has already sacrificed so much to get here. She has lost her family, and then again. She killed Agagkantor, and spurned her own sister for this. For Nattaskur, and the Dark Forest. For the home that would have her without reservation.

In her mind's eye, Queen Hilda's axe rises – and falls.

With aching slowness, Sýstir reaches for her knife. Her fingertips brush the edge of its handle. She strains towards it, pain racing through every line of her body as it fights the trolls' magic. She will not be sedated. She will not lose now.

Fulgir's eyes flicker downwards and her singing cuts off. "Wait—"

Sýstir grabs the handle of her knife – and thrusts.

It is a clean wound, direct to the heart. Hot blood spills over her fingers. Fulgir – *she is your friend, Sýstir* – looks down at her with wide-eyed shock.

Fulgir, who has been kind at every step of this long and treacherous road. Who braided her hair for a crown once. Who Sýstir twice saved and would have again.

So why is there a knife in her hands? Why is there blood?

Something fragile stirs under her ribcage. And, for a moment, she is Sýstir again. Not the anger that has worn her face like a mask, nor the Rotinn that has wound its tendrils through her thoughts. Just Sýstir, half human, half Väsen.

You have killed her.

"No!" Sýstir cries.

She presses her hands against the wound, readies the words for the protection spell she had once used on Fenrir. She can save her. She can fix this mess she has wrought.

But Fulgir shakes her head, gasping at the pain. "I will not... walk as you."

Not like this, she means. Losing her mind in pieces to Rotinn, to spook at the ghosts of her past and eye the future warily. To become a cruel shadow of herself, and commit atrocities as a vengeful wraith. To be the creature that terrorises the Dark Forest. Alone.

"Don't leave me," Sýstir begs.

But the shock of what she has done is already fading; her thoughts are slipping. She tries desperately to return to them. This is not who she is. This isn't what she *wants*—

Fulgir levels her gaze at Sýstir. "Will we not go together, my friend?"

A sharp breath between them.

Fulgir throws herself at Sýstir. They fall into the hollow of the stump.

Sýstir cries out just once, a punch of breath snatched from her lungs. Then she lands hard on the packed dirt beneath her. The walls of the hollow are just broad enough for her to stretch fingertip to fingertip; the trolls must have spent all night digging deep, tearing at Nattaskur's roots. And Fulgir's meeting on the burial hills? A distraction.

Frantically, Sýstir scrambles upright, looking for a foothold to climb out. But Fulgir digs her fingers into the edges of the stump, her sturdy body wedged into the entrance. Though her face is screwed tight in pain, her eyes are still bright.

"I told you, Sýstir," she gasps. "I do not give up."

"Let me out!" Sýstir says desperately. "You cannot stop me – you cannot—"

But Fulgir does not move.

"Peace, Sýstir," she whispers, and Sýstir cannot tell whether it is a command or absolution, reproach or plea.

She exhales one last time and her eyes slip shut. They do not open again.

Fulgir – her greatest, most loyal friend, her bitterest enemy, her kin through love if not blood – is dead.

Something within Sýstir shatters. She is fury. She is grief incarnate.

This is Grendel's fault. This is Fundin's fault. This is—

It is your fault. It is all your fault.

She scrabbles at Fulgir's body, desperate to escape, but it is too late. Fulgir is already losing the cohesion of what she was, features etched away before Sýstir's furious gaze. Within moments, the only part of her that Sýstir recognises is her parted hands, dawn ribboning through.

From above the bars of her new prison, Fundin and Grendel look at her.

"You can cause no harm here, huldra," Grendel says, his mouth thin. "Fulgir will be hailed a hero for her sacrifice."

"I am sorry, Sýstir," Fundin says, and there is genuine sorrow in his voice. "I sought to avoid this at all costs."

Fulgir is dead. Her friend is dead.

It cannot be her fault. Because if it is, then Agagkantor, her *sister—*

No. She is the Dark Forest's protector. Whatever the cost, however bloody her hands have become, and all she has sacrificed along the way – it will be for nothing if she remains here.

"No prison can keep me," she snarls. "I will be free, and you – you are already a dead creature."

Fundin shakes his head. "Goodbye, Sýstir."

Then he vanishes from view. The sound of his footsteps, always light despite their heft, fades with the other Väsen until she can no longer hear them. Above, the wind whistles faintly.

Sýstir screams until her voice is hoarse. But no one answers.

She is trapped.

. . .

For the first few days, she is certain she can escape. She is not unfamiliar with the trolls' magic; her Väsen, loyal to the last, will surely come for her; and she herself is resourceful, powerful.

But the magic within the stump's hollow is laced with a

powerful sedative, stronger even than Sýstir's own resolve, buried deep in her core. Eventually, she succumbs to it, unable to fight the tide of exhaustion that tugs at her. Her hunger diminishes, whittled away to a feeling that she only occasionally recalls, and so, too, does thirst. Although the cold and damp creep over her, there is only a light touch of both on her skin. The trolls have tried to be merciful in their magical workings, and as such, they have become unfathomably cruel.

She exists, mostly, in a suspended state. Like the deepest ice in the caverns, that never melts even at the height of summer.

When she is awake – lucid enough to remember her name, unswayed by magic – she rages. But this, too, is just as futile, with nowhere to place her energy, and no one upon which to exert her fury. It is better, she admits in her despair, to let dreamless sleep wash over her once more. At least there, time does not cling to her so viciously.

And there are no more impossible decisions to make. No more sacrifices to wrench at the cold remains of her heart.

No more friends to die at her hands.

Fine. She will sleep. Let her aches ease with the passage of time. Let her mind drift, so that it may heal. Let her friend's blood flake from her fingers, and her guilt with it. Let it all wash away.

She closes her eyes, curls in on herself. The ground is cold and hard, but she does not feel it. She does not feel anything at all, these days.

Let her sleep. Let her dream.

For now.

· EPILOGUE ·

Sýstir sleeps.

She wakes, briefly, when rain patters into the hollow, or when a lynx passes by above with her noisy kits. But with waking comes pain, surfacing from some deep tidal place within. It is easier to give into the magic, to let herself fall back into bottomless, dreamless sleep.

There is no more running.

Sometimes, she senses the briefest notion of her future, coiled tight in the fist of her heart. There will be a true waking, and then retribution; she knows this like she knows little else with such utter certainty. But for now, Fulgir's embrace holds, kindness and cruelty so entangled she knows not where each begins and ends.

But tonight, Sýstir's eyes flutter open for the briefest moment. Between the fissures of stone, the stars dance across the night sky, the constellations as familiar to her as the sound of her own heartbeat. There goes the Bear, Jörmungandr's Scale, the Maiden and the Draugr. So many stories of heroes and villains, and those who would walk the line of both.

She catches sight of one of the sister stars, alone in the void. But perhaps a millennia has passed, because on the other side of the sky, still long out of reach, is the other sister star.

Ada, she thinks at last, and sighs.

Spring is coming.

ACKNOWLEDGEMENTS

Thank you to everyone at Trollheim, but particularly Björne, Jacqueline Dalunde and Åsa Sandoval for letting me into the Dark Forest to glimpse some of its wonders. Thank you for your invaluable guidance on Swedish wild plants and animals, and for showing me the beauty of Tiveden. It's such a privilege to wander into someone else's world, and I'll always be grateful that you entrusted me with a piece of it.

Thank you to the team at Titan, including Daquan Cadogan, Bahar Kutluk, Caitlin Storer, Katharine Carroll and Hannah Scudamore, for taking Sýstir through that crucial process between Word document and typeset novel. A special thank you to Sharona Selby, the forensic queen of copy-editors – long may she reign.

Thank you to Robbie Guillory, for taking this boat out to adventurous seas, and Kiya Evans, for taking over the helm with such steady hands. (I'm sorry about the ship metaphors, but not enough to stop using them.)

Thank you to my friends and family, who let me be very mysterious about this book for a year and a half. Thank you for your support and love, and for lending your ears and shoulders and wisdom at all hours requested. Not to be sappy on main, but I'm so very glad I have you all.

Finally, thank you to you, reader. I hope you find the Dark Forest when you need it most.

ABOUT THE AUTHOR

Georgia Summers is a half-British, half-Trinidadian writer, who spent most of her life living across the world, including Russia, Colombia and the US. When she's not doing bookish things, she's planning her next great adventure. She currently lives in London, but she dreams of one day living in a haunted château with a ghost that cleans.

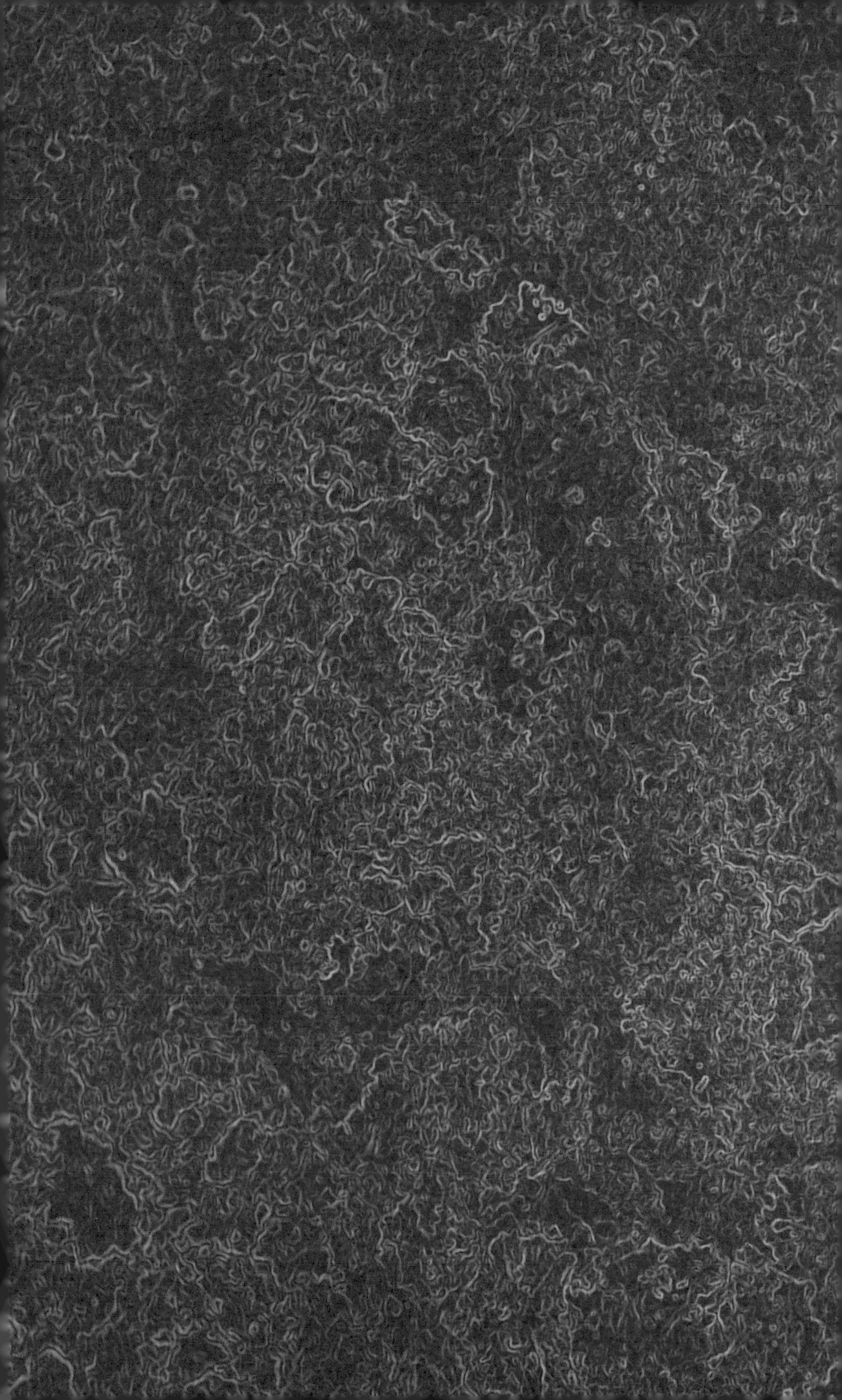